# Jess Cameron,

# I Love You

Mila Natalie

Mari House Publishing

Mari House Publishing

ISBN 979-8-9942140-0-8 (Hardcover)
ISBN 979-8-9942140-1-5 (Paperback)
ISBN 979-8-9942140-2-2 (eBook)

Library of Congress Control Number: 2025926981 (Hardcover edition)

Published by Mari House Publishing
Enoch, Utah

Cover design by Mila Natalie

First edition 2026

Visit the author's website at www.marihousepub.com

# Dedication

For my Dad, who taught me to never stop chasing my dreams. And for the person who taught me to love reading the most, I hope I've made you proud.

# Content Warning

This work contains mature themes and situations intended for adult readers. It includes strong language, explicit sexual content, references to substance abuse, and depictions of violence. Reader discretion is advised.

Jess Cameron,

I Love You

# Prologue

Despite the uncomfortable pressure building behind my eyes, a few heavy thoughts manage to pass through my mind, and the more I think about everything, the less I fight against the cold that surrounds me.

I guess contemplating your own importance mid-death can really put things into perspective for you. It's funny though, I always thought it would feel different, dying, I mean. Or I imagine this is what the feeling is like, I guess I wouldn't know since I've never really experienced it before.

Honestly, I always figured that when the lights finally went out, it would be a bit more dramatic, you know, like life flashing before your eyes, or thinking about all your regrets in life—*that* type of dramatic. But all I feel is the sharp bite of the cold water on my skin, and the unsettling sensation in my ears as they threaten to burst from their ringing.

Darkness encroaches until it almost envelops me completely. I can't tell if my eyes are open or closed anymore, just that the pressure that throbs behind my eyes is now almost unbearable.

I can feel my body jerking from its lack of oxygen, and the feeling is calming in a twisted sort of way as the intensity of the burning in my chest almost fades to zero.

I tell myself I want the darkness to take me, that I'm ready for it, and that it's better this way—better for everyone.

The burning in my chest is still a dull ache, but I feel the imploding pressure surrounding my body lessen as the cold slowly begins to turn into warmth, and I suddenly feel the warm rays of the sun on my numb body. My skin tingles, and when I open my eyes, all I see is green.

Not green like grass or the leaves on a plant, but green like the ocean in a storm. I've seen them a million times before, but never did I feel like they saw me back. Not until now.

Someone's calling my name, and someone's crying, but all I see are green eyes.

*His* green eyes.

# Chapter One

The sunlight streams through the curtains as I open my eyes. I look up through the bright rays shining across the room, the glare blinding me as it slices through the plastic of the thin blinds.

I sit up and rub the sleep out of my eyes.

*Shit, where the hell am I?*

I look around the room, trying to place myself, still trying to remember how I got here.

*That's right. I'm at Daniel's.*

Daniel is my current boy... friend? I guess boyfriend is a loose term. I hate to say it, but it's more of a "friends with benefits" situation. Though after last night, I think we unofficially made it official. When I asked him if he saw our relationship going anywhere, he kissed me and then bent me over his living room couch. So, I guess it was sort of an unspoken thing, but I really feel like we made some actual progress.

I throw off the covers and stand, stretching my hands above my head as I let out a yawn. I start to rummage around Daniel's room looking for the dress I had on last night, not wanting to walk around his house naked this early in the morning—not that he'd mind, though.

I hear my stomach growl and suddenly notice just how hungry I am. *I guess being twisted up into a pretzel for most of the night will do that.*

The thought has me laughing to myself. If future Sam had told me a few years ago that doing the walk of shame would become a regular thing for us, I probably wouldn't have believed it. I guess a lot can change in just a few short years.

When I first got to college, it took me all of five minutes to get with the first heavily inked, tall, dark, and handsome asshole I could find. Though I didn't realize it at the time, he'd prove to be a majorly toxic d-bag down the line. I'd never dated anyone who'd possessed violent tendencies before, so when he started breaking things and punching holes in walls after I tried to break things off with him, it was enough to scare me off for good.

I was in a weird place when we met, so I suppose that I was just so lonely that I was willing to overlook all of the obvious red flags that were there from the start. I thought it was love for a while until the fighting became such a regular occurrence that it made me wonder if real love was supposed to be that exhausting all the time. He never put a hand on me— at least not one that I didn't ask for—but I decided that I wouldn't ever let it escalate to that kind of violence, so I ended things.

That's when I met Daniel. He's been my *sort* of boyfriend for the last few months. We started talking about a year ago but didn't actually hook up until more recently.

We met in my 8 a.m. Intro to Econ class, which is ironic because I hadn't originally intended on taking it. By the time I realized it was an early morning class, it was too late for me to drop. I'd usually roll out of bed with just enough time to brush my teeth and put some pants on, hell, I'd even be lucky if I managed to put on matching shoes for the day.

Almost every morning, I'd just barely make it on time to class, which in turn resulted in me having to cross the room in front of everyone, inadvertently interrupting the professor just to get to the only seats left. Of course, they'd usually end up being the ones in the first or second rows. Daniel always sat in the front, always volunteered for things, and was *always* on time to class, so basically, he was my exact opposite.

Up until then, Daniel and I had never actually spoken before, except when paired off for group projects or when we had to pass papers to each other. One day, he saw my midterm test results and asked if I wanted to join his study group. My score wasn't *that* terrible, but I figured that it probably wouldn't hurt to get some more studying in anyway. Even though I'd already been at school for almost a year, I still hadn't made many friends, so I welcomed the thought of company.

Every time our study group met, it progressively got smaller and smaller until eventually, we were the only two left. After spending some time with Daniel, I realized that he'd be a nice change from the pricks I'd usually dated. He was definitely white bread, but at least he was safe. I figured I wouldn't mind sacrificing the parts of myself that liked the danger and drama that I'd usually gravitate toward if it meant that I would be kept out of harm's way.

One thing I will say is that even as vanilla as Daniel seems, he's almost even more of a freak in the bedroom than I am, which was honestly a nice surprise. It was something I definitely didn't expect when we first got together, but I guess you know what they say, you shouldn't judge a book by its cover, right?

A few months ago, when we were studying in the library one night, I remember watching Daniel as he diligently sorted through one of his notebooks, his brows furrowed together in concentration. We had been spending a lot of time studying together for finals, and I'd have been lying if I said I wasn't attracted to him. Sure, he wasn't the usual type I'd go for, but he was pretty good-looking beneath the stuffy collared shirts and perfectly gelled blonde hair, especially with those crystal clear bright blue eyes of his.

The more time I'd spend with Daniel, the more I'd imagine what it would feel like to wrap my legs around his lanky form. Even as smart as he was, he didn't seem to be able to take a hint, even when I had basically spelled it out for him several times before.

It was pretty late that night, so we were the only ones left in the library, aside from a few stragglers and the occasional janitor with a vacuum. Daniel had gone to look for a book in the far section of the library, so just like every college cliché, I followed him. I figured I'd try one last time to get his attention. One thing led to another, and we ended up banging against the dusty bookshelves in the back of the library.

I won't say I completely forced myself on him, but it seemed like he wasn't ever going to pick up on my subtle hints unless I did something drastic, and I guess shoving my tongue down his throat is what finally did the trick.

Since then, our relationship has been purely academic in the fact that we're strictly study buddies when it's study time, and any fun stuff is reserved for weekends, or late-night booty calls only. His rules, not mine. He said he couldn't afford to let his grades suffer because of a relationship, and that if I wanted something more than no-strings-attached, I'd be better off with someone else. In the beginning, I'd only agreed because I figured he'd eventually change his mind, hopefully after finals were over.

That was last semester.

After searching around Daniel's room, I finally find my black dress in a heap in the corner and slip it back on, not bothering with my underwear. They're definitely trash now since I distinctly remember Daniel literally ripping them off me last night.

I'm still rummaging around the room for my shoes when I hear a laugh through the door and wonder who's here this early on a Sunday morning. I give up on trying to find the rest of my clothes and let my curiosity get the best of me.

When I walk into Daniel's kitchen, I recognize the face of a girl who goes to our university, Alyssa, I think her name is. I've seen her around campus a few times but didn't realize that she and Daniel even knew each other.

"Morning," I say, trying to sound normal, but it comes out a little too cheery, especially for me.

Daniel looks over from where he and Alyssa are sitting, papers and textbooks spread out all over the table. "Oh, hi, you're up," he says, giving me a hesitant smile paired with an annoyed look, like I'm interrupting something super important.

"Good morning," Alyssa says as she looks up from her papers. She gives me a friendly smile, and I fight the urge not to strangle her.

"It's pretty early to be studying already," I say, trying to keep my tone light, not letting my simmering jealousy show.

"Yeah, well, Alyssa is taking the makeup exam for Professor Meisner's class tomorrow, and she asked me to help her cram. We've got to take advantage of what little time we have left," Daniel says with a shrug, and goes back to sorting through the stack of papers on the table.

"So, I guess breakfast is off then...?" I ask, trying not to sound too disappointed.

We had made plans yesterday to go out on a real breakfast date this morning. Well, it was more like I suggested it, and he didn't outright say no this time.

7

"I know, but I forgot that I'd already said yes to Allie yesterday, and with the makeup's being tomorrow, it's just bad timing right now. Sorry, Sam," he says, his nonchalant attitude suggesting that he's obviously not that broken up about missing our breakfast date.

*Allie? Okay, what the actual fuck? You're telling me he already has a nickname for her?*

It seems like they definitely know each other better than he's letting on, and I tell myself to chill out before I make a scene.

"Sure, I get it," I say with a shrug, barely able to hold my jealousy at bay. "Seems like more of a *study group* thing though, doesn't it? I'm also in that class too, remember?" I say, getting angry again at the fact that Daniel purposely left me out.

"It's fine, Sam, we can just study later," Daniel says, half ignoring me as he sorts through some papers on the table.

"Oh, but I did make coffee," Daniel says, looking up. He turns and looks over to the now-empty coffee pot next to the kitchen sink, before looking back at me. "Well, there *was* coffee... You can just brew some more real fast ...unless you're on your way out?" he asks, raising his brows at me.

Considering that I don't have any shoes on and I'm not holding my bag, it sure feels like I'm being asked to leave. I'm starting to feel annoyed, and glance at the two mugs of coffee on the table next to all the textbooks and papers. I notice that both mugs are nearly empty and wonder how long she's been here if they've already gone through an entire pot of coffee.

"Right... Daniel, can I talk to you for a sec?" I ask and give a forced smile as I gesture to his bedroom behind me. Daniel follows me into the room and shuts the door behind him as he lets out a heavy sigh.

~

*Sorry, Sam, you knew we weren't that serious... I think it's time we take a step back from things...*

Daniel's words keep replaying in my head.

As if being rejected in front of his new friend wasn't humiliating enough, I had to go and make things worse by losing my shit when I realized that *Allie* was using the new mug I'd just bought Daniel for his birthday last week.

Any normal person would've taken what was left of their dignity and left without a word after being dumped like that. I, however, did not do that.

After I'd practically ripped the mug out of her hand, I poured Allie's remaining coffee right onto the table, ruining most of her papers. Definitely not my finest moment by any means, and I do recognize that taking my relationship frustrations out on her was completely unfair. She seems like a nice enough person, and I really have no reason to believe they're even sleeping together, but I was just so mad that I couldn't help it. I'd sure save myself a lot of trouble in life if I had a little bit more impulse control.

*...we weren't that serious...*

The line that's been used on me more times than I'd like to recall. It's usually my own fault, though. I tend to take things way too fast, way too soon. Besides the fact that we were already screwing, I don't know how much slower I could've gone with Daniel. Maybe I should have clarified my feelings earlier on since it's obvious that I had the wrong idea about where our relationship was headed. He flat-out told me what he wanted, and I chose to ignore it anyway.

No matter what I try to do, it seems like I'm only able to attract emotionally unavailable assholes who end up not really wanting anything to do with me. I thought that things were going well between Daniel and me, but now I realize that it was clearly just wishful thinking on my part.

After graduating from high school, I vowed to myself to only date nice guys from then on out, which only lasted about five seconds. I was determined to start my college career on a good note, and it was actually pretty good once I was able to settle into my schoolwork and classes.

This year is only my second year being at school, and even though I'm enjoying my time for the most part, I was supposed to be here with my best friend Sophie. She had decided last minute to go to an East Coast school, and where I wasn't ready to leave yet, I decided to take some time off before starting college.

I ended up taking a gap year—or three, in my case—and settled on staying within a few hours of my hometown. I didn't want to go too far away, just far enough to pretend like I was living my own life, even though I still had one foot in my hometown. I told everyone that I needed the time to figure out who I was outside of the hell that was the last four years of my life before jumping back into another four years of potentially equal torture.

If I'm being completely honest, though, I had hoped my older brother, Chris, would leave for school before I did. With my brother gone, I figured that my dad would finally notice me and want to spend longer than two minutes speaking to me every day.

Ultimately, my brother kept putting it off and eventually never left for school. The little time I did manage to spend with my dad made me realize that some things can't be fixed overnight, or really ever for that matter.

Since my motivation to return to school kept fading with each passing season, I knew if I didn't leave when I did, I probably wouldn't ever. So, I packed up my car and enrolled in the first school that would accept me on short notice, and luckily it only ended up being a few hours away. Things with my dad seemed to only get worse no matter what I did, so I knew that it was time for me to leave.

Relationships within my family have been strained for the past few years, to say the least. A month after my fifteenth birthday, my mom left. Our family dynamic was all but destroyed, and my brother's and my relationship with our dad quickly changed as well.

The initial story my dad had told us was that my mom was going to live with a cousin out of town for a little while, saying that it had something to do with work. They both assured us it was only temporary, of course, but my brother and I soon realized that "cousin" was actually code for boyfriend and that the "work" that was supposed to be temporary, was actually permanent.

Of course, I didn't believe it. How could I? This was Mom, after all. The same mom who would stay up with us at night when we were sick, the same mom who helped me get ready for my first date, and then through my first breakup. I knew she wouldn't just leave us out of nowhere without a good reason to back her up. It was so unlike her that I knew something had to be wrong.

It was around the time I turned sixteen that my mom had stopped returning my calls, so I set out to find her like the heroine of any story would. Only, instead of the movie cliché—me, crying as I stare at my mom and her new family through the window, everyone laughing and having a grand ole' time all while I stand out on the corner in the pouring rain—I actually confronted her.

While it *was* raining and I could in fact see her through the window smiling and laughing, I didn't let it stop me—I couldn't.

I marched straight up to the door and rang the bell like a crazy person until someone answered. I kept telling myself that I hadn't gone all that way for nothing and had to talk to her myself before I could accept that she really wasn't coming home ever again.

In the end, she was more bothered by the fact that I had interrupted dinner and had tracked mud into her new house than the fact that I had just taken a three-hour bus ride—alone—in the dark, with nothing but a description of the house and a general idea of where to look for her.

I realized the woman I knew as my mother was gone, replaced by a plastic robot who only cared about dinner parties and her new BMW. As if the way she was dressed wasn't clue enough, the house and fancy new husband were a dead giveaway to the status of her new life. Growing up, our family was by no means "poor" but evidently, she wasn't satisfied with the life my dad had spent years building for them.

After being chastised for making her guests uncomfortable, I lied and said that I had already arranged for a ride home and excused myself back into the rain. The realization that she was really gone hit me when she let me leave like that without question.

I spent the night alone on a bus station bench, still soaking wet from the rain, and if it had been winter, I likely would've gotten pneumonia.

At that point, I didn't have many options since I hadn't exactly planned for a return bus ticket. I naïvely thought that once my mom saw me, she'd snap out of it, we'd go home together, everything would be right in the world, and I would be forever regarded as the one who singlehandedly saved the family.

I called my dad the next morning after asking a stranger for some change to use the payphone and was ready for an earful from him. Only he didn't yell or scream at me, he just asked me where I was and if I was all right. When I told him I was about three hours away, he just sighed at me through the phone and asked if I wanted him to pick me up, or if I'd rather take the next bus home.

Already feeling guilty about the whole situation, I told him I'd take the bus, not wanting to inconvenience him any more than I already had. He told me to use the emergency credit card that he'd already given me to buy myself a bus ticket and something to eat before our call ran out of time.

When my dad picked me up from the bus station a few hours later, he didn't ask me about what I was doing so far from home or what I'd hoped to accomplish, even though I'm certain he already knew. He didn't look over at me or say a single word the entire ride home, except to say that he was glad I was safe. Later on, I learned that my best friend Sophie snitched to my brother Chris about what I was up to and then told my dad.

After that, I stopped attempting to contact my mom, figuring she would eventually come around after she got whatever she needed to out of her system, but she never did. I told myself I was better off, but I knew that was a lie. I was grateful for the good memories I did have of her, but I no longer held out hope that things would ever go back to the way that they were before.

I really should have just left it alone because things only got worse after that. In my head, everything was just supposed to be a weird misunderstanding, but I was naïvely mistaken. My dad slowly stopped eating, and his appearance became scraggly, his beard and dirty blonde hair each with a mind of their own.

My brother Chris and I progressively saw less and less of our dad, and most of the time he'd stay late at work, even going in on weekends when he wasn't required to. Any small amount of free time my dad did end up having was spent at Chris's baseball games or locked away in his office at the house.

I tried my best to take on the role of the "woman" of the house, but it was difficult for me. I was supposed to be thinking about college applications and boys, not *what should I make for dinner?* and *oh, I forgot to pick up Dad's dry cleaning.* Not that he would've minded, though, if I had forgotten to do either.

13

Looking back, I wonder if my dad purposely didn't want to know where my mom was that entire time, and the fact that I found her made it all too real for him.

He never asked me about that day, what her new husband was like, or even what was said between us. It was only when I was tidying up his office one day that I found pictures from a PI that he hired—pictures taken of my mom and her new life.

My dad caught me looking at the photos before I was able to put them back where I found them and was furious with me. He went on a rampage and destroyed his entire office, breaking everything he could get his hands on, the desk, the other furniture in the room, and half of the bottles and glasses on his whiskey cart.

I saw a side of my dad that day that I never knew existed, and it scared me, making me think that maybe I didn't really know him as well as I thought I did. I knew that his anger wasn't necessarily directed toward me, just at what I'd done.

Blind rage consumed him, and I couldn't help but feel partially responsible for it all. If I didn't go poking the bear looking for my mother, he might not have tried either, still hoping she'd eventually find her way home. I'm sure that the possibility of the unknown was ideal to learning what she'd chosen over him.

Even though I wasn't a kid anymore, I'd still hid in my room and cried until the sounds of breaking furniture subsided.

That night after his angry outburst, I found my dad curled up in a puddle of his own tears on his office floor. I remember that his hands and knuckles were all bloody from the destruction of his office and couldn't believe that I was seeing him like that. My father, my protector and provider, the one who always seemed to have it together, broken and lost within his grief.

It seemed to me that whatever had happened between my mother and him, wrecked him beyond what I was even able to comprehend, and

I couldn't bear to see it. I had always looked up to my father, and as a little girl, he was my everything. What little girl *doesn't* see her father in that way? I knew that no matter what had prompted my mother to leave, that didn't mean that he deserved to suffer like he was.

I decided that day that taking care of him now was the very least that I could do for him, especially after all he had done for me as a child. After all the late-night talks and drives we'd gone on, all the joking around and good times we'd spent together over the years, I knew that I couldn't just leave him alone in his despair. I knew that I had to show him that even if my mother was gone, *I* was still here. Even just as his daughter, I wanted to show him that I still loved and appreciated him.

That night, I'd searched for my brother, but in the end, it was me alone who had drug my dad into the bathroom to clean him up. It was definitely a struggle, but eventually I was able to get my dad into his bathtub where I ended up having to pick the shattered glass out of his skin before I bandaged up his swollen hands.

Miraculously he didn't break all of the alcohol bottles in the house like I originally thought he did, because I remember the potent stench of whiskey on him when I helped clean him up.

I'll never forget the sad look in his blue-gray eyes when he mistook me for my mother, desperately grabbing at me and asking what he'd done wrong. He sobbed to the point of hyperventilation, and I had to keep reminding him that I was Sam, not Helena, thinking that it might calm him down, but it only seemed to confuse him more.

Of course, it didn't help that in the looks department of the family, I strongly take after my mom and her Italian side. Dark hair, and olive skin with hazel eyes. I guess you could say that I'm a taller, slightly more freckled clone of her in her younger years.

The more I corrected my dad, the angrier he got at me until eventually I gave up arguing with him. After all was said and done and I'd gotten him bandaged up and changed out of his soiled clothes; he fell asleep in the bathtub before I was able to get him to his bed. Whether it was from exhaustion or the alcohol, I'm still not sure.

As cliché as it sounds, that night was the first and last time I ever saw my dad cry.

Our relationship was never the same after that. He didn't really want much to do with my brother or me besides the bare minimum. He stopped going to Chris's baseball games altogether, and I often spent most of my nights at home alone, usually eating dinner by myself.

I always told myself that he was probably just trying to give us space to be teenagers and that I shouldn't read too much into his disinterested attitude.

My dad seemed resolved to stay in his office for hours on end and "crunch numbers" whenever he managed to be home from the office. Though, "crunching numbers" was code for obsessing about his failing investment accounts while drinking cheap whiskey.

One day, after I had turned eighteen, something changed, and he suddenly began caring about his appearance again. He got a haircut, a gym membership, and some new clothes that actually fit him for once. It was like he was a new man.

I was hopeful at first, wondering if the dad from my childhood had finally worked through what was weighing him down for so long, but soon realized that it was all just a façade. He looked one hundred times better, but still wasn't himself. He wasn't okay and I knew that.

At the time, I didn't know what ended up triggering the changes, just that I was more worried that the "new" version of himself was in much more pain than he was letting on.

As I later found out, it seemed that all the time and effort my dad was putting into his investments had finally paid off as well. His crypto accounts spiked one night and rose almost 30,000%. He never told me any specific amounts, nor did I ask, he just alluded to the fact that he probably wouldn't have to work again for the next hundred years or so.

After that, I felt like I saw even less of him—if that was even possible. He quit his job and started spending all of his time at the Westview Hills Country Club in town, saying he was "networking" or whatever bullshit.

The summer after graduation, Sophie scored a job there and said that his "networking" mostly consisted of him playing golf and sipping martinis with all the self-important assholes of the town. Not to mention all the gold diggers that seemed to constantly flock to him after he started throwing his new money around.

For a while, my dad would bring home a new woman every week, and by woman, I mean that she usually only looked to be a few years older than me. He'd joke and say, "Kids, meet your new stepmother," never failing to make everyone uncomfortable, but that never stopped him from saying it anyway.

After each and every breakup, at some point, I'd get a call from the manager of the club bar, asking me to come collect my dad. He'd usually have one too many, and before too long, he'd always start to make a scene. Even though my dad looked like a new man—and acted like one for the most part—I knew he was still broken on the inside. It crushed me to see him like that, but I knew that there was nothing I could do to fix it, which only made me feel worse.

My breakup with Daniel, if I can even call it a breakup, comes at a good time since finals were last week and I was prepping to head home for the break anyway. I was hopeful that by now things would've gotten more serious between us, and I'd have been able to persuade him to come home with me. I was going to introduce him to my family as my first ever normal, nice, strait-laced boyfriend, but I guess those plans went straight down the tubes.

I wasn't going to leave for a few more days, but after moping on my couch for the last three days, I'm starting to feel like I'm going to turn into a vampire if I don't get some sun. I also don't want to risk running into Daniel or his new friend at all if I stick around campus for the summer, so I feel like getting away for a bit will do me good.

I'm currently renting a small studio apartment that's only a few blocks away from the college and campus bar where I work, so it's not unlikely that I'll run into Daniel at some point this summer. Though the apartment is small and in definite need of some TLC, I don't mind. It's my safe space and I'm happy with that, rusty door hinges and all.

Before I decided to leave for school, I'd saved most of my money from all the odd summer jobs I'd done over the last few years and was able to pay a year's worth of rent up front. My dad had offered to help pay for everything, but being able to do it all on my own felt pretty damn good. I was lucky and got a scholarship that helped pay for half of my tuition and most of my textbooks, so the tips from the bar have been enough to get me by for now.

Normally, I would stay home and veg out just like I do for most of the school breaks, but since Sophie graduated a semester earlier than she thought she was going to, I want to spend some time with her before she heads back to NYC in the fall. If things had gone to plan, she'd be starting grad school in August, but she had to push it back a year because she was too busy enjoying her senior year that she missed all the deadlines, even though she graduated early.

She still assumes that I'll eventually join her there once I finish my degree, but I just haven't had the heart to tell her yet that I don't want to go so far away. It's been a while since we got to spend any real time together, so I figure I might as well head home for a bit anyway and maybe try to find a time to bring it up with her.

I pack a large suitcase, not deciding just how long I'm staying yet, but also not wanting to underpack. When I talked to my dad last week, he mentioned wanting to take our annual family camping trip since it's been a few years since we've all been together. Because of everyone's school and work schedules, we've not been able to go camping in a few years, even though it was always a steadfast tradition in our family.

Since Sophie is finally back, my dad suggested we squeeze in a weekend trip, which, these days, seemed uncharacteristically thoughtful of him, but I guess I'll take what I can get and not complain.

We don't usually go this early in the season since it can still get cold up on the mountain at night, so I decide to bring a few extra sets of sweats just in case. I smile to myself as I fold my clothes into my suitcase, thinking back on the fond memories I have from my childhood of sleeping under the stars, and how I long to smell the crackling wood of the fire pit.

I almost forget but decide to include one nice dress with my other clothes since there's a pretty good chance that Sophie will try to get me to go out dancing with her one night.

By the time I'm done packing, I end up with two large suitcases and a small duffel bag filled with shoes. I look down at my bags and think that I might've slightly overdone it, but I feel like you can never be too sure of the weather this time of year, especially in the mountains.

I haul my bags out to my car and decide to get on the road before it gets too dark, not wanting to get lost on the unfamiliar roads at night.

# Chapter Two

It's about a three-hour drive from South Jamestown University to my hometown of Cedar Hills, if traffic is flowing nicely, that is. I've only made the drive back home twice over the last two years, once for Thanksgiving just after I'd left for school, and once when Sophie's Grandpa Millard died last year.

I'm about halfway there when I get a call from Sophie, who's probably already bored out of her mind in our dinky hometown. After spending five years in the bustling metropolis of New York City, there's not much our small town has to offer, at least not to a party girl like her.

I welcome the conversation, though, since I'm starting to get drowsy from the drive. The second I get into a car, it's usually lights out unless I down at least two Red Bulls and then chew through an entire pack of bubblegum to keep myself awake. I don't know why I'm like that, it's just always how I've been. But then again, I feel like I'm chronically sleepy from always staying up too late, so maybe that's why.

I unintentionally yawn into the phone as Sophie prattles on and on about her last few weeks of college. I just laugh and give the occasional *yeah, uh-huh,* and *right, right.*

She tells me about the wild graduation party her college friends threw for her and how she managed to pull two of the hottest guys on campus before seducing them into making a Sophie sandwich out of her, which makes me laugh.

Whoever they are, those guys had better count themselves lucky because Sophie is gorgeous, to say the least. She seriously got the best of both worlds from her parents' genes. Her dad's dark brown skin and curly hair mixed with her mother's light eyes and complexion, made for a brutally dangerous combination. To say she turns heads wherever she goes is an understatement, especially with the voluptuous curves she inherited from her dad's side of the family.

I don't say anything, but I feel a shred of worry when Sophie neglects to mention anything about grad school or the internships she was supposed to apply for before coming home for the summer.

Sophie's a smart girl, but her grades usually suffer due to her constant need to party and sleep around, hence why her degree took her longer to complete than normal. There's definitely no judgment on my part, though. I could only ever dream of being half as confident as she is. She knows what she wants and goes after it, and somehow everything always seems to work out in her favor.

I decide to bring up the internship anyway. I'm curious to see if she has any real intentions of finding one this summer, or if she plans on just stalking the cute guy she saw at the grocery store she was telling me about earlier.

I hear a heavy sigh on the other end of the phone, followed by silence before she finally answers me. "Shit. Can we talk about something else?" she asks.

"Why? What did you do?" I ask, teasing her.

"Nothing!" she says defensively, and I can hear her smile through the phone.

"You're so full of shit," I say. "Now spill. What did you do?" I ask and try to hold back a laugh, already guessing what trouble she's been up to lately.

"Babe, did I mention that Jess is seeing someone new? She's reportedly on the modeling scene in Alaska. Weird right? Who would've thought there'd be any modeling agencies all the way in the middle of nowhere?" Sophie says, obviously trying to change the subject.

*Typical Sophie. Always all up in everyone's business, especially Jess's.*

"Uh-uh, no way, you're totally deflecting right now," I say, calling her out. "Out with it."

"Ugh, *fine*," Sophie grumbles. "If you're insinuating that I slept with the director's son and got kicked out of the program—like you had predicted I would. You're wrong," she says with a pause. "I slept with his wife," she says with a huff.

"*You slut!*" I say, laughing. "Isn't she like on the board of directors for the school?" I ask in disbelief.

"Correctamundo," she says with a sigh. "Good thing my graduation was already a done deal, otherwise I'd have been screwed," Sophie says, and I don't say anything as I try to stifle my laughter.

"Don't you say another word, I know exactly what you're thinking!" she says, and I can hear her trying not to laugh as well.

Sophie lets out another huge sigh, and I know her well enough to know that she's rubbing her temples right now, probably stressing herself out over it all.

"I dunno Sam, I think I just need a reset before I make a final decision on what I'm gonna do next with my life. I know it's an important choice, but it all feels like too much to deal with right now." Worry is heavy in her voice, and I know exactly what *that* means—she'll be looking for a distraction.

"I hear Trevor's back in town this summer," I say and raise my eyebrows, teasing her through the phone even though she can't actually see me. "That could be fun for you," I say, knowing that I really shouldn't be encouraging her bad behavior. Honestly, she'd probably end up doing it anyway, though, even without any help from me.

"Been there, done that," she says, and I can practically see the eye roll of disinterest through her voice.

"Okay, well, how about tomorrow we hit the town and browse for a man you can take home, to *reset* with. And if you're a good girl, I might even just buy you a treat from Leonard's," I say teasingly.

"You wouldn't *dare* tempt me like that," she says, and I can just imagine the hair flip she probably just did, and how it perfectly accompanies her feisty attitude. "Hmmm, I have a better idea, though."

"Okay, let's hear it," I say, wondering what shenanigans she might be cooking up.

I hear Sophie take a large inhale, and smile to myself as I prepare for whatever "Sophie" thing she has planned for us tonight.

"Okay, check this, Babe. You come straight over, and we make a fort in the living room just like we always used to," she says, and I can tell that she's waiting for me to agree before continuing with the rest of her plans.

"Okay, okay, I'm definitely listening," I answer, already knowing I can't blow off my dad, but still curious as to where she's going with this.

"Then, onto the most important part, we order some takeout. I'm talkin' something chalked full of carbs and MSG, I'm talkin' egg rolls, crab rangoons, an extra extra large container of chow mien, and maybe even some of that deep fried shrimp you love so much from the Red Dragon," she says, and I smile to myself as I picture her dramatically counting off the list on her fingers.

"*Then*, tomorrow I won't have to pick you up, and we'll have more time to browse for hunks," she says as she lets out a relieved breath, like she had just delivered a long-winded speech or something.

"Just text your dad and tell him you had more important places to be," she says, annoyance prevalent in her voice at the mention of my dad.

Sophie's no stranger to the weirdness that's been my home life for the past few years. She tries to hide it, but I know that my mom's leaving had an effect on her as well. Sophie was raised by her grandpa, so my mom was sort of her mom by proxy because of how close our families were.

He sure tried his hardest, but poor Grandpa Millard was not equipped to raise a teenage girl. When things like periods and puberty started to come up, he turned most of that over to my mom.

Regardless of the nontraditional situation, Sophie still managed to have Grandpa Millard wrapped around her little finger. That man would've done anything for her; all she had to do was ask.

In a strange turn of events, Sophie's cousin, Jess, was also raised by a grandparent of sorts. Both of Sophie's parents and Jess's dad were all in a head-on collision and died when they were both six. Jess's mom had passed away a few years earlier due to complications with his birth, so Grandpa Millard's sister, Judy, took full custody of him after the accident when he was just seven years old. Jess and Sophie's moms were sisters, so Grandpa Millard was technically Jess's biological grandfather, but there was no way he would've been able to handle two kids in his old age.

Jess was the only one in the car who had survived the crash even though he was thrown from the vehicle. Though he was in critical condition for a few weeks, the doctors were amazed that he didn't have more injuries than he did. The only physical reminder from the accident he was left with is a large scar across the left side of his waist.

Because of the weird parenting situation, Jess, Sophie, and I were basically all raised together, since Judy and Millard needed all the help they could get.

Aunt Judy had spent most of her life in the military, and for every year for as long as I can remember, she would spend a good portion of every summer volunteering at a military boot camp for troubled teens. During that time, Jess would stay with Sophie and Grandpa Millard until school was back in. It was clear how much Aunt Judy really loved Jess, but I'm sure she enjoyed the time to herself. To say he was sort of a handful is putting it lightly, which is kind of ironic if you think about it.

"That actually sounds a thousand times better than the plans I have tonight, but I'm afraid I can't bail on this one. Dad says it's *important*," I say sarcastically.

When I'd originally told my dad I was coming home for a few weeks, he gave me his usual halfhearted *yay, can't wait to see you* reaction, which was fine because, honestly, I wasn't really expecting much more than that. It surprised me when he invited me out to dinner tonight, though, no doubt to introduce me to his new lady friend of the month. Normally, I wouldn't go since I made it clear to my dad a long time ago that I wasn't interested in meeting his flings anymore, but since it's been almost a year since I've seen him, I figure I can smile and fake my way through dinner for his sake. Just this once.

"Okay fine, we're still on for Leonard's tomorrow, though, right?" Sophie asks. "You can't tempt me like that and then leave me hanging."

"*Absolutely yes* we're still on for tomorrow, I'll pick you up at nine?" I ask, but when I say nine, I actually mean ten thirty, since two hours is about the standard wait time before Sophie even starts getting ready to go out.

"Better make it ten just to be safe," she says. "Since you're not coming over tonight, I might as well call Trevor," Sophie says with another heavy sigh.

*Poor Trevor, she's gonna eat him alive.*

"Oh, and say hi to your new step-mommy for me," Sophie jokes through the phone, and I roll my eyes.

"Sure thing," I say sarcastically.

"Byeee, love you," she says before hanging up.

I'm almost to town when my dad texts me the address of the restaurant where he wants me to meet him. He's usually pretty predictable when it comes to food, so I figured that he'd go for one of his usuals, either Texas Roadhouse or Red Lobster, but instead, tonight he chose Adolfo's.

Adolfo's is a crazy fancy Italian restaurant that takes months in advance to get a table reserved at. I've only been once before, and that was on prom night my senior year with a group of friends. We were obviously pretty dressed up, so I didn't think much about a possible dress code at the time. I look down at the clothes I have on—gray sweatpants and a purple tie-dye hoodie.

*Yikes.*

I look at the clock in my car and debate what to do. I'm only a few blocks away from the restaurant, and since my dad's house is on the other side of town, I have no doubt I'll make myself late if I try to go home and change first. I pull over a block away from the restaurant and try to make up my mind amid the sounds of my growling stomach.

If we were eating literally anywhere else in town, my current wardrobe wouldn't be a big deal. I think back to all the times I purposely rolled up in sweats to dinner to meet my dad's new girlfriends, and snicker to myself.

I don't want to make him lose his reservation, and I feel bad for even considering wearing my sweatpants to this dinner after thinking about how long it must've taken my dad to get a table reserved. Though the more I stop to think about it, the more irritated I get. If it really did take him forever to get a table at Adolfo's, then he had plenty of time to let me know in advance to dress appropriately for tonight's dinner. Which also makes me sort of irritated because the man is not forgetful, at least not with the things that he considers important to him.

I know he said that *tonight* was important, but I try not to let my imagination run wild and hope that by that he's just referring to us not seeing each other in forever as being a special occasion.

I let out another breath and look down at my clothes again.

*Shit.* I'm going to either have to go in as I am or get changed in my car.

I glance out the window and look around. There are too many people walking around for me to just change right here out in the open. Even though my windows have a bit darker tint than normal, I don't intend on giving a free peep show to some random strangers on the street.

I quickly scan the shops around me, looking for somewhere that might have a good bathroom to change in. When I spot Mona's Food and Drug across the street, I hop out of my car. Mona's is a small mom-and-pop grocery store that by some miracle survived when a Target opened up on the other side of town last year.

I know the owners because they live in the same neighborhood as my dad. I also used to cat-sit for them when they went on vacations when I was a kid. The Hendersons are a nice elderly couple, and I can't imagine they'd have anything against me quickly using their bathroom.

I rummage around in my duffel bag looking for the dress I packed just in case Sophie made me go out and remind myself to thank her for that later.

The dress is made of a silky wine-colored fabric that bunches just underneath the cowl neckline, and it has spaghetti straps that crisscross across the back. I grab the dress out of my duffel bag and the black strappy heels that I brought to wear with it before zipping my bag back up.

I got the heels a few weeks ago to go with a *special* outfit that I'd bought to wear for Daniel's birthday. It's safe to say that the outfit didn't stay on me long enough to break the shoes in properly, though. I sigh and try to shake the thought from my mind, Daniel being the last thing I want to think about right now.

I shut the trunk of my car and cross the street toward Mona's. I hear the familiar tinkling of the bell on the door as I open it and step inside, the door shutting gently behind me with another soft jingle.

It's empty inside the store, save for me and Mrs. Henderson, who's sitting behind the register on a small stool, completely lost in whatever book she's reading. She looks the same as when I saw her last, gray hair in a fancy updo, and still sporting her signature dark red nail polish and lipstick.

Seeing her perched on her stool behind the register with her nose buried deep in a book is super nostalgic in the best way possible. The familiar smell of the fresh produce in the store and Mrs. Henderson's continued presence here, just as if she'd never left, makes me smile and wish for those simpler times as a kid when I'd come here to buy candy with Sophie and Jess.

"Hello," I say hesitantly, not wanting to startle her.

She doesn't seem to notice me at all, and I wonder if she's in the middle of a particularly good part of her book. The thought makes me smile to myself, wondering just what kind of books she reads.

I clear my throat and speak a little louder when she doesn't look up. "Hello, Mrs. Henderson," I say, and when she finally looks up from her book, I watch her eyes light up as she registers who I am. "How have you been?" I ask, smiling at her.

"*Oh my word*, is that you, Samantha Ryan? My goodness, you're so grown up!" she says. "Just look at you! You're so beautiful!"

Her compliment makes me happy even though I'm sure that she's just being nice, given that I'm wearing old sweats and Crocs.

She frantically searches for her bookmark before calling over her shoulder. "Richard! Come quick, you'll never believe who's here!" she says excitedly.

"How long have you been back in town? I feel like we haven't seen you in ages! *Richard!*" she calls behind her again as she rushes around the counter to hug me.

When she hugs me tight, I feel a pang through my chest, and suddenly I can't remember the last time someone has hugged me like that, or was this excited to see me.

Mrs. Henderson lets me go but holds one of my hands with both of hers as she smiles warmly at me. "When did you get back, honey?" she asks, seeming to be genuinely interested in the answer.

"Since tonight, actually. I've got a little break from school, so I thought I'd visit my dad," I say, and before I can elaborate, Mr. Henderson makes his way out of the small office and heads around the counter toward us.

"Well, I'll be damned, if it isn't Quincy's favorite person," he says through a smile, his usual gruff demeanor softening at the mention of Quincy. And as if summoned from thin air, Quincy the Cat appears beneath my feet, rubbing himself along one of my ankles.

"Quincy!" I exclaim excitedly as I clutch my dress and shoes to my chest with one hand and squat down to pet him with the other. He purrs loudly, the bell on his collar ringing as I scratch his neck.

"My gosh, you've gotten fat in your old age, haven't you?" I say with a chuckle and continue scratching his neck, the black fur on his nose now peppered with little gray hairs. Quincy meows at me before rubbing his head on my hand and then slowly meanders away, his chubby body swaying as he walks. I stand back up and turn to Mr. and Mrs. Henderson with a smile.

"It's sure nice to see you darlin, but I figured you'd have that troublemaker with you, seein' as though you two were usually tied at the hip," Mr. Henderson says, looking around suspiciously as if someone's going to jump out from behind one of the shelves.

"Oh, you mean Sophie? No, she's at home tonight," I explain.

He shakes his head. "I meant the *other one*," Mr. Henderson says, his eyes narrowing as he says the words.

*Ahhh*, that would be *Jess* he's referring to.

I think back to the last time I babysat Quincy for the Hendersons when I was around twelve years old. I used to do it for them all the time, but that sort of came to an abrupt end when Jess insisted on coming with me to help one time.

Since it was the last day of the Hendersons' vacation, I told Jess that he could come with—only this once. It was supposed to be a quick visit since Mr. and Mrs. Henderson were set to be back sometime that afternoon. We were just going to check Quincy's litter box, his food, and his water, and be out.

I had warned Jess that Quincy was quite skittish and to approach him slowly, just until he got used to him, at least. Jess said I was too much of a worrywart and went straight for Quincy the second he walked into the Hendersons' house.

Long story short, in the commotion of Jess trying to catch Quincy, and me trying to catch Jess, Quincy escaped and ran up the tree in the Hendersons' front yard. Jess was determined not to give up, so he scaled the tree trying to reach him, which only resulted in Quincy climbing higher and higher up through the branches.

Just as the fire department showed up, so did the Hendersons. Jess was still trying to save Quincy, all while being scratched in the face, when they both slipped and fell out of the tree. Jess was able to slow himself down on a branch he caught on the way down, right before landing flat on his back in the grass, luckily not breaking anything in the process. Quincy, however, broke his fall on the head of one of the firefighters standing beneath the tree.

Mr. Henderson thanked me for taking care of Quincy and for keeping him safe up until then, but I could tell that he was pretty unhappy about the whole thing. Jess tried to explain that I had nothing to do with it and that he was trying to save Quincy, not hurt him, but Mr. Henderson wouldn't hear any of it. He ignored Jess's apology and told me to say hi to my dad for him and then went inside the house with Mrs. Henderson. That was the last time I was ever asked to watch Quincy the Cat again.

"Ohhh, you mean Jess?" I say and laugh, remembering the look on Mr. Henderson's face when Quincy landed on the firefighter's head. "No, he's not with me, he's actually working in Alaska right now," I explain, certain that Mr. Henderson couldn't care less, just that Jess is far, far, away from his precious Quincy. Mr. Henderson just gives me a nod in response, still eyeing the shelves behind me like he doesn't believe a word I'm saying.

For a second, I forget what I'm even doing there in the first place and think that if I don't hurry this up, I'm going to be even more late than I already am.

"Anyway," I say, and gesture to the dress and shoes in my arms. "The reason I came in is because I was wondering if I could use your bathroom to change my clothes," I say, and Mrs. Henderson raises a brow at me.

"Oooohhh, so you've got a hot date tonight, then?" she asks, wagging her brows up and down at me.

"No, nothing like that," I say and smile. "I'm meeting my dad for dinner, but I didn't have time to change before I got to town," I say, quickly checking the time on my phone, and see that I'm already ten minutes late. *Shit.*

"Well, you'd better get a move on then. You don't want to be late for dinner with your *dad*," Mr. Henderson says with a wink.

I playfully roll my eyes and smile at him before heading toward the bathroom near the back of the store.

"Wait just a second, Sam. Why don't you change in the office? There's a bigger mirror in there. You won't be able to see anything in that stuffy little bathroom," Mrs. Henderson says, nodding toward the small bathroom, and then gestures to the small office behind the cash register.

"Are you sure? Isn't that for *authorized personnel only*?" I tease as I turn to look at her and nod at the small sign hanging on the office door.

"Oh, *hush*," she says and waves me on around the front counter toward the office.

I close the old wooden door and look around, the decor of the small office making me smile. The office is equipped with a small velvet couch, its orange floral pattern the ugliest thing I've ever seen, which ironically enough probably means that it's comfy as hell.

I see that there's a small gray metal desk in the corner with a dinosaur of a computer on it, right next to a large bookshelf filled from top to bottom with framed photographs.

The old floorboards creak beneath my feet as I walk over to the bookshelf to take a look at the pictures. I haven't ever been in this back office before, and who knows when I'll be back here again, so I tell myself that a little innocent snooping won't do any harm.

I smile to myself as I look at the photos, thinking it's cute how Mr. Henderson still manages to rock his 60's style greaser look even now after all this time. For always being "old" in my mind, Mr. Henderson never betrayed his sense of style due to his age, and it definitely shows in his photos.

I look at the pictures on the shelf and notice that most of them include a black cat. It seems pretty unlikely that the cat in the photos is Quincy, at least not the Quincy *I* know, otherwise he'd have to be at least over forty years old by now.

Richard and Mona never had any children, they only had each other—and Quincy, of course. I've never asked, but I heard rumors that Mrs. Henderson had tried but wasn't able to stay pregnant for very long. The thought makes me sad, and I can only imagine what she went through.

The photos are beautiful, and a good majority of them are even in black and white. There's one of them at Petra in Egypt, one on the Great Wall of China, and even one of Mrs. Henderson on an elephant. It seems like they'd been traveling the world long before I became their cat sitter, and the thought makes me smile to myself. I notice a more recent colored photo of them in Machu Picchu, old age clearly not slowing them down one bit.

The way they look at each other in the photos is endearing, and it's not hard to tell how much they love each other. Seeing the photos makes me very aware of just how lonely I've been, even before everything that went down with Daniel, hell, maybe even before when I was with my previous ex.

I sigh and wonder why I keep trying to fill the void I feel in my chest with people who are obviously all wrong for me.

I quickly undress and slip my dress on over my head. After struggling with the straps that cross in the back for what feels like ten minutes, I finally get the dress on and zipped up. I step into my heels and look in the full-length mirror that's hanging behind the door as I run my hands down the dark, silky fabric. It fits my body well, hugging it in all the right places, the long slit up the thigh making my already long legs appear longer than they actually are. The color of the dress complements my skin tone nicely, making me feel grateful that I'd inherited my mom's Italian olive skin instead of the pasty white skin that runs on my dad's side of the family.

I didn't grab any sort of jacket to match with the dress, and since all I have with me is my tie-dye hoodie, and a few other sweaters in my car, all I can do is hope that it doesn't get much colder out. Even with the slit up the thigh, I'm grateful for the dress's length, hoping that it will at least help keep my legs warm.

I put my hair up in a clip and leave a few face-framing pieces down, trying to make myself look semi-presentable. I didn't bring much jewelry with me, but I decide that the small gold hoops and braided chain necklace that I'm already wearing will do just fine for tonight.

I gather up my clothes before giving myself a final once-over in the mirror and let out a steadying breath before I step out of the office.

"How do I look then?" I ask Mr. and Mrs. Henderson as I do a quick twirl.

Mrs. Henderson gasps and covers her mouth as she smiles, and Mr. Henderson puts a hand to his heart, staggering backward dramatically as if he'd just been hit. I smile, thinking it's so cute how over the top their reactions both are, and thank them before Mrs. Henderson gives me another hug.

"Say hello to your dad for us! Come by and see us again now that you're back in town!" They call after me, and I wave as I exit the store, the bell jingling on the door as it shuts behind me.

When I step out into the cold air, I immediately consider putting my hoodie on over my dress when the cool night breeze hits me, blowing a freezing gust through my dress and across my bare legs.

*Damn, it's cold out here.* "So much for my legs staying warm at least," I mutter to myself. A small shiver passes through me, and I wonder why I didn't bring a nicer jacket after bothering to pack a fancy dress and heels.

I cross the street and leave my sweats in my car, ultimately deciding against the hoodie. I grab my small crossbody purse and throw my phone and keys inside before heading up the street toward Adolfo's.

As I walk, I wrap my arms around myself to keep warm, glad that the restaurant is only a few blocks away. Friday nights are the literal worst for trying to find parking downtown, especially this time of night, and nearby Adolfo's no less. So I tell myself it's a good thing I decided to park by the Henderson's store.

I'm lost in my own thoughts as I walk, but after a few minutes, I get the strange feeling that someone is following me. When I turn and search the streets, twice, there's no one there. I try to convince myself that I'm just being paranoid and that nothing ever happens in this boring little town.

It's not until I'm almost halfway to the restaurant that I hear footsteps on the pavement closing in behind me, followed by a slow whistle.

"Ryan, is that you?"

I curse under my breath when I instantly recognize the voice behind me and decide to pick up my pace, annoyed more than anything.

The streets are dark, and even though it's just after dusk, most of the streetlamps aren't on yet. I look around and notice that my stalker and I are the only ones in sight. I hear thunder in the distance and wonder if the busy streets cleared out because of the downpour that's threatening to start at any minute.

*Dammit, why tonight of all nights?* I speed up, still grumbling to myself, my heels clacking down loudly on the sidewalk.

"So, she's a runner," he says with a snicker.

I quicken my pace further without turning around but quickly feel a hand on my elbow before it yanks me back roughly. My ankles wobble, and I almost fall because of my shoes.

*Damn heels, I could've run if I were still in my Crocs.*

"I knew that was you, Ryan. I'd know that ass anywhere," he says as he scans my body with his eyes, making me uncomfortable.

"Don't call me that," I say as I try to pull my elbow from his grasp.

He jerks my arm roughly before he forces me backward into a wall, and the cold brick of the building bites into my exposed back as I continue to push against him with my other hand.

"What the hell do you want, Elliott?" I ask angrily, trying to keep my cool, even though I'm starting to freak out.

"Nothing, just wondering where you've been. Seems like you've been avoiding us," he says, licking his lips as he brings his face closer to mine.

"We've been worried sick, you know," he purrs into my face, and my reflexes cause me to recoil, but with nowhere to go, I feel the rough brick of the building scratching deeper into my back.

"You're fucking delusional," I scoff in his face with disbelief. "Kyle knows we're done, *now let me go*," I say and pull against him, struggling to free myself from his uncomfortable grip.

My arm is starting to go numb from how tightly he's squeezing it, and I force myself to show annoyance instead of the cold fear that's starting to creep in.

Elliott whispers as he leans in closer to me. "I warned him that this would happen, you know. I told him you'd rather be with a real man, someone who could really keep you... *satisfied*," he says, pinning me against the wall with his body, his breath rank of cigarettes and cheap alcohol.

*Seriously? Could he be any more unoriginal?*

"What? Someone like *you?*" I mock, and scoff at his greasy long hair and wannabe punk rocker getup as I quickly look him up and down. "In your dreams, asshole. I told you to let go of me, now get *OFF!*" I spit, pure venom in my voice as I try to knee him in the crotch.

Elliott dodges my attack with his thigh before he wedges one of his knees in between my legs instead, causing the slit in my dress to ride up from the tension on the fabric.

"I guess you said it yourself, Sam. If you and Kyle really *are* done, there's not much stopping me from having my own taste then, is there?" he says with a look that makes my stomach turn.

Elliott's words infuriate me, as if I'm some object to be claimed without my permission, and even though I'm scared, I refuse to let him have the satisfaction. I struggle against him, frustrated, unable to knee him again from the way he has me pinned against the wall.

"Fuck you, asshole," I say as I thrash angrily and push against him before he grabs my jaw with his hand, putting a painful amount of pressure on it. He roughly shoves my head back against the brick wall, my hair clip painfully digging into my scalp, my other arm still in his tight grasp.

Elliott leans in close, staring at me wildly with his cold, vacant eyes. "*Hmmm*, my boy always did tell me you were a wild one, you know… said you liked it rough," he whispers in my ear.

Elliott starts to rub his knee against me, and I want to vomit at the unwanted closeness of our bodies.

"Is this turning you on, princess?" he asks as he presses his nose up against my cheek before licking up the side of my face.

My panic and the smell of his breath make me feel nauseous, so I attempt to turn my head away, but can't, my jaw still forcefully retained in his grasp.

I try formulating a plan, thinking if I can somehow get away, it's not far to the Hendersons' store. Hell, I just need to get within earshot of literally *anyone* at this point.

Elliott suddenly releases his grip on my elbow, leaving my arm throbbing. He slowly drags his hand down my body, pinning me at the waist as I fight against him still.

"*I said get off*—" I seethe through my teeth to which he responds by tightening his grip on my jaw. The force of his grip makes me wince in pain as he forces me to look at him, and I feel like at this rate I'm going to end up with his fingerprints permanently engraved into my cheekbones.

"Who would've thought that underneath all of this…" he says, his free hand now trying to slip under the slit in my dress. I push against his chest and try to yell for help, but my voice comes out muffled through my tightly clenched teeth.

"…would be such a dirty whor—"

Elliott's words are cut off, and before I can process what's even happening, he's being dragged backward, and I fall onto the sidewalk, my ankles giving out on me. I grit my teeth as I feel the painful bite of the pavement dig into my palms, but manage to catch myself before my knees hit the ground too forcefully.

My head spins from the stress of the situation, and I decide to sit myself down on the sidewalk, afraid my ankles might just give out again in my woozy state. I try to calm my breathing, and as my eyes start to focus again, I watch as Jess roughly shoves Elliott backward, causing him to stagger back off the sidewalk and into the street. I'm met with a disturbing sight as Elliott smiles menacingly at Jess, blood now dripping down his face.

*Wait, Jess? What is he doing here?* And for a second, I wonder if I'm seeing things.

Even though it's been a while since I've seen him, he still looks like himself. His wavy hair's a lot longer now, long enough to be put in a small bun or ponytail. It's strange to see since he usually never let it get past his shoulders before, which makes me wonder when he decided to grow it out.

I shake my head, trying to bring my focus back to reality and the gravity of the current situation.

"Where do you get off thinking you can put your hands on a lady like that?" Jess says angrily and I watch as he turns his head to the side before spitting a small mouthful of blood onto the ground.

Elliott charges at my rescuer, who manages to dodge him effortlessly with a quick sidestep, causing Elliott to almost trip from his own momentum.

"Sorry man, I didn't realize the bitch was your property," Elliott huffs out with a snicker as he puts his hands up defensively, trying to catch his breath as he turns to face Jess again.

"She's not," Jess says before he lunges, punching Elliott square in the nose. "She's no one's property, you asshole," Jess says as Elliott staggers backward up onto the sidewalk, almost tripping over his own feet. He grasps at his face, more blood now trailing down his mouth and chin from Jess's last blow.

I sit on the sidewalk, a little in shock as I watch Jess and Elliott take a few more swings at each other. I'd call it a fight, but it's not really even fair to say that. Elliott just keeps mindlessly swinging his fists at Jess, who keeps dodging him with ease, before landing his own hard blows straight into Elliott's face each time.

I haven't seen Jess since Grandpa Millard's funeral last year and decide that he's put on quite a bit of muscle since then, especially after seeing him fight, and wonder just what kind of work they have him do on the rig for him to be so fit.

Jess quickly turns toward me. "Are you all right?" he asks, and I give him a quick nod, still wondering what he's doing here. He turns back toward Elliott before grabbing him by the collar of his leather jacket and slams him up against the brick wall of the building.

"She told you to get off her, didn't she?" he asks Elliott as he presses him up against the wall.

"Look man, no reason to get all worked up over a piece of ass," Elliott says through a laugh. "You're welcome to have her when I'm done—or better yet—we can share her," Elliott says, and the sound of his laugh is cut short by the loud crunch of Jess's fist colliding with his face, Elliott's nose undoubtedly broken now.

"I don't share," Jess seethes at Elliott, who's now struggling to get away, his tough guy act quickly disappearing after witnessing Jess's intensity close up.

"Don't you ever, and I mean ever, look at this woman again, you disrespectful piece of trash," Jess says threateningly, his chest rising and falling with his quick breaths, like he's trying his hardest to keep his anger in check.

His hands are fisted tightly in the leather of Elliott's jacket as he holds him up against the wall. "Do you understand me?" Jess angrily whispers the words into Elliott's face.

Even after just being warned, Elliott tries to glance over at me, and Jess slams him against the wall again, this time Elliott's head hitting the brick with a hollow thud.

"What the fuck did I just say? Huh?" Jess says, and Elliott looks like he might be concussed at this point.

When Elliott doesn't answer, Jess leans in and grabs him by the jaw, the action giving me a small sense of satisfaction as I watch.

"Look at me," Jess says to Elliott, who's struggling to focus and looks like he might lose consciousness if he sustains even the smallest of blows.

"Look. at. me," Jess demands as he shakes Elliott's head roughly.

Jess leans in and whispers something to Elliott that I'm unable to hear. I watch as Elliott's eyes widen and he nods his head frantically at Jess, who then nods back at him.

After being released, Elliott trips over his own feet as he tries to get away and falls onto the sidewalk. I hear his black jeans tear as he falls before he gets back up and runs down the block, disappearing around a corner without a single look back.

It's only then that I realize that I'm still on the ground, my body shivering from my bare legs against the cold sidewalk.

I look up at Jess and shake my head, wondering if *I'm* actually the one who's concussed. *Isn't he supposed to be in Alaska?*

"Jess, what're you..."

I watch as he walks over to me before offering me his hand. "Are you all right?" he asks with a look of genuine concern on his face.

"I should be the one asking you that, you're the one who's bleeding," I say, noticing the small cut on the corner of his lip.

"Eh, I'm fine, he barely grazed me," Jess says before touching the corner of his mouth with his thumb to check for blood.

I take his hand, and he gently yanks me to my feet. I wobble for a second, and he catches me by the waist when my ankles try to give out again.

"Whoa there, you good? You wanna sit down for a sec?" he asks as he steadies me and then looks around for a place for us to sit.

"No, I'm okay, I think I just twisted my ankles in these damn heels when I fell," I say as I cling to him and scowl down at my feet.

Jess grabs onto the sides of my face gently as he looks me over. "Are you sure you're okay? That douche had you pinned pretty good," Jess says with a worried look as he inspects my jaw before lightly touching it. I wince and he immediately pulls his hand back.

"Yeah, I'm all right. I still think you got it worse than me, though," I say and nod to his cut lip.

"Eh, it's nothing," he says with a shrug.

*Calm and collected as always. I should expect nothing less from him by now.*

"Were your ears burning?" I ask, changing the subject as I give him a small smile, thinking it's ironic how I was just talking about him at the Henderson's store and now he's right in front of me.

"Huh?" he asks and raises a curious brow at me.

41

I shake my head at him and give him a *forget about it* look. "Your hair, it's longer than usual," I say, and stop myself before I reach up to fix the few pieces of hair that are now out of place from his tussle with Elliott.

"Yeah, I know. I'm seriously overdue for a haircut," Jess says as he casually reaches up to run a hand through his hair.

"Don't," I say, and Jess quickly meets my eyes with his own.

For a second the world feels like it stops, and I forget how easily I'm captivated by his dark emerald eyes, almost like they're able to hypnotize me with just a simple glance.

I feel Jess's hand tighten around my waist before he speaks, the action grounding me back into reality.

"You look really beautiful tonight, Sam," Jess says as he searches my eyes, and my heart melts a little at his soft words.

Jess holds my gaze, and before I can call him out for teasing me, I shiver involuntarily as the cold breeze brushes past us and instinctively lean in toward him to shield myself from the wind.

Jess lets go of my waist and grabs my hands as he brings them to his mouth before breathing hot air into them. He rubs our hands together, looking me up and down before raising a brow, and I try not to blush at his close proximity.

"Ryan, where the fuck is your jacket? Aren't you freezing right now?" he asks with a scoff and I just shrug, figuring I'll spare him the whole tie-dye hoodie debacle from earlier.

"Here, put this on. You're making me cold just from looking at you," he says as he takes off his hoodie before handing it to me.

It's been a while since I've seen him, so I try not to drool over how big his arms have gotten since I've seen them last.

*Looks like they've got him working real hard on the rig…*

I open my mouth to protest but stop when he gives me a disapproving look. I put on the hoodie and zip it up, already feeling ten times better with it on. It's soft and warm and smells nice too, so I don't complain.

"Come on, I'll walk you the rest of the way to Adolfo's," Jess says as he grabs my hand and pulls me along behind him before I'm able to say anything.

*Wait, what the hell? How does he know where I'm going… and also, where did he even come from in the first place?*

"Wait, hold on just a second," I say, and try to pull my hand from his grasp, wanting him to slow down.

"If we don't hurry, your dad's gonna be suuuper mad at you for ruining his dinner," Jess calls playfully over his shoulder, still holding onto my hand tightly as he tugs me along behind him.

I roughly yank my hand from Jess's grasp, and he stops walking and turns to face me finally.

"Fuck you," I spit and try to walk around him as I shake my head in disbelief.

"Whoa whoa whoa, hold on a sec," he says, grabbing me.

I turn and look at his hand on my arm and then back to his face before narrowing my eyes sharply at him. He's lucky, because if looks could kill, he'd definitely be a goner.

Jess immediately lets go and puts his hands up in a surrender. "Shit, I'm sorry," he says apologetically, and I can see that he means it from the look in his eyes.

Determined to be dramatic, I unzip the hoodie and quickly take it off before throwing it at him. He catches it and tries to reach for me as I walk around him angrily, dodging his touch.

"Wait, Ryan! Wait!" Jess says as he runs in front of me and starts to walk backward down the sidewalk in front of us. He stays close but doesn't touch me this time, clearly sensing my hostility.

"Look, I'm sorry, I didn't mean it like that. I was just—"

I stop walking and fold my arms across my chest. "You just what?" I ask angrily. "Do you think I *planned* on being assaulted tonight?" I raise my brows at him. "Do you think that I *wanted* to be late to this

43

stupid dinner that I didn't even want to go to in the first place?" I ask as I gesture up the street toward the restaurant with my hands dramatically.

Jess's eyes soften. "No, of course not. I know that wasn't your fault. I'm sorry, Sam, really. You know I'm always on your side. Always. No matter what," Jess says, and his words come out gentle. "If that prick had actually hurt you, you know I would've done much, much worse to him," he says, the softness in his eyes now laced with a simmering fury.

I sigh and cross my arms again, knowing that I could never stay mad at him for very long, also feeling like I might've slightly overreacted. "Fine, I forgive you," I say and roll my eyes. "I guess you did take a hit to that gorgeous face for me, so I guess I can let it slide," I say sarcastically as I reach up and attempt to poke him on the corner of his mouth.

"Hey!" Jess says, trying to dodge me as he lets out a laugh.

"Now give me that back," I nod to the hoodie. "I'm freezing my baguettes off out here," I say as I rub my hands together, and he lets out another small laugh at that. I take the hoodie from his outstretched hand and zip it up as I put it back on, happy to feel its warmth again.

"How did you even know where to find me earlier? Also, when did you get back in town? Aren't you supposed to be in Alaska right now? Does Aunt Judy know you're back? What about Sophie?" I ask, and put my hands on my hips, realizing that this conversation is starting to turn into an interrogation.

"Well then, aren't we inquisitive tonight?" Jess says, placing my arm around his before we start walking again. I don't fight it, but I raise my brows in question at him. "What? We can't have you falling over those heels again. I'd hate to have to carry you the rest of the way," he says, gesturing to our interlinked arms. "Unless you want me to," he says with a wink.

I roll my eyes and look away. "You're doing that thing where you avoid my questions and then try to distract me with flirting," I say flatly as we continue walking, our pace slowing to a leisurely stroll.

"Is it working?" Jess asks with a smirk, and I just give him a look.

"Wellll, to answer your question, it just so happened that I was in the area when your dad texted me asking if I'd heard anything from you. I didn't even know you were back and had to find out from him that you plan on staying in town for a bit. Funny, I don't remember getting that text," Jess says, putting a finger to his chin, and I smack him gently on the arm with my bag. He just laughs and adds, "When I told your dad I hadn't heard from you, he said that he tried calling, but you weren't answering. He said you were running late and that he was getting worried about you."

*Yeah right.*

Silence falls between us for a few seconds before Jess continues. "The only reason I knew where to find you, was because I'd already predicted that your cheap ass wouldn't want to spring for valet at Adolfo's," he says, scoffing to himself. "I was just down the block at the hardware store when your dad texted, so I figured I'd poke around and see if you ended up having to park down the street," Jess says and looks over at me with a smirk.

*Well, I guess he's got me there.* I sigh to myself and wonder if I'm really always that predictable.

I can feel his gaze on my face as I look straight ahead, not saying anything as we continue walking toward the restaurant, my arm still laced through his.

"Look, Jess, thank you for what you did back there. You know I don't usually condone violence... but I don't know what would've happened if you hadn't been there," I say, meeting his eyes.

I feel a bit embarrassed about the whole thing, but he just gives me an understanding look before smiling at me with his perfect teeth. I look back ahead and try not to let my nerves get to me.

"Now don't get mad, but do you know that scumbag?" Jess asks, concern prevalent in his voice. I turn my gaze back toward him and see his smile drop into a frown before he continues. "That guy seemed like he already knew you with the way he was talking."

"Sort of, he's one of my ex's cronies," I say and let out a heavy sigh. "I knew he'd had a thing for me for a while, but this is the last place I thought I'd run into him. He's always been kind of a weasel, but I never expected he'd ever actually try anything."

"Your ex sounds like he's dangerous," Jess says, his voice heavy with disapproval. "What the hell are you thinking getting involved with someone like that, Ryan? With someone who has friends like that dirtbag back there?" Jess asks, and I can tell he's starting to get worked up again. At this point, I wouldn't put it past him to run back down the street to find Elliott for a round two.

Jess seems like he's just about to really lay into me about my questionable boyfriend requirements when we make it to the corner of the restaurant. I stop to face him, wanting to dispel his concern.

"Don't worry, I ditched his sorry ass ages ago," I joke, smiling at Jess. "He had like a million girls after him, so I'm sure that I'm ancient history to him by now," I say, giving Jess a reassuring smile.

"Right, well, tell me why that sentence doesn't make me feel any better," he says, shaking his head.

I let go of Jess's arm and unzip his hoodie before handing it back to him. "You never answered my other questions. Why are you back?" I ask, and the chill of the night breeze creeps up on me again, causing me to shiver. Jess notices and tries to hand his hoodie back to me, and I shake my head. "It'll ruin the look," I say, and he raises his brows before shaking his head.

"I can leave town if it's bothering you…" he says with a smirk as he slowly starts to walk backward, back toward the way we came.

"Oh, shut up, you know that's not what I meant," I say and grab his arm to stop him, his skin unbelievably warm under my touch.

"Can I buy you a coffee tomorrow?" he asks as he looks at me before playfully rolling his eyes. "Sorry, what I meant to say is, can I buy you a sugary milk beverage topped with whipped cream that mayyybe has a *hint* of a coffee flavor in it?" he says, smiling. "*Then*, I'll answer all of your questions," he says and winks at me.

"Actually, tomorrow I can't, I already promised Soph I'd take her to Leonard's to make up for tonight," I explain and give him an apologetic shrug.

"So, you blew Sophie off for your dad tonight?" he asks.

"Well, not exactly, I already had plans with my dad when she asked me to come over," I say.

"Okay, so don't feel bad then. You shouldn't feel like you have to make anything up to her. You're not obligated to give her all of your free time just because she says so, you know," he says, sounding slightly annoyed, and I wonder if they recently had a fight or something. They butted heads a lot as kids, but in the end, they always worked it out.

"No, I know, you're right," I agree, and nod. "But regardless, tomorrow I have errands to run before Friday's trip. Which brings me to my next topic." I fight the urge to anxiously pace and wonder why I feel so nervous all of a sudden. "It looks like my dad wants to start the annual camping trip to Bass Lake back up again this year. I know we'd usually wait until the end of the summer, but apparently, he has another trip planned that he can't miss or something like that," I say, and roll my eyes as Jess watches me intently.

"It'll be just like the old days, me, Sophie, Chris, my dad... and you, if you want. I didn't text you about it because I thought you were still in Alaska," I say with a shrug. "But obviously you're welcome to come, just like you always are," I say and smile. "It'll be fun to be all together again," I say, trying not to come across as desperate. I know that before, Jess had always looked forward to this trip when we were growing up, but I don't want to make him feel obligated if he already has other plans.

"Okay. I'll come on one condition, though," he says with a mischievous grin.

"No, I will not piggyback you around the lake barefoot like you made me do that one year—that was a one-time thing only," I say, smiling as I hold up a finger at him.

Jess just laughs. "With those ankles?" he asks, gesturing to my feet. "I wouldn't dream of it," he says with a smile.

"What do you want then?" I ask and put my hands on my hips.

"It's a simple request, really," he says, shrugging. "Ride up the mountain with me. We'll have a chance to talk for real, and I'll tell you why I'm back in town," he says, a hint of mystery dancing in his eyes.

"Okay, fine, but I get to pick all the food. I'll not be having any trail mix or any of your other old man snacks," I say and wag a finger at him.

"Deal." He nods, trying to hold back a laugh.

"I'll text you the details tonight," I call over my shoulder as I turn and head up the walkway toward the doors of the restaurant.

I grab the handle but hesitate for a second before I turn around and see Jess standing with his hands in his pockets, still watching me from his place on the sidewalk where I left him.

I slowly make my way back over to him, my heels clacking against the walkway, and he gives me a confused look.

"Ryan, is everything—"

I snake my arms around his waist and pull him into a tight hug. At first, he doesn't move, but then he slowly wraps his arms around me before hugging me back tightly. After a few seconds, I feel him exhale and he relaxes into me, and it's a real hug. I hold him tight and think about how I've forgotten how much I've missed him over these past few years, not realizing just how much until I heard his voice again tonight.

The longer we hug, the less I want to go to this dinner. I'm half tempted to ask him to play hooky with me so we can catch up right now instead of in a few days. I nestle into him, enjoying the warm comfort of his embrace, an embrace that feels like home.

I let go and step back, our eyes meeting.

"What was that for?" Jess asks, looking at me, his mouth turned up in a half smile. I can't tell if he's blushing or if his cheeks are just flushed from the cold, but my stomach does a small flip at the thought that it could be from our hug just now.

"I'd forgotten how much I've missed you, is all," I say as I stare into his dark green eyes, before I feel my own cheeks start to redden.

"Missed you too, Ry," he says as his mouth widens into a perfect smile.

Jess gives my hand a light squeeze before letting me go, and I turn and make my way back down the walkway to the restaurant, this time heading inside for real.

I let out one last steadying breath before walking up to the host stand.

"Hello, I'm here to meet John Ryan."

# Chapter Three

I quickly check my phone as the hostess shows me to the table and curse under my breath when I look at the time. Shit, Jess was right. I'm forty minutes late now. I see two missed calls from my dad and one text message, including quite a few from Jess himself.

*Great, my dad is not going to be happy.* I groan internally as I follow the hostess through the restaurant.

From across the dining room, I spot the top of my dad's dirty blonde hair and notice that he's wearing a rather fancy suit, even for a restaurant as swanky as Adolfo's. Even now, sometimes it's still a trip to see him put together and presentable, especially after looking like a total slob for the last few years.

I see that my dad is sitting opposite a tiny blonde woman, and I let out a defeated breath, dreading this dinner and the ensuing small talk I already know is in store for me.

The woman's back is facing me as I walk through the restaurant, so the only thing I'm able to make out is the sparkly blue dress that she's wearing and the dopey expression on my dad's face as he looks at her. I watch as he smiles from ear to ear at whatever she's just said before leaning in toward her.

They share a kiss that's borderline inappropriate for a restaurant, and I shudder at the sight.

*Great, some night this is turning out to be.* I scream internally at the thought of having to sit through any more PDA than what I'd just witnessed from them. I watch as my dad holds her gaze like they're the only two in the whole restaurant, and I roll my eyes.

*Give me a break.*

I hate it when he gets like this, it always makes it that much more complicated when he decides to dump them after a few weeks. It's always head over heels full speed ahead and then quickly moves on to detached nothingness once he can't open up. I let out a heavy sigh, wondering if it isn't too late to just bail and go home, especially since I haven't been spotted yet.

I walk up to the table and clear my throat. "Hello," I say hesitantly, looking from my dad to the blonde. My dad snaps his head up to look at me, my sudden appearance breaking his trance.

"Sam, you're here! I'm so glad you made it okay. Jess texted me and said you had a flat? Why didn't you say anything? You know I would've come to help you," my dad says with mock concern, standing, before pulling me in for a hug.

"Well, I guess I didn't want to bother you…" I say and hug my dad back apprehensively, wondering when Jess had time to cover for me. I'm grateful he didn't tell my dad the real reason I was late, not that my dad would make much of a fuss about it anyway.

My dad lets me go just as quickly as he pulled me in and slides my chair out for me. "Here, sit," he says, gesturing to the padded chair. I try not to read too much into it, since this Father of the Year shit is obviously just a show for Blondie over there.

I take a seat at the small round table and turn to look at the woman sitting next to me. "Who's your friend tonight, Dad?" I ask, trying to sound friendly. I give her a polite smile as I unfold my napkin and place it across my lap.

One look and I already hate her. Well, *not actually*. To put it lightly, she's stunning. She looks like she just walked out of a Victoria's Secret catalog, pouty lips, blowout, and all. I quickly give her a once-over and try not to make it too obvious when I try to take stock of her. Almost everything about her appearance is perfect, and although she's very pretty, her hair is obviously bleached. I scoff to myself. I don't care who you are, no one's hair is that blonde naturally.

"This is my—"

Before my dad can finish, the blonde sticks out her hand for me to shake, the tacky bracelets on her wrist jangling together.

"Rebecca," she answers for him in a nasally voice. "But you can call me Becca," she says, giving me an all-too-friendly smile as I shake her hand awkwardly. "It's so nice to meet you finally. Your dad has told me *so much* about you, Samantha," she says.

*Jesus, could she have picked a more cliché thing to say to me?* I have to physically restrain myself from rolling my eyes at her, and it's almost painful.

"It's Sam... by the way," I say, correcting her, trying my best not to sound rude. "...And, he has?" I ask and scrunch my brows together in disbelief.

"Well, obviously. You and Chris are practically *all* John talks about," she says with a fake smile as she lifts her wine glass and takes a sip before looking away. I narrow my eyes at her, still trying to decide if I like her vibe or not—and so far, all of my senses lean toward no.

"Are you sure he's talking about me and not some *other* daughter?" I say jokingly as I let out a nervous laugh before taking a sip of my water.

"Of course, you're much prettier than John described you, though," Rebecca says, and I notice my dad look away when I try to meet his eyes, which tells me that never happened.

"Really? *Hmm*, must be because I take after my mother," I say lightly, trying to bait my dad, and Rebecca's eyes widen at my comment, confirming my suspicion that my dad hasn't told her the first thing about me or my personality.

I watch as my dad quickly cuts me a warning glare from across the table, his true self finally showing through the bullshit show he's putting on.

An awkward silence falls over the table, and I clear my throat nervously before taking another drink of my ice water. I feel stupid for playing right into Rebecca's trap, especially right off the bat. I set down my water glass and look around for our waiter, thinking that I'm definitely going to need something stronger than water to get me through the night.

An uncomfortable silence takes over the table again after a few minutes of idle small talk, and at that point, I don't really know what else to say. The last time I talked to my dad was a few weeks ago when I managed to catch him on his way home from his Sunday tee time at the club. Which, as you can guess, was a pretty quick call. "Business never sleeps," he'd said before cutting me off, saying that he had work he had to get to.

We used to talk all the time, but where these past few years have been—for lack of a better description—*literal dog shit* in the communication department of our family, I doubt he even knows the first thing about adult Sam. Hell, I'd be surprised if he even knew what I was studying in school. It was a bit of a surprise to hear Rebecca say that my dad talks about me at all, which makes me think she really was just making it up for the sake of small talk. Either that, or he actually does talk about me, just maybe not in the way I'd like him to.

I watch as my dad and Rebecca smile at each other like lovesick puppies, seeming to forget that I'm sitting right in front of them, and wonder why they even invited me if they just intended on ignoring me the whole time.

Even though most of my dad's flames only lasted maybe a month at max in the past, I always tried my best to be friendly even though I knew they wouldn't be around for long. The women usually aren't the issue; it's the emotional unavailability from my dad that inevitably sours things pretty quickly. I'm predicting this one will end up a mess just like the rest of them do, but right now—at least in this moment—it's important to my dad, so I guess that in a way, it's important to me too.

I clear my throat to get their attention, and they both look over at me like they forgot that I was literally sitting right in front of them. "Tell me about yourself, Rebecca. How long have you been seeing my dad?" I ask and thank the waiter after he brings me another water, along with the glass of red wine I'd ordered.

"Let me think…" Rebecca says as she puts a finger to her chin. "Right, well, last week was our one-year anniversary, so that means—"

I cough as I choke on my water, spitting some of it on Rebecca by accident, and I'm glad that I didn't decide to take a drink of my wine instead to wash down the bread I was eating.

Rebecca closes her eyes and lets out a deliberately slow breath as she grabs her napkin and dabs at the small droplets of water on her face.

"You okay, Bec?" my dad asks Rebecca as he reaches over to hand her his napkin to help clean up the water I'd accidentally spat at her.

I'm still trying to get my coughing under control when Rebecca stands up. I see a look of worry take over my dad's face and hope I didn't just royally mess this up for him.

I'm still half choking when I try to apologize. "Oh my god—*cough! cough!*—I'm so sorry, Rebecca—"

"It's fine. It's just water ...*and spit*," she says, muttering the last bit under her breath. She sets her napkin down on the table a little too aggressively before excusing herself to the restroom, leaving me alone at the table with my dad.

He looks beyond annoyed as he sits back in his chair. "Please tell me that was actually an accident," he says, raising a brow at me.

"Are you kidding me right now? Please tell *me* that you haven't had a secret girlfriend for an entire year without saying anything," I say, trying to keep my voice down even though I'm a little upset, not wanting to cause a scene in the middle of the restaurant. "Not to mention that that *secret girlfriend* looks like she probably went to the same high school as me!" I say and throw my hands in the air dramatically.

"You couldn't have gone to school with her, Bec was raised in New Jersey," my dad says with a frown and takes a drink from his wine glass. He's still obviously annoyed by my reaction—and doing a piss poor job of hiding it, I might add—even for him.

"That is soooo not the point, and you know it," I say and give him a look of disbelief.

"It's a good thing it's not up to you then, is it?" my dad says with a condescending look.

"Are you for real right now, Dad?" I say, my whispers starting to get more heated the more I try to calm myself down. "It's obvious what she's after, can you really not tell—"

"That's pretty presumptuous of you to assume she's just after my money, Sam. You don't even know her," my dad says, and the color of his face tells me that I'm probably pushing my luck with this conversation.

"I'm just trying to look out for you, Dad. I know you don't want to be alone, but... but wouldn't you rather be with someone who actually wants you for you?" I ask as I let out a heavy sigh.

I watch as he clenches his jaw before he shakes his head and straightens his suit jacket before glaring at me. "Right, because that turned out so well last time," he says with an annoyed scoff before finishing off the last of the wine in his glass.

I'm just about to apologize again when Rebecca returns to the table. I watch as my dad quickly stands and pulls her chair out for her, his annoyance with me momentarily muted as he jumps back into doting boyfriend mode.

Watching their interactions tonight has me a little confused, to say the least. He was never this way with any of his other lady friends in the past, since they were always the ones chasing *him*. That's not to say that he mistreated them by any means, but he usually did little more than lift a finger, and they were all over him.

Rebecca sits down in her chair, but before my dad is able to return to his, she grabs him by his collar and pulls him down into another borderline inappropriate kiss. Rebecca opens her eyes and glances sidelong at me before breaking their kiss and releases the collar of his shirt.

*What the fuck is wrong with her?* I cringe and look away, feeling uncomfortable.

When the waiter brings out our food, I stare down at my pasta, no longer feeling very hungry—especially after the heated conversation between my dad and me. I play with my noodles for a few minutes before pushing my plate away and grab my wine glass instead. I feel like the night couldn't go any slower, so I down the contents of my glass before signaling for the waiter to bring me another.

I watch as my dad gives me a disapproving look from across the table, and I cut him a warning glare, daring him to say something to me about it. After all the times I was left to sober him up, he has absolutely no room to chastise me about a few measly glasses of wine.

I thank the waiter after he pours me another glass and clear my throat. "Sorry I was late tonight. That *flat tire* took a little longer to handle than I'd anticipated," I say, trying my best at some small talk to ease the tension. "I'm curious as to why you chose such a fancy place, Dad, I don't think we've ever had dinner here before."

My dad gives me a forced smile and I'm already dreading his answer. I have a sneaking suspicion of what he's about to tell me so I'd rather he just get on with it so we can leave already.

"Well, this is a special place for Bec and me," he says as he reaches across the table to grab Rebecca's hand, smiling at her.

*Here we go.* I take a quick look at Rebecca's hand in his and can't believe that I didn't notice it before.

*You have got to be kidding me.*

My dad doesn't say anything, like he's just waiting to see how I'll react. What does he expect, for me to jump up and down with excitement and then cry, or some shit? *Give me a break.* I roll my eyes internally.

I look at the giant ring on Rebecca's hand and then back at my dad, who's still staring at me intently, which makes me feel a little guilty for my previous comments about her. He's made it clear over the last few years that he has no interest in my approval or opinion about things, much less his girlfriends, so the look he's giving me is somewhat confusing, especially after the argument we had earlier.

It's strange to see, but he looks happy with Rebecca, and this time it seems like it's actually reaching his eyes, which is definitely a first. I know that I accused her of only having an interest in him because of his money, but judging by the way he looks at her, I don't think he really cares about that at all—even if it is true.

"When?" I ask, unsure of what else to say, looking between them both.

"Last week," Rebecca says cheerfully as she lets go of my dad and shoves her hand in my face so that I can see the gaudy thing for myself up close. "It was on our anniversary. We met at this very restaurant," she says matter-of-factly as she straightens in her chair.

The ring is nice, and by nice, I mean it looks expensive as hell. Anything flashier and you'd need sunglasses to sit in the same room as her. I'm relieved to see that the ring isn't the one that belonged to my grandmother, though. If it were, I can just imagine myself leaping over the table before ripping the ring off Rebecca's bony finger and laugh to myself at the ridiculous visual.

Don't get me wrong, I'm not necessarily unhappy for my dad, but this all just seems a little rushed to me. I've wanted him to be happy for as long as I can remember, because ever since my mom, there's been this perpetual sadness about him, which has always been difficult for me to witness.

Even in his Playboy phase, it was clear that he was still heartbroken. Even if he didn't act like it, I could always see it in his eyes. It was like he was looking for something that he'd lost instead of being open to something new. But this ...*Rebecca*... person, I'm not too sure about.

"Well, Rebecca, to be honest, I don't know the first thing about you. I don't know if I can let you marry my dad," I say, completely serious as I fold my hands neatly in my lap. My dad and Rebecca both just stare at me.

"John, you did say she was a jokester," Rebecca says to my dad and gives a fake laugh as she squints her eyes at me. "It's not really up to you, is it now?" she says and gives another humorless laugh. "*A joke*, of course," she says, looking between my dad and me, and grabs my hand out of my lap. "But I would really like your blessing, Samantha. Christopher has already given us his."

*No shocker there that they told Chris before me.* I wonder why in the hell that jerk made me come to this dinner alone, especially since he probably knew it was going to turn into some weird family celebration.

Rebecca's stare intensifies as she tightens her grip on my hand, and I pull it away, pretending to adjust the napkin in my lap.

*He can't be serious about her. This bitch is crazy.*

"Look at this, my two girls already cracking jokes together," my dad says and reaches over to pat me on the shoulder but stops himself halfway there.

The rest of dinner is as awkward as humanly possible, even though it mainly consists of chatter about the weather and how crazy it is that the town is growing so fast. My dad is in a pretty cheery mood despite our tense argument earlier, so I mostly stay quiet and try to behave, not wanting to ruin this for him. I remind myself that even as broken as our relationship is, he still asked me here to tell me his big news, so I figure that's got to count for something, at least.

When my dad asks if I have any particular plans for the summer, I tell him that, besides hanging out with Sophie, and the camping trip that's coming up in a few days, I don't really have any. He just nods and then proceeds to tell me all about the trip he has planned for him and Rebecca in a few weeks. I should've known that he wouldn't actually care what my plans were, and I try to shake off my disappointment before I let it get me down.

Since he and Rebecca have *so many* upcoming trips coming up in the next few months, my dad says that it's for the best that we decided to cut the camping trip short by a few days. He tries to blame it on everyone's busy schedules, but I know he's just making excuses, especially since Becky's vibe doesn't really scream outdoorsy.

Rebecca starts to drone on and on about wedding plans, and I let myself zone out, not really interested in listening anymore. I can sense the four glasses of wine I drank earlier starting to get to me, my eyes and head starting to feel heavy. My body feels all warm inside, the chill from being in the breezy outside air earlier all but gone now.

I think about before and how it felt so nice to see Jess again after such a long time, and how I'd much rather be here with him instead of with two lovesick teenagers.

My dad breaks my thoughts away from Jess when he lets me know that he's going to stay the night at Rebecca's place, which means that I'll have the house to myself tonight since Chris is out of town with his friends.

I sigh to myself. *Great, so I'll be alone. Again.* So much for spending any time with my dad this summer.

As we're leaving the restaurant, my dad offers to give me a ride down the block to my car since the air has only gotten colder outside. I tell him not to worry about it since I opt to take an Uber home instead of driving, still feeling a little buzzed from the wine. He offers me a ride to the house but doesn't insist. From what I've learned, Rebecca lives on the other side of town, so he'd have to backtrack quite a bit after dropping me off. I tell him to just go on home with Rebecca and that I'll be all right getting back on my own.

I have the driver stop by my car on the way and I get at least one of my bags, so I have something to wear for the night and tomorrow morning.

After I quickly grab my things and get back in the car, I keep checking behind us every few minutes to make sure we aren't being followed. I know I'm just being paranoid, but I can't help it. I'm aware that it's unlikely that Elliott waited all throughout our dinner just to follow me home, especially after the beating and whatever warning Jess had given him.

I let out a heavy sigh as I stare out the window of my Uber and think about how I can't wait to be home, safe behind locked doors already.

# Chapter Four

When I get to my dad's house, all of the lights are off and the house is empty, just like he said it would be. I didn't expect Chris to throw me a welcome home party, but I also didn't expect him to be out partying on a Wednesday night. For not going to college, he sure likes to act like he's in some kind of frat.

I drop my bag in my old room and look around. It still looks pretty much the same since the last time I was here, which surprises me. I guess Rebecca hasn't decided to redecorate the entire house just yet, and I make a mental note to pack up anything I don't want *accidentally* donated while I'm not here.

I pick up the small picture frame that's sitting atop my dresser and think back to the day it was taken. It's a photo of me, my mom, Sophie, and Jess at the aquarium when we were all about seven years old. I remember it was taken just a few months after the accident with Jess and

Sophie's parents. We're all smiling in the photo, but I remember that the day didn't originally start that way.

Sophie grew up in the house next door to mine, so it was only natural that we became best friends pretty early on. After the accident with her parents, even though she went to live with her grandpa, she still ended up spending a lot of time at my house while he worked on getting the guardianship situation sorted out.

One day, when my mom brought Sophie over, she also brought along a new face with them. The day the picture was taken was the first time I'd ever met Jess. And even though I'd heard about him multiple times before from Sophie, I still wasn't sure what to expect. I had overheard my parents talking about Jess and how his aunt needed a small break from his violent outbursts. When I had asked my mom about it, she told me that I must have heard them wrong and that everything was fine.

Even though Grandpa Millard's sister, Aunt Judy, had volunteered to take custody of Jess after the accident, she was facing some difficulty from the courts since she wasn't a direct grandparent of his. In the end, she fought like hell for him, because if she hadn't, he would've most likely ended up in the foster system.

While Judy and Millard were preoccupied with fighting the unhelpful state court system, my mom volunteered to take both of the kids for a few days to give them both a break, saying it would be good for all of us to have a change of pace for a little while.

The boy who walked into my house that day wasn't the Jess that Sophie had talked about so many times before. The dark circles under his eyes, and the pale skin and ratty curls around his head were nothing like what I'd pictured in my mind, nothing like the mischievous little rascal Sophie had made him out to be.

That day, I remember watching from around the corner, still wary of what I'd heard my parents talking about earlier, and wondered if he really was violent like they'd said he was. Even though he seemed sad, he didn't look *mean*. I remember thinking that if he were, would they really have agreed to bring him over?

Jess didn't say much when he first got to the house and had only asked to be shown to his room, where he didn't come out for the rest of the night, not even to eat.

Sophie and Jess both seemed to deal with their grief in different ways. Sophie would cry a lot, and according to what I'd overheard, Jess had a bad habit of breaking things.

When I'd first heard the crash, I was so terrified that I didn't know what to do. My dad had just taken Chris to the store with him, so I ran to get my mom instead. I remember that Sophie and I hid around the corner to the kitchen, still unsure of what was happening.

When my mom walked in on Jess, he was smashing her favorite plates straight onto the kitchen floor, they were her lemon-colored ones, the ones she had brought back from her trip to Italy with my dad the previous summer. It was the first time I'd ever seen anyone so upset that they broke something with such intent the way that Jess did that day.

I stare at the photo of us as I hold the picture frame in my hand, the memories of the day flooding back in like it was only yesterday.

"Jess, honey, what are you doing?" my mom had asked. Jess turned around to face her as she approached him slowly from the living room. He was red-faced, tears streaming down his cheeks, as he held one of the glass plates in his right hand.

"I hate these plates! I hate them!" he screamed the words at her as he smashed the plate against the kitchen countertop, the glass shattering against the marble.

Though I didn't realize it at the time, Jess's hatred of the color stemmed from his mother's love of it, and the subsequent use of yellow roses at his father's funeral. He'd later told me that the color itself repre-sented the ensuing finality that they were both gone and how he felt all alone in the world.

"It's not fair! I hate these plates, and I hate *you!*" he'd yelled at my mom through his tears.

My mom had just stood there, not saying a word as she watched him. I thought for sure his ass was grass when she caught him, especially when I found out just what he was destroying.

I watched my mom closely, confused by why she wasn't getting mad or trying to stop him. She just stood there, staring at him, her breath-ing calm and even as she watched him.

Jess stood his ground as if challenging her, with a piece of the broken plate still in his hand. He'd held a pained expression on his face, hot tears and snot still running down his chin.

I'd cowered with Sophie in the doorway, who seemingly got more distraught the more she saw how upset Jess was getting, and I held tightly onto her hand when she began to cry.

Very slowly, my mom walked over to him, and Jess adjusted his stance aggressively as if warning her that he'd throw another plate at the slightest provocation. My mom put her hands up in defense before she grabbed a plate off the counter next to him. She ran her hands over the face of the plate, admiring the beautiful craftsmanship of the glass before dropping it onto the floor in front of them.

The sound of breaking glass against the tile echoed throughout the kitchen. Shock and silence filled the space as none of us dared to say a word. It was like the air itself was holding its breath, waiting for her alone to speak.

Jess gaped at my mom, his jaw hanging half open in disbelief at what she'd just done. I'd watched as she slowly knelt down in front of Jess, making it so they were eye level with each other. She held his eyes with hers as she grabbed the other end of the broken plate in his hand before she gently pulled it from his grasp, and the sound of the fractured piece clinked as she placed it on the counter behind them.

"I never really liked those plates anyway," she lied—and I couldn't understand why.

Jess continued to gape at her, his eyes looking like they were about to pop out of his skull.

When my mom spoke, she spoke to him so gently, as if he were about to shatter as her beautiful yellow plates had against the cold tile flooring.

"Let's get you a bandage for this, yeah?" she'd said as she lifted his hand that was holding the glass, a tiny stream of blood now dripping down his pinky from a small cut across his palm.

Jess looked down as he sniffled and wiped his nose on his other sleeve, not able to meet her eyes anymore.

My mom gently lifted his chin while holding his other hand in hers. "It's okay to be sad, Jess," she'd said, and slowly nodded at him as he finally met her eyes. "Everyone gets sad," she'd said before pausing as she held his gaze, "even *I* get sad sometimes."

"You do?" he'd asked her quietly, followed by another sniffle.

"I do." She'd nodded at him again before she lightly placed one of her hands on his cheek. "I know it doesn't seem like the truth, but sometimes there is no one to blame for the bad things that happen, and that sometimes very bad things happen even when they shouldn't," she'd said gently as a few tears ran down her face.

"*Especially* when they shouldn't."

Jess's face contorted in pain as he held back a sob, his little frame jerking from his hiccups.

"We just need to remember, Jess, that there are people who love us and need us to be strong, even though we're sad. And even though it seems hard right now, and that this pain you feel—this pain right here," she said as she placed her hand on his chest, "feels like it's never going to end. It will."

My mom softly patted the back of Jess's head as she continued to hold his gaze. "I can't promise that it will ever go away completely, but I can promise that someday it won't hurt you so much anymore, okay?" Jess looked up at my mom with his bloodshot eyes and gave her a small nod in understanding.

I remember the sadness on her face in that moment, and I had wondered what she meant by all that. In hindsight, I realize that she wasn't just empathizing with Jess, it was much, much more than that for her.

My mom looked over to Sophie and me huddled by the kitchen's entryway and waved us over. She'd pulled Jess into her chest for a hug and opened her arms to Sophie and me before pulling us all into her embrace.

We stayed there a while, all huddled together in the kitchen, a big mess of tears and runny noses, before my mom wiped them all away and instructed Sophie and me to take Jess to the bathroom to get his hand cleaned up.

One Hello Kitty band-aid and a semiofficial introduction later, and Jess had finally calmed down. He'd apologized to us both for making us feel scared earlier, and for breaking my mom's plates.

Sophie, however, was still on the verge of tears, saying that she was worried that my parents would send Jess away after what he'd done. I'd told her not to worry and that there was no way that my mom would do that to him, not now, not after everything.

When we came back to the kitchen, the broken plates were all cleaned up, and my mom was putting on her coat. "Okay, everyone! Shoes!" she'd ordered as she clapped her hands together. "I *accidentally* dropped the meatloaf that I'd made for dinner in the sink—so obviously—there's only one reasonable solution. Ice cream for dinner!" she'd said cheerfully, and I could see that her eyes were red and a little puffy from crying, but she still gave us her biggest smile anyway.

When Chris and my dad got home, we all went out for ice cream. After that, my mom even took us to the aquarium, where she let us each pick out a stuffed animal to take home.

Following that incident, Jess never had another violent outbreak at our house again, or ever again, from what his Aunt Judy had said. She'd said that though he was definitely a handful, he never got violent, even when he was upset.

I look at the picture frame in my hand and sigh, wishing I could go back to that day and tell my mom the same things that she'd told Jess. As an adult now, I realize that she probably needed someone to say those same words to her. I doubt it would've made a difference, but now knowing what I do, she was likely going through something of her own back then, too.

I decide to take a hot bath and try to read a little bit of my spicy romance novel but can't seem to focus. After reading the same page four times, I decide to call it. I stand up to dry off and wrap my robe around myself in a hurry, the cold draft in the bathroom making me shiver.

I hear a creak and startle myself for what feels like the hundredth time in the last hour, my imagination running wild with every little sound in the house. I'm seriously on edge but keep reminding myself that everything is fine and that my dad has a top-of-the-line security system that not even Tom Cruise could get past.

I've never told any of my college friends, or exes, my dad's address, least of all people Elliott, so there's no way anyone even knows where I am right now. I'll admit, though, that it *was* a seriously freaky coincidence running into Elliott tonight. *Unless it actually wasn't...*

I jump at the sound of someone knocking on the front door and lose my footing just as I'm stepping out of the tub. I slip and fall on my ass straight back into the water, cursing as I look down at myself. Robe and all, I'm soaked again.

*Well, shit.*

I sigh and look around for a towel.

I climb out of the bathtub, careful not to let myself slip again, my tailbone aching, and peel off my sopping robe before tossing it to the floor in a wet heap. I find the biggest towel I can and wrap it around myself, my hair a soaking mess around my shoulders.

I curse my dad under my breath for not giving me access to the Ring camera yet, making it so that I can't check who's at the door without checking the peephole.

I peek around the corner once I'm down the stairs, hoping that whoever it is will just go away on their own if I ignore them long enough.

*Knock! Knock! Knock!*

I slowly walk toward the door and grab a golf club out of my dad's bag that's in the entryway of the house. I tiptoe myself up and look through the small peephole on the back of the front door.

Jess.

I unlock and open the door, my shoulders hunching forward in relief as I let out the breath I was holding. "Thank god it's you."

"*Well hello there,*" Jess says as he looks me up and down, followed by a catcall whistle.

His sweeping eyes distract me until I feel the breeze from the open door behind him. I shiver, noticing that it's still cold as fuck outside and that me standing in the doorway half naked and wet isn't helping that fact.

I realize that I'm still holding the golf club in my hand and toss it to the ground before I grab Jess by his arm, pulling him inside the house before shutting the door and locking it behind him.

"If I'd have known you'd be this eager to see me, I'd have come over sooner," he says and winks at me.

I walk over to the couch and grab the small throw that's draped over its side and wrap it around my shoulders. "In your dreams, buddy," I say, narrowing my eyes at him.

"What were you planning on doing with that?" he asks as he raises a brow before nodding over at the golf club I'd thrown on the ground.

I shrug. "I had to improvise, it was either that or one of these god-awful pillows," I say, gesturing to what seems like one of forty covering the couches in the living room.

I guess Rebecca has been here redecorating after all, and I wonder how I didn't notice the ugly things before.

We both laugh, and then a thick silence fills the room, both of us immediately aware of just how naked I am under my thin towel. I wrap my arms around myself, suddenly feeling very exposed in my current state. I look over at Jess, who clears his throat as he looks away from my towel-clad body.

"I thought we weren't getting coffee for a few more days, or did you want to go right now instead?" I joke as I look at the invisible watch on my wrist before stepping toward the door, trying to break up some of the awkwardness. "Should I get my things, or…?"

"You're insane if you think I'd ever let you out of the house looking like that," he says and scoffs.

"What? My hair can't be that messy, can it?" I ask, joking as I put my hands on my hips, and I cringe just thinking about how bad the tangled mess must look right now.

"That's not why," Jess says as he gives me another once-over, lingering a little too long on my exposed legs.

Jess's flirting always gets to me, and he knows it. *So annoying.* I blush and try to change the subject. "What's in the bag?" I ask as I gesture to whatever it is that he's holding in his hand.

"This…" Jess says as he holds up a small brown paper sack, "…is from Aunt Judy. I swung by to see her tonight after I'd finished my errand at the hardware store. I told her you were back in town, and she was all bent out of shape that she wasn't able to make you anything, so she sent me out to get you something instead," he explains, followed by a wink.

A few years ago, just after our high school graduation, Aunt Judy fell down her porch steps and broke one of her hips. Jess had insisted on taking care of her himself, but the stubborn old bat wouldn't let him, as Jess had put it.

She'd said that she was afraid that if he stayed home to take care of her, he'd never leave our miserable little town and make something of himself. At the time, he'd just gotten the job offer on the oil rig, and since it was so far away, he almost didn't take it.

Judy said she didn't want to be the one to hold Jess back from living an extraordinary life. She really pushed him to leave, even if it only ended up being for a little while, she wanted him to go out and see what the rest of the world had to offer before he settled down.

Apparently, Judy had been hoarding most of her money for the majority of her life. Because of that, she was able to afford to move into a pretty nice assisted living community after she was discharged from the temporary ortho rehab facility she was in.

Jess was pretty upset about the whole thing, but they'd agreed that she would go live there *only* if Jess was allowed to pay at least half of her living expenses. He'd originally wanted to pay for it all, but Aunt Judy wasn't having it.

Jess walks toward me and hands me the small bag. I take it from him, immediately recognizing the logo from Leonard's Bakery. I take a look inside and let out a squeal of excitement.

"White chocolate chip macadamia nut cookies! My favorite! Jess, you have no idea how much I've missed these!" I say as I hug the bag to my chest as I spin around, jumping up and down.

My excitement is halted when I feel the throw blanket fall off my shoulders, my towel almost going down along with it. I stop moving and clutch the material to my chest right before I almost flash Jess.

"Careful there, I wouldn't want to make you have to use one of those golf clubs on me for accidentally sneaking a peek at you," he says and smirks as he nods to my dad's golf bag.

I squint my eyes at him and shake my head as I watch him trying to stifle a laugh. "Pervert," I say, and Jess just laughs before bending down to hand me the throw blanket.

I smile to myself, opening the bag again as I inhale the sweet scent of the cookies inside. "*Mmmm*," I hum and close my eyes. "Tell Aunt Judy thank you. Obviously, nothing could ever compare to her homemade ones, but these are definitely a close second. I haven't had the chance to go see her yet, but I was planning on stopping by tomorrow afternoon."

"I'll be sure to tell her you loved the cookies the next time I talk to her, but if you want to see her, you'll have to wait until sometime next week," Jess says, and I raise a brow at him. "She's leaving on a ski trip with a group from her building in the morning. It's like their annual old people field trip," Jess explains, and laughs to himself, as if he's trying to picture retirement-home-aged people all with hip and knee replacements trying to ski.

"I know what you're thinking, and *no*, most of them don't actually ski, they mainly just sit around the fire and play cards," he says. "You didn't hear this from me, but reportedly, Aunt Judy has a boyfriend," Jess says and shakes his head in disbelief as he backs toward the door.

"You're joking," I say, trying not to laugh.

"Dead serious, his name is Phil. Apparently, he's a retired fire-fighter," Jess says, also trying not to laugh.

Aunt Judy always did like a man in uniform. They weren't married long, so I didn't ever get to meet him, but her previous husband, Frank, was in the Navy.

"Damn, Judy, you've still got it," I say and shake my head as we both laugh.

I move toward the doorway to see Jess off for the night when he turns to face me, rubbing his neck nervously as he stares at the ground.

"What's wrong with you? Why are you acting all weird?" I ask and give his shoulder a playful shove.

"It's nothing—it's just that… Aunt Judy did ask me to bring you those cookies, she just wanted me to stop by tomorrow instead," he says.

"Why would that matter? You tryna give me stale cookies or something?" I joke.

Jess shrugs. "She said it would be too late if I brought them by tonight—and not that I give two shits about what they think—she'd said that the neighbors might get the wrong idea about me or something, and she didn't want it to make you uncomfortable."

Even though Jess rolls his eyes, he still seems nervous and won't meet my gaze completely. I don't say anything, wanting to know where he's going with this.

"Anyway… I guess the real reason I came by tonight was to see if you were all right. You know, after everything that happened earlier," Jess says as he looks at me with concern in his eyes.

*So that's why he's acting so weird, it's because of what happened earlier.*

I'm not really sure why, but I feel sort of relieved, unsure of what he was really trying to get at. I wouldn't mind a booty call right about now—especially from Jess—but I know that's not what this is.

He's practically a chiseled god with his beautiful dark wavy hair and jawline that could cut diamonds, to go along with the rest of his flawless features. Honestly, he might be the most gorgeous thing I've ever laid eyes on, male or female, for that matter.

Whenever I'm around him, I have to mentally restrain myself from thinking about him in *that* way because I know that it wouldn't be reciprocated. I have no doubt that he cares about me, he's proven that much tonight at least, but I don't think I could handle being rejected by him, at least not in that way. Not only would things be super weird after a confession like that, but Sophie might never speak to me again if anything ever did happen between Jess and me.

"I didn't know you'd be home alone, so I'm sorry if I scared you. I figured that either your dad, or Chris would be here," Jess says and shrugs apologetically. "It kind of threw me off when I didn't see your car. I wondered if you were still out to dinner with your dad and considered a rescue mission for a second," he says with a laugh.

"You must've been picking up on the telepathic messages I was sending you." I groan and rub my tired eyes with my fingers. "I was *dying* for a rescue from that dinner," I say with an exhausted scoff.

"That bad, huh?" Jess says as he leans back against the door, folding his arms over his chest. The action makes his biceps look humongous and I have to force myself not to ogle him.

"You have no idea," I say and sigh. "Looks like John is in love again, and this time there's even a ring involved," I say and shake my head, closing my eyes momentarily.

"No shit?" he asks in disbelief. "But not your grandmother's ring, right?" Jess never knew my grandmother, but he knows how important she was to me, even though she passed away when I was little.

"No, thank god. If it were, I think we'd probably be having this conversation from jail right now," I say, and we both laugh.

Jess scratches his head and suddenly looks serious again when he speaks. "Look, Ryan, I don't wanna overstep or make you feel weird... but if you don't want to be alone tonight, I can stay if you want. I'll just crash on the couch or something, you won't even know I'm here," he says, nodding toward the living room.

The way he's acting so weird makes it feel like the last few years we've spent apart might've really put a fair amount of distance in between us.

I consider his offer and realize that he's right. I don't want to be alone. I was already planning on not sleeping at all tonight, paranoia still running rampant through my head. I would really like to actually get some rest, and I know that I would for sure feel much safer if Jess were here with me, even if he just stays on the couch for the night.

I feel bad for possibly inconveniencing him a second time to-day, especially since I've only been back in town for less than twelve hours now. *This is probably the last place he wants to be tonight... But, he is the one who offered...*

I raise my eyebrows. "You don't have a pretty little redhead wait-ing up for you or something?" I tease.

"She'll just have to wait," Jess says as he winks, and just like that, he's back to his usual charming self.

"Okay, you can stay, but only on one condition," I say with a cheeky grin as I hold up a finger.

"Seriously? Last I checked, I'm the one doing *you* a favor here," he says sarcastically.

I'm already halfway up the stairs when I call over my shoulder. "Just give me five minutes."

I change into some comfy pajamas and throw on my pink bunny slippers before heading back down the stairs toward the living room where I left him. When I reach the bottom of the steps, I see Jess stand-ing at the fireplace in the living room. He's looking at the picture frames that line the narrow mantle, a good majority of them including him throughout the years.

"Alrighty, sir, you ready?" I ask and he turns around, both hands tucked in his front pockets.

"Oh boy. Ready for what? You're not gonna braid my hair or something, are you?" he says and gives me a come on look as he tilts his head to the side.

"I guess you'll just have to see, then, won't you?" I say cryptically as I walk through the living room toward the kitchen.

"Fine, but only if you let me braid your hair, too," Jess says in my ear from behind me, purposely getting too close.

I swat him away and shake my head at the tickle in my ear from his breath. "Hard pass then on the hair braiding tonight. Do you remember what happened the last time you tried to braid my hair?" I ask and Jess gives me an innocent look, like he has no idea what I'm talking about.

"You're lucky Judy was able to get those knots out, otherwise I'd have ended up sporting a pixie cut for most of the fourth grade," I say, and Jess throws his head back as he lets out a menacing laugh.

I pull two wine glasses out of the kitchen cupboard and fill them with milk. I place a glass plate in front of Jess and one in front of myself before putting two cookies on each of them.

The thing about Leonard's, is that one of their cookies is equivalent to maybe four regular-sized cookies, but that's honestly the best part. You can't feel guilty if you've only eaten *one* cookie, right?

"Would you look at that, I didn't know that grown-up Sam even knew what wine glasses were," Jess says as he picks up a glass and swirls it before sniffing it like it's the world's finest red.

I smile and give his shoulder a playful shove as I dunk one half of my cookie into the milk in my wine glass. "Yeah right, like you're some wine connoisseur now," I say and scoff. "Last I heard, you still hold the reigning title of keg champ around these parts," I joke, remembering back to our high school days.

"And for your information, I am a very sophisticated adult," I say over a mouthful of cookie and laugh.

*If only he knew what I was up to earlier at dinner...*

"Clearly." Jess laughs and gestures to our wine glasses filled with milk.

I finish chewing and swallow my huge mouthful of cookie before speaking. "One more smartass remark, and your cookie privileges will be revoked for the night, maybe even forever," I say as I give him a side-eyed glance before taking another swig from my wine glass.

"I'd like to see you try." Jess challenges me with a smirk as he grabs his plate, holding it to his chest while trying to turn away from me. I playfully grab at it, and in the struggle, we end up dropping it. It cracks straight down the middle as it falls onto the marble countertop, breaking it into almost two perfect halves. I stay silent and glance up at Jess, wondering if he remembers that day from all those years ago.

"She helped me a lot, you know," Jess says without looking up from the two halves of the broken plate, and I don't have to ask to know exactly who he's talking about. "I think eventually I would've gone down a pretty dark path if it weren't for her and Aunt Judy, Soph too ...and you," he says and looks up at me. Jess's green eyes are glossy, and I can see the pain that's there.

I reach up and place a hand on the nape of his neck, holding his gaze intently as I speak. "You know I'd do anything for you, right, Jess?" I say, and a look of surprise flashes across his eyes, like it's the last thing he'd expected to hear from me right now. His features shift, and he looks like he wants to say something, but doesn't.

"Let's get some sleep, okay? It's been a long day," I say, and he hesitates for a moment, as if still wanting to finish his thought first, before eventually nodding at me. I stand and remove my hand from the back of his neck, electricity tingling in my fingers from where his skin was touching mine.

We clean up the wine glasses, and I throw the broken plate in the trash before putting the leftover cookies back in their bag for later.

I head toward the stairs as Jess makes his way to the large sofa in the middle of the living room. "Jess?" I call from my place on the stairs as he starts unfolding the pile of blankets I'd left on the couch for him.

"Yeah?" he asks as he stops fluffing up the pillow he's holding and meets my eyes.

"Thank you, for everything—I don't just mean the cookies—I mean for what you did for me earlier, too," I say, trying to fight the urge to run down the stairs and hug him. "I mean it, Jess, you saved me today, I won't ever forget that."

The corners of his mouth lift into a small smile. "You're welcome," he says and gives me a nod. "Night, Ryan."

"Night, Jess," I say and smile before turning back up the stairs.

When I make it to my room, I collapse onto my bed, exhausted by the day. I don't feel as uneasy as before, but I'm still not able to sleep, even with how tired I am. Not because I'm afraid of Elliott showing up, but because Jess is downstairs asleep on the couch right now. I try not to picture if he's wearing a shirt or not ...or if he's wearing any pants either...

I think about the way his short-sleeved shirt tightly hugged his arms and chest today ...and oh, *what I wouldn't give* to see his butt in a tight pair of Wrangler jeans...

*What the hell?* Jess isn't a cowboy, why would I even picture that?

Telling myself not to think about a rugged, manly cowboy version of Jess only makes me do it harder instead.

*Dammit.*

I sigh and roll over in my bed, still unable to get comfortable. I haven't had thoughts like this about Jess in a long time, not since our junior year of high school, at least.

I once overheard him and some of the neighborhood boys joking around about which of the girls on the block they'd sleep with if they'd had the chance. My interest was piqued until I heard my own name come up. I didn't stay long enough to listen to their entire conversation about me, only that the other boys said that sex with me would probably be boring as hell since I didn't have nice enough "assets" to make it very worthwhile.

In my defense, I looked flat as a board compared to Sophie, who was blessed with a full figure the second we hit puberty. It wasn't until a few years later that I finally grew into my own womanly figure more fully.

I'd cried myself to sleep that night but decided not to mention it to Jess since I was the one eavesdropping after all. The second I heard them talking about girls, I should've just left. When I told Sophie about it, she just brushed it off as them being asshole teenagers. I could've guessed that would have been her reaction since when her name came up, Max, the neighbor boy from across the street, said he'd smash, one hundred percent, no questions asked. Jess was grossed out by that since he and Sophie are cousins, and that's when my name came up.

I was pretty upset by it, but then again, I never told Sophie how I really felt about Jess, so she couldn't have realized how hurt I was by what they were saying about me. And to be fair, I didn't actually hear Jess say anything negative about me, but one can only assume that he joined in with his friends.

Ever since then, I've tried to keep a clear line drawn in my head when it comes to Jess, not wanting to ever accidentally ruin things between us just because of a silly little crush I had on him.

*...have on him...*

*ENOUGH!* I smack my forehead with my palm. *What is* wrong *with me tonight?*

I try forcing myself to sleep but just end up tossing and turning. I groan in frustration as I sit up and look at my alarm clock, the time flashing 3 a.m. I huff and lie back down and decide to check the app I have on my phone that tracks my cycle.

*Typical.*

Just as I'd suspected, I started ovulating today. It's no wonder I keep having these weird thoughts about Jess and his stupid muscles.

I put my phone down and reach into the top drawer of my nightstand. I tell myself that I'll just make it a quick one and be off to sleep in no time. I'm definitely feeling a bit deranged getting myself off to the image of Jess punching Elliott in the face for me today.

What can I say, though? Hormones can really fuck with a girl's mental state, and to be honest, I myself have always wanted to punch Elliott in the face, so I feel like it's a win-win.

It doesn't take long for me to take care of things, and my body is still humming from the aftermath as I finally start to drift off. I close my eyes and feel my body starting to relax and think about how I hope to find some other poor sucker to be the subject of my perverted thoughts tomorrow night instead of Jess.

# Chapter Five

When I wake up, Jess is gone, and all the blankets I'd left for him to use are folded neatly on the couch.

Walking into the kitchen, I notice a yellow sticky note on the countertop next to the coffee machine. I smile to myself knowing he predicted that the first place I'd go would be straight to the coffee maker. The man knows me well.

> RY,
> THANKS FOR LETTING ME STAY THE
> NIGHT
>
> I HOPE YOU'RE FEELING BETTER TODAY
> I'LL GLADLY JOIN YOU FOR A MIDNIGHT
> COOKIE DATE ANYTIME
>
> SEE YOU TOMORROW MORNING
> -J

*Tomorrow?* But we're not going up the mountain until Friday. I look at the calendar hanging on the fridge. *Shit, that* is *tomorrow.*

I sigh and grab my phone to text Sophie, thinking we've definitely got our work cut out for us. I ask if her regular coffee order from Leonard's is all right or if she's feeling adventurous and wants to try something new today.

I'd texted her last night after I went to bed asking why she didn't tell me that Jess was back in town on our phone call before I met my dad for dinner. She claimed that the thought just slipped her mind, but I get the feeling that she's hiding something. She's always the first to let me know what he's up to. Obviously, Jess's new Alaskan model girlfriend was important enough to mention but not the fact that he's in town, and I shake my head at the thought. Typical Sophie, only ever relaying the information that's important to *her.*

I plan on grilling her about it all when I pick her up, thinking I'll use coffee and pastries as blackmail. If Sophie thinks she can hide things from me, she's got another thing coming.

The more I think about everything we have to get done today, I figure it would probably be better if I place an online order and we eat on the go. I'm already starting to overthink things when Sophie's text reply comes through.

> Sorry bitch. Rain Check?
> Trevor ended up staying
> the night and wants to
> make me waffles.

> Seriously? I thought you
> said you were only using
> him for his—how did you
> put it—abs/acrobatic
> bedroom skills?

Yeah, well now I'm using
him for his cooking skills
too. Sue me lol.

Okay fine. You're off the
hook this time, but you're
still coming on the trip
though right?

Girl yes, chill. Send me your
location when you get up
the mountain before you
lose reception so I know
which turnoff to take.

Have fun with abs.

We'll see how good his
cooking skills are first.

I shake my head and laugh, but there's no real humor behind it. I can't say I'm surprised that Sophie blew me off yet again. The older we got, the more notorious she was for doing things like that. I've mentioned it to her before, but she claims that I'm just being overly sensitive, so I've just left it alone.

I decide not to let it get me down and quickly get dressed before I make a shopping list of the groceries we need for tomorrow. I guess my dad did make it home sometime between last night and this morning because he left a note and his credit card taped to one of the fridge doors. I look over the list he left for me and notice that it's more of the same things I already have on mine, aside from the extra case of beer he wants me to get, which was probably as per Chris's request.

At the bottom of the list, the word, marshmallows, is underlined and circled a few times underneath beer and beef jerky. For always being such a tough steak-eating manly man, my dad sure does have a soft spot for a sugary treat.

I guess some things do run in the family, and the thought makes me smile.

I head outside to my car and panic for a second when I don't see it in the driveway. I kick myself internally as I let out a frustrated groan, forgetting I'd left it parked down the street from the restaurant last night. I sigh and sit on the porch steps before ordering a car to pick me up.

After waiting for what feels like an hour, my Uber finally pulls into the driveway. When my ride drops me off at my car, I head to the local grocery store, Lim's. I still feel guilty shopping at Target, knowing that many of the smaller businesses in town went under when it first opened. I think about the Hendersons' store, and I'm glad they're still able to keep their doors open even though they don't seem very busy anymore.

I put my car in park and take another look at my list as I scan over the items, hoping I didn't forget to include anything. I grab my purse and step out of my car, when I spot a green Jeep from across the parking lot. I only caught a small glimpse of the Jeep parked in my dad's driveway last night when I let Jess in the house, so I can't be sure if it's the same one. It was pretty dark out, but I could've sworn it was the same green color as the one I'm looking at across the parking lot.

Hoping it's just a coincidence, I shut my car door and head into the store. My pulse rises a little at the thought of seeing Jess again today, especially after I basically flicked my bean to the thought of his face last night. I shake my head, trying to clear my mind of the thoughts of Jess in full cowboy garb.

I grab a shopping cart and make my way over to the produce section first, not wanting to forget the potatoes like I accidentally did one year. After securing the potatoes, I'm just about to heave a large bag of onions into my cart when I see a familiar leather jacket approaching me from out of the corner of my eye.

I tell myself that I'm just seeing things, but my feet freeze in place, and I start to feel my body warm with panic. My heart slowly begins to thunder in my ribcage, and suddenly, I feel dizzy. My chest feels constricted, and my breath starts to catch in my throat as images of last night flood my mind.

Bile starts to rise in my throat as I remember Elliott's foul breath on my face and the unwelcome feeling of his hands as they touched my body. My stomach starts to churn, and I think I might throw up.

*I need to get out of here.*

I turn to make my exit, but my legs wobble underneath me when I try to force them to move. I take a step but don't make it very far before a wave of nauseous vertigo takes over my senses. Apples tumble to the ground, spilling over the shelf and onto the floor as I accidentally ram into the display with the corner of my hip.

I'm still trying to will my unstable legs to move when I slip on a stray apple and slam into the display again. I drop the bag in my hands, and onions tumble to the ground along with the apples already there.

I manage to catch myself on the corner of the shelf before I completely eat it, causing more apples to roll onto the ground as they fall off the display.

Elliott grabs me, and I feel a scream rising in my throat.

"Ryan?" I snap my head up and see Jess standing next to a beautiful brunette on the other side of the produce stand.

So that's why he left early today. *He was meeting up with someone.* The thought has jealousy rising hot inside of me.

Hearing Jess's voice momentarily stifles my hysteria, and I turn to look at the man in front of me. It's not Elliott. He honestly looks nothing like Elliott. There are no other similarities between them besides the leather jacket.

"Are you all right, Miss?" he asks as he gives me an apologetic look. I look down and see that his hand is on my upper arm and think he must've grabbed me when I was falling.

"I—I'm fine… sorry—" Embarrassment stains my cheeks when I realize the scene I'd just caused and how the poor man was probably only trying to help me.

I pull my arm from his grip and stumble backward, falling on my ass this time. The man steps back and raises his hands in a surrender, sensing my discomfort. A small crowd has amassed around us, probably to witness *crazy girl on aisle 2*. I pull myself to my feet and try to avoid eye contact with anyone. I leave my cart and spilled onions, and rush out of the store as fast as I can.

"Ryan, wait! Hold up!" I hear Jess calling after me as I hurry across the parking lot toward my car.

I'm pulling on my car's door handle when I turn around to look at him, praying he's alone. "Oh, hi there, Jess, what's up? Fancy seeing you here," I say, trying to joke with him. I try to put on my most convincing, *everything is great, no crazy girl here* face. My pulse is still elevated from before, and I try my best to keep my voice even when I speak.

"Are you all right? I saw what happened in there," Jess says, gesturing back toward the store with a look of concern.

"Oh, that?" I jab to the grocery store behind us with my thumb. "That was nothing, I just tripped on a loose apple. They really shouldn't stack those so high, I mean, *what* a hazard, am I right?" I say, still trying to play the whole thing off, wondering how much he saw.

"Okay, well, was that before or after you dropped that bag of potatoes and ran off without all your groceries?" Jess asks as he narrows his eyes at me, no doubt able to see straight through my lie.

"Well, for your information, they were onions, not potatoes," I say, and Jess frowns at me, still not believing my bullshit. "Look, it's fine, I just thought I saw someone I knew, that's all… It just startled me a bit," I say and shrug.

"You mean that creep from yesterday?" Jess asks, and I see a flame of anger light behind his eyes as he looks at me.

"Nah, don't worry about it, you wouldn't know the guy. Goes to school in Canada," I joke, trying to lighten the mood, already with one foot in my car.

Jess's features soften as he exhales deeply, and he takes a step closer to me and starts to reach out with one of his hands. "Look, Ry, if you—"

The curvy brunette who was with Jess earlier walks up beside him and grabs onto his arm. "Jessy! Who's your friend? Introduce me!" She leans her petite stature up against Jess as she hugs onto his arm and looks at me with a smile. Her features are stunning, and I can't help but instantly feel insecure about my apparent lack of makeup skills compared to hers.

Wait. Are they… *together?* Is *she* the Alaskan model Sophie was telling me about? The way she's clinging to him sure makes it seem like they're more than just friends. I feel a small surge of disappointment at the thought that they might be seeing each other.

I must have an insane look on my face because Jess clears his throat, and I snap out of it, trying to rein in my expressions. I try to keep calm, but my jealousy from first seeing them together earlier still lingers.

"I'm Madison, it's nice to meet you!" she says cheerfully, introducing herself when Jess doesn't do it for her. She lets go of Jess and leans in toward me, looking like she's about to go in for a hug, and I back myself up against the door frame of my car.

*What the hell?*

I'm about two seconds away from shutting the door in her face and hauling ass straight outta there when Jess grabs her arm and pulls her back.

"We're leaving," he says sternly as he backs them away from my car.

"Oh, but Jessy, introduce me to your pretty friend!" she says and snickers as Jess cuts her a stern look. "Oh, come on, you're no fun," she pouts, puffing out her perfectly glossed lips.

Jess then lets out an annoyed sigh when she gives him puppy dog eyes. "This is Samantha, she's a friend of Sophie's. Now let's go," he says coldly, pulling her away.

"It was nice seeing you," he says nonchalantly and turns away, pulling Madison along behind him by her wrist. "See you around," Jess calls over his shoulder to me. Madison turns and smiles as she waves good-bye, and I slowly wave back, still a little bit in shock from Jess's cold words.

*What the fuck was that?*

Jess has never treated me like that around any of his other girl-friends before, which makes me wonder if maybe he didn't want me to know about her. I wonder if he didn't tell her where he was last night and wanted to separate us before I had the chance to spill the beans. I never really pegged Jess for a cheater, but then again, nothing hap-pened last night. The only reason he stayed over was because he felt sorry for me.

Over the years, I've gotten used to seeing Jess with other girls, finally accepting that I would probably never get to be one of them. I made peace with the fact that if I only ever got to be friends with him, I would count myself lucky that I still got to have him in my life, no matter what that looked like.

But that's not what bothers me about our interaction just now. Jess has never called me by my first name before—sure, sometimes he calls me Sam to annoy me—but never Samantha. It's always been Ry or Ryan, and

I made it clear to everyone a long time ago that he was the only one allowed to call me that. Hearing Jess say Samantha just now felt unnatural.

The way he said "See you around" definitely made it sound like he doesn't want Madison to know that he and I are actually friends. That also suggests that she has no idea that we have plans to drive up the mountain together tomorrow, followed by a weekend-long camping trip.

I try not to worsen my mood further by imagining if he's going to invite her to tag along with us before I finally get in my car and shut the door. I know it's unlikely, but I can't help it.

I rub my palms over my eyes, feeling angry with myself.

*Stellar job, Sam.* Not only did I not get any groceries for the trip, but I royally embarrassed myself in front of half the town, along with Jess and his gorgeous new girlfriend.

The feeling of embarrassment is still lingering in my chest, and I hope there aren't already any videos of me circulating online. I sigh and put my car into reverse. *I guess Target it is.*

~

I decide on a grocery pick-up instead of doing any actual physical shopping. I'm still a little on edge from earlier and don't really feel like causing another scene. I feel like I got lucky before at Lim's, but if I freak out in a Target, there'll most certainly be some asshole recording, and I have no intention of becoming an internet meme.

I have a little time to kill before my groceries are ready, so I consider what to do in the meantime. If I head back home to my dad's, I'll just have to turn right around and come back by the time I get there, so I rule that out.

I'm only about a five-minute drive away from Aunt Judy's retirement community, and if she weren't on her old people ski trip, I'd head over there for a bit. I really do want to see her. She was already like a surrogate grandma to me when I was growing up, but after my mom left, I realized just how much I really appreciated and needed her in my life.

Judy's definitely a little rough around the edges, but that's what I love about her so much. What you see is what you get, there's no bullshit with her. And not only does she know how to make the best cookies known to man, but she also always knows the right things to say to make everything feel not so terrible. I sigh just thinking about it, and how I sure could use that right now.

I'd also wager that Judy knows exactly why Jess is acting all moody, and I'm guessing it has something to do with his pretty new friend. Aunt Judy always knows the hot gossip of the town, so I guess I'll just have to ask her about it when I see her next week.

I'm still wallowing in self-pity in the Target parking lot when I feel my stomach grumble. After being ditched by Sophie this morning, and in my hurry to get to the store, I realize that I'd never eaten anything today. I still don't feel mentally stable enough to be in a public place, but decide that I need to get some food.

I spot a small café nearby that I haven't seen before and enter the drive-thru line with my car. I take one look at the menu and decide that it's definitely my kind of place with the number of sugary drinks and customizable options on the menu.

After I get my food, I sit in the Target parking lot and drink my coffee. Now, I call it coffee, but it's mostly sugar and cream with a smidge of actual coffee and about fourteen pumps of caramel syrup.

I take another sip of my drink as I rest my head back against my car's headrest and let out a long breath. Without meaning to, my mind wanders to Daniel. I think about the steamy night we shared together just a few days ago and wonder what he's doing right now.

*Probably showing Allie all of his sexy bedroom moves.* I scowl to myself at the thought.

*Stupid Daniel. Stupid Allie.*

I try to think about something else, but my mind keeps jumping from Daniel and Allie and then to Jess and Madison. I sigh and decide to blast my music, cranking my car stereo up to an almost painful level, and try to force myself to stop thinking about any of them.

After waiting for about forty minutes, I receive a notification that my grocery order is ready for pickup. I thank the Target worker and give him a twenty-dollar tip as an apology for all the heavy things I had him put in my trunk.

As expected, when I get to my dad's house, there's no one home. I sigh and put my keys on the kitchen counter. I can't explain this feeling, but every time I come home to an empty house, I feel so... I dunno... *empty?* It's like the feeling you get waking up to an empty bed after you expected them to be there in the morning. So, maybe *disappointed* is a better word for it?

For once, it would be nice to have someone waiting for me— someone who actually wants to see *me*, and not just because I'm conveniently the only one around.

I pack all the groceries into the kitchen and force myself to start the prep for tomorrow as I fight the urge to nap instead. I figure I might as well chop and peel everything while I still have access to running water and electricity, and I have to keep reminding myself that if I don't get things ready today, I'll just be making it harder on myself tomorrow.

Between thinking about what happened at the store with Jess, and my nonexistent relationship with Daniel over the past few months, I feel mentally exhausted. Even though I'm feeling tired, I'll admit that the camping prep is a nice distraction to keep my mind busy for the time being.

After about five hours, I've chopped, peeled, diced, and sliced almost everything you could ever need for a top-notch dutch oven meal. I put all the food away into sorted containers in the fridge, trying to make it easier on everyone tomorrow when it comes time to cook.

I check the time and wonder why my dad still isn't home yet. In the note he left me, he mentioned having to run a few errands today, so I wonder if maybe it's taking him a little longer than he expected. I sigh and wonder when I'll stop subconsciously making excuses for him.

*Never. That's when.*

I sigh and shake my head to clear the thought away.

I decide to be helpful and rummage around in the garage for the plastic totes filled with the camping gear. I figure I can help make things a little easier for my dad if I at least make a pile of stuff for him to load up into his truck when he gets home later.

I pull down a few totes labeled "camping" and notice that they're unusually light. I pop the lids of a few of them, but don't find anything of much use. I know it's wishful thinking, but I wonder if my dad already took care of sorting through things yesterday and has everything loaded up into his truck ...wherever he is. The more I think about it, the less I believe it. *Oh well, I've done my part.* I shrug to myself before putting the half-empty totes back up on their shelves.

When I walk back into the house, I let out a big yawn and tell myself that I've earned some time to relax on the couch for a bit while I wait for my dad to show up. I head into the living room and shake my head when I get to the couches.

*Who even needs this many pillows? Like seriously.* I shake my head again as I look at the ugly patterns covering most of them. After aggressively shoving all of the pillows onto the ground, I grab the TV remote and take a seat on one of the leather couches.

Between school and work, I haven't had much downtime in the last few months. I've been meaning to catch up on my Korean soap operas but haven't been able to since it's a premium channel, so I'm grateful that my dad is still a diehard cable fan. I finally persuaded him to at least get Netflix a few years back, but that's as far as he'd go.

I'm about three episodes in when my eyes start to get heavy, and before I know it, I fall asleep.

It feels like it's only been about five minutes when something soft smacks me in the face, waking me up. "What the fu—" I inhale sharply as I sit up and shove one of the pillows I'd thrown on the floor off my face.

Once my eyes adjust to the light, I notice Rebecca standing right above me.

"Oh my gosh, Sam, *I am so sorry*, I didn't even see you there," she says innocently as she stares down at me through her fake caterpillar lashes.

*Sure you didn't.* I narrow my eyes at her as I look up, picking some of the fuzzies from the pillow out of my mouth.

"I was just trying to tidy up," she says as she gestures to the pillows littering the living room floor.

"Sorry about that, I must've knocked them off by accident," I say and shrug.

"There's still a lot to be done before tomorrow, I'm surprised you had time for a nap," Rebecca says, putting her hands on her hips. "I figured you'd at least want to show your dad some gratitude, seeing as though he's letting you stay here for free," she says as she gives me a condescending smile.

"Sam, did I hear you're up? Great job on getting the food so organized," my dad calls from the kitchen, and we both turn to look in his direction.

I look up at Rebecca and squint my eyes at her. "What was it you were just saying…?" I ask, and she sneers at me before walking off toward the kitchen, her heels clacking loudly against the hardwood flooring.

I look out one of the living room windows and see that it's already dark outside.

*Damn, how long was I asleep for?*

I let out a yawn, still feeling exhausted. If it's dark already, that means we don't have much time to get everything packed up. If I say I'll do it in the morning, chances are that I will *not* do it in the morning.

I peel myself off the sofa and rub my sore neck as I enter the kitchen behind Rebecca. I pull my sweater off before tossing it onto the back of one of the kitchen chairs, my body all hot and sweaty from the nap.

"Hey, Dad?" I say, rubbing my eyes as I take a seat at the bar, and I watch as he carefully puts a few bottles into his fancy new wine fridge.

"What's up, kid?" he answers, but doesn't stop to look up from what he's doing.

"Did you already pack up the gear that was in the garage? I was going to help sort through things, but I was having a hard time finding anything," I say.

"Oh yeah, I forgot to tell you—" my dad starts, but Rebecca chimes in before he can finish his thought.

"We donated that old junk—well, most of it anyway. John and I agreed that a fresh start is the only way to start our new lives together," she says. She walks over to where my dad's still crouched down by his wine bottles and puts a hand on his shoulder possessively. "Right, sweetie?" she asks my dad.

"Uh-huh," he says, not really listening to either of us.

"Okay...? So, what's that supposed to mean? That you got rid of a bunch of perfectly good, *usable* things that we needed for our trip tomorrow? So, what? Are we all just sleeping on the ground then?" I ask, starting to get heated.

"Don't be silly, Samantha, we replaced everything with upgrades. Obviously," Rebecca says as she sneers at me.

I look around the kitchen for the so-called "upgrades" but come up empty. I keep trying to make eye contact with my dad, but he's still too preoccupied with the temperature settings on his wine fridge.

"*Dad—*"

I'm about to lose my shit on Rebecca when I hear a loud horn honking outside. My dad stands finally and claps his hands before rubbing them together.

"He's here!" my dad says, and I can only assume that he's talking about my brother, Chris. I figured it was about time that he came home already, but my dad rushes out of the kitchen and through the front door before I can even ask.

I follow my dad outside, brushing past Rebecca's shoulder maybe a little too aggressively on my way out of the kitchen. As I reach the front steps of the house, I watch as Chris hops out of the driver's side of what looks like a giant shiny tour bus, and I almost have to do a double take.

I take one look at my brother and almost can't believe my eyes. Instead of his usual Shaggy Rogers haircut and baggy clothes, his dirty blonde hair is shaved into a buzzcut, and he looks like he's put on about twenty pounds of muscle.

I shake my head as I look at him. Looking like a meathead gym bro really isn't helping him beat those frat guy allegations.

"What the hell is that thing?" I ask and slowly walk toward the giant bus. "And what the hell are you wearing?" I ask as I give his cutoff gym crop top and basketball shorts a once-over.

"This…" Chris shuts the door and pats the metal paneling as he speaks, "…is Betty." Chris stares up at the thing in awe, ignoring my presence completely. "Isn't she amazing!" he says without turning away.

*Well, nice to see you too, brother. It's not like it's been over a year or anything.*

"I'm confused. Can someone please explain what the Backstreet Boys' tour bus is doing in our driveway?" I ask, gesturing to the large rollin' turd blocking the entire driveway and part of the street.

Chris looks over at me with his arms folded and shakes his head. "You're so dramatic," he says, and I stick my tongue out at him like a five-year-old.

My dad interrupts what's about to potentially become a fight between the two of us before patting Chris on the shoulder.

"Bec and I got to talking, and I think she's right about a fresh start to things for us. She's not been exposed to many outdoor activities, so I wanted to make sure she felt as comfortable as possible," he explains. "Chris's friend down at the lot got us a screamin' deal on Betty here. Isn't she great?" my dad says as he and Chris stare up at the monstrosity like it's the coolest thing since sliced bread.

"We picked her out today, along with all the stuff to fill 'er up with. That's why we were out so late," my dad continues, still admiring Betty.

"Dad, aren't these things, like, outrageously expensive?" I ask. "What happened to 'Tent camping is the only real camping?' Isn't that one of the main reasons we liked it in the first place, for the open air? For the freedom? Wasn't it always the dirtier we came home, the more fun we had?" I ask and throw my hands up in the air dramatically. "I don't get it, Dad. What's changed?" I ask, trying not to get emotional as everyone stares at me with blank looks.

"What's changed is that Rebecca is a permanent part of my life now, and I want her to feel comfortable with our family since she's going to be part of it now, whether you like it or not," my dad says sternly, and the mood quickly shifts.

Rebecca clings to my dad's arm as she gives me a satisfied look, and I feel like I've just been scolded like a small child.

I stand there and clasp my hands together nervously. The weight of everyone's eyes on me makes it increasingly difficult not to cry, and I try to find the right thing to say to diffuse the situation.

"I'm sorry, Dad. That's not what I meant at all. I just don't understand what was wrong with the stuff we already had," I say, trying to lighten my tone so as not to set him off again.

"You're right. That stuff was perfectly fine, but most of it—it was your *mother's*. It's time I had my own things. *Our* own things," he says, and looks at Rebecca lovingly. When he meets my gaze again, his expression changes to an aggravated glare, so I just nod and decide to keep my mouth shut.

After a brief tour of Betty the Bus, we all head back inside the house. I'm corrected half a dozen times by Chris that she is, in fact, not a tour bus, but a top-of-the-line *Entrega Coach Cornerstone RV.*

*Whatever the fuck that means.* Insert eye roll.

I show the guys where all the food is so they can pack the coolers with ice in the morning before we leave, already knowing I won't be awake when they do it. I was surprised they didn't want to load everything into the massive fridge inside Betty, but apparently, Rebecca doesn't want dirt tracked inside whenever someone wants a hot dog or a beer. If she's actually worried about things getting dirty while we're literally *camping*, she's in for a big surprise.

Since Rebecca and my dad donated all of our sleeping bags and tents, I text Sophie asking if I can borrow an extra one from her family's stash. Surprisingly, she answers me back pretty quickly, saying she'll bring the gear with her tomorrow, along with some extra junk food.

I figured she'd still be too busy with Trevor to answer me back so fast, so I'm wondering if she's kicked him out for the night already.

Sophie's always been known for having a good time, but when she's done, she's done, and she's not afraid to kick anyone out—myself included.

Because of my late nap, I can't sleep even though I'm still mentally drained from the last few days, so I check my phone to see if Jess has texted me. I keep on waiting for the message that says, *Oh yeah, I forgot to mention my girlfriend is in town and wants to come with us. You don't mind sitting in the back, right?*

I'm really hoping that doesn't happen, otherwise, I'm going to have to fake a sudden illness or break my own leg to get out of tomorrow. I know it's cliché, but there's really nothing worse than being a third wheel.

I try reading for a bit and then switch to TV but can't focus on either. I decide to put myself out of my misery and text Jess already. Before I can even click on his name, a message from him comes through.

Your dad told me we're
heading out at 10 tomorrow.
Please don't make me wait
forever for you to get ready.

As if. I don't know if you
know who you're talking to.
I'm never late.

Yeah right. We have a strict
schedule to uphold ma'am.

So it'll be just you picking
me up tomorrow, then?

If you're asking about Soph,
she told me she already let

you know she was coming
up later.

Oh, but she did mention
bringing someone with her.
Trent, I think it was?

No, you're right. She did tell
me that, my bad. See you in
the morning then.

See you in the morning.


She's bringing Trevor? *That's weird.* Why didn't she tell me anything about it earlier? Bro better be bringing his own tent, otherwise he's sleeping outside.

 I thought talking to Jess would set my mind at ease, but if anything, it's only made things worse. He seemed normal for the most part, but then again, sometimes it's hard to judge emotions through text. I guess we'll see what tomorrow's vibe is like. Maybe I'll try to find a way to casually bring up Madison without making it weird.

 I can already tell it's going to be a long night and an even longer day tomorrow if I don't get any sleep. I lie in my bed and try to count sheep or whatever, but I just end up tossing and turning for most of the night.

# Chapter Six

After a restless night, I finally managed to fall asleep around 4 a.m., so when Jess texts me that he's outside, it feels like the ass crack of dawn even though it's already ten o'clock.

Thanks to my dad's incessant need to be "on schedule" for everything, he wanted to leave much earlier. I *almost* convinced him that later was more leisurely, more "vacation-like" but in the end, he still insisted on leaving at eight o'clock and said that he'd meet us halfway up the canyon for lunch later.

I'll never understand why everyone is always in such a hurry to be "on time" getting to an unassigned campsite in the middle of the wilderness every year. We've made the drive countless times, so I can only think that maybe my dad is a little nervous about how Betty will handle the curves heading up the canyon—especially with Chris's side-by-side trailer attached to the back.

I don't mind since I figure we'll catch up to them pretty quickly since Jess is notorious for having a lead foot. I already knew I'd accidentally sleep in and didn't want my dad and Chris waiting for me, so this works out better anyway.

Even though I was able to get *some* sleep last night, I am most definitely not a morning person. Not for Disneyland, not for the airport, and *most certainly* not for Mother Nature. Chris had to practically drag my ass out of bed every time we took a family vacation anywhere that involved an airplane.

I rush to gather up my things and make sure that I'm at least wearing pants before I set foot outside. When I step out of the house, Jess is leaning against the passenger-side door of his Jeep, the same green Jeep I thought I'd recognized yesterday at the grocery store.

In high school, Jess always cruised around in Grandpa Millard's old red CJ7 Jeep, so this shiny green one sitting in my dad's driveway is definitely a much-needed upgrade. It seemed nice yesterday when I saw it, but the dark olive paint and glossy black trim are much prettier up close. It's nice without being too flashy, like those Jeeps that are obviously overcompensating for something by having 12-inch lifts and size 100 tires, or whatever the hell.

"Well, don't we look chipper this morning?" Jess says and smiles at me. "That is, if you can even call ten o'clock morning," he says and scoffs, arms still folded across his chest as he leans up against the Jeep. "You just woke up, didn't you?" he asks, eyeing my sweats.

*So, I guess we're just ignoring what happened yesterday, then?* The thought has me feeling slightly annoyed.

Even though I'm tired and a little grouchy, I can't help but notice how good Jess looks today. His shoulder-length hair is in a low messy bun with a few loose pieces tucked behind his ear. He's wearing his signature black boots, dark blue jeans, and a navy shirt that looks two sizes too small for him.

It's obvious that the guy works out, but *come on* with that compression shirt. One flex and his sleeves look like they'll rip.

*Show off.*

I roll my eyes again and he gives me a questioning look that I ignore as I walk toward the back of his Jeep with my bag.

I quickly glance down at my sweats and could kick myself for not wearing something cuter, even if we are just camping. It's my own fault though, I would've had more time to get ready if I hadn't snoozed all fifteen of my damn alarms this morning.

I was still half asleep when I got Jess's text saying he was already out front. I was hoping I'd get at least a ten-minute warning from him to let me know he was on his way, but I had all of five minutes to do a quick braid in my hair and brush my teeth. It's a good thing I packed my bag yesterday, otherwise I'd be rocking the same pair of dirty sweats all weekend long.

I'm struggling to get my bag on the Jeep's roof when Jess takes it out of my hands before effortlessly tossing it onto the rack. He secures my bag next to his other camping supplies, and I spot a camp chef and some dutch ovens with his gear. I'm still trying to fight the simmering anger I feel toward Rebecca for getting rid of all our camping stuff, so I'm grateful that Jess unknowingly planned ahead.

"Is that everything? Where's the rest of your stuff? No tent or sleeping bag?" Jess asks as he looks around and eyes me quizzically, like I didn't just forget to pack the most essential things needed for camping. "You *are* planning on staying the whole weekend, right?" he asks, raising an eyebrow.

"No, I am," I say and nod. "Soph is bringing some extra stuff with her when she comes up later today. She's got the nicer tent, which, thanks to daddy's new girlfriend, happens to be the only tent between the two of us at the moment."

Jess gives me a questioning look, and I figure I'll tell him later about my growing dislike for Rebecca, before continuing. "Sophie also happens to have my sleeping bag from three Thanksgivings ago when we tried to sleep out on the trampoline," I explain.

"Wait, for real?" he asks, looking at me like he can't believe we tried to sleep outside in mid-November. "You guys still do those?"

"Yeah, I've actually been meaning to plan one now that I'm back in town for a bit... Why? Is that really so hard to believe?" I ask, putting my hands on my hips when I notice him giving me a weird look. Of course, I don't let him know that immediately after Sophie and I went outside, we turned straight around and ended up having a sleepover in the living room instead.

"I guess," Jess says, scratching his head as he shrugs. "You two are still pretty close then, huh?" he asks, his expression hard to read.

*Weird.* I swear I can sense a touch of jealousy in his tone.

Jess never seemed particularly fond of mine and Sophie's sleepovers when we were kids. Sophie never let him hang around for long, saying that our sleepovers were only for the girls, and unless he wanted his nails painted or hair braided, he had to get lost. I think he always wanted to be included so badly that he always said yes to being the subject of a makeover, but Sophie never would actually let him. I'd always secretly wanted her to say yes so he could stay with us, makeover or not. It'd always made me feel bad the way she'd shoo him off every single time.

"I mean, yeah, it was hard when she was away for school, but we still managed to keep in touch. We're definitely not as close as we once were, but I guess that's what happens when you grow up. It's sort of inevitable, I think," I say and shrug. "I am glad that we're back in the same town again though, it definitely makes it easier to see each other," I say, only now realizing that I haven't actually even seen her yet.

"You guys probably froze your asses off if you really slept out there in November, but it couldn't have been the same without her sexy cousin, though, right?" Jess asks and winks at me before heading around to the driver's side of the Jeep.

I roll my eyes and shake my head as I open the passenger door before climbing inside. I flashback to the time when Jess caught a garden snake in Grandpa Millard's backyard and snuck it onto the trampoline with us.

"I think the word you're looking for is *annoying*," I say and give a sarcastic sneer, not wanting to admit he's right. That "annoying" cousin was one of the main reasons I always wanted to hang out at Sophie's house during the summer instead of at my own.

*Too bad I'd never admit that to him.*

"So, now that we're all grown up, are you still gonna threaten me with makeup and nail polish if I don't leave, or can I actually be invited this time?" he asks, raising his brows at me.

"We'll see," I say and turn away from him, trying not to smile as I adjust my seatbelt after clicking it into place.

We're only on the road for a few minutes before Jess offers to stop for coffee, and I wonder if he noticed my head starting to bob. When I ask if he's going to get something to drink as well, he declines, and I remember that he doesn't drink coffee, or any other form of caffeine for that matter.

*What a weirdo.*

My head's starting to pound from its lack of sleep and coffee, and I wonder how Jess is able to survive without an ounce of caffeine in his system. I think back and remember that Jess was always sort of like that. While I practically lived off Red Bulls and Slim Jims in high school, Jess was all about protein shakes and celery.

So when he offers to stop again, I tell him I'll be fine, not wanting us to have to go out of our way just for my stupid caffeine dependency. I *am* tired, but I'll survive.

Jess gives me an *Are you sure?* look, and I just nod, hoping he doesn't make a fuss about it. He smiles and nods in response, and we keep on driving. He's just as bright-eyed as before and somehow still annoyingly cheerful for someone who had to get up early.

I look over at him and try not to stare before returning my focus to the road ahead. I'm assuming he got up early. How could he not have and looked *that* good when he picked me up? Then again, he could be one of those 7-in-1 guys with a beauty routine that takes all of three seconds.

*Typical. Man looks like a frikin' model and probably doesn't even use moisturizer.*

I know that Jess has been living on the oil rig where he's been working, so he hasn't had his own place, so to speak. I let my mind wander, imagining what it would be like if he did. It'd probably be a mess, just like any typical bachelor pad. I picture rings on his coffee table and unwashed dishes in the sink, and scoff to myself.

He's probably the type to leave his clothes in a pile on the floor, too. *How annoying.* I can just picture the navy shirt and dark jeans he's wearing in a heap on the bathroom floor, along with a pair of checkered briefs and black socks. I don't know why I'm getting so worked up about a mess in Jess's hypothetical bathroom, but I am.

I think about the shower and all the soaps in it—or possible lack thereof—and I let my mind wander, imagining what the rest of his bathroom might be like.

Jess always did love the color blue, so I wonder if that's the color he'd choose for his towels, or if he'd choose something darker like black or olive green, just like the color of the Jeep.

I picture matching bathroom rugs and think that's probably a stretch, knowing that most men couldn't care less about matching colors in a bathroom. I imagine how the steam from the shower would roll down over the dark material of the hypothetical rugs and out into his bedroom, slowly escaping underneath the door. The heaviness of it already starting to fog up the mirror in the small area as the air grows thicker.

I hear the sound of the shower curtain opening before it closes and watch as Jess's lean form steps into the steaming water. He takes a deep breath as the hot water streams down his skin, and he flexes his stomach as he puts his head into the water and closes his eyes. His dark locks stick to his face as the water cascades down and over his shoulders, and he lets out another long breath as the water continues to wash over him.

Steam rises off his skin from the heat, and the water runs down the length of his forearms as he reaches his hands up to smooth the wet pieces of hair out of his face. Jess keeps his eyes closed as he leans his head back, the water running down his neck and chest before it streams down his torso, flowing dangerously low, down past the V cut of his lower abdomen.

His breathing is slow and heavy as he braces himself with both hands against the wall of the shower, the water now flowing down his face as he lowers his head back into the steady stream. Jess takes a long steadying breath before slowly reaching a hand down, the other still bracing the wall in front of him. He lets out a breathy gasp as he grips himself, wincing at the contact.

His eyes are still closed, his brows furrowed together as he pumps his hand up and down his length. The movements progressively grow faster each second, along with the sounds of his breathy moans as they echo off the tiled bathroom walls.

His head hangs down between his shoulder blades, as the water drips off his perfectly shaped nose in small streams. Jess's body starts to tremble and his breathing hitches as he throws his head back, the veins in his neck and arms straining forcefully against his skin. He lets out one last groan as his brows pinch together in blissful agony.

Jess's shoulders shake as he pants, still trying to catch his breath. He turns his head to the side, one hand still gripping his length, the other bracing the wall.

With open eyes at last, a piercing green escapes his half-lidded gaze as he tilts his head to the side. He's trembling and breathless as he starts to whisper, Ry...

"...an. Hey, wake up, we're stopping."

I open my eyes and feel Jess's hand on my shoulder as he gives me a gentle shake. I stir and sit up from where I was slumped against the window and feel a sharp pain running down the side of my neck. I've got a killing headache and is that...? Yep, I drooled on myself.

*Well, this is embarrassing.* I start to wipe the corner of my mouth with the sleeve of my hoodie and...

*OH MY GOD, WHAT WAS I JUST DREAMING ABOUT?* Mortified, I panic, and I feel my cheeks instantly flame hotter than the sun.

Jess still has his hand on my shoulder and looks like he's about to make some joke about me drooling all over his Jeep like some freak. Before I can think straight, I recoil from his touch, slamming myself further up against the door, even though I'm already pressed tightly up against it.

I fumble to unlatch the door handle and trip over the ledge of the doorframe as I fall out of the Jeep, not fully aware of whether we're parked or not. I stumble, but catch myself before I fall face-first onto the asphalt. Thankfully, I fell asleep before I was able to take my shoes off, otherwise, I'd be picking gravel out of my feet right now.

*So parked it is, then. Good.* I feel relieved that I didn't end up finding that out the hard way.

I rub the sleep out of my eyes and recognize the monstrosity that is Betty the Bus parked next to us, along with Chris's truck and his small camper. I don't bother shutting the Jeep door behind me, not able to look Jess in the eye at the moment, and stalk toward the small building in the middle of the parking lot.

I recognize the building as the diner we always stop at on our way up the canyon. I head straight for the restaurant without looking back to see whether or not Jess is behind me. I'm hoping the others are already inside so I don't have to spend any alone time with Jess for a bit, at least not until I can get a hold of myself.

I try to convince myself that the only reason I had such a vivid dream like that was because I wasn't able to get myself off last night. After TV and reading had both failed me, I was still so in my head that I couldn't get off without the help of my vibrator, which was conveniently left without a charge due to the night before and my pervy thoughts about Cowboy Jess.

As I walk into the diner, I can feel an uncomfortable wetness between my legs and can already tell it's probably a Niagara Falls situation down there right now. Ovulation week is seriously no joke, if I don't keep to a regularly scheduled program during the week, all hell can break loose.

Apparently, it only took me about five seconds to pass out in the front seat of Jess's Jeep after we left my dad's house, because according to the time, I was out for about two hours. Even though my dad and Chris left a good few hours before us, it seems we still managed to get to the diner around the same time, which is nice since I was worried about us getting separated.

I spot the others chatting in a booth in the back corner of the diner and make my way over to them. I head back to their table and almost bump into a waitress holding a tray of drinks when I let out a massive yawn. I apologize to the waitress, and she cuts me a glare before walking over to a table on the opposite end of the dining room. I shrug to myself.

*Oh well, can't win 'em all, I guess.*

I yawn again and keep walking, and this time my eyes water a little. *How am I still this tired?* I know I need to get to bed earlier, but it's always been a struggle for me, and by get to bed, I mean to *sleep*. I'm *in* my bed at eleven, but that doesn't mean that's when I actually go to sleep. By the time I end up going to sleep, it's usually half past two in the morning since I get off work so late most nights. So, I guess I've inadvertently trained myself to be a night owl these last few years.

I let out another large yawn, and feel like I should've taken Jess up on his offer for coffee this morning, then maybe I wouldn't have fallen asleep and had such an awkward dream about him...

I greet the others when I get to the table and take a seat, not realizing that Jess was probably right behind me the whole time. He sits down next to me, and we both scoot in toward the middle of the booth. It's large enough to fit all five of us comfortably, but I still try to scoot away from Jess as much as possible, when I accidentally crowd Chris.

"Do you mind?" Chris asks and gives me an annoyed look as he peers down to where our arms are touching.

"Sorry..." I say and scoot back over, putting myself closer to Jess than I want to be right now. I can feel Jess looking at me, but I don't make eye contact with him. I refuse to turn my head in his general direction at all, afraid I'll give myself away.

I pretend to look at my menu, even though I already know what I'm going to order. My cheeks still feel heated, and I don't know why I'm so embarrassed. It's not like I can control what I dream about, and it's not like Jess even knew that I was dreaming about him when I pulled away.

By no means was that the first ...*strange*... dream I've had involving Jess, they're just usually a lot less x-rated than that. I sigh and could smack myself for making this into a thing when it shouldn't be.

We all order the special, which, much to no one's surprise, is a burger and fries. It's *always* a burger and fries. There aren't many restaurants or places to stop at out here, so it's sort of become a tradition to stop at this diner every time we pass through. The food's not terrible, but it's always pretty predictable, which is oddly comforting to me. The entire world seems to be in a rush to change and evolve, but not this place.

I sit quietly through most of lunch, only offering the occasional *uh-huh* and obligatory *wow, that's crazy*, since my dad decided that it was time to rehash every detail of the cruise he and Rebecca just took to Mexico.

I'm grateful, though, because it's saving me from my self-perpetuated awkwardness with Jess. He's not really a breakfast kind of guy, so I tell myself that there's no way he wouldn't be hungry by now. I try to sneak an inconspicuous glance at him when the waitress brings out our food and hope he's paying more attention to his burger than to anything else.

I quickly look up at him, which I immediately regret doing. Jess meets my eyes briefly before I look away, focusing intently on my chocolate shake. I thought that the sugar overload might make me feel better, but I mostly just played in it, and now it's all melted.

Lunch drags on and on, and I'm forced to listen to Rebecca and my dad talk about things I couldn't care less about, like how apparently this isn't the first time Rebecca and Jess are meeting. It sounds like he's been back in town for a few weeks now, and whenever my dad needs help moving something or another, and Chris isn't home, he'll call Jess instead.

Although I'm slightly irritated at Rebecca's flirtatious attitude toward Jess, I know he'd never go for her, even though she's around our same age. He's just being his regular charming self, which I'm sure she's misconstruing as reciprocal flirting, but it's obvious to me that he's just trying to be polite.

I'm surprised at how okay my dad is with Rebecca's blatant flirting. It seems unlikely that he's not picking up on it, especially since he's usually the one flirting and making eyes at women everywhere we go—or at least he used to before he got together with Rebecca.

After listening to Rebecca's incessant bragging for what felt like two hours too long, we finally get back on the road again. She was telling us the story about how she and my dad had met for the second time around when I started to nod off. After my head fell onto Jess's shoulder by accident, Chris couldn't help but make fun of the embarrassed look on my face, and my dad had to break up what was brewing to be a fight.

We've been back on the road for a little while, and the more time passes, the less tension there seems to be between Jess and me. I don't say much, and neither does he, which tells me he's definitely picking up on my weird energy.

When he met my eyes back at the diner, I swear I saw a flash of hesitation in his eyes, like he wanted to say something, but didn't, or maybe like he *couldn't*. Probably because of the present company we were in. I broke away too fast to be able to tell for sure, though.

I pull my hood up over my head and rest it against the window as I close my eyes. I'm still tired but don't want to fall asleep again, afraid of what dreams might manifest now that I've imagined Jess naked while saying my name.

We're on the road for about an hour when I sit up and stretch, the pain in my neck from earlier returning due to being hunched to the side for so long. I yawn for the thousandth time and notice a big sign that I haven't seen on this road before. It reads: Uncle Wayland's Crystal Trinketry, and the like.

"Looks like they must've finally torn down that old rickety shed that passed for a gas station," I mumble, more to myself than to Jess. It's been a few years since I've been out this way, so I guess it's only natural that some things will have changed.

"What was that?" Jess asks, turning toward me before looking back at the road.

I gesture to another sign advertising the shop as I look out the window. "Can we stop?" I ask, and my nose is basically pressed up against the glass when we pass by a third sign.

*Hot damn. I do love a trinket.*

When I look over at Jess, he has a giant smile plastered across his face.

"What?" I ask.

"Nothing," he says as he shakes his head. "I just like it when you're like this," he says, looking over at me, still smiling widely.

"Like what?" I ask.

"Excited," he says as he shrugs. I roll my eyes at him before looking back out the window.

The shop really isn't anything special, which honestly makes me like it all the more. Even though the sign suggests an abundance of crystals and the like, it's more like a small flea market threw up in here, with only a handful of crystals for sale by the front door. The inside of the shop is relatively the size of a small gas station, but even so, there's still plenty to look at.

I look across the various tables set up around the shop and shake my head.

*Yep, I'm in trouble.*

I guess it depends on one's own definition of the terms—but I am by no means a hoarder or junk collector; I just have a real soft spot for whimsical trinkets. There's something so special to me about seeing something handmade that borders on ridiculousness. Somewhere out there, someone thought it up and created it, regardless of what anyone thought, not caring if it was weird or unconventional. It strangely makes me feel less alone in the world, like there are other weirdos like me out there somewhere.

Forget about it if it's something mini—because man, oh man, there's nothing I love more than a random thingamabob that's also in mini form.

I'm looking at my third stand of taxidermy sea creatures, these ones dressed like mariachi players, when Jess walks over to me. "You've got to be kidding me with that," he says, nodding to the small puffer fish in my hand. The fish is wearing an oversized sombrero with a black bob cut wig underneath it.

"What?" I shrug and give a small giggle as he raises his brows at me. "The Lord Farquaad cut of his tiny wig is… *everything*," I say, scrunching my nose as I hold the puffer fish up to my face, smiling.

"We're literally hundreds of miles away from the ocean right now. Why would you even want that? It's so… *strange*. Not to mention, it has nothing to do with anything in, like, a five-hundred-mile radius of here," Jess says and puts his hands up, gesturing around us dramatically.

"When you said you wanted to stop because the sign said, '*Crystal Shop*' I figured you'd go for moon pebbles and sage, or whatever it is that basic bitches these days like," he says and scoffs quietly, gesturing to a group of girls that just walked into the shop now congregating around the small crystal display at the front of the store.

"I'm going to pretend that you didn't just call me a basic bitch," I say as I hold up a finger toward him. "And also, I like this little guy," I say and look down at my little sea creature as I cradle him in both my hands. "He's so whimsical, *I freakin' love it.*"

"But you're right though, he is *so* weird," I giggle, smiling to myself as I head over to the checkout stand to pay for my new treasure.

I got a handful of other small things at the shop, and honestly, I probably would've gotten even more if a text from Chris hadn't snapped me out of my unnecessary shopping spree.

He tells me that they decided to stop up the road a ways to take pictures of some rock formations my dad spotted off the main road. Since this is Rebecca's first official "family" trip with us, it seems my dad is in full tourist mode. I'm surprised that Chris bothered with letting me know, and I wonder if he's just as annoyed with my dad and Rebecca as I am.

I check the time and realize we've spent almost two hours in the shop, which means that now it'll probably be dark by the time we get to the campsite and get everything all set up for the night.

*Shit, what was I thinking?* I kick myself for wasting so much time.

Jess wasn't too far off with his comment about "moon pebbles" or whatever he'd said. I don't know if I put much belief into all that astrological stuff or not, but I do think that the crystals are beautiful. Whether they actually do anything or not, is sort of irrelevant to me. I'll welcome any good juju I can get, and if they don't end up working, then oh well, at least I'll have something pretty to decorate my bookshelf with. No harm done, right?

So, when Jess goes to the bathroom before we leave, I buy a few crystals I eyed on our way in and stuff them into the pocket of my hoodie, not wanting him to mock me for doing exactly what he predicted I would. Though I know he'll just roll his eyes, I pick one out for him anyway. I sort of did freak out earlier, so I tell myself that I'll test the waters and give it to him later as an apology.

"Ready to go?" Jess asks from behind me, and I shove the green crystal I got into my pocket before Jess sees me admiring it, not wanting him to make fun of me just yet.

"Uh-huh," I reply and nod as Jess holds the door open for us to exit the shop.

# Chapter Seven

We spend the rest of the drive up the canyon in relative silence, with only the occasional question from Jess, asking if I need to stop for the bathroom. Which, out here, equals the bushes, so I politely decline. I won't pretend that I'm too high maintenance to pee in a bush, I'd just rather not do it in front of Jess, so I resolve to hold it until later.

Whenever it seems like he's about to say something, I turn the music up or pretend like I'm sleeping—which I'm aware, is very childish.

I'm still a little embarrassed about earlier and don't really have the energy to talk about it right now. At least when we were stopped at the souvenir shop, I was able to keep us both distracted with all the random knick-knacks around us. But now, there's nothing to keep us distracted besides each other.

My mind keeps going back to when I pulled away from Jess and the look of hurt that came over his face before I decided to run away. I didn't mean anything by it, but I wonder if I accidentally upset him for real. Jess usually has a thick skin for things like that, so why do I feel like his reaction was so weird? He seemed fine when we stopped at the shop, so I tell myself that maybe I'm just overthinking it.

I think I just need a real nap and some caffeine, and then we can talk if he wants to. If not, I might accidentally put my foot in my mouth and say something like *Sorry, I've actually had buried feelings for you for a long time, and they've just now decided to manifest themselves in the form of smutty dreams.*

Yeah right.

After a while, the tension in the air feels like it's mostly gone, making me think it really was all just a figment of my imagination. Jess has stayed pretty quiet most of the day, so I wonder if sleep is finally catching up with him. I'm hoping that's actually the case and he's not just unhappy to be spending the weekend sleeping on the ground.

I had just assumed he'd want to come with on the camping trip since it's been tradition with our family for forever, but I wonder if he's rethinking it now. He probably only agreed out of pity. I had literally just been assaulted and was all cold and sad when I asked him to come on the trip. How could he have said no when I really didn't give him much of a choice?

I'm sure he has much better things to do than to hang out with my sorry ass all weekend. He'd probably rather be hanging out with Madison instead. Maybe I should tell him to forget about the camping trip and let him off the hook. He's probably realizing that I'm not that much fun to hang out with anyway, given our silence in the Jeep this whole time. It's just like when we were younger, Jess is the cool one everyone wants to be around, Sophie's the adventurous fun one, and I'm just the awkward extra.

I sigh to myself. *I guess I can always hitch a ride back with Sophie later...*

"Hello? Earth to Ryan, you in there?" Jess asks as he knocks on the top of my head, breaking my spiral of thoughts.

"Sorry, I guess I must've just spaced out for a sec," I say and shake my head as I turn back toward the window. I can feel him looking at me, and I don't know why, but I start feeling self-conscious.

*How long was he trying to get my attention?* My mind immediately goes back to earlier today when he had tried to wake me after I'd dozed off.

"Come on, I know that look," he says.

"What look?" I ask.

I turn to face him, and he frowns slightly, but it doesn't reach his eyes. That's one of my favorite things about Jess, no matter his mood, his beautiful eyes always seem to hold a bright shine behind them.

Madison's a lucky girl, she gets to see those eyes whenever she wants, and I get a weird feeling in my chest at the thought. I try not to picture them staring longingly into each other's eyes or the intensity in them when he's holding her, or when he's going in for a kiss, or when they—

"You're either being way too hard on yourself about something that's already happened, or you're overthinking something else completely unrelated. Or both," Jess says and smirks.

"You think you've got me all figured out, don't you, mister?" I ask and shake my head as I give him a squinty-eyed look.

"Maybe, or maybe you're just really, really easy to read," he says. "*Or...* maybe it's because I've spent most of my life learning your cute little ticks," he says and winks, reaching over the center console playfully jabbing me in the side. I swat his hand away, and we both laugh, the weirdness from earlier all but gone.

I smile to myself but try to ignore that last part, an obvious joke to get a reaction out of me, just like it always is.

"So, you're really not going to tell me why you freaked out earlier then?" Jess asks finally, raising a brow at me.

"I don't know what you're talking about, there's nothing to tell," I say, turning my gaze back out my window.

"Oh really?" he says sarcastically. "Were you… were you having a sex dream?" he asks, his voice dropping low.

"Wha—*no*, why would you even ask that—I—y-you—" I stammer and watch Jess laugh as I stumble over my words. I'm sure I'm red as a tomato and decide to stop talking before I make things worse for myself.

"Oh my god, *you so were*," he says, and gives me an incredulous look when our eyes meet. "Who was it about? Was it about me?" Jess teases, looking over at me intently as he waits for my answer.

*Shit.* He's got me cornered, only this time I can't jump out of the vehicle unless I wanna die.

"Sorry, no. You wouldn't know the guy," I say. "And anyway"—I gesture to the road with my hand—"eyes back on the road, mister."

"Right, because let me guess, he lives in Canada or something?" Jess says and scoffs, ignoring my comment about focusing on his driving.

"*Mmm hmm*," I reply and nod.

I can feel Jess's heavy gaze on my face, and I rush to change the subject. "If you keep staring at me, you're gonna miss all this *pristine land-scape*," I say sarcastically and gesture out the window. Both Pine trees and Aspens now heavily line the sides of the road the deeper we get into the forest.

What can I say? Sure, the view is nice, but the wilderness really isn't my jam.

I continue sarcastically as I clutch my hands to my heart while I look out the window. "I mean, have you ever *seen* anything more—"

"Breathtaking? Never," Jess says, finishing my sentence for me as he gives me a quick once-over in my seat, followed by a wink. He smiles and turns his head back toward the road.

One of the reasons I liked going on this trip growing up was because it was the only time my dad was away from all of his distractions. While we were up on the mountain, I knew there weren't going to be any cell phones or TV, and especially no Wi-Fi or ESPN either. It was the only time I felt like I could actually get my dad to look at me, even if it only ended up being for a few minutes at most. That, and the other obvious reason.

Sophie and her stupid sexy cousin.

~

We only have about another forty-five minutes left before we get to our campsite near Bass Lake, so I decide to sit the entirety of that time pretending to be asleep. I'm glad we aren't too far away, otherwise, I might literally combust if Jess looks at me again like he did earlier.

*That jerk, he so knew what he was doing.*

I try not to picture Jess's perfect smile when he looked at me and those sharp canines of his that I wish he'd just bite me with alrea—

*Oh. my. god. Enough already, Sam. GET IT TOGETHER, GIRL.*

I decide that I am wayyy too pent up to be in the same vicinity as Jess right now and can't wait to get out of the Jeep already. At this point, even the slightest hint of his cologne might be enough to cause me to pounce on him, so I make sure that I keep my face turned toward the window.

*Better safe than sorry.*

I don't know why I thought I could actually keep it together. If Jess keeps flirting and smiling at me, I'll be a permanent shade of red for the entire weekend. He always loved pushing my buttons, but I usually don't let it get to me like I did today, which makes me wonder what's changed.

I let out a huff, my eyes still closed, as I try not to overanalyze Jess's behavior over the last few days. I swear it's been so hard to get a

119

clear read on him. One minute he's staying the night on my couch, saying he's worried about me, the next he's pretending not to know me, and then he's back to making flirty eyes at me like nothing ever happened.

I have to remind myself that's just how he is—how he's always been. He's friendly and charming and flirts with everyone—and not just girls, from what Sophie tells me. That does have me curious to say the least, so I remind myself to ask him about it later.

The only difference is that even though Jess constantly flirts with me, nothing ever comes of it. That's how I know I'm different from the others. He obviously doesn't see me in a romantic way like he does with them, otherwise he would've said something by now. It's not like he's the shy type who keeps their feelings in, if Jess wants something, he always finds a way to get it.

When I feel the momentum of the Jeep slowing, I open my eyes and see that we've finally made it to the super-secret campsite that Chris had told my dad about yesterday.

Jess pulls in behind the other vehicles, and we both get out to stretch. I let out a yawn and reach my hands over my head as I watch my dad and Chris argue over how to situate the layout of our camp for the weekend.

"Are you seriously still tired?" Jess asks from beside me as he leans up against his Jeep, folding his arms across his chest. "You practically slept the whole way up," he says, and I can sense a tinge of annoyance in his voice.

"What can I say? I am, and forever will always be, a sleepy bitch," I say, shrugging my shoulders, and Jess just rolls his eyes.

I lean against the Jeep beside him and try not to stare at how much bigger his biceps look with his arms folded across his chest, and wonder when I developed a thing for arms.

My mind darts back to my dream from earlier, and I wonder how I was able to make up such details about his body. I haven't seen Jess shirtless in I don't know how long, but somehow, my mind was able to paint a perfect picture of the sculpted abs I know are underneath his clothes.

We watch Chris as he backs up his truck and small camper, strategically trying to block the entrance to our campsite from any unwelcome campers trying to set up next to us.

"RIGHT! TO THE RIGHT, I SAID!" my dad yells at Chris, waving his hands around in frustration, and it's evident that we probably all need food and some sleep.

I look around at our little area and think that Chris did a pretty good job finding this place. I wonder how we haven't discovered the spot until now and notice that there are plenty of trees for shade, for which I'm incredibly grateful. The only thing I hate more than the obvious bugs, dirt, and lack of toilets that go along with camping, is having to sit around in the heat with no shade.

I glance back at the way we came and see that the campsite's turnoff is almost completely covered with trees, making it hard to see if you didn't already know it was there. It makes me wonder how Chris even knew about it.

I imagine he probably discovered it one of the times he was up here with his buddies for another one of their mid-week ragers. I spotted a few beer cans on the way in and can't help but wonder if those were from Chris and his friends. I do worry about him partying too hard, but "nagging" him about it, as he puts it, only ever makes it worse, so I try not to overstep and give him his space.

Ever since our mom left, he's been sort of a mess. I mean, hell, who in this damn family isn't? I try to be there for Chris, but he's always so irritable that it usually makes any attempt at a normal conversation almost impossible. I try not to take it personally because I know that deep down, like *deep, deep down*, he loves me. I know he'll get through it eventually, it's just hard to sit back and watch his self-destructive behavior. Maybe it's just the maternal side of me trying to—

"You're doing that thing again," Jess says as he snaps his fingers in front of my face.

I jump a little when he breaks my trance, my eyes refocusing as I look at him. "Oh, uh, sorry. Long drive, I guess," I say, and run my hand over my face, rubbing my eyes.

I turn away without meeting Jess's gaze, my embarrassment just barely at bay after thinking about what his naked body might actually look like in person just a few minutes ago. I shake the thought away and try to focus on what's at hand.

"We really need to get our tents set up before we lose what little sunlight we have left, not to mention how long it'll take us to get dinner going," I grumble to no one in particular as I walk around the side of the Jeep and reach up to unclasp the ties that are holding everything down. I knew I shouldn't have made Jess stop at that shop earlier. Now we'll be setting up in the dark thanks to my need for dumb souvenirs.

I can't quite reach the strap on the side of the Jeep's roof rack and walk around to the back to use the bumper as a ledge to stand on, but before I can, I feel Jess's hand on my left arm. He stops me from making the step and quickly whips me around, sandwiching me in between himself and the spare tire of the Jeep, our bodies pressed lightly up against each other.

"What's going on with you today? Really?" he asks as he stares at me with a little more intensity than I was expecting. I'm sure my eyes are bugging out of my head because when I look at him and then down to where he's gripping my arm, he immediately lets go and steps back a foot. "Sorry," he says, before putting some space between us.

Even though he let go of my arm, I can still feel the heat of his touch on my skin. I don't know what shocks me more, the look of concern on his face or how he was able to spin me around and discombobulate me so effortlessly.

"Honestly, what's going on with you? Do you not... *want* me here?" he asks, his eyes still holding their same intensity.

I give him a look of confusion. "Why would you even ask me that?"

"I was looking forward to today because I thought that we'd finally have a chance to talk, but you've barely said two words to me the entire drive, not to mention you keep spacing out every time I *do* try to talk to you and you can't even look me in the eye for longer than two seconds," Jess says as he leans in closer to me, the words rushing out of him in exasperation. He holds my gaze, refusing to break eye contact, almost as if he's daring me to even try.

"No, I…"

Shocked and flustered by this sudden confrontation and the closeness of our bodies, I'm at a loss for words. I want to look away, but I don't, especially now that I know it's been bothering him every time that I do.

*So, he* was *hurt earlier.* I feel like an idiot for thinking any differently. Of course he would've been hurt by my strange reactions all day long, *I* definitely would have had our roles been reversed.

"*You* invited *me* here, remember? Why did you invite me anyway if you didn't really want me to come? When John—or whoever—suggested it, you should've just said no or made up some excuse," Jess says and puts his hands on his hips as he shakes his head.

I see the same look of hurt from earlier flash across his eyes as he tries to turn away from me, and wonder if I possibly misread this entire thing. "Maybe I should just go—"

"No, wait!" I say and grab Jess's arm to stop him. "*Please* don't," I say, and it comes out more pleadingly than I expect, but I mean what I say.

"I really do want you here! Honest! I thought *you* were the one who didn't want to be here. I thought you only said yes because you felt sorry for me …for what happened the other night outside Adolfo's." I fidget nervously with my hands and fight the urge to look away from Jess.

"I—I figured you'd want to hang out with Chris instead, or that you'd rather be home with—with *Madison*," I say, feeling that burning embarrassment again, and hate the jealousy that's starting to well up inside of me at the mention of her name.

123

"I'm here because I want to be, and because you asked me to, not because I wanted to see Chris," Jess says, and scoffs like it's the most ridiculous thing I could've said.

"I wanted to see *you*, to spend time with *you*, not with anyone else," he says, his eyes softening as he speaks, and the pressure in my chest eases a little at his words.

I let out a heavy breath. "I'm sorry I've been sort of spacey today," I say, rubbing my eyes with my hands. "If you're still up for it, we can talk after we set everything up? Or, better yet, let's go on a walk tomorrow by the lake, just like we used to," I suggest. We haven't done that since we were twelve, so I hope he doesn't think it's a dumb idea.

He smiles at me, and it seems like Angry Jess is no more. It's only a half-smile, but it's still enough to make my stomach do the thing it always does when he looks at me like that.

"It's a date." Jess winks at me. "But you're not forgiven just yet," he says, giving me a squinty look.

"Wait, what—"

Chris cuts me off as he yells over to us. "Hey, Jess, get over here. I need a hand," he shouts, probably wanting help before my dad tries to take over.

Chris is trying to get his camper's awning open, but it's stuck on one side, and the material looks like it's about to rip from how roughly he's pulling on it.

Jess braces a hand above my head against the Jeep and leans in close to me. My heart starts to race, and I panic before I hear one of the straps on the Jeep's roof rack unlatch. "Coming," Jess calls to Chris halfheartedly without breaking eye contact with me before he turns away with another wink.

I seriously can't believe he just threw a tantrum like that, and now he's already back to his usual self? *How typical, and he says* I'm *the moody one.*

I roll my eyes as I lean back against the spare tire of the Jeep, trying to compose myself. I feel all flustered and borderline woozy from being in such close proximity to Jess and can't help but fantasize about what would've happened if he'd leaned in any closer to me. My face feels all hot, and I decide to check my phone, trying to find a way to distract myself from my own thoughts.

I check the time, and at first, I consider waiting for Sophie to get here before starting on dinner, but decide against it. I know I could ask the guys for help, but they're busy getting everything set up, and if I wait for them, we might not end up eating until midnight.

*Great.* That only leaves Rebecca to help me.

Since Rebecca's culinary delicacies consist of spaghetti or tuna casserole—I'm still not quite sure why she chose to brag about those things, but to each their own, I guess—I figure that most of tonight's cooking falls to me. Honestly, it's so predictable.

It used to bother me to do all the cooking and prep alone after my mom wasn't around anymore. However, when the guys started talking about making it a guys-only trip, I was so grateful to still be invited that I'd usually volunteer to cook for everyone. I have to give some of the credit to Sophie, though. Even though she's not much of a cook herself, she at least tries to help out the best she can. I let out a sigh and wish that she were here already.

I look over and see that Chris is busy setting up his hammock, and my dad and Jess are still trying to get Betty leveled. I watch for a good ten minutes as they both argue over the manual, pushing random buttons, and crawling under the RV trying to figure it out.

I scoff to myself at the sight of Betty. You'd think something that costs the same amount as a small house would be fancy enough to level itself.

*What a colossal waste of money.*

I spot Rebecca standing off to the side, watching Chris curse and struggle with the strings of his hammock, which is somehow more tangled now, but doing nothing to help him.

I walk over to Chris's truck and lower the tailgate before pulling one of the coolers onto the ground with a heavy thud. I grab another and gesture at Rebecca to help me pack them over next to the fire pit where I'd already drug our small prep table.

It surprises me when she doesn't complain or flat-out refuse to help. I figured she'd spout off some bullshit about not being able to help because of her nails or something. Maybe I judged her too quickly, and wonder if she isn't as bad as I initially thought she was.

I set up our small prep table and open up a few chairs for us to sit on as we start on dinner.

"So, your dad tells me you've been single for a while. Why is that?" Rebecca asks as she looks at me from the fold-up stool she's perched on. "Is it that you're not interested in—*all that?*" she says as she waves her hand around in the air. "Or is it that you play for the other team, then?" she asks, raising a judgmental brow at me.

*Seriously?* I internally smack myself in the face at her words. The way she asked has me thinking it won't make a difference how I answer the question. And not that it's any of her business, but I did date a girl during my first semester in college. It didn't end up working out, so we decided to stay friends, but I feel like that's neither here nor there in this conversation.

I feel like I could really use some backup right about now, and sigh as I look up at the sky. *Soph, where the hell are you?* I silently pray to the teleportation gods that Sophie will magically appear to save me.

Immediately, I regret thinking that Rebecca wasn't actually the worst, and I shake my head to myself. Like, what the hell is my dad thinking with this bitch? I know that Rebecca and I got off on the wrong foot, and at this point, I don't really have the time or patience to act like I want to get along with her. Not anymore. I give their relationship the shelf life of a slice of bread—sorry, Dad.

Don't get me wrong, she's probably an okay person, that is, when she's not constantly judging others, or making every single condescending jab she can think of.

I pull two cutting boards and a few knives from one of the clean totes, and I'm glad I already prepped and washed most of the veggies yesterday to save myself some work. I only left a few things to chop because I wanted to make sure they stayed fresh for today. The less time I spend cooking, the less time I have to suffer my way through this incessant small talk with Rebecca.

"Actually, no, I *haven't* been single for a while, and honestly, my dad wouldn't know the first thing about any of my relationships," I say, unsure why I'm even explaining myself to her.

"And why is that?" Rebecca asks me defensively, and I regret bringing it up.

"It's not important," I say, and she sneers. I have no doubt she takes my comment as it being none of her business, instead of the fact that my personal life doesn't interest my dad very much, so he doesn't usually bother with finding out the details.

Rebecca ignores my obvious irritation and keeps pushing. "Right, well, you know you really should put more effort into the way you look. A little help would go a long way for your... *situation*," she says, and there she goes again, waving her hand around at me.

*Situation?* Okay, I know I'm no supermodel, but damn, she so didn't have to go there.

"Just look at that cutie Jess. It's no wonder that he already has a girlfriend even though he just got back. Madison, is it? I hear she's gorgeous. John told me all about her and how they're perfect for each other. They've practically been inseparable since he's been back in town," Rebecca says as she picks at her manicure. "John also told me about your little childhood *crush*, but it really is sad you know. Unrequited love is such a bitch, isn't it? How cute though that you thought you'd end up with Je—"

I slam a cutting board down onto the table in front of her. "Would you rather slice the potatoes, or start on the bacon?" I ask, cutting her off before I *actually* cut her. I'm not ready to give up my knife just yet, so I hope she opts to start on the bacon instead of anything requiring a blade.

*Seriously, how did my dad end up with this witch? You're telling me this is the nicest one he could find?* I think as I fight the urge to slap her.

Rebecca stops eyeing her nails and looks up at me, completely unfazed by the loud noise of the cutting board being slammed down in front of her.

"Honestly, neither. I don't really enjoy cooking," she says.

*No shocker there.*

Rebecca hops off her stool, uncrossing her legs before making her way toward Betty, now all set up and leveled. I just watch as she walks away and figure it's better this way. She wasn't really helping anyway, and I'm afraid I'd accidentally end up murdering her if she messed up the food.

"Be right back, hon, I just need to grab something really quick," Rebecca calls over her shoulder without looking back at me.

I cringe internally as I watch her walk away. Being called "hon" by someone close to your own age is another level of cringe.

A little while passes, and just as I'd suspected, Rebecca, in fact, did not come right back. My dad said she suddenly came down with a *horrible* migraine and had to go straight to bed.

*Poor thing.* I scoff to myself. The biatch can stay in the RV for the rest of the weekend for all I care. She doesn't really strike me as the outdoorsy type, and I'm guessing that being this far away from her precious country club already has her on edge.

Making dinner alone tonight doesn't bother me like it usually does, though. The sound of the breeze blowing through the trees and crickets chirping in the background is relaxing to me, therapeutic, even. It takes me back to when I was younger and would play in these woods with Chris and Jess and Sophie, back before everything eventually went to shit with my family.

I try to use the time alone to clear my head and stop myself from overanalyzing every interaction I've had with Jess over the last few days. It's difficult not to think about it, but I can't help but let Rebecca's words from earlier get to me.

*Where does she get off calling me out on something she knows nothing about?* The thought makes me angry, and I continue taking my frustrations out on the potatoes I'm slicing.

So *what* if Jess has a perfect girlfriend who happens to be gorgeous with nice hair and skin and a nice personality and nice-looking boobs? What do *I* care if she volunteers at the terminally ill children's ward on her days off and helps out at the local soup kitchen three days a week before nursing abandoned kittens back to health at the local shelter?

*Humph.*

I let out a frustrated groan and tell myself to chill out before I make up any more ridiculous assumptions about Madison, knowing I'm just going to make myself feel worse, even if it is all made up.

As much as I'd like to believe that Jess only came on this trip for me, I just can't imagine that's the whole truth. He's been on this camping trip with us a thousand times before, so it would honestly be weird if he weren't here right now.

I wish he wouldn't joke so much about stuff like that with me. I've forgotten how hard it is to keep my guard up around him, especially without Sophie here as a buffer. If I let myself get my hopes up, I know it'll just be that much more painful when he has to let me down, and I'd rather not be known as the pathetic friend who couldn't take a hint.

I know Jess made it sound like he didn't want to hang out with Chris, but they *did* used to be friends, before Chris turned into such a sourpuss—

"I think you're doing that wrong," Jess says from behind me, startling me a little at his sudden appearance.

*No no no no!*

I got so distracted by my thoughts again that I accidentally dumped the bacon pieces meant for the potatoes straight into the peach cobbler mix. "Well shit," I say with an exhausted sigh.

I look toward the sky, feeling like an idiot, knowing that I didn't bring any extra ingredients this year.

*Great.*

I rub a hand over my forehead in frustration and think that if I don't get some sleep soon, I'm gonna end up accidentally poisoning one of us or something with my next screwup.

"Here, give me that," Jess says as he gently takes the metal spatula out of my right hand and replaces it with a bottle of water. "Drink," he instructs. "Let's just focus on one thing at a time, yeah?" he says, and I obediently crack open the water bottle and take a long drink. I watch as Jess grabs a paper plate and some tongs and starts picking the bacon pile out of the peaches.

"Wait, what are you doing—" I ask, almost choking on my water. "You can't seriously be trying to save that?"

I was sort of on a mincing rampage after Rebecca's comments earlier, so I can't imagine that he'll actually be able to get all of the tiny pieces.

I watch him patiently pick the small pieces out with the tongs as he drops them onto the paper plate in his other hand.

"Shhh." Jess puts a finger to his lips and gives me a mischievous grin.

"But it's ruined. We should just throw the whole thing out," I say, looking around to see if anyone else was close enough to see what had happened.

"I'll just lie and tell my dad I forgot the peaches or something and had to throw it out," I say walking over to Jess as I try to take the tongs out of his hand. He turns and holds them out of my reach, facing me as he looks down with half-lidded eyes.

"They'll never know," he says as he winks before giving me a cheeky smile. I try not to flush and quietly return to my post stirring the chicken.

"Chris is already on his fifth beer, so I doubt he'll notice much else tonight, and your dad is probably grateful to be eating anything besides one of Rebecca's casseroles for once …and as for the Wicked Witch of the West herself, I saw her eat a handful of almonds earlier so I'm guessing she's already full," Jess says, his concentration back on the bacon.

The way he says it in all seriousness makes me erupt with laughter as I look over at him. I realize that I must *really* be sleep-deprived if I'm laughing this hard over something so stupid. Jess looks over at me like I've lost my mind. A large grin spreads across his face, and then he's laughing, too.

We're both cackling like a bunch of idiots when Chris walks up to us as he cracks open a fresh can of beer. "Yooo is the food ready yet? It smells incredible!" Chris says, sniffing the air around the sizzling food.

It sucks that the only time he's ever in a good mood is when he's three sheets to the wind. Though it's a pretty fine line between Happy Chris and I'll fight you Chris, judging from the way he's acting right now, it seems we get Happy Chris tonight.

Chris eyes the open dutch ovens and rubs his hands together after setting his can down on my small prep table. He tries to sneak a piece of food from one of the open pans, and I swat his hand away with the wooden spoon I'm holding. Chris lets out a giggle as he scurries away toward his hammock that's swinging gently in between the two trees it's tied to.

I'm still struggling to regain my composure from my laugh attack with Jess earlier and wipe the tears of laughter away with my sleeve, when Jess looks over at me and winks.

When he's not looking, I check to make sure that my water was actually filled with water and not some crazy fever-inducing liquor.

I wonder why my head feels so fuzzy when he looks at me lately. *Nothing's changed, right? He's always looked at me like that, hasn't he?*

I tell myself to blame it on the day's exhaustion getting to my head and try to convince myself that the feelings I'm picking up on between Jess and me aren't actually there. He's just being nice and I'm reading way too much into it, just like I always do, and remind myself to rein my emotions back in before I do something I'll regret.

After we eat and finish cleaning up the mess from dinner, I watch my dad make a plate of food for Rebecca. She'd told him she wasn't hungry, but he said he wanted to make one up for her just in case she changed her mind later.

Regardless of my feelings toward her, I will say it's sort of sweet seeing how my dad dotes on her. I know he's wanted to have that again with someone for a long time. I have to remind myself that we're all human, and at the end of the day, we all just want to be loved and cared for, just like anyone else ...*even* the evil stepmothers of the world.

It's hard to tell where I don't really know Rebecca all that well, so I can only hope that her affections toward my dad are actually sincere.

"Did you do something different to the food tonight?" my dad asks from his camp chair from across the fire. "I think this cobbler was your best one yet," he says as he finishes off the last spoonful of his dessert.

"Just a few secret ingredients this time, thought I'd try something new tonight," I say, struggling not to laugh as a small smile crosses my face when Jess meets my eyes.

I can see the reflection of the fire dancing in his eyes and wish I knew what he was thinking right now. He's giving me that look again, and my heart skips a beat. I try not to notice and turn back to the washing station to finish drying what's left of the dishes.

# Chapter Eight

"What do you mean you're not coming?" I whine into my phone.

After dinner, I wandered around to see if I could get any cell reception to call Sophie with since she'd never answered my texts from earlier. She was supposed to be here by now, and I was worried she wouldn't be able to find our location in the dark, especially with all the trees that are practically blocking the entrance.

It took me a while, but I was finally able to get one bar of service at the far end of our campsite. My dad had Wi-Fi installed in his RV for Rebecca, but I wasn't about to ask her for the password. Honestly, it's unlikely she'd even give it to me, and I so do not want to end up owing her a favor.

I sigh and prepare myself for whatever bullshit excuse I'm about to hear from Sophie as I loosely hold my phone to my ear.

"I'm so sorry, girl, they called me super last minute. Someone dropped out, so a spot finally opened up. You know how much this internship could mean for me, for *us*. We can finally move to L.A. like we always talked about!" she says, laying the guilt on heavy. "I *promise* I'll make it up to you."

I know Sophie well enough to know that her apology is about as fake as a three-dollar bill and shake my head for expecting anything different from her.

"I'm sorry, I know this is important to you," I say, feeling a little guilty for making it seem like a stupid camping trip would take priority over her future.

Sophie's been trying to get into the grad program at UCLA since last semester. Her grades have always been subpar, so the only way she can get in, is if she has good extracurricular activities and an impressive internship under her belt. L.A. was never my dream, but I always went along with it because I didn't want to be left behind.

*A lot of good that's done me.*

I usually don't think about it much, but I'm a little annoyed with myself for always agreeing to go along with whatever Sophie wants us to do. After she'd changed her plans and left for an East Coast school at the last minute, I figured she'd forget about L.A. and move on to something else, but it seems I was wrong. In the end, I guess I did get left behind in a way, even if it was by my own choice.

Sophie doesn't apologize again, she only tells me that the sacrifices we have to make now will make it all worth it in the end, *blah blah blah*... I sigh and tell her it's fine, letting her off the hook for the millionth time in our friendship before ending the call.

I let out a dramatic groan as I look toward the night sky. "Dammit, Sophie!" I shake my fists at the sky and wobble, almost falling off the wooden stump I'm perched on.

*Well shit, there goes my tent and sleeping bag.*

I feel like crying because of how tired I am right now and rub my burning eyes with my hands.

Since by the grace of the gods we were blessed with Happy Chris tonight—and as long as I wake up and leave before I have to deal with the wrath of Hangover Chris—I figure he'll probably have no problem with me crashing in his camper. At this point, it's my best alternative because I sure as shit will not be staying with my dad and Rebecca. I would rather sleep naked on a bed of sharp tree branches than witness what happens at night between those two.

*Bleh.* I shudder at the thought.

"What the hell are you doing up there?"

Startled, I lose my balance and slip off the tree stump. I almost land flat on my ass before Jess catches me in his arms. I cover my mouth with my hand when a startled squeal accidentally escapes my lips, and when I turn to face him, I feel like I've had the wind knocked out of me. The fact that he scooped me up so effortlessly and the feeling of his sturdy body next to mine catches me by surprise.

Jess is holding me so close that I can feel the warmth of his body through my thin sweats and hoodie, causing a shiver to run through me at the contact. I wonder when it got so cold out here, when I notice how the heat of his hands sears me through the fabric of my clothing.

"I uh—w-well I…" I swallow hard and my words come out breathlessly as I try to remember what I was even doing up there in the first place, the feeling of Jess's strong arms making my head fuzzy.

We're face to face as he cradles me in his arms, and my words catch in my throat as I try to say something—*anything*. I remember how hot his hand felt earlier when he grabbed my arm, and even though it's freezing out here, he's still just in his t-shirt and jeans.

*Has he always been this warm?*

"You really should be more careful, Ryan," he murmurs as he leans in closer, our noses almost touching. "I wouldn't want you to get hurt," he whispers, and I feel his lips move as they gently graze the side of my ear, sending another shiver down the length of my body.

"Sorry, did I startle you?" he whispers against me when I don't respond.

Everything starts to slow down, and I feel myself waiting for Jess to make some wisecrack about how it's so easy to tease me, but he doesn't. Instead, he stays still as he holds me in his arms, and I can feel his uneven breathing against me. His seriousness takes me by surprise, and I decide to see how far I can push my limits.

Unsure if I'll ever get the chance again, I move a hand from where it's resting on Jess's chest, up to the top of his shoulder. The bright moonlight glints off the gold chain Jess has around his neck, and I can't stop myself as my fingers reach out to touch the cool metal.

I run a light finger underneath the thin chain and notice the goosebumps that spread across his skin as I touch him. Jess closes his eyes, and I feel his breathing hitch. I hesitate, but then slowly let my fingertips wander to the edge of his shirt collar and trace the small birthmark on the side of his neck that just barely peeks above the soft navy material. I've always loved the strangely shaped splotch and notice it's much lighter than usual, despite how bronzed his skin is right now.

I sense Jess's eyes on me, and I feel myself pulling him in closer when he doesn't stop me. My right hand grips the back of his neck, and a small noise leaves his throat, something between a gasp and a groan, and I'm rewarded with a small sense of satisfaction at the sound.

Even though my hand is resting on the back of his neck, I'm half tempted to remove the small elastic that's holding his hair back. I want to pull him in by his soft waves, knowing if they were loose, I wouldn't be able to stop myself from tangling my fingers through his hair.

My breathing feels rushed but also calm at the same time, and I wonder if I might actually be losing my mind. It's like I keep waiting for the other shoe to drop, and for him to call me out in a *gotcha!* moment, but he doesn't. I tilt my head up to face him, and even through the dark, the intensity of Jess's stare scorches through me.

My entire body feels hot, and all I want is *him*. I want to *touch* him, to *smell* him. I want to taste the salt on his skin as I run my mouth up and down his birthmark.

Jess tightens his hold under my legs as he pulls me in closer to him, and I imagine what his hands would feel like if they gripped my hips like that. I imagine the pressure of his hands against my skin, wanting him to almost bruise me from his strength. The thought makes me shiver again, and I swear I hear a small growl escape Jess's lips as my body trembles against him.

He's so close now that I can feel his hot breath on my face, which is a stark contrast to the cold mountain air around us. I can feel his heart thundering through his chest from where he's pressed against my body and wonder if he can feel mine doing the same.

Jess lets out a labored breath, his voice coming out gravelly as he speaks, finally. "*Sam*—"

My heart starts to race faster in my chest as I continue to stare at him through the dark, and I can feel his eyes searching mine.

*Is this actually happening right now?*

"Jess, can you—*oh*, I'm sorry, am I… interrupting?"

Our gazes break, and I feel the embarrassment burning through me as it works its way from my cheeks down through my body. "N-no, um, the stump had reception and then I f-fell. Okay I'm going over here now—goodnight!" I say as I practically jump out of Jess's arms and make a beeline for Chris's trailer.

Fucking Rebecca. Isn't she supposed to be asleep or something? I wonder if she just has shit timing or if she purposely interrupted us. Probably the latter.

"Hey, wait—" Jess calls after me, sounding out of breath.

"Not the most articulate girl, is she?" I hear Rebecca mocking me as I run away, and I don't bother turning back to see Jess's reaction.

My words rushed out of me so fast, I feel like I can barely breathe, but then again, I think I stopped breathing the second Jess scooped me up in his arms. I'm grateful it's dark enough out that Rebecca couldn't see my face clearly, all I need is to give her more ammunition to berate me with about my little "crush."

*Whatever that means.* I scoff to myself. *What crush?* I'm obviously just hormonal. Anything within a two-mile radius would probably look good to me right now.

I bang on Chris's camper door and notice that all the lights are off inside, and I cross my fingers that he's still awake.

I knock again. Nothing. *Well, shit.*

I check the doors and they're all locked, including the doors of his truck.

*Double shit.* I rub my hands over my eyes as I groan silently to myself.

"I think he had one too many tonight. I saw him turn in a bit ago," my dad says as he gets up from his chair by the fire. He walks over to me and smiles, his eyes glazed over.

*Seems like Chris wasn't the only one who might've had one too many...*

"Everything all right? Did you need something from Chris?" my dad asks, nodding to Chris's camper.

"No, I just wanted to ask him something. It's nothing that can't wait until tomorrow," I lie and give my dad a halfhearted smile.

139

"Are Sophie and Ted still coming?" he asks, looking around as if they're going to magically appear. *If only.*

"Yeah, they should be here soon," I lie again, not bothering to correct him about calling Trevor by the wrong name. Since they aren't coming anymore, it's not like it really matters anyway.

I tell my dad goodnight and head over to Jess's Jeep to try the doors.

"SON OF A BIIITCH!" I yell to the sky as I throw my hands in the air in frustration. My voice echoes through the trees and I notice a few birds scatter into the sky above me.

"*Seriously*, who does everyone think is going to break in out here? *The fucking bears?*" I call out loud to no one in particular as I continue to throw my hands in the air dramatically after trying the doors, only to find them both locked as well.

"You all right...?" Jess asks from next to his tent as he finishes setting up the rain cover, securing the last Velcro strap to the body of the tent. I didn't realize he was watching me, and the thought has me a little embarrassed that he witnessed my mental breakdown.

"Can I please have your keys?" I ask as I let out an exhausted breath when Jess walks over to me, eyeing me suspiciously.

"What for?" he asks as he raises a brow.

"Because I'm exhausted and cold and just want to sleep already," I say, shivering. I wrap my arms around myself and rub my hands up and down, trying to generate some warmth with the friction.

"I'm guessing Soph bailed?" Jess asks, seeming annoyed. "Did she say what was more important than this?" he asks, and I wonder if he's disappointed by the fact that she's not coming or that he's stuck with me all weekend.

I try to shake the negative thoughts from my head. I doubt he's upset about having to spend time with me, I guess he already said as much when he got upset earlier. And… I mean, we did sort of have a moment back there…

*Ugh, stop thinking about it already, Sam!* I shake my head again, trying to physically shake the thoughts of Jess's strong, sturdy body from my mind.

"Intern stuff. Now enough with the questions. Keys. Now, please," I demand as I hold out my hand impatiently.

"Sorry, no," Jess says as he turns away from me, heading back to his tent.

"What do you mean *no*…?" I ask, following him closely. Jess turns around to face me and I almost bump into him.

"You'll freeze to death. Not to mention it's way too small to sleep in there, especially in that tiny back seat," he says. "Trust me, I've tried." Jess winks and returns to whatever he was doing with the rain cover.

"Just sleep in my tent with me, there's plenty of room," he says over his shoulder and nods to the tent.

I shake my head. "Not happening."

"It's no big deal, Ryan. It'll be just like when we were kids," Jess says as he bends down and starts to unlace his boots.

"Thanks, but I'd rather sleep outside," I say, putting my hands on my hips, even though I'm starting to rethink the backseat of the Jeep after his earlier comment. I'm beginning to get angry, but I feel like I don't have many other options, and Jess's smug attitude only makes me feel more annoyed.

"Have it your way. You can always bunk with John and *Bec*…" Jess says, and snickers as he turns away, disappearing inside the tent. He leaves it partially unzipped after he ducks inside, leaving me to consider my options as I stand there shivering from the cold.

Maybe I'll just wait for him to fall asleep and then take the keys. *Yeah, that's what I'll do.* I'm sure I can find an extra sleeping bag lying around here somewhere, and if not, I'll just double up my sweats for the night. *It's really not* that *cold tonight.* I lie to myself as my teeth lightly chatter against each other.

"*Fuck*," I huff and duck inside the tent after pulling my shoes off, leaving them outside.

The tent has a surprisingly small interior despite how big it looks on the outside, probably from the fancy windows and rain cover.

"Hey, what the—"

I glance down at Jess on his sleeping bag. He's already shirtless, lying on his side with his cheek propped up on a fist, wearing only a pair of dark-blue flannel-patterned pajama pants. He's taken his hair out as well, and it rests perfectly tousled around his head.

*Well, damn, he sure doesn't waste any time, does he?* And I'm left wondering how in the hell he got changed so quickly.

"*Why* is your shirt off?" I ask as I feel redness creeping into my cheeks again and try not to stare at his body. I'm afraid of where my perverted mind might take me this time, and I try to remember how to breathe as I avert my eyes.

*Hold it together, Sam.*

Though there's only a small lantern on inside the tent, I can still see the chiseled lines of Jess's upper body and abs as the shadows dance off his skin. It's honestly annoying how good-looking he is, even in such poor lighting.

I struggle not to stare at him, and my heart rate slowly starts to pick up, as does the heat between my legs when I think about how accurate my dream was about how good his body looks without a shirt on. I can only wonder if my imagination was right about another particular body part as well…

Jess shrugs before answering. "My tent, my rules," he says as he gives me a cunning smile.

*Here we go.* "And what rules are those?" I ask impatiently with a heavy sigh.

"Just one," he says, winking before flexing his pecs. "No shirts allowed."

"That's it. I'll take my chances with the She Devil," I say flatly, and quickly unzip the tent before I pull my shoes back on.

As much as I love the sight of Jess like this, I'm having a hard enough time as it is being in close quarters with him, forget about it if he's half-naked, too.

"When did you get so touchy about everything?" Jess calls after me, sounding like a whiny kid. "*My* Sam used to be more fun!" he says, and I try not to read into the way he said "*my*" Sam.

I step out into the cold air and wish I had a better jacket on. "Damn, how in the hell did it get so much colder in like the five minutes since I've been out here?" I grumble to myself.

I'm still trying to will the heat forming between my legs to dissipate and realize that it won't take long with the brisk night air around me, and I shiver.

I make it partway to my dad's RV, when from behind me, I can hear Jess swearing as he trips out of the tent, followed by his half-tied boots clomping after me in the dark.

"Wait a second! Hold on, Ryan! I said wait!" Jess calls after me, and I turn to see him almost fall as he still tries to get his left boot all the way on. I turn and keep walking before he finally catches up to me and grabs the back of my arm. "Hey, come on, Sam," he says.

*Great, not this again.*

I'm starting to get beyond agitated and consider if punching him will even do anything. I turn around and get right in Jess's face, and he quickly releases me as I angry whisper at him with all the energy that I have left in my body.

"Listen up, you! I am *tired* as hell, so unless you want to experience Cranky Sam all day tomorrow, I NEED SLEEP. *Right. Now,*" I say, and Jess gives me a look of surprise as I wag my finger in his face, causing him to step back a foot.

"Here's how this is going to work. We're going back to the tent where, *for the sake of my sanity,* you're going to put on a damn shirt, and you're gonna get in your sleeping bag and go to *sleep* and not bother me until I have my nine hours. Is that clear?" I say, out of breath, both from the cold and my rant.

"Nine hours? Seriously? You do realize we're *camping*...?" Jess says and starts to scoff but stops himself when I cut him an abrupt glare. He puts his hands up in surrender when I raise both my brows dramatically at him, giving him a *Sorry, what was that?* look.

I notice his pajama bottoms hanging dangerously low on his waist, and I try not to stare, especially when I realize I can't see the waistband of any underwear.

"Okay, okay, I'm sorry. Let's just get back inside before one of us freezes a tit off," he says and blows into his hands as he rubs them together. Before I can protest the gesture, Jess grabs onto one of my hands and drags me back through the dark toward the tent.

It really is pretty chilly outside, and my hands *are* freezing... I tell myself that's the only reason why I don't pull away from him.

Once we're back inside the tent, I make Jess turn around and cover his eyes so that I can change into my thermal pajamas. Sophie gave me so much shit when I bought them a few summers ago, saying that they were a fashion nightmare.

We were at the T. J. Maxx yellow tag sale, and it was pretty obvious why they were on clearance: yellow with brown polka dots. Of course, at the time, it made no sense to buy thermal pajamas in the dead of summer, let alone the ugliest ones on the face of the earth, but I knew they'd come in handy eventually.

*Take that, Soph.* I'll have to remind her of that fact the next time we talk.

I finish changing and pull on some fuzzy cat socks as I sit down on the edge of Jess's fluffy red sleeping bag. "Okay, it's safe to look now," I say.

Jess removes his hands from his eyes hesitantly and turns around to face me. "You do realize that I've seen you in next to nothing before, right?" Jess says as he watches me remove my hair from its braid.

"Don't remind me," I say, rolling my eyes as I sit cross-legged across from Jess on the soft sleeping bag, and continue to fight the tangles in my hair. It was partially damp when I braided it this morning, so it's sort of a mess now.

"What, no witty reply?" I scoff, waiting for a smartass remark from him about my various skimpy swimsuits over the years, and the thought makes me smile to myself. After getting inside the warm tent and putting on my comfy clothes, I feel like I've definitely calmed down quite a bit, making me feel bad for the come-apart I had on him earlier.

Jess says nothing as he lies on his side with his body turned toward me, his head propped up on one fist. Thankfully, he agreed to put his shirt back on as soon as we got back into the tent. Being in a tent alone with him is distracting enough. I don't need the thought of all he's got going on under his clothes getting in my head again, especially since now I know that my imagination was pretty accurate with its details.

"Seriously. What?" I ask. When I look over at Jess, he's staring right at me, and his eyes lock with mine in the low lighting.

"It's nothing, you just look really beautiful, that's all," he says completely straight-faced as he continues holding my gaze.

"Ha. Ha," I say, rolling my eyes as I finish taking the rest of my braid out before giving the waves a good shake to loosen them from each other.

A sad look crosses Jess's face, but I have a difficult time seeing his expression clearly since it's so dark in the tent.

"Why do you always do that?" he asks.

This time I don't need to see Jess's face to know precisely what expression he's making, just from the tone of his voice.

*So, what, now he's mad, then?* Seems like we're both cranky tonight.

"Do what? Roll my eyes? You should've been able to predict that by now, I'm surprised you could even see it in the dark—"

Jess sits up and cuts me off before I finish my snarky reply. "Why do you discount everything I say to you? It's like you always love to make a joke out of every compliment I ever give you. I swear to god, Ry, when you mock literally every nice thing I say to you, how could you *not* take it the wrong way every single goddamned time?" he says frustratedly, throwing a hand up in the air.

"Well, I'm… *sorry*. I guess I figured that was just sort of our thing," I say hesitantly. His sudden seriousness catches me off guard, especially after his playful antics from earlier, and I quickly try to find the right thing to say to him.

"You say something to get a rise out of me—I come up with some smartass reply—you know… it's this witty back-and-forth thing we've always had. That's just …*us*, right?" I say, still unable to read his expression clearly with only the tiny lantern illuminating the inside of the tent.

"I mean, yeah, that *is* our thing. Only, *you're* the one who decided all on your own that my compliments were insincere, which by the way are *not*, they never have been. I've meant every nice thing I've ever said to you, Sam," Jess says, and the harshness in his voice softens a bit at that.

The use of my first name instead of my nickname sort of throws me for a loop. While Jess occasionally calls me Sam, it's usually only when he's trying extra hard to annoy me or when he's upset with me.

*Damn, he must actually be serious then…*

"Look, I'm sorry, Jess. I don't mean to be an asshole to you, I guess I'm just not used to real compliments, is all," I say and let out a breath I didn't realize I was holding. I watch as Jess shakes his head at me in annoyance and lets out a *tsk* sound.

"Can I please just have your extra sleeping bag so I can pass out already? I promise to be more sociable tomorrow. I really just need some rest," I say apologetically. I hug my arms around my knees as I bring them in toward my chest, and glance around the inside of the tent. When I don't spot any other bedding, a flicker of panic—mixed with hopeful anticipation—washes over me.

"Sounds like a great idea, but I didn't bring an extra," Jess says as he looks at me, his playful tone from earlier returning, along with a mischievous glint in his eyes.

"That's funny, it sounded like you just said that you *didn't* have an extra sleeping bag. I probably just heard that wrong," I say, raising my eyebrows in question as I look at him. "*Right?*"

"This"—Jess gestures to the sleeping bag underneath us and shakes his head—"is the only one I brought. Remember when I asked you last week if you needed to borrow any gear and you said that Sophie was bringing your sleeping bag, so you didn't need—how was it you put it— my stinky boy camping gear that's probably full of cooties?" Jess says and sits up, brows still raised as he folds his arms, and the tightness in my chest from earlier subsides a little at the return of our usual banter.

"Okay, well, in retrospect, I don't recall ever having a conversation with you about borrowing one of *your* sleeping bags, but I do remember asking Sophie to bring *mine* up with her. So, maybe you just overheard our conversation incorrectly," I say, and let out a small laugh while rubbing my chin quizzically.

"Ya know, that may very well be a possibility," Jess says with a casual shrug. "But, might I remind you, though, who's been the one kind enough to do you the *extreme* favors of giving you a ride, helping you with dinner, providing you with shelter for the night, and now you're practically forcing me to share my bedding and precious body heat with you as well?" He gives me a crooked smile as he tilts his head in question, his anger from before seemingly gone now. "Is that all, or did I happen to miss something?"

"No, that's quite all right"—I raise my hands to stop him from continuing—"I think I've heard enough," I say, and I watch him try to hold back a laugh as he smiles.

"But just know that any funny business will not be tolerated, understand?" I say and Jess points to himself before looking around innocently.

I nod and give him a *yes, you*, look.

"I've been practicing my self-defense lately, so unless you want an elbow to the face..." I pause to elbow crush an imaginary skull, before hyping up the invisible audience that's cheering me on. "I suggest that you keep your hands to yourself, got it?" I challenge him with a smile.

"Watching WWE doesn't equal self-defense," Jess says as he scoffs at me and uncrosses his arms, leaning back against his palms on the sleeping bag.

"Well, that's not what you used to say when we'd spend hours watching it in Grandpa Millard's basement, now is it?" I retort.

"That's because that's the only channel we could get on that dinosaur of a TV he had," Jess says, and we both laugh at the memory.

"Okay... well let's see you get out of *this one*—" I say as I leap at him from where I'm sitting on the other end of the sleeping bag. I try to get behind him, but Jess uses my own momentum against me before I can. He grabs me and swings me around, and before I know it, I'm on my back and he's sitting on top of me, straddling my waist as he pins one of my hands above my head.

Jess leans down, smirking, his dark eyes half-lidded. "I'm sorry, was that how that move was supposed to go?" he asks, panting gently against my face from our tussle.

*What a chump.*

I reach my other hand up and hook a finger under Jess's gold chain that's now dangling above my face. I lower my lashes, inviting him closer as I give him my best seduction eyes. Warm breaths linger in between us as I continue slowly pulling him toward me.

Pinned beneath his weight, I can't sit up very far, so Jess leans down until our faces almost touch, our eyes still locked onto one another. Just before our noses collide, I feel Jess unintentionally loosen his grip on my wrist ever so slightly as he shifts his weight forward. He lets me go just enough so that I'm able to slide my hand out of his grasp.

I seize my moment, using my hips to throw him off balance. Quickly, I twist us around and flip him on his back. I swing a leg over his waist, and suddenly, I'm straddling him instead, breathless and triumphant as I stare down at him.

My hands fall to either side of Jess's head as I lean over him, my wavy hair a curtain around our faces. Neither of us is laughing anymore, and we're locked in an intense staring contest again, both out of breath from the effort of trying to overpower one another.

I watch as Jess's eyes dilate and realize that the usual playfulness there has been replaced with a raw heat that I've never seen before. The air around us feels thick as it hums with an electricity that makes my skin prickle.

Jess slowly starts to slide his hands up the sides of my legs before they lightly grip onto my waist, and the muscles of my inner thighs clench involuntarily at his touch. I almost want to laugh at the fact that he's unknowingly feeding into my fantasy of wanting to feel the rough grip of his strong hands on my body.

He looks up at me through his dark lashes and makes small strokes over my skin with both thumbs, my stomach now partially exposed from our struggle.

His dazzling green eyes catch the light of the small lantern next to us, and suddenly I feel exposed by the weight of his stare on me.

Our breathing slows, almost synchronizing with each other, and it takes every bit of self-control in me not to grind my hips down into him. Jess pushes himself up onto his forearms, putting our faces in a dangerously close range of one another.

His gaze drops to my lips, lingering there before meeting my eyes again. He's giving me *that* look again as he reaches up to tuck a stray piece of wavy hair behind one of my ears.

I notice his jaw tense before he leans in, our noses practically touching at this point. "Ryan, I…"

Jess doesn't finish his thought as his breathing picks up, and he's near enough now that I can smell the minty scent of his toothpaste on his breath. I watch as Jess bites his bottom lip and inhales sharply before looking down at my mouth, his eyes aflame with a wild longing.

"I… I think…" I struggle to speak, and any words I try to form end up getting caught in my throat. My head is foggy, making it feel like I might pass out from lack of oxygen, and I'm almost positive that I've forgotten how to breathe. It's almost as if Jess has taken all of the oxygen from my lungs and from inside the tent—maybe even from the entire world.

He's so close now I can feel the flutter of his soft eyelashes on my right cheek as he tilts his head and leans forward again.

"I-I think we should go to sleep," I say in a rush as I scramble to get off him, seconds away from doing something I know I only would've half regretted.

Whatever Jess was about to say, I cut him off before he could say it. The way he leaned in toward me didn't seem like a rejection, but I don't think I'd be able to handle it if it turned out to be one. Jess is always such a tease, but I feel like he took the joke way too far this time.

After I jump off him, I scoot as far away as I can and pretend to look for something in my bag. I'm unable to make eye contact with him at the moment and feel like my nerves are shot to hell.

"You're right, it is pretty late," Jess says quietly, and I don't look over to see the expression he's making, even though I have a pretty good idea of what it looks like from the sound of his voice.

I hear the faint *zipppp* of the sleeping bag's zipper and see Jess climb in from out of the corner of my eye. I watch as he moves all the way to one side and turns his back toward me.

Jess ends up using his rolled-up hoodie as a pillow since he only brought one and insisted I use it. Without turning to face me, I watch as he rolls it up and lies his head down onto it with a huff. It looks uncomfortable as hell, but he doesn't budge when I ask him to trade with me.

The sleeping bag is a two-person sleeping bag, but it could easily fit three people given how large it is. I climb in, grateful for the warmth on my cold body, even though I'm much warmer now than I was earlier. The sleeping bag has a soft thermal lining on the inside and feels all warm and cozy from Jess lying on top of it earlier.

I pull the zipper up the side after I climb in and reach over to shut off the lantern in the corner of the tent. I tug the edge of the bag up to my face and snuggle in before a familiar scent hits me. It's the same smell that was in the jacket he let me use last week, and the same smell as the inside of his Jeep.

The scent is him, it's—Jess.

I try not to squirm from my nervousness, but I can't seem to hold still. I'm afraid to turn around, not only because that means I'll have to face him after what just happened, but because I know that his scent will envelop me completely if I do. Being this close to Jess and feeling his body heat has me hardly able to keep it together, and now I have to worry about accidentally sniffing him like some creeper. *Great.*

"I'm sorry if I took that too far," Jess says with his body still turned away from me, and part of me wishes I could see his face. He sounds sincere, but it's hard to tell if he's still just messing with me or not.

"No, *I'm* sorry. I shouldn't have jumped on you like that, I don't know what I was thinking," I say quietly and wrap my arms around myself, suddenly feeling self-conscious.

We both lie there in silence for a minute, neither saying a word. The slight rustle of the trees and the crickets the only background noise between us.

"Hey, Jess?" I ask nervously, and it comes out scarcely more than a whisper.

"Yeah?" he says.

"I wanted to thank you…"

"For what?"

"For letting me crash your tent and for helping me save dinner… and for saving me from falling on my ass when I tripped off that damn tree stump, and for the other night, too." I ramble on and can feel my cheeks burning as my eyes start to water. I sniffle and cover my face with my hands, not wanting Jess to see me cry, even if it's too dark in here for him to actually see my face.

"Hey hey hey." I feel Jess's hands as they gently pull mine away from my face. He props himself up on his elbow, and even though the lantern is off, I can feel the intensity of his stare through the darkness.

"Don't worry about it, okay?" he says softly.

"God, I'm so embarrassed," I say, muffling my words as I try to put my hands back over my face. "I acted like a real jerk to you today and I'm so sorry. I haven't seen you in forever and that's the last thing I wanted to do to you, honest." I cover my face with my hands again as I try to turn away from him, and my body starts shaking as I begin to full-on cry. "I blamed it on sleep deprivation or whatever stupid bullshit, but I think I'm actually just a *bitch*."

Jess laughs gently as he pulls me toward his body and slowly turns me to face him. "You are not a bitch," he says, hugging me tightly to his chest. "Maybe a bit of a crybaby, but not a bitch," he says, no doubt trying to make me feel better by joking around.

"But I am!" I say, ignoring his joke as I continue to cry, having thoroughly lost it at this point, and my body is racked with small sobs.

"Stop saying that, you are *not* a bitch," Jess says as he strokes the back of my head, and I can hear the smile in his voice.

The way he holds me makes me feel like he's not actually laughing *at* me, just at my ridiculousness, which I am fully aware of but can't seem to stop. I'm supposed to be grown up, but I feel like a toddler who's way overdue for a nap and the thought only makes me cry harder.

I don't know why I don't pull away from Jess, maybe because I'm too exhausted to, or maybe because deep down I know I don't really want to. *I mean, when will I ever have this chance again?*

We've never been physically close like this before, at least not since we were kids and used to wrestle over who got to have the last slice of pizza or control over the TV remote.

Part of me feels guilty. I feel guilty for wanting this, for wanting *him*. I know he doesn't see me in that way, so pretending that this is real only makes me feel worse.

Just for tonight, I want him to hold me like I'm his Madison. Like there's nowhere he'd rather be than calming my crazy ass down in the middle of the wilderness with the threat of bears and mountain lions looming all around us.

My crying subsides after I'm finally able to let it all out, and my breathing eventually starts to even out as well. I begin to relax into the warmth of Jess's body, and my mind drifts off. I let it wander to the alternate universe where I'm his and he's mine, one where he loves me back—one where I'm not afraid to tell him how I really feel.

I'm sure Jess also starts to feel me relaxing, but he doesn't let me go. "Are you—is this ...okay?" he asks, seemingly unsure of how I'll react, no doubt wondering which version of me he'll get.

Even if I wanted to, I'm too tired to fight, so instead I say, "Just for tonight..." *Please, just for tonight... let me really be your Sam...*

I try, but only manage to get half of the words out before my body and mind start to feel unbearably heavy.

As if Jess can read my thoughts, I feel him pull me closer to his body, his strong arms still wrapped tightly around me. I press my hands up to his chest, clutching his shirt in my fists, before I feel the blissful wave of sleep finally pulling me under.

# Chapter Nine

## Jess

I let out a long breath. Jesus Christ, what a fucking day.

I started off pretty optimistic about how this trip would go, but now I'm not sure. Don't get me wrong, I love Soph, I do, and I feel like an ass even thinking it, but I'm sort of glad she bailed last minute.

It's been almost a year since I've seen Sam, and even longer before that, so I won't say that the idea of spending time alone with her doesn't have me excited.

*Too* excited almost.

Thinking about her in *that* way doesn't take long to get me going. Though the circumstances of how we met up a few days ago were definitely not ideal, all I've been able to think about is how good she looked in that red dress and those black heels. She's so damn gorgeous I feel like there's not a supermodel out there that she doesn't put to shame. I didn't imagine she could look any more perfect than she already does, but I guess I stand corrected on that front.

That red dress has been enough to trigger filthy shower thoughts about her these past few days. The soft fabric hugged her curves in all the right places, and I'd be lying if I said I didn't wish I could explore every one of those sweet curves with my fingertips.

I'll admit to feeling a little bit guilty thinking about her in that way, but I can't seem to stop doing it, either. I figured that by *taking care* of things this morning before I picked her up, I'd be able to suppress any urges I might've had while on this trip. That all went out the window the second I saw her in her purple sweats and bed head when I rolled up to John's house this morning.

After seeing Sam like that, I wanted to say fuck the camping trip before I carried her back into the house, slowly ripping said sweats off her beautifully long legs. I stare at the condensation on the canvas of the tent wall and let out a long breath as I try not to think about everything I wanted to do to her in that moment.

Growing up, Sam always hated her height, saying she was like some gangly giraffe or something. Personally, I think her legs are one of her best assets and can't even count how many times I've imagined her crushing my skull between her precious thighs. I swear to god, the way she tightened her legs around me earlier when she was straddling my waist was almost enough to make me blow a load right there.

I take another deep breath and groan silently, forcing myself to drop the image of her sitting on top of me before I lose my mind to the world of "what ifs."

I reach between us and brush a few messy strands away from Sam's face as I stare down at her through the dark. She mostly seemed like her regular bratty self today, but after what happened earlier on the drive, I'm not too sure where things went wrong. Okay, so sure, I might've called her out on her dream, but I don't think that was really the issue. Sam was acting weird way before that even happened.

Although we've spent a few years apart since we all split up for college and work, things couldn't have changed *that* much between us, could they?

*Maybe I really was just part of a childhood phase for her…*

I continue to watch Sam through the darkness, and even though my eyes have adjusted I still can't make out her features as well as I'd like to. She looks so peaceful and I'm glad that she's finally resting. I reach up and gently pull the sleeping bag up around us, wanting to make sure the cold air inside the tent doesn't wake her.

I sigh to myself at the thought that she might just consider me a "childhood" friend. The possibility makes my heart ache, and I hope I'm dead wrong about that.

Sophie was constantly having to run me off after we got older because she said I was being too clingy. Even so, it still seemed like we managed to stay pretty close, all things considered. After we had all graduated and gone our separate ways, Sam wasn't obligated to talk to me anymore, so I guess that explains why she never called.

I was surprised by what she said about Sophie and their almost trampoline sleepover, though. I was under the impression they didn't talk as much anymore, but I guess that I just must be the odd man out now. Then again, I only just got back into town a few weeks ago. I mean, I still talk to Sophie on a regular basis since she's basically my sister, and then there's the fact that I'm living with her at the moment. But as far as things with Sam go… I remind myself that *she* invited *me* here and wonder why she's suddenly acting so strange.

I really hope it's not the case, but I wonder if my invitation might've just been out of obligation. Sophie was supposed to be here, so I can see how Sam would've felt bad if I'd found out they took the trip without me. But even still, we aren't kids anymore, so we aren't required

157

to hang out or be nice to each other if we don't want to, which is kind of a bummer if that's actually how Sam feels toward me now.

I stare up at the roof of the tent, the bright moonlight glowing through the canvas. I watch as the small beads of condensation that formed just above the window slowly trail down the tent wall as they drip.

I turn back to face Sam when I think I hear her rousing, but her chest rises and falls gently as the soft sound of her almost snoring escapes her pouty lips. I reach up and gently trace the outline of her mouth with my thumb before I instinctively pull her in closer to me. Even though she's asleep—and as embarrassing as it is to admit—her simple presence makes me all giddy inside.

I've never wanted to make Sam uncomfortable, so I've never pushed my feelings onto her, especially after hearing from Sophie time and time again that Sam didn't see me in a romantic way whatsoever. I didn't want to ruin all the years we had spent together, let alone potentially ruining any future plans—if Sam even wants me in that future, that is. The possibility of that sends another sharp pain through my chest. I couldn't imagine my life without the three of us, let alone never seeing Sam again, or worse, having to watch her with someone else.

I know I have no right to be upset about it, but picturing her in another man's bed still infuriates me. That's part of the reason I left right after high school. I knew she was going to find someone to make her happy, and I didn't want to be forced to watch from the sidelines.

I am glad, though, that I didn't have to witness the last jerk Sam dated, because according to Sophie, he was a real tool. I likely would've beat his ass if I were around, so it's probably better that I never met the guy.

Thinking about our high school days makes me smile to myself. It really wasn't all that long ago, but somehow still feels like a lifetime ago. A lot has changed since then, but strangely, some things haven't changed at all. Sophie is still Sophie; bratty, bossy, and possessing enough attitude to rule a small country.

And Sam? Sam is still perfectly Sam. Still the brightest light in any room, and somehow even more devastatingly beautiful every time I see her. I take a deep breath before letting it out slowly, still intently watching Sam sleep peacefully beside me.

I'm trying to stay grounded in the present, but I can't help my mind from drifting back to my past moments with the girls. Since there's no shortage of daddy issues between Sam, Sophie, and me, I've always felt a responsibility to protect those two troublemakers—even though they didn't ask me to.

I smile to myself again, thinking about how many times they were the ones getting *me* out of trouble instead of the other way around. I think about how many nights Sam helped me sneak out of the house whenever Judy would ground me, and how we'd sit on John's roof and look at the sky together. Even if Sophie wasn't there, it's always been us three, always together, always looking out for one another—I guess up until the last few years, that is.

The way Sam flinched today when I touched her shoulder in the Jeep was... *weird*. I mean, I was just giving her shit, but maybe she really *was* having a sex dream. Why else would she have reacted so strangely—unless maybe she was having a nightmare instead? I know she sometimes has issues with waking up and being confused, but I've never seen her react the way she did today. I wanted to seriously ask her about it, but she never gave me the chance to.

Sam fidgets in her sleep and I feel her cold feet on my leg and the sudden sensation makes me flinch. I chuckle quietly to myself and shake my head. It seems that even in her sleep she finds ways to torment me.

I'm pretty sure that something has been bothering her lately and I wish she'd open up to me. Even if we aren't together romantically, I want her to always feel like she can come to me with things, just like I know that I can do the same with her.

Since the moment I found out she was back in town, I've been pulling my hair out wanting to run over to John's house to see her, just like I did every summer break when we were growing up. Sam's house was always the first place I wanted to go. I'd always said it was so that I could see Chris—which was an obvious lie. I can count the number of times Chris and I have actually hung out on one hand.

Being away from Sam all that time only solidified the feelings I always kept hidden from her. I thought that moving away and not seeing her anymore would make it easier for me to move on, but if anything, it only made me want her more. I know it's a fucked-up thing to do, but I can't help but compare every person I get into a relationship with to Sam. Lately, I find myself wanting to be alone rather than force unrealistic expectations on someone who could never in a million years measure up to her.

Though just one look at her long legs is enough to get me as hard as a rock, it's not just her body that gets me going. It's the way she smiles at the simplest of things, and the way her nose crinkles as she smiles her real and true smile, especially when she doesn't know anyone is watching. It's the way the sound of her laugh is like music to my ears and makes my heart beat just a little bit faster.

I stare hard at her through the dark, straining my eyes as I will them to make out the small freckles that pepper her cheeks and nose. She's told me before that she doesn't like them, but I wish she only knew how much I'd love to kiss each and every one on her body.

But the thing I love most about Sam, above all else—including the physical—is the way that one look from her beautiful hazel eyes can truly make a person feel seen. I'm sure she really has no idea of the effect she has on people, and at times, I wish I could keep that part of her all to myself, as selfish as that may seem.

I don't know if I didn't always feel that way, or if I was just in denial, but something shifted inside me after what happened that day at the lake when we were seventeen. I never wanted to see Sam hurt like that again, and the thought of losing her was almost enough to break me. Which, in hindsight, makes me realize I was seriously deluding myself by thinking that moving away from her would've made those feelings just disappear.

I told myself that I would never, ever, put Sam in a position to have to choose between a friendship and romantic feelings for me, so I put those sentiments in a box and buried them in the deepest pit I could imagine. Then I left.

If she'd found out my real feelings for her and rejected them, I don't know what I'd have done. Being away from her was torture, and I realized that there was no way I could stand it being a permanent situation, so I promised myself that I'd never tell her.

Sophie, of course, has had her suspicions over the years, including the time she almost caught me with my pants down jerking it to a picture of Sam that I'd stolen from her room. It was a picture of Sam and Sophie on prom night from our senior year, which I'd considered cutting Sophie out of, but ended up just folding the photo in half. It was taken right before Sam's date got drunk and puked all over her sparkly pink dress, or so I was told. I would've pummeled the bastard, but I was out of town for the state baseball championships that weekend.

After the close call with the photo, I made Sophie swear on the grave of her childhood dog, Tootie, that she'd never breathe a word to Sam about her suspicions. She agreed on the condition that I gave the photo back—which I did—after making myself a secret copy, of course.

Since then, I vowed to myself that I'd always be there to protect Sam whenever I could, even when she didn't want it, and wouldn't let anything or anyone, including myself, mess that up. That's why her being in my tent, wrapped up in my arms and clinging to my chest while she sleeps, is causing me a bit of a problem.

I was certain that after what had happened between us earlier tonight, I'd royally fucked up, afraid she'd refuse to sleep in my tent altogether, let alone in the same sleeping bag as me. I'm sure that Sam would've left had she another option and I'm glad she didn't spot the extra sleeping bag I had stashed in the back of my Jeep just in case Sophie flaked out last minute. I kind of feel like an asshole for not telling Sam about it, but I got greedy, knowing I might not have the opportunity to sleep next to her like this ever again.

I know I got a little carried away with the wrestling, but for the record, she was the one who started it. I was just playing along, like I always do, but I should've known that it'd end up making her feel uncomfortable.

I'm glad she acknowledged "our" style of banter earlier, solidifying that it's not just all in my head. We've always been like that, which I'm grateful for since it's always given me a way to disguise my flirtations as jokes.

It was a relief to finally admit to her that my compliments are always honest—whether or not she believes me now is unclear. The same goes for when I flirt with her, though I know she probably wouldn't believe that either. I just wish that Sam knew those comments were always genuine as well. Sure, I tease her a lot, but it's never out of maliciousness. There's so much more I want to tell her, to *show* her.

I let out a quiet yawn and tighten my grip around Sam's waist just a little. I'm tired, but don't want to sleep, not at a time like this. Morning will already be here too soon, and I don't want to miss out on a single second of this time I have with her.

She'd fallen asleep pretty quickly after she calmed down and had stopped crying. I took a chance, unsure of how she'd react to me pulling her into my arms, but after I did, I realized how cold her body was by how she'd responded almost instantly to my warmth. She was shaking pretty badly as well, but it was obvious to me that it wasn't from the cold alone.

She's so close to me right now that her hair lightly tickles my chin, and I can smell her shampoo without even trying to. I inhale deeply as I indulge in the sweet smell of coconuts radiating off her body and hair. I feel her chest as it gently moves up and down as her breathing grows heavier, and I'm having a hard time believing that any of this is real life.

I watch as her lips part, soft and inviting, and all I can think about is how badly I want to taste them. Sam stirs a bit before she snuggles into me and lets out a small *hmmm* noise. Her breathing returns to a peaceful rhythm as she settles in against me, and I let out an exhausted breath.

*This girl is going to kill me.*

Heat continues to seep through Sam's clothing and into my own and a shiver passes through me. I inhale her sweet scent again and pull her closer to me as I tighten my hold on her.

I try to steady my breathing, struggling not to let myself get too excited thinking about how she's literally asleep in my arms right now and how it was actually on purpose. Well, I guess it wasn't necessarily on purpose... I think she was just too tired to push me away before she fell asleep.

Either way, I don't think I've ever held her like this, at least not intentionally. Sure, we've wrestled plenty of times growing up, but this feels different—more intimate. Though I've always wanted this to happen, I just wish Sam were awake and consciously choosing to be this close to me right now. I know beggars can't be choosers, so I'm grateful for the situation, no matter how it manifested itself.

I try not to picture Sam earlier, straddling my lap, her shirt pushed up just above her belly button. It's a good thing she was only on top of me for a second—because if she felt my hard-on beneath her from where she was sitting on my hips, she didn't say.

I think about the way I would've flipped her over and kissed around her exposed skin before peeling off those god-awful pajamas, had she let me. I try to sear the memory into my brain, willing myself to never forget just how warm and soft her skin felt beneath my hands.

I know what I saw in her eyes when my hands gripped her waist. It wasn't quite desire, but it was definitely more than lust. Lust specifically for *me?* Unlikely. Maybe for my muscles, at least. Subtlety is not one of Sam's strengths, especially since she's been making it pretty obvious that she's been ogling my physique every time we've seen each other these past few days. I'll admit that I sort of love the idea of all those hours at the gym finally paying off if I was able to get Sam all hot and bothered with a simple display of my abs.

Regardless of all that, it was probably just a physical reaction to the position our bodies were in. Gaslighting myself into thinking it was just a purely physical thing instead of something more helps my overthinking a little, but somehow still makes me feel like shit. I consider the possibility of a purely physical relationship with Sam for a second and then lowkey want to jump off a bridge. Obviously, I want her in that way, but not just in that way. If she ever suggested it, I would probably jump at the chance, but I know that I would always be left wanting more.

The thought of getting to touch the silky soft skin I know is underneath her hideous pajamas has my fingers buzzing with electricity. For a second I picture her beautiful olive skin and how I'd love to kiss down the length of her spine, all the way down to her feet, and then all the way up again. I shiver at the thought of how I long to dig my fingertips into her thighs as I'd wrap them up over my shoulders...

An uncomfortable tightness in my pants has me scrambling to calm myself down before it's too late. If Sam wakes up to a raging hard-on pressed up against her, I'm sure she'll never let me hear the end of it.

I try thinking about algebra, or ice water, or whatever the hell else you're supposed to think about to get rid of boners, but obscene images of Sam whimpering out my name with my face buried between her legs keep invading my mind.

A few minutes pass, but it's too late, my pants somehow uncomfortably tighter than they were before.

*Fuck, this is bad.*

I know that I need to get away from Sam, because the mere fact that she's physically touching me—let alone pressed up against me—has got me already teetering on the edge. I tell myself it's fine, and that as long as I lie still and try to calm my breathing, it'll eventually go away.

I consider trying to maneuver carefully around her without waking her up but remind myself that this isn't the first time I've had to hide a boner from Sam before.

*Just breathe, Jess, just breathe. You can do this.*

I let out a slow breath and try to think about every unsexy thing I've ever seen in my life—about the cold uncomfortable ground beneath us, the distant chirp of the crickets outside, the rattling of the tent canvas against the slight breeze. I try to think about literally anything besides the breathtakingly gorgeous girl that's in my arms right now.

Every time I try thinking about something else, my mind goes straight back to her, her cute frizzy hair from the braid her hair was in, her ugly polka dotted pajamas, the look in her eyes when I had her hand pinned above her head... the feeling of her warm body pinned underneath mine...

Ultimately, all of my efforts are in vain, and I feel myself losing it again just as Sam begins to stir. I'm hoping it's a good thing, thinking that maybe she's starting to get overheated or something and wants to scoot away from me to cool herself off. That would be great, then I could take care of my ...er... *situation*, or at least try to get myself under control until morning. If not, there's no way I'll ever be able to get any sleep bricked up like this, not that I really want sleep anyway, I guess. I'm sure a few minutes standing out in the freezing air will fix the problem pretty quickly and consider doing that instead.

Sam turns in her sleep without breaking contact with me, so her back is now pressed tightly up against my chest. I try to scoot away from her, this angle even worse for my erection, which is now pressed up against her lower back.

*Shit.* I inhale sharply, panicking now, knowing there's nowhere for me to escape. Because I got into the sleeping bag first, the zipper is on the other side of Sam's body, and I know there's no way she wouldn't wake up if I tried to get around her to unzip it.

Sam continues to shift, and I'm praying she doesn't wake up while I'm like this. Angry would be an understatement, she'd most likely threaten to cut my dick off and feed it to the wolves, along with the rest of me.

Sam stirs again, and I try turning myself around so that our backs are facing each other, but before I can, she grabs hold of my left arm and wraps it around her waist. She holds my arm tight to her body and wiggles her ass into me, getting herself comfortable again, her breathing still heavy as she sleeps.

*Okay Jess, don't panic, don't panic. DO. NOT. PANIC.*

I fight against myself internally because I most definitely *am* panicking. My heart is racing unbelievably fast, and I feel like I can't breathe. Somehow, my dick gets even harder, making my hard-on almost painful at this point.

I continue to feel the uncomfortable tightness in my pants as my bulge strains against the fabric of my pajamas. I tell myself that Sam's obviously so out of it she doesn't know what she's doing, because there's no way in hell she'd ever do anything like this if she weren't. My mind starts racing again, my pulse rises as it hammers in my ears, and I think if my boner doesn't wake her up, the sound of my heart thundering in my chest just might.

Sam's murmuring something in her sleep, which might've even made me laugh if I weren't so fucking tense right now. I had forgotten she was a sleep talker, and it makes me smile to myself despite the precarious situation I'm currently in.

Sam moves in her sleep again, and this time when she speaks, her speech is a little less slurred, but the words are hardly audible.

*"Jess, please."*

I freeze, and my smile instantly fades. Did I hear what I think I did just now? Please? Please *what?* Now I know this has to be a fucking dream.

She's saying it again and again, each time more breathless than the last, and before I can process what's happening, I feel her hips as they start to move against me.

Wait, is she... *grinding* on me?

A sharp jolt of sensation zaps through me, confirming that she *is* indeed grinding on me. Sam moves back against me again, and I inhale sharply as I hold back a moan at the sensation.

*HOLY FUCK THIS CAN'T BE HAPPENING.*

How many times did I jerk off to this exact scenario, never thinking it would ever actually happen? Now I know there's no way she's awake. Sam would never in a million years say something like "Jess, please" and actually want sex from it, from *me*. This has to be some kind of sick joke, something that she and Sophie cooked up to try and actually kill me with.

*This cannot be real.* Wasn't she the one who said no funny business earlier?

I groan and move my hands to stop her waist from its grinding motions, the sensitivity driving me mad from the wicked hot friction she's creating between our bodies. "*Ugh, Sam… stop…*" I grit out, breathless, in a sort of half-whimper half-groan.

If Sam is *actually* asleep, she'll murder me if she finds out that I let her do this while she was incoherent.

"*Ryan*, no, wait what are you—" I feel her grab my left hand from its place across her waist as she slowly pulls it around the front of her body, dragging it lower and lower until it's positioned right between her legs.

It's quite possible that in this moment I die, leaving my body temporarily as I cross over into the afterlife. I have a cool glass of water on the other side, pet a dog, ponder on the meaning of life, and then enter back into my body, simultaneously, all while having a stroke.

"*Sam, please,*" I say, and it comes out as a desperate plea as I struggle to form coherent thoughts. "You have to stop… you don't know what you're… *doing…*" With every movement of her hips, I find it growing increasingly difficult to hold myself back, and my words come out in a breathless groan.

As bad as I want this with Sam, I refuse to take advantage of the situation and decide it's best to try and get out of the sleeping bag, even if it ends up waking her. She might not believe me if I tell her she's the one who started this, but I can live with that. What I *cannot* live with, is her thinking that I took advantage of her without her consent while she was sleeping.

I'm starting to feel dizzy and feel like my vision is hazy, but I can't actually tell because of the darkness of the tent. I tug at my wrist that's still hovering right between Sam's thighs, and as I go to move, I hear her speak, her words causing me to freeze up again.

"I do," she says. Her words are still breathless, but I hear them clear as day.

"I want this, Jess. I want *you*."

# Chapter Ten

After crying like a loser in Jess's arms, the exhaustion from the day finally pulled me into a blissful sleep.

When I open my eyes again, I see that pink cotton candy lines the sky around me, and my body feels weightless as I lounge on the fluffy clouds.

I don't think I've ever been more relaxed, and it makes me think that I quite like it here. I look around at all the other weightless clouds in the sky and think that this wouldn't be a terrible place to spend forever.

I stretch my arms and legs out long in a snow angel formation, but I quickly sit up when I realize that something's not quite right. I look from cloud to cloud, and as far as I can see, I realize that I'm the only one up here, and an uneasiness slowly starts to creep in. Everything around me starts to feel strange, almost as if things are moving in slow motion, but somehow in fast forward at the same time. The peacefulness I feel starts to disappear, along with most of the clouds, and I realize that I really am all alone.

The few remaining clouds quickly darken, lightning and thunder crashing down through them onto a rocky shoreline below. I can feel the electricity radiating through the air and watch from my cloud above as the storm floods down onto the dark waters below.

The water beneath crashes onto the rocks in a steady rhythm, and the feeling connects with my senses, rippling through my body. I can sense each wave as it washes up roughly over the cliffs below, causing my body to tighten at the sensation. I feel a warm heat starting to take hold deep within my body, working its way up through the length of my spine as my stomach starts to tighten.

I close my eyes from the intensity and yearn for the waves to continue their strong friction against the jagged rocks below, wishing the storm would keep raging on. But something is wrong. Something feels hollow—*vacant*, almost. I look down at my body and see that there's a throbbing hole in my chest, right where that *something* is supposed to be.

I grasp at the gaping hole in my chest and pull at my suddenly wet clothes, and the more I pull at them, the more difficult they are to remove. Panic starts to take over as I try to remember what it is that's missing, knowing that it's something important.

I look around and try to call out for help, but I can't speak. The harder I try to cry out, the less sound comes out of my chest, and my throat feels raw from the soundless screams trying to escape my body.

I shut my eyes and try to cry out one more time, sound finally exiting my lungs as it comes out in a high-pitched shriek. The sound pierces my eardrums, and I flinch as I cover my ears with my hands.

When I open my eyes again, both the sea and clouds are gone. The sky is now a brilliant blue, and I can feel the sun's warmth as it shines down brightly on my skin.

I grasp at my clothes, no longer soaking wet, and search my chest for the void that was there only moments ago. I'm beyond confused, but don't question it, glad to be rid of the discomforting sensation. I look down at my body and realize that the hole is now gone, leaving no trace, as if it were never there in the first place.

I run my hands across the sheer silk dress that now shrouds my body and wonder where it came from. The material is a soft cream-colored fabric, and I notice a slight iridescent shimmer as I run my hands across it.

When I look around, the dark clouds and waves from earlier are nowhere to be seen. Instead of rocky cliffs laden with lightning and thunder, what stands before me now is an incredibly lush forest.

I find myself standing in a clearing, surrounded by flowers and trees, each one's foliage more beautiful than the last. I wiggle my toes into the soft grass beneath my bare feet, the blades so smooth they feel like they're made of the softest strands of silk. The bright colors of the flowers and the lush greenery of the forest are almost blinding in their vibrancy.

I see that before me stands a large weeping willow tree, towering high off the ground, long branches hanging around its trunk in a beautiful green cascade. The branches slowly sway in the breeze, and I hear the tree calling to me, asking me to touch its soft leaves.

I run my hand over the soft leaves before me and realize they're just as silky as the grass beneath me. I pluck a single leaf, hold it to my nose, and get a vague sense of déjà vu as I inhale the soft fragrance.

I greedily inhale again and let the smell consume me. My body starts to react as my eyes roll back into my head, and I feel a tightness returning in the pit of my stomach. The scent grows stronger, causing me to gravitate toward the willow tree, my body craving more of the delicious aroma.

But the closer I get to the tree, the weaker it grows.

I catch a single whiff on the gentle breeze and turn around to face it, confused.

Standing in the small clearing directly across from me is a man. He stands watching me, silent and unmoving as the breeze slowly brushes past him. He's a handsome man—in fact, he's the most handsome man I've ever seen. His beautiful dark brown hair cascades in waves just past his shoulders, unruly pieces framing his angular face.

I notice that he's wearing clothing similar to mine, white linen pants and a shirt, which starkly contrast with his beautifully sun-kissed skin. His shirt is partially untied, leaving his muscular chest exposed, the strings of his shirt swaying gently against him each time the breeze passes by.

I tilt my head to one side as I look at him, and he continues to watch me, still unmoving and silent. I notice something familiar about the man, and I'm sure that we've met before, but I'm not certain where.

I don't take my eyes off him as I raise the willow leaf to my nose and inhale once again, seeking the same satisfaction as before, only this time, I get nothing. Confused, I look at the willow tree before turning back toward where the scent came from earlier—back toward the man.

He notices my confusion, and I watch as he slowly approaches me from his side of the clearing but stops just before we're close enough to touch. I try to step back, unsure of his intentions, but I can't move, my feet held to their place on the forest's floor by an invisible force.

He watches me still, no words leaving his mouth to explain who he is or what he's doing here, and he gives me a curious expression, like he can't quite place me either. Logic tells me I should want to leave, that I should be scared, wary of the stranger in front of me, but I'm not. If anything, I want him to come closer.

The dizzying scent hits me again, and it's almost overwhelming this time.

I close the gap between us, willing my feet to move, willing myself to recognize the handsome stranger standing across from me when I realize the origin of the warm aroma.

He watches me without a word as I slowly reach up and run my fingers through his long, wavy hair, wanting to see if it's as soft as it looks. I let my impulses get the better of me, but he doesn't stop me, he just closes his eyes and takes a deep breath, his face relaxing with his exhale. It's just as I'd suspected, his hair is as soft and smooth as the velvety grass we're standing on.

When the man opens his eyes again, I raise both hands to either side of his neck, feeling the warmth of his skin under my hands. I drag both hands over his shoulders and down the front of him as I rest my palms on the front of his chest. His skin feels unbelievably warm from the rays of sunlight that bathe us through the gaps in the trees, and I feel it sharply through my palms, as if he's intentionally sharing his warmth with me.

He holds my gaze as I stare back into his eyes before moving my hands to the string holding his shirt closed. I slowly unlace the material and pull it down around his shoulders until it falls to the ground behind him.

I let my hands wander over the man's body, feeling up and down his shoulders and back as I circle him. I gently run my fingertips across his skin, searching for an answer to the familiarity I feel for him, thinking I might find it in the contours of his solid frame.

He stands completely still as he lets me continue, never interrupting me. He only blinks at me with curiosity when I stop in front of him again.

I stare into his eyes, asking his permission as my fingers reach for the button on the front of his pants. We lock eyes as I undo the button, and his pants drop to the ground in a soft heap around his ankles before he steps out of them.

He takes his turn as he circles me slowly, eyeing my body through the sheer fabric of my dress. I'm almost completely exposed, and even though the thin material doesn't hide much, I don't feel the need to cover up.

My body is starting to react to his presence, and I want him to see it. I don't want him to just look at me; I want him to *see* me—*all* of me.

My breathing hitches as he reaches for the buttons on the front of my dress and gently undoes them. The anticipation is almost too much as the thin fabric finally falls to my feet. The man steps toward me, and I can feel his hot breath on my face as he reaches up and cradles my right cheek in his hand.

I lean into his touch and step toward him, closing the gap between us as I place my hand on his opposite cheek, holding his face as well. His emerald eyes pierce into mine, their brightness almost putting the forest to shame with how breathtaking they are.

We hold each other's faces as we breathe together, the passing time a blur, and I wonder how long we've stayed like that. Is it minutes? Hours? It feels like time doesn't exist. It could've been forever, and I'd never have wanted to leave him.

The man leans in close, his soft eyelashes brushing my cheek, and in the softest whisper, he finally speaks, his words fading as the breeze carries them away.

*"I'm right here…"*

The second I hear his voice, everything comes flooding back in. *Jess*.

The sound of his voice pulls me out of my dream, and everything from earlier comes rushing back—picturing Jess in the shower, straddling him on the floor of the tent, and the man from the clearing in my dream.

My body feels hot, and I'm suddenly very aware of the throbbing sensation down in between my legs. I'm vaguely aware that Jess is saying

175

something to me, but I'm having trouble focusing on his words, still half asleep and reeling from my dream.

"...*Please*, you have to stop... you don't know what you're... *doing*..." Jess says, and his words come out breathlessly, almost like he's in pain.

Only when I hear his words do I realize what's happening. I'm so horny that it seems even in my sleep, I have no control over my physical actions.

I can feel Jess's hand between my legs, and the panic in his voice makes me wonder if he wasn't the one who put it there to begin with. I feel him trying to pull his arm free but can't because I've got a death grip on his wrist.

Before I realize what I'm asking Jess for—or more like—before I'm able to talk myself out of it, I say, "I do. I want this Jess, I want *you*."

Lust mixed with the delirium of sleep takes over me and I pause my movements momentarily, waiting for his response.

My body is in desperate need of a release, and from what I can feel pressed up against my ass, I'd wager that Jess needs one as well. Clearly, missing a night with my Rose is affecting me more than I'd anticipated.

"*Please*, Jess, I want to come," I say as I practically beg him when he says nothing. I start to grind back into him again, still half asleep. I know it won't take me much longer to get there, I can tell that I'm already close.

*So... close...*

I struggle to get my words out as my breathing starts to pick up. "I... need..."

"You don't know what you're asking me for... you—you're— *shit* that feels so good," Jess says under his breath, and he's practically moaning in my ear now.

He's no longer trying to pull his wrist away from where it's wedged in between my thighs, but he's not moving it either, and I can tell that he's trying hard to restrain himself.

I take Jess's moans as a good sign, hoping he's just as into this as I am. If he didn't want this, he'd stop me, plain and simple.

*Wouldn't he?*

Shame hits me like a brick, temporarily knocking me out of my lust-controlled trance. The poor guy was probably sound asleep until my horny ass woke him up, and here I am practically assaulting him in his own tent.

I immediately stop moving and release his wrist. Jess hesitates for a second but eventually pulls it away. I feel his body move as he tries to scoot away from me, but since we're both still zipped up in the sleeping bag, he's not able to get very far. I move away from him, pulling myself over to the other side, giving him as much space as the sleeping bag will allow.

My cheeks are burning, and I can't bear the thought of turning to look at him. I don't even know what to say, maybe something stupid like, *Oh, sorry, I was just accidentally having a sex dream—and about you no less. I wasn't able to finish, and now I'm asking for your help to get me off, because, evidently, I'm such a goddamned horn dog that I can't go a single day without an orgasm.*

*Facepalm* *You idiot.*

Fear grips my chest, and I'm praying that I didn't just ruin our entire friendship in the span of only a few minutes.

"I... uh... I'm sorry, I don't know what I was thinking—I mean, of course I obviously wasn't *thinking*, I was supposed to be sleeping," I say and feel like my cheeks are on fire.

"Of course you wouldn't want *that* from me. I'm sure the only reason you're ...*excited*... right now is because you woke up to someone grinding on you. Which I'm not mad about obviously—since it was completely my fault—I guess it's only to be expected, right? It's just biology, right?" I ramble, the words rushing out of me so fast I can hardly catch my breath. I feel like such an idiot, wishing I were anywhere but here right now.

*Why the hell can't I stop talking already?*

Jess says nothing from beside me as I continue with my word vomit. "I-If you want me to leave, I'll go sleep in the Jeep for the rest of the night. I'm sure it's almost morning by now, so it's not a big deal, it's really not even that cold outside. I'll just—"

"No," Jess says, interrupting my ramblings. "Don't leave."

His words come out so quietly that I can't decide if he sounds angry or not. I'm sure I heard him wrong, if he *were* mad, wouldn't he *want* me to go?

What he probably said was, "*No*, you can't sleep in my Jeep, and *yes* please leave." I move to unzip the sleeping bag, tears burning behind my eyes, wishing I could just disappear.

*Fuck, he hates me.*

I tell myself to hold back my tears, just at least until I can get out of the tent.

"I said no," Jess says firmly, and I feel his arm snake around my waist as he pulls me back into the sleeping bag with him.

*Huh? What the hell?* Okay, so *this* is the part where he psycho murders me and leaves my body in the woods for the bears to fight over...

My back is pressed tightly against Jess's chest, his arm still wrapped around my waist, keeping me from going anywhere. He's so close I can feel his jagged breathing against my back, and his warm breath tickles my neck.

"You're wrong," he whispers as he pulls me in closer to him. "I do want you like that. It's *all* I want." He practically moans the words into my ear, his breath hot against my already burning skin.

I don't even have the chance to form a response when I feel Jess's hand move from its place around my waist to the waistband of my pajama pants. I feel his fingers slide gently along the edge of the elastic band, dipping below the fabric just slightly, teasing me.

"Ryan, do you still want… *need* to come?" he asks, his voice husky with desire as he continues to tease the skin of my stomach with his fingers. I'd only ever dreamed of hearing Jess's bedroom voice, so it's enough to send shivers through my entire body.

I begin nodding before I can stop myself, but then wonder if I'm making a mistake. "Jess… I… but aren't you mad at me…?" I ask as I try to turn to face him, my embarrassment momentarily taken over after getting caught up in the moment again.

"I'm sure you'll find a way to make it up to me," he murmurs, and I hear a wicked smile in his voice as his fingers now trace slow circles around my lower abdomen, making my head spin.

"Just let me take care of you, Ryan. Please," he says, the desperation in his voice getting me closer to my edge already. "Please let me," he almost begs through his gravelly voice.

I'm starting to get dizzy, and if I don't come soon, I'm going to pass out either from delirium or from using up all of the oxygen in this tent. *Fuck the tent, I feel like I've used up all the oxygen on the whole damn planet.*

I try to focus on my breathing, but I can hardly think straight anymore. I only manage to let out one breathy syllable. My head is fuzzy, and my body is hot, making it hard to concentrate, so it's a wonder that I'm even able to say anything at all.

"*Jess.*"

The second his name leaves my lips, I feel Jess stiffen behind me, his dick still rock hard as it's pressed up against my ass. I reach a hand back between us to feel him, but he grabs my wrist, stopping me before I can. If he won't let me touch him, then fine, but it's only fair that he gets off too. I'm a lot of things, but selfish isn't one of them.

I start grinding back against him again, only this time he doesn't protest but instead takes my action as the permission he needs to continue the assault between my legs with his hand.

Jess cups me over my pajamas, and I grind into his palm, craving more friction, and the feeling is almost unbearable now.

*Enough teasing.*

I grab his hand and shove it down the top of my underwear. Jess finally takes the lead, my guidance no longer needed, and I spread my legs slightly to make room for him.

He runs his fingers up and down through the folds of my pussy, the slick sounds of my wetness echoing off the walls of the tent.

"Why are you already so wet, baby? Who were you dreaming about?" Jess says darkly, and I hear a smirk in his voice. "Anyone I'd know?" he asks, and he's breathing so hard into my ear that it sounds like he might combust at any second.

His words mixed with the feeling of his body pressed up against mine sends me, and my back arches as my climax approaches.

*How pathetic, he's barely even touched me, and I'm already about to go over.*

I feel incredible and wish this could last forever, not wanting to come just yet, even though that's what I'd basically begged him for.

"No, not yet, baby, not yet. Hold it. I'm not done touching you like this," Jess says as he groans into my ear.

"Wait for me, do you think you can wait?" Jess purrs, his fingers slowing as they make torturously long swirls around my clit. I nod, unable to form any words, still shamelessly grinding back against him.

I feel Jess's other hand as he reaches up and around my body, cupping a breast underneath my shirt. He kneads my soft skin in his hand, and I let out a small gasp when he pinches my nipple.

My skin starts to throb from the pressure of his fingertips as they continue to squeeze, the sensation causing a welcome ache. I rock my hips into him and let out another breathy moan as I picture his teeth there, pulling on the sensitive skin of my nipples, twisting and biting until he almost draws blood…

"*Fuck*, baby, make that noise again," Jess says, and he gently bites my earlobe, causing my back to arch. I feel his dick start to twitch, and I know he's seconds away from his own release as well.

"Come, baby…" Jess moans into my ear. "Let's come…"

I'm mindlessly grinding back against him when his fingers switch from swirling around my clit to teasing my entrance, almost driving me insane. His fingers pick up their pace, and I feel my body starting to go over as I grind myself down into the palm of his hand.

"Jess—I …*oh god*… JESS!" I cry out, and Jess groans into the crook of my neck as release crashes through both of us. My back arches hard against Jess's body, and I throw my head back against his shoulder involuntarily. I try to cover my mouth with my hand to muffle the sound but end up clinging to his arms instead as the shockwaves of my orgasm ripple through me.

We're left trembling in the aftermath, both sweaty and panting hard as we cling to each other. All I can think about is how good it felt to have his hand down in between my thighs, even if he *was* just teasing me the entire time—which, let's face it, is pretty on brand for him. Jess's fingers made my trusty silicon boyfriend seem like garbage in comparison. I can only imagine what else those hands can do…

We're both spent, panting hard, neither saying anything, likely because we're both physically unable to. We stay like that for a while before Jess goes to remove his hand from between my legs, and I stop him.

"No, wait, let's just… stay…" I say and close my eyes, still trying to catch my breath.

I feel a hum of approval against my ear as Jess pulls his hand out from underneath my shirt. He wraps it over my shoulder and across my chest before hugging me tightly to his body. He pulls me firmly against his chest, and I continue to cling to him, afraid that if I let go, he'll disappear, just like in my dream.

After a while, we both come down from our highs, and I can feel sleep pulling me under once again. As I start to drift off, thoughts of the green forest from before cross my mind, and I wonder if I'll ever be able to go back there again. I think about the version of Jess that exists there and how I'd like to see him again, though I'm already certain that nothing could ever hold a candle to the version of him that I just experienced.

# Chapter Eleven

When I wake up, I'm sweaty and a little out of sorts.

*Where the hell am I? Am I... in a tent?*

I pull the covers off myself, desperate for some air to cool me off. *That's right, we're camping.* I remember where I am and try to shake some of the grogginess from my brain.

Whenever I sleep in a new place, my head is always kind of muddled when I wake up. You'd think I'd be used to it by now, but it still affects me sometimes. That's why I never liked traveling much. By the time I get familiar with a location, I leave and have to start readjusting all over again. Which, as you can imagine, has caused many a sleepless night, thus inconveniencing everyone involved. Enter Cranky Sam.

I sit up and rub the sleep out of my eyes as I look around, my body feeling uncomfortably hot. The sun glares through the canvas of the tent, and I feel like an ant under a magnifying glass.

I look around for my phone, wondering what time it is. I check the clock and wonder how it's already hot as balls in here when it's only a quarter past nine.

*So much for the nice weather my dad predicted.*

I roll my eyes. Man thinks he's a meteorologist, but I should know better by now that the mountain nights are freezing cold while daytime temps are usually blazing, go figure.

My throat feels hoarse, and I search around the tent for my water bottle, desperate to quench my thirst from the rising temperature inside the hot tent. I feel like I just woke up from one of those couch naps that feel amazing until you wake up in a puddle of your own sweat and don't know what year it is.

Aside from my damp PJs and sore throat, I actually feel pretty good, like, *really* good. Considering I slept on the hard ground and in an unfamiliar environment at that, I feel pretty rested.

*Man, I really did conk out yesterday, didn't I?* I look around, yawning, and give up on looking for my water bottle. *I wonder where Jess...*

*Fuck me.*

Images from last night flash through my mind, along with the feeling of Jess's hands all over my body, along with his hot breath on my neck.

My cheeks warm at the thought of the filthy words he whispered into my ear.

*"Come, baby..."*

Okay, that couldn't have actually been real. *Right?* I've been known to have a pretty active imagination, not to mention the ...*vivid*... dreams I sometimes have when I'm pent up. Yesterday's dream I had on the drive is a prime example of that. *Only, why does last night feel like it was different than usual?* I look around the tent.

One sleeping bag.

*That's right, we* did *share a sleeping bag, right after I… was sitting on top of him…* Okay, so that much actually did happen, but, as for the rest…

I try to backtrack the rest of the night and struggle to piece everything together through a rising headache I feel coming on.

The heat of the tent is starting to get to me, so when I move to unzip one of the windows, desperate for some fresh air, I'm suddenly very aware of the slickness between my thighs.

I hear Jess's voice in my head again, and my body instantly remembers the feeling of his warm hands on me. My skin prickles with the memory of how his fingers felt as he ran them up and down the warm wetness in between my legs.

I swallow hard.

*So maybe last night was real. Okay, Sam, just chill out, there's no need to overreact.*

I feel my heart rate starting to pick up, and I try to talk myself down. From what I can remember, last night we both got off. *It's what we both needed, right?*

I try convincing myself that there should be no weirdness since it was just two platonic friends helping each other out. Granted, I'm pretty sure that I was the one who provoked the situation, but to be fair, Jess also seemed pretty into it in the moment.

*And, it's not like I confessed my love or anything…* I try to recall if I might've accidentally said something along those lines, but I come up short.

I can hear muffled voices not too far from the tent and wonder if the guys are going over their plans for the day. Their inaudible chatter is followed by an occasional high-pitched racket that I'm sure is none other than Rebecca, who's likely wondering when we're leaving.

I roll my eyes just as my stomach lets out a grumble. I can't say I'm avoiding Jess, but the heat of the tent makes me realize that I can't stay in here forever, even with the windows open.

I catch a whiff of what smells like bacon through the mesh windows of the tent and hope they're getting breakfast started without me. It's probably just wishful thinking on my part, but a girl can dream, right?

I try to hype myself up, but can't bring myself to leave the tent just yet. I tell myself that everything between Jess and me is fine, and that there's no need to overthink things.

*There's no reason we can't be adults about this, right?*

I'll just go out there and ask him about it. I'll walk up to him and say, *Hey, awesome job making me come last night. That was really, really, great, by the way. Also, we're good, right? Okay, cool, see you next weekend for Aunt Judy's birthday dinner.*

As if.

I have no problem with a good one-night stand or a no-strings-attached type of arrangement, I mean, hell, just take a look at my last relationship. I feel like it's none of my business, so I never ask about it, but by Sophie's account, Jess is always with a new girl whenever she talks to him. So, maybe he's all right with casual.

*As if I could do casual with Jess of all people. That's a laugh.*

He might be okay with those types of relationships, but it wouldn't be possible for us, especially where I already have some pretty hardcore feelings for him. Then it hits me.

Madison.

Jess has a *girlfriend*, and I basically forced myself on him last night. Now, not only did I potentially ruin our friendship, but Jess also cheated on his partner because of me.

I'm left weighing the terrible options I have to choose from—either walk all the way home or hitchhike—and wish I'd driven my own car for a quick escape.

When the tent door suddenly unzips, it makes me jump a little. Jess pokes his head inside and he gives me a look as if he's surprised to see me awake.

"Good, you're up. Breakfast in ten if you're interested," he says with a smile, acting like his usual charming self.

*Maybe I did just imagine last night.*

I try reading his energy for any strange vibes but come up empty-handed.

"Okay, yeah, just let me change real quick," I say, looking down at my pajamas and then back up to Jess, when he gives me a slow once-over.

"Don't take too long, Ry," he says. He winks before leaving and zips up the tent behind him, already exuding typical flirty Jess behavior this early in the morning.

I fling myself back against the sleeping bag in a dramatic huff and cover my face with my hands. I let out a low groan mixed with a humorless chuckle.

*Dammit, Sam. What have you done.*

I change into a heather gray cropped tank top and black leggings before climbing out of the tent. As I pull my shoes on, I realize that my nose didn't deceive me earlier when the delicious smell of bacon wafts my way. I can see the Camp Chef already set up near the prep table with Jess standing behind it as he stirs something in one of the large dutch ovens.

I take one sniff of whatever is sizzling in the pans and my stomach starts to growl. Whatever Jess is cooking smells delicious, and it's already making my mouth water in anticipation.

I notice that someone's started a fire, and I walk over to warm my cold hands. Although it was a million degrees inside the tent, the morning air outside is still pretty brisk, especially in the shade of the canopies.

Too lazy to walk back to the tent for my hoodie, I stand by the fire and roast myself rotisserie chicken style, slowly warming my body as I turn. From my place by the fire, I sneak the occasional glance at Jess, still trying to sense any weird vibes coming off him, but still get nothing.

Jess is acting his usual cheery self, smiling and chatting with the others while he cooks breakfast. He's somehow still looking fine as ever, while I'm sure that *my* appearance is less than glamorous at the moment. He traded in his navy shirt for a white one, this one still just as tight as the other, layered with a long-sleeved dark green flannel. His hair is pulled back in a tiny man bun just like yesterday, and a few extra stray pieces are tucked behind his ears.

Jess catches me staring and gives me a wink. I look away, a little embarrassed that I was caught, and turn back to face the fire, holding my hands out even though they're not cold anymore.

*Stupid sexy jerk in his stupid sexy tight t-shir*—

"If you're cold, you can borrow this," Jess says from behind me, placing something on my shoulders. I look down and see that it's the flannel shirt he was just wearing. I turn and blink up at him, a little stunned by his sudden appearance.

"No, I uh… I can go get my jacket," I say, and he walks away before I can hand the flannel back to him.

"Just wear it," Jess says as he calls back to me. "Also, if you don't hurry and come get some food, it'll get cold," he says, still not turning around as he calls back in my direction.

He's right, but I'm not so much worried about my food getting cold as I am about the menfolk eating it all before I even have a chance at any. I am grateful though that I didn't have to make breakfast this morning, so I guess I'll take what I can get, even if it ends up being the scraps. I'm not too concerned about Rebecca either since I heard her yesterday yapping about having an intolerance to any pork byproducts. Insert hard eyeroll. I guess that just means more bacon for the rest of us.

I let out a defeated breath and pull my arms through the sleeves of the flannel. I try not to think about how the warmth inside of it was generated from being in direct contact with Jess's body. I take a steadying breath and try to shake the feeling of said warm body wrapped around me last night.

The sleeves are way too long for me, and it fits more like a dress than a shirt—even with my height—but it's warm and it smells nice, so I don't mind that much. I hug myself and give the collar a quick sniff before looking around to make sure no one saw.

I walk over to the small table next to the food and try to grab a paper plate off the pile just as Rebecca goes to grab one as well.

"Are you feeling better today?" I ask her, more to diffuse our awkward interaction rather than from any actual concern.

"Much," she says. "Your dad *really* knows how to take care of me," she says and winks at my dad, who's preoccupied with drowning his eggs in hot sauce.

*What the fuck?*

Jess drops the spatula in his hand and Chris chokes on his orange juice.

"You okay, son?" my dad asks, obviously not hearing what Rebecca had just said, and pats Chris on the back as he continues to cough. Chris, Jess, and I all exchange uncomfortable looks before I pick up the spatula Jess dropped and hand it back to him.

"Well, that's… *nice…*" I say to Rebecca, regretting my question, my appetite now starting to fade at the thought of Betty the Bus being christened last night.

I turn away from the food when Jess shoves a paper plate into my hand. I look up at him, wondering if he's asking me to hold it for him, but then I realize that he must've made it up for me instead. It's piled high with hash browns, bacon, two over-easy eggs, and a small stack of pancakes. There's so much food on the plate that I have to hold it with both hands to keep it from bending in half.

*He doesn't expect me to eat all of this, does he?*

I look up at Jess, and he gives me a look that just says, *Oh yes I do,* as if he can read my mind.

I stare at him with curiosity and wonder if it's just a coincidence or if he actually remembered how I like my eggs for breakfast.

"Thank you for cooking, Jess, it looks great," I say, and he nods at me with a smile before bowing. I roll my eyes at him, and he flashes me a crooked smile in return. I feel my cheeks start to flush and quickly look away.

I notice most of the food in the pans is almost gone, and I reach for an empty plate. "Aren't you gonna eat?" I ask Jess, trying to split my food with him. "Here, have some of mine. You gave me way too much," I say before he stops me.

"No, it's okay, don't worry about it. I already ate what I wanted to earlier," he says. "Just promise that you'll eat some of the real food before drowning your pancakes in sugar," he says, smiling as he chuckles at me.

"We'll see." I playfully stick my nose in the air before making my way to an empty chair next to Chris in front of the fire.

"So, John, is it the regular spot today, or are you finally gonna trust us with your top-secret fishing location after all these years?" Jess asks my dad as he takes a seat next to him across from Chris and me.

Since Jess was mainly raised by his aunt, my dad always took him under his wing whenever it came to manly things like camping and fishing, especially since Grandpa Millard was never interested in being outdoorsy. My dad always treated Jess just like a second son, which I know meant a lot to him, even though he's never said as much. Chris didn't really act like it affected him either way, and I'm sure he wouldn't have minded trading me for Jess in a heartbeat.

The fishing part of our Bass Lake trip has always been a tradition for the guys since it's the reason we started taking these trips to begin with. Jess once told me that he doesn't necessarily like the fishing itself, claiming it's a little boring, but that he mainly enjoys spending time with the guys out on the water.

Though they've never explicitly barred me from joining, I always felt like I'd be intruding if I asked to go with. I figured I'd be a nuisance as the only female on the boat since there's no way in hell that Sophie would ever touch live bait with a ten-foot pole. That, and I didn't want to leave her all alone at the campground.

So, instead of asking to go with, every year I'd always beg Jess to tell me what they did besides just fish, but he never would. That is, until he lost a bet to me and had the choice of either eating an entire jar of mayonnaise or letting me in on the tea.

From what it sounds like, they mostly just sit around and talk, have probably a few too many beers—or root beer back then—and the occasional cigar. After that, I never considered asking to tag along again. I don't mind a cold beer, but that's a hard pass on the cigars for me.

I'm glad Jess got back into town not long ago, so he didn't have to miss the trip. I know he always looks forward to it, which makes me feel like an idiot for ever thinking he'd want to skip it, especially since we've missed the last few years.

The guys usually go fishing for an entire day, which would typically be fine, except that this year, I'll have Rebecca to keep me company instead of Sophie.

*Fantastic, I can't wait to see how she'll verbally attack me today.*

"Sorry, boys. Maybe next year," my dad smiles at Jess from his chair as he shovels a forkful of hash browns into his mouth.

My dad has always been pretty secretive about his special fishing spots, so it's no surprise that he still won't say anything. He quickly changes the subject before Jess can press him on it further.

"So, Sam, it looks like Sophie and Tanner didn't make it up last night, then. Is everything all right?" my dad asks in between mouthfuls of his hash browns.

I set my plate down on the small side table that's attached to my chair. "Yeah, she had some intern stuff she had to deal with, so she won't be able to make it this year," I say as I stand and make my way over to the stack of cups on the prep table.

"Well, that's too bad. It's a good thing Bec's here to keep you company while we're out today, then," he says, rubbing Rebecca's shoulder as he smiles at her.

I grab a plastic cup and pour myself some orange juice before putting the bottle back into one of the coolers. I don't reply to my dad's comment and hope that someone changes the subject again since I'm not in the mood to disguise my stink face with friendly Sam at the moment. I notice that Rebecca's been uncharacteristically quiet and wonder what she's scheming.

"So, if Soph didn't make it up last night, I'm guessing that means you let Sam crash your tent then?" my dad asks Jess as he looks over at him.

"I brought my large tent by mistake, so there was plenty of space," Jess says and shrugs casually before taking a sip from his water bottle.

*Liar. That tent barely fit both of us in it.*

Good on Jess for having the best poker face of all time, but the fact that he's not acting the least bit suspicious has me wondering if last night was just a meaningless hookup to him. I mean, he's acting completely normal like nothing happened, but then again, so am I…

My dad raises his eyebrows disapprovingly as he looks over at me from across the dying fire. "I thought I taught you to plan better. It looks like you owe Jess big time for letting you borrow his extra gear, Sam."

There's no way that my dad would ever suspect anything between Jess and me, even if what Rebecca said the other day about him being able to pick up on my "crush" is true. I'm hardly Jess's type, so I'm sure that my dad just assumes it's a one-sided thing.

I swallow hard and try to keep a straight face as I mumble a small apology to my dad, not wanting my expressions to give me away. I take my seat back in the chair next to Chris before taking another drink of my juice, wishing it were coffee instead, and kick myself for forgetting the most important thing on my list.

"It's a good thing Jess planned ahead. I hope you two were able to stay warm enough last night," my dad says, and this time it's me who chokes on the orange juice.

I start coughing and Chris reaches over, repeatedly smacking me on the back just a tad too roughly. "Okay, *enough, enough,*" I say, still trying to catch my breath as I try waving him off, his smacks doing more harm than good at this point. "It's fine—*cough! cough!*—I'm fine!"

"You all right?" my dad asks, and I see Rebecca roll her eyes as if I'm just being dramatic.

"Sorry, yeah—*the pulp*—" I say, gesturing to my plastic cup, still trying to rein in my hacking as everyone stares at me.

"It was no bother. I think we stayed plenty warm," Jess tells my dad, who's oblivious as to how it was that we were able to keep warm last night.

My eyes meet Jess's, and he winks at me before taking another drink from his water bottle. And, since I'm still unintentionally making a scene with my cough attack, no one notices the small exchange between us.

I try to ignore Jess and get up to search for the maple syrup, having gotten tired of trying to eat the "real" food Jess piled high on my plate. I look at what's left of the food and think that Jess really outdid himself today, especially if he cooked this all on his own.

I think he may have overdone it with the meats, though, having cooked bacon, corned beef hash, and not one but two different types of sausage, and it makes me smile to myself. I guess he knows my dad and Chris pretty well, given that they'll usually have a fit if there's not half a pig served with their wilderness breakfast every year.

I smear a massive chunk of butter onto my pancakes and struggle to clear my throat, still trying to get the last of the orange juice—or more like *acid*—from my burning lungs.

"If you're looking for the syrup, I just finished what was left of the bottle. Sorry," Chris says through a mouthful of food, now standing next to me as he makes himself a second plate with what's left in the dutch ovens.

I search through one of the smaller totes I'd packed, mumbling to myself as I continue rummaging through it. "I know I put two bottles in here…"

"Bec helped me organize most of the dry storage totes into the RV before we left the house. Wasn't that nice of her?" my dad says as he beams at Rebecca.

"We figured it'd make things much easier to find if they were put away neatly instead of tossed into a plastic bin," Rebecca says as she sneers sweetly at me.

*Clearly.*

"Yep, that was *super* nice of her," I say, trying not to make a face as I hide my irritation and head toward Betty to find the syrup.

I don't care if Rebecca says she was trying to help, I know her well enough now to know that she probably did it just to aggravate me. She probably put all the important things in the trailer on purpose, knowing that I wouldn't want to set foot in there.

*Bitch.*

I hear the chatter behind me starting up again as I open the door and climb the steps into my dad's RV. I pause and look around.

*Wow, this thing really is gaudy.*

Who the fuck needs two flat screens and a leather couch for camping? I wouldn't be surprised if the thing even has satellite TV, too. I roll my eyes and start sifting through the cupboards looking for the maple syrup.

I'm able to find literally everything else I'd packed with the dry storage—including shit you would never even need for camping—and try not to think about why there's a drawer in the kitchen with a silk scarf, a blindfold, and a large roll of duct tape in it. I quickly shut that drawer and resolve to wash my hands after I leave.

I'm crouched under the sink, irritated, as I search still for the syrup. I wonder if Rebecca hid it somewhere crazy on purpose, like with the cleaners or bathroom supplies. I'm afraid to search anywhere besides the kitchen, so I sigh and stand, prepared to admit defeat and eat dry pancakes.

"Any luck?" a voice says in my ear, making me jump. I whip around, my nose almost colliding with Jess's face, putting us only inches apart.

"What the hell are you doing in here? Stop sneaking up on me like that, you scared the hell out of me," I say, and smack his arm as I put my other hand to my chest as I try to catch my breath.

"Sorry, you were taking a while, so I thought you might want some help looking," Jess says innocently as he bats his flirty eyes at me.

He's standing so close that our chests are almost touching, and I'm finding it hard to catch my breath properly.

"No, uh—it's okay, I don't need any help," I say as I stare up at him, willing myself not to let his shiny eyes hypnotize me.

"So, you found the syrup, then?" he asks, raising a brow.

"Uh-huh," I say and nod, trying not to seem too flustered.

*Why is he standing so close? Like, damn, boy, give me some space.*

Without stepping back, Jess slowly glances down at my empty hands as they hang at my sides. He smirks as he braces his hands against the countertop on either side of me and leans down. His breathing is slow and even as he stares at me, and I try not to panic as he continues to lean in closer, slowly closing the gap in between our faces.

I close my eyes and rise up on my tiptoes to meet him halfway, the world now moving in slow motion. My pulse thunders beneath my skin, and I feel his chest brush against mine just as he whispers in my ear. "You mean *this* syrup?"

My eyes snap open, and I feel Jess's body pull away from mine as he puts a foot of space in between us. I look down, and he's holding a glass bottle of maple syrup in his hand. I take it from him and notice the corner of his mouth twitching upward. I sense my cheeks flaming as I look up at him, feeling like I just got played.

"You didn't look very hard, Ry, it was on the counter behind you," he says, winking at me before he turns around and heads down the RV's metal steps. "Better hurry, Ryan. Didn't I tell you your food would get cold?" Jess calls behind him with a chuckle.

*Okay, that bottle was sooo not there five minutes ago.*

Embarrassment continues to stain my cheeks as I think about how it's possible that I was looking so hard for the syrup that I completely missed it. I feel sort of guilty blaming Rebecca for hiding it from me, but she shouldn't have messed with my organizational tote system in the first place.

I let go of the breath I was holding and slowly slide my back down the wooden cabinets before landing on my butt. I sit on the floor of the RV, clutching the small glass bottle of syrup to my chest as I try to pull myself together.

*What the hell was that? I don't even want the damn pancakes anymore.*

I shake my head, positive that Jess was just trying to get a reaction out of me. He usually doesn't take it that far, and it makes me wonder if it's payback for my attitude yesterday. I feel my cheeks flush even more as I think about last night.

*No... I don't think that's it.* Even though he got a little angry at me at one point, we sure didn't end the night on that note...

"What are you doing in here?" Rebecca asks after clearing her throat aggressively, and I look up. "Can you leave? I need to get ready," Rebecca says, looking down her nose at me with her hands on her hips.

"Yeah, sorry," I mumble as I pull myself up off the floor and head down the camper's steps, my shoes clunking against the metal as I walk.

Jess was right, and my food's long since gone cold. I douse my pancakes in syrup but only manage to take a few bites. I don't feel great and think I should just lie down for a bit.

Not wanting to be antisocial *just* yet, I sit in one of the camp chairs near the smoldering remnants of the morning's fire. I sit and watch the men as they gather their fishing supplies for the day before loading everything up into Chris's Razor.

Seeing Chris gather up his small beer cooler reminds me that I made a bunch of sandwiches for the guys yesterday when I was prepping

197

the food. I don't know how I could've forgotten because I was pretty damn proud of those sandwiches. They looked delectable enough to put even the meanest Jersey Mike's sub to shame.

I hop up out of my chair and search through one of the coolers before I find the large brown paper sack I'd put them in. I grab the bag out of the cooler that I'd filled with ice packs instead of ice to keep the subs from getting soggy and head over to where my dad is standing next to the Razor.

As I approach him, I laugh to myself and watch as he slathers an unholy amount of sunscreen all over his nose and face. Say what you will about him, but the man doesn't play when it comes to sun protection.

"Hey, Dad," I say, and he looks up at me after squirting another stream of sunscreen onto his palm. "I forgot to tell you earlier, but I made you guys sandwiches to take out on the boat. I figured you might want something besides beef jerky and Pringles," I say. I smile at him and hold out the large paper bag containing the sandwiches for him to take. "I made them just how you like with extra—"

"Thanks, but Bec already made us our lunch for the day," he says apologetically, now lathering sunscreen all over the tops of his ears and neck.

"Oh, okay… sorry, I didn't know," I say, and immediately feel stupid.

*Wait, why am I the one apologizing?*

The guys usually take a butt load of chips and jerky, among other snacks with them, but this year I felt like doing something different. He's not obligated to eat my dumb sandwiches, so why do I care so much?

I still have my hand half outstretched, holding the sack of sandwiches awkwardly, unsure of what to do with them at this point.

"Make any with ham?" Chris asks from behind me as he snatches the paper bag out of my hand.

"*Umm*, yeah, there should be a few ham in there," I say, knowing full well that ham is my dad's favorite, so I made extra.

"Good, ham makes for decent fish bait," Chris says, stuffing the bag into the back of the Razor next to their other snacks. I watch as he roughly loads his beer cooler into the back as well, flattening the sandwiches underneath it in the process.

*Well okay then. That's the last time I ever do something like* that *again for the guys.*

I look around for Jess and consider telling him about the sandwiches but decide to just forget about it. I hear the door of his Jeep slam shut and watch as he makes his way over to us, tackle box and fishing pole all ready to go. Jess looks at me for a second and pauses, no doubt seeing the tears in my eyes that are threatening to spill over.

"Hey, Ryan—" he says as he tries to step toward me, but not before my dad cuts him off, clapping him on the back of his shoulder enthusiastically.

"All right, boys, let's go get 'em," my dad says before climbing into the passenger seat of the Razor.

*You okay?* Jess mouths the words to me as he puts his things into the back seat. He looks at me with genuine concern, which makes me feel guilty for overreacting over something as silly as some dumb sandwiches.

I nod at him and shrug. "Have fun today, boys," I say, and force a smile before turning around, not wanting them to see me cry.

"Be safe out there," I call over my shoulder, and don't look back as I continue walking toward the chairs by the fire pit.

I hear a door shut, followed by the roar of the Razor's engine and the bass of the stereo before Chris speeds past me, leaving a trail of dust behind them as they leave our camp.

The small boat dock is only a few miles away, so it shouldn't take them long to get there. My dad used to drag his old beater of a fishing boat along every year but got an upgrade earlier this year and even had the shop deliver it to the lake for him. I think about all the times Chris and Jess helped him patch up the holes in that old tin can and laugh to myself. I'm glad that my dad got something better, now at least I don't have to worry about them sinking in the middle of the lake.

I sit in my camp chair long after they've gone, and the trail of dust settles. I sit there for a few more minutes, unsure of what to do with myself.

Usually, Sophie would be here with me, so when the men would leave, we'd either nap for most of the day or sit in our tent and flip through trashy magazines while eating our weight in marshmallows. I sigh, wishing she were here but at the same time glad that she isn't. *If she were here, last night with Jess never would've happened...*

I'm not really in the mood to do anything, but I figure I'd better find something to distract myself with to keep from thinking about Jess. I wish I'd gotten a chance to talk to him before he left, because now I'm going to be stuck overanalyzing all of our interactions for the rest of the day.

*Great.*

I've never really been up on the mountain alone by myself before, so the silence definitely feels strange. I guess Rebecca's here, but she doesn't count, obviously, and I hope that she just ends up staying inside my dad's RV for the rest of the day. With my dad not around, who knows how she's going to act, or how *I'll* act, for that matter. I won't purposely pick a fight with her, but I'm sure as shit not going to let her push me around either. And, forget about it if she starts talking about Jess again, because I am not afraid to throw hands with a bitch.

The chilly mountain air from earlier is gone now, along with most of the dying embers in the fire pit. I decide to pour a small bucket of water onto what's left of the smoldering wood, just to be safe, and watch as a small plume of steam rises up from the ashes.

I set the small water bucket down and turn toward the entrance of our campsite when I hear the sound of a car approaching. I hear the car before I see it, and wonder if Sophie might've changed her mind and made the drive up anyway.

The second I see the car, I realize it's not Sophie and shake my head in disbelief.

*You have got to be kidding me.*

A silver Honda with an Uber sign in the window pulls up next to me just as I hear Betty's door open and then slam shut.

I turn back to Rebecca. "How did you even get service to call a car way out here?" I ask incredulously as she walks past me.

I know my dad's trailer has Wi-Fi, but considering how fast the car got here, and also how far away we are from civilization, I'd wager that Rebecca scheduled her ride in advance. I realize that if that's the case, she was probably planning on ditching me the entire time then.

"Um, hello? Where are you going?" I call after her, waving my hands around.

Completely ignoring my question, Rebecca turns toward me, and I roll my eyes at her appearance. She's in full glam makeup, hair done perfectly, wearing a tight red skirt and heels.

She grasps the door handle of the Uber and gives me a threatening glare. "Unless you want me blabbing to everyone, *including* Jess, about those silly little feelings you have for him, you'd better keep your fucking mouth shut, all right?" she says with a sneer.

Without another word, I watch Rebecca climb into the Uber, slamming the door shut behind her. The car quickly zips away, leaving me to eat another trail of dust for the second time today.

*That was weird.* And, I'm wondering where in the hell she could possibly be going.

It'd be impossible for her to try to make it back home, so I'm guessing that she has to be going somewhere nearby. Come to think of it, there is a ski resort up the road a ways, but they're usually closed at this time of year, and I wonder if the spa at the lodge is still open. Something like that definitely seems more her speed than camping.

I can't help but think if we hadn't gotten off on the wrong foot—and if she didn't have some personal vendetta against me—that we might've been able to get along. I think saying we could've been friends is a stretch, but with everything that's on my mind right now, I wouldn't say no to a spa day at some fancy wilderness lodge.

*Whatever, good riddance.*

Rebecca will probably out herself all on her own, and I won't even have to say a word. If the guys get back before she does, she'll be busted, and it'll be her own fault. As for her threats about Jess, I don't put too much stock into them. Her suspicions about my feelings for him are literally the only dirt she has on me right now, which I doubt she'd be willing to let go of just yet. I don't really want to waste my energy fighting her, so I'll let her think she's won this round.

For now.

# Chapter Twelve

Though there's not much left to do, I start on what remains of breakfast cleanup. I decide that Jess must've taken care of it earlier while I was still preoccupied with finding the maple syrup for the stupid pancakes that I didn't even eat. I try not to think about our interaction in my dad's trailer and let out a breath as I put away the pan I'm holding.

After I finish drying the rest of the dishes, I decide to tidy up a little to keep myself busy. I refill one of the large drink coolers with cans and some water bottles. The guys have already decimated half the soda and beer we'd brought with us, so it's a good thing I decided to get extra this time.

I consider walking around the lake but decide against it because I still get a little nervous around large bodies of water. I really don't mind the water anymore, it's just that I'd rather not go alone, even though I'm a pretty strong swimmer.

I've only been awake for a few hours, but I'm starting to feel sleepy, and at this point, I wonder if it's just because I'm bored. I let out a long yawn as I stretch my hands above my head, thinking that maybe I'll rest my eyes for a bit since there's nothing else for me to do.

Apart from the other day at my dad's house, I can't remember the last time I actually had the time to take a decent nap. Lately, I've been so busy with school and work that I haven't really had room for much else. I don't count Daniel since he was starting to limit our booty calls to weekends only.

I lazily make my way over to Jess's tent and take my shoes off, leaving them just outside. When I unzip the canvas and step inside, a nice cool cross breeze flows between the windows, making it feel less like an oven than it did this morning. It's late enough in the day that the sun has shifted, so the tree that the tent is under provides some nice shade as well.

I spread myself out on the sleeping bag, my arms outstretched by my sides as I run my fingers across the soft material. I close my eyes, trying to force myself to sleep, but all I can think about is how the entire contents of the tent smell like Jess.

*This sleeping bag… This pillow…*

I sit up and cross my legs in front of me before clutching the pillow to my chest. The faint aroma smells of wood and sage mixed with something sweet that I can't quite put my finger on, like vanilla or some type of flower. I raise the pillow to my face and inhale lightly.

*Wow, so I've officially crossed over into obsessive weirdo behavior.*

I'm feeling like a creep as I continue to sniff the pillow, but I don't let that stop me from doing it anyway.

I put the pillow behind my head and let my body fall backward onto the sleeping bag with a huff. I sigh and roll over onto my side, clutching at Jess's flannel shirt that's wrapped around me.

I let out another heavy yawn, and now that I'm lying down again, I realize just how tired I really am. Even though I'm sleepy, my over-analytical brain is still in high gear. I can't help but think about Jess, and how I wish we would've had a chance to talk. It's not that I'm worried about him getting the wrong idea, I'm more concerned about *me* getting the wrong idea.

I wonder if maybe he doesn't think there's anything to even talk about, and that's why he didn't bring up last night.

Even though I try not to, my brain can't help but make a list of why things couldn't work out between us. I'm already aware that it probably won't make me feel any better, but at least doing so helps me sort things out in my mind.

*Fact #1: Jess has a girlfriend—see Madison, the Alaskan supermodel. Though not actually confirmed just yet, it's incredibly likely.*

*Fact #2: Jess has never acted toward me in a serious romantic way before. Ever. And last night doesn't count since I'm the one who came on to* him, *and it was purely physical.*

*Fact #3: I am in no way, shape, or form his type. Height, body shape, hair, eyes, you name it. All are complete opposites of every girl he's ever dated.*

*Fact #4: HE PROBABLY HAS A GIRLFRIEND.*

I rub my hands over my eyes and groan in frustration. *What the hell is wrong with me?* I shouldn't be thinking about this, what I *should* be thinking about is how to apologize to Jess for what happened.

In the moment he seemed into it, but that still doesn't change the fact that I crossed a line that I probably shouldn't have. Half asleep or not, I still can't help but feel like I took advantage of the situation last night.

Part of me kind of wishes that Sophie were here so I could ask her what to do. I already know she'd tell me to enjoy the casual sex thing and not to worry so much. She'd tell me to keep him around until I got bored and then move on to some other poor sucker.

*That's easy for you to say…*

I sigh and wonder if Sophie's ever actually had an emotional attachment to anyone she's slept with. I'm sure her advice would be different if she knew the target this time was Jess. Honestly, she'd probably be furious if she knew the truth.

I try steering my thoughts away from my lame boy problems and wonder how Sophie's internship is going. I'll admit that I was pretty upset at her yesterday, but I'm not really anymore. I know she's worked hard for this, and I don't want to make anything more difficult for her by seeming unsupportive. Especially since it's kind of a miracle that she even managed to find a lawyer's office that offers intern positions in our small town, let alone one with an opening.

*Maybe I should call her and let her know that I'm not mad.*

Where it's daylight out, I won't have to worry about getting lost walking around looking for reception. Though I'm sure there are a few people in our party who wouldn't mind if I wandered off and got eaten by a bear.

I halfheartedly feel around for my phone before remembering that I left it in one of the cupholders of my camp chair. I try to sit up, but I've gotten so cozy I didn't even realize that I'd closed my eyes. I snuggle up to the sleeping bag and inhale the faint aroma of Jess's cologne through the flannel.

*I'll call Soph in a minute, I just need to rest my eyes for a little bit first…*

The sound of tires on dirt stops me just before I'm about to drift off, and I sit up, wondering if Rebecca's back already. For making such a nasty threat earlier, she returned a lot sooner than I'd anticipated. I only get up mainly out of curiosity to see if she's brought anything back with her. I doubt she found anywhere to shop up here, but I guess you never know with those shopaholic types.

I unzip the tent and peek my head out slowly before looking around, wanting to make sure it's safe before exiting. All I need is a black eye because I *startled* her or something.

"Well, this is unexpected," I say, not anticipating Jess to be standing just a few yards away from the tent. He doesn't answer and stands with his back facing me as he watches the dust trail left behind by Chris's Razor, and I catch a glimpse of my dad's hair in the driver's seat.

"You forget something?" I ask and smirk even though Jess can't see my face, the sarcasm heavy in my voice. "Who would've thought that you'd—" I stop myself just as he turns around to face me.

Blood trickles down a cut above Jess's left eyebrow along with a small tear on the outer left corner of his mouth. The neckline of his shirt looks stretched out, and his hair is slightly out of place as well. Honestly, he's a mess, and I don't think I've ever seen him this disheveled in my life.

I jump out of the tent and rush over to him. "What the hell happened to you? Are you all right?" I ask frantically and have to stop myself from grabbing his face with my hands and grab onto his shoulders instead.

"Is that *concern* I hear?" Jess says through his cracked lip, and I can tell it hurts by the way he winces as he speaks. "And, for *my* well-being from Her Royal Highness Sam Ryan herself?" he says sarcastically, trying to make a joke.

I put my hands on my hips as I frown and lower my eyebrows. I stare at him, and he lets out a small chuckle at his own joke before I turn around and walk away, not really sure where I'm going, just *away*.

"Aren't you gonna help me? I'm injured," Jess calls after me, and I can hear the smirk in his voice.

"I'm sure you're going to be just fine," I call back without turning around.

"*Dammit!*" I hear Jess say through a pained whimper, and I spin around. He's clutching the side of his face with one hand, the other out-stretched to steady himself like he might fall.

*So he really is hurt, then.*

I rush toward him just as he starts to wobble. He looks like his knees are about to give out, and I run to him, barely managing to catch him by his side before they do.

"Damn, you're a heavy son of a bitch, you know that?" I grunt the words out as Jess leans against me heavily.

I drape his arm across the back of my shoulders as I clutch onto his side, trying to keep him upright. His eyes are half open, brows scrunched together tightly, and I can't tell if it's from pain or a possible concussion since I don't exactly know what happened.

"Do you think you can make it to one of the chairs over there?" I ask and nod to the camp chairs positioned around the fire pit just a few yards away from us.

Jess nods, any hint of humor in his face gone, now replaced with a pale grimace of pain instead. I go to move him and we both sway, almost losing our balance. My knees threaten to buckle under the weight of trying to hold us both up.

"You've gotta help me out here or we're both going down," I say, slightly out of breath, my strength waning from trying to keep us both standing.

*I know he works out, but damn, the hell is this dude made out of? Rocks?*

Jess tries to take a step forward. "I think I can make it," he says, but sounds like he's not really even convinced of that himself.

If we both eat it, I won't be able to get him back up on my own, so I decide that I might end up playing nurse while he's lying on the ground.

*Here goes nothing.*

We start to move forward, and most of Jess's body weight still leans against me. He's a little wobbly at first, but we manage to make it to the chairs, where I try to gently transfer him down into one of the more comfortable ones.

I bend over, my hands on my hips as I breathe hard, trying to catch my breath.

"Damn, what's wrong with you?" Jess asks as he closes his eyes. "You really ought to do more cardio, you know," he says, only the teeniest bit out of breath.

"I'll have you know… that I do… *plenty*… of cardio…" I manage to say in between huffs.

Jess cracks an eye at me. "*Hmm*… is that so?" he says as he closes his eye again, and a small smile crosses his lips.

*Ugh, jerk. I walked right into that one.*

My cheeks start to flame, so I leave Jess sitting in the camp chair and go to find a first-aid kit and some ibuprofen, wanting to cool myself off.

I can't find a single first-aid kit anywhere, and—shocker—Rebecca moved everything I had in my medical supply tote into the RV's bathroom cabinets.

I gather a bunch of supplies out of the cupboard, not wanting to have to come back, and fill a small sandwich bag full of ice from the ice maker. I still feel like Betty was an unnecessary splurge on my dad's part, but I'm grateful for the access to some clean ice that's not been floating around in a cooler.

I grab a small kitchen towel and wrap it around the plastic baggie, not wanting to freeze Jess's face off with the ice, and head back to assume my role of nurse.

I walk back over to him, set my supplies down on an empty chair next to him, and then make my way over to the small dishwashing station before I wash my hands. I can feel Jess's eyes on me the entire time, and I try pretending not to notice.

"Has anyone ever told you that you're very thorough?" I hear him ask and roll my eyes as I dry my hands off with a paper towel.

I ignore him and rip open a disinfecting wipe from inside the first-aid kit. I clear my throat and gesture for him to sit up straight so that I can begin his medical aid. Jess glances at the wipe in my hand and then back to my face before I raise a challenging brow at him. He looks at me with uncertainty like he's afraid I might smack him—which I still might just do—before nodding at me to continue.

"But first, here, take this," I say, handing Jess a water bottle and three ibuprofen tablets from my pocket.

"*Uh…*" Jess hesitates, eyeing the side pocket of my leggings and then the pills resting in my outstretched hand.

"Oh relax, they're from my private stash. Light hallucinations only. Nothing hardcore, I promise," I say sweetly, trying to hand him the pills again.

"Whatever," Jess says as he shakes his head. He takes the pills from my hand before popping them into his mouth and washes them down with the bottled water. After he takes a long drink, he sets the water bottle down in the cupholder of the chair and closes his eyes again.

"Okay, you may proceed," he says as he rests his head back against the chair, his arms outstretched on the armrests.

I scoff. "And you have the audacity to call *me* your majesty?" I say before bending down, and I start to wipe the crusted blood off the side of Jess's face. I try my best to be gentle, but I can tell it's sensitive with the way he flinches every time I pass the wipe over his skin.

"I never called you your Majesty, I referred to you as My Royal Highness," he says matter-of-factly, eyes still closed.

"Her," I say as I gently pass the wipe over Jess's skin again.

"Huh?" he asks, trying to raise one of his brows but stops himself halfway, no doubt due to the pain.

"You called me *Her* Royal Majesty, you never said that I was *your* Royal Majesty," I say, and it comes out quieter than I mean it to.

I furrow my brows and keep wiping gently, wanting to kick myself for ever saying something so cringy, and try to think of a way to change the subject before I die of embarrassment.

*Why am I even saying all of this? It's not like it really matters anyway. It was obviously just a joke.*

Jess gently grabs my wrist. "Do you want me to?" he asks as he stares at me with his deep green eyes, and they sparkle as he looks up at me.

"Want you to what?" I say, pulling my wrist from his hand as I look away, continuing to wipe his cuts with the disinfectant. "I'm taking this out, you've got blood in your hair," I say, and without asking or making eye contact again, I gently pull on the elastic band holding Jess's hair back.

His shoulder-length waves fall down around his face, and the deep musky scent of pine and firewood mingles with the sweet scent of what smells like vanilla. I try not to make it obvious that I'm smelling his hair, but we're so close it's not like I can really help it.

"What I want…" I say, ignoring his earlier question, and I try my best not to pull his hair as I wipe the blood out of it. "Is for you to stop moving so I can get this out…"

I turn and rummage through the first-aid kit, looking for another wipe after tossing my old one to the side, and stand tall to stretch my spine out. I let out a sigh and roll my neck before turning back to Jess. Normally, I'd be fine, but my back's been bothering me a little since sleeping on the flat ground last night, so being hunched over isn't really helping things at all.

"You know it'd be much easier if you just sat in my lap," Jess says, and I frown at him in response. "Easier on your back, too," he says, and gestures to my aching spine. "Just look at it this way, the sooner you're done with this, the sooner you can get away from me, isn't that what you want?"

I can't read his expression, so I playfully smack him on the arm with my hand, trying to lighten the mood. "I never said that," I say and give him a light smile. "Now quit moving around so much," I say as I scold him teasingly.

"I'm sorry. You're just so far away. It's not my fault you can't reach me," he says innocently, dodging me as I try reaching for his face with a fresh wipe in my hand.

I let out a sigh of defeat and put my hands on my hips. I hate to say it, but he's right. Hunching over is killing my back, and if I try to sit in a chair next to him, the stupid armrests will be in the way, so I'll just end up leaning over him anyway.

"Fine, have it your way," I say as I squint my eyes as I point the empty wipe packet I have in my hand at him. "But, hands where I can see 'em, all right?"

"Scouts honor," he says before doing a made-up version of a Hail Mary.

"What the heck was that?" I ask and laugh as Jess shrugs at me like he's not sure either.

I roll my eyes and lower myself onto Jess's lap. I sit perpendicular to his chest, hanging my legs over the armrest of the chair, and quickly realize that the angle is a lot more comfortable.

Now that I'm up close to him, his injuries don't seem so bad. If anything, the cut above his eyebrow is more irritated than in need of stitches, making it appear virtually nonexistent with all the blood wiped out of it.

The cut on his lip is another story, though. The skin is starting to swell, and it looks painful every time he moves his mouth to speak.

I can feel Jess staring at me, but I don't look down to make eye contact with him. "What?" I ask. "Spill it."

"Nothing, you just didn't answer my question," Jess says and shrugs.

"Do I think you're annoying?"—I put my index finger to my chin and pretend to contemplate for a second—"the answer to that would be… yes," I say and laugh as I go back to disinfecting the rest of the small scratches on Jess's cheek one last time.

"Very funny," he says with a sneer, and I just laugh. "No, what I meant was, would you rather me call you just plain old Ryan, or Ryan, My Royal Highness, Ruler Supreme, Queen of the Known Universe, Mother of Dragons and Breaker of Chains," he says.

"I think you have me confused with someone else," I say with a laugh and smile down at him.

"No… I don't think I do," he says, pulling his lower lip between his teeth as he looks up at me through his dark lashes.

I blush and look away, my body starting to feel warm, when Jess suddenly winces in pain and grabs at his temple.

Startled, I drop the small wipe in my hand. "*Ah, shit,* what's wrong? Are you all right? Was I too rough?" I ask as I frantically grab at him when Jess looks up with a sly grin on his face.

"Seems like the only way I can get you to look at me these days is if you think I'm dying or something," he says with a mischievous smile.

"Not cool," I say, smacking him on the arm as I stand to leave. My heart rate was already elevated just from sitting in his lap, but after thinking that he might be in mortal distress, my pulse is through the roof.

Jess wraps his arms around my waist and pulls me back down onto his lap. I struggle in his arms, which only makes him hold onto me tighter.

"What are you—"

"You're right, I'm sorry, total dick move," he says. "I promise to be a good boy from here on out and let you finish your treatments, Nurse Ryan, just... please don't go," he says.

I crane my neck to the side to look at him, ready to rip him a new one for scaring me like that. When I turn to look at him, he's staring at me with those eyes again, and any anger I was feeling before quickly dissipates.

I break eye contact and raise my nose in the air. "That's *Doctor* Ryan to you," I say, referencing an imaginary name badge with my hand. "See?" I ask and raise my brows at him.

"My mistake, *Doctor*," Jess says, trying to stifle a laugh.

I finish disinfecting his cuts and put a little bit of Neosporin on each of them, deciding against any bandages since they aren't that deep, that, and I doubt he'd be okay with pink Hello Kitty band-aids all over his face. Jess still has his arms loosely draped around my waist, but I don't protest since he's finally behaving and letting me do what I need to.

I try to keep my mind out of the gutter, but Jess calling himself a good boy might be doing something for me. *What the hell is that about...*

"So, are you going to tell me what happened out there?" I ask. I dab a little more Neosporin on his forehead and try to think about something else besides the warmth of his body beneath me and the feeling of his toned arms around my waist.

"Nothing too exciting—just an unfortunate run-in with a tree branch," he says nonchalantly.

"Right," I scoff. "You expect me to believe that you *accidentally* ran into a tree on a trail that you've been on dozens of times before?" I say, narrowing my eyes at him.

"You should've seen it, the damn thing came out of nowhere. It was... *massive*..." he says, widening his eyes in exaggeration before flashing me his perfect grin.

"You know what would really make me feel better, though?" he asks, and I stop my ministrations temporarily and raise my brows in question. "If you would kiss it better," Jess says with a wink.

"Ya know, you wink awfully well for a person supposedly in immense facial pain," I say, and he gives me an innocent smile.

"Fine then"—I sigh—"don't tell me what really happened," I say.

I roll my eyes as I try to stand, knowing full well that unless some random tree magically grew a fist, someone else is responsible for Jess's cut lip. The thought makes me angry, especially since it's not exactly difficult to pinpoint who it was. That would explain why my dad was the one who drove Jess back to camp instead of Chris.

Jess tightens his grip on my waist and pulls me back down onto his lap just like he did before. "What the hell, Jess, you're all better now. Dr. Ryan is officially off the clock," I say, and struggle against him as I try to pry his hands from my waist.

"But you still haven't let me repay you for your kindness, *Doctor*," Jess whispers against my ear, and I can hear the smile in his voice.

The feeling of his lips so close to my ear makes me shiver, and I try to shoo him away. "Cut it out, Jess, I've had enough of your teasing to last me a lifetime already," I say.

"Duly noted, so *teasing* is off the table, then. Anything else off limits?" he asks, and I stop struggling long enough to turn and give him a wide-eyed look.

His eyes are dark, and a half smile tugs at the corner of his mouth as he stares at me, arms still tightly wound around my waist. Heat starts to bloom between my legs at the way he's looking at me, and I feel my face growing warmer.

*What has gotten into him?*

215

I try to stay assertive, but the feeling of his warm breath on my skin makes it hard for me to keep my voice even. "Look, Jess, I think we need to talk…"

"What's there to talk about?" he asks, and I can feel his lips as they gently brush up against the side of my neck. "You needed my …*assistance*… and I was happy to oblige," he says before he peppers a few light kisses down the side of my throat.

I fight the urge to lean into him, the feeling of his lips on my skin sending electric waves throughout my body, short-circuiting my brain.

"Tell me you don't want this. Tell me to stop, and I will," he whispers before gently biting the top of my ear, sending a shiver through my body.

"Jess, y-you're injured. You should rest," I say breathlessly as he continues to bite and suck at my earlobe.

"You're gonna regret this later, I promise. You might be concussed, or maybe you're… *confused*," I say, inhaling sharply when he bites down gently on my ear.

The thought makes me a little sad, thinking that it might not actually be *me* that he wants in this situation. I only half struggle to get away, still wanting to enjoy the feeling of Jess's strong arms wrapped around me while it lasts.

"I am not concussed *or* confused. Ry, you took care of me so well, now let me take care of you," he says, and his breath feels hot against my already burning skin.

Jess moves a hand from my waist to my knee before he drags it torturously slow up the inside of my thigh. His voice comes out gravelly as he speaks. "Tell me. Tell me to stop," he says, practically begging me.

I know that I should be thinking about how someone could catch us out here in the open at any second, but I'm not. If anything, that possibility only makes me want to do it more. I know we need to talk about things, but we can always do that later. *Right…?*

Jess's hand is slowly wedging its way in between my thighs, and all I'm able to focus on is how I want more friction there. The second I let my thoughts wander back to last night and how good his fingers felt on my sensitive bundle of nerves, I feel my sanity starting to disappear. I can't believe this is happening again, and I don't want it to stop. Ever.

*Rational Sam has now officially left the building.*

I'm feeling almost delirious as I continue to think about Jess's fingers, and I can feel his heartbeat thundering in his chest as I press myself back into him. I grab his hand and remove it from its place between my thighs, and grab his other wrist, removing it from my waist as well, making my decision.

I stand with no protest from him—no begging or grasping at my body. His heavy breathing is the only sound between us as he watches me in silence. I have no reason to doubt Jess, but I guess he really meant it when he said he'd stop if I wanted him to.

I turn to face him, and a look of concern is splayed across his handsome features. I grab onto either of Jess's shoulders and step over one of his legs, straddling one of his thighs before lowering myself back down.

The look of concern on his face quickly fades away as he realizes what I'm about to do, and I watch as his eyes darken in anticipation as he scoots us to the edge of the chair. I grab Jess's hands and place them back on my hips, and I feel him squeeze me gently between them.

I don't break eye contact with him as I begin to grind back and forth against his thigh slowly. The friction of his Jeans against my clit sends wave after wave of pleasure through me the harder I grind against him, and I struggle not to come instantly.

Even though the fabric of my pants is thin, I find myself wishing that my leggings weren't in the way so that I could rub my bare pussy against his leg. A small gasp escapes my lips at the thought, and I grasp at his shoulders to steady myself.

"*Fuck*, make that noise again," Jess groans through his ragged breathing, his chest rising and falling with each quick breath that he takes. Jess grips my waist tightly as he continues to grind me back and forth on his leg.

I can feel his impressive bulge through his jeans with my left knee and push my leg harder against it. Jess throws his head back at the increased sensation and lets out a low moan. His brows pinch tightly, and I can see that he's struggling to keep himself together.

The sounds he made last night were like nothing I could've dreamed up on my own, but there's something so sexy about actually getting to watch his face this time while he's making them. My pulse feels like it's about to burst through my skin as I think about how I'd do anything to keep seeing him like this—almost about to come undone from a little bit of friction.

My leggings feel wet, and I can tell that I'm getting close, a familiar tightness building at the base of my spine. I claw at Jess's biceps and try to grind myself down harder as my eyes start to roll back into my head.

"Wait. Stop," Jess says, breathless as he halts my movements, stopping me just before I'm able to go over.

"Why? What's wrong?" I ask him, out of breath and slightly lightheaded, and I worry that he's suddenly changed his mind.

"Hand me that bag of ice," he says, pointing to the half-melted bag I'd left on the chair next to the first-aid kit.

"*Shit*, what was I thinking? I can't believe I forgot to give you the ice for your head! Are you okay?" I ask frantically. "Are you in pain? *Dammit*, I should've—"

I go to stand before Jess stops me, gripping tightly onto my waist again. "It's not for my head," he says, his voice low as he stares at me intensely. "Don't get up, just hand me the bag," he says, nodding over to the small Ziplock bag as he holds my eyes.

I look at him momentarily and make sure he's not bleeding again or about to pass out before I reach over and grab the bag of ice off the chair. I hold it up, and water drips off the corner from the condensation that's accumulated on the outside of the plastic.

Jess takes the bag from me, opening it up, and even though most of the ice is melted, he manages to fish out a decently sized piece. I watch him closely, curious about what he's planning to do with the ice before he lifts the chunk of frozen water to my neck. He gently traces small circles with the ice, causing me to shiver when it comes into contact with my skin.

Jess continues his slow movements as he glides the ice down over my neck and across my collarbone. I shiver as I stare at him, and I start moving my hips against him in slow grinding motions once again. Goosebumps now cover my body, even with Jess's flannel shirt still on, and I'm not entirely sure they're from the ice alone.

He pulls the ice away from my skin, and I watch as the water runs down his arm and slowly drips off his elbow, the warmth of his fingers quickly melting the ice.

"Do you want more?" Jess asks, the husky tone of his voice laced with desire as he stares at me. A fire burns behind his emerald eyes, and I feel as though I'm almost entranced by them. I don't say a word as I nod and continue my grinding motions against him.

I watch as Jess fishes out a larger clump of ice from inside the bag before tossing away what was left of the other melting piece. Jess holds the ice to the side of my neck, and I whine at the feeling of the cold temperature against my skin a second time.

We maintain eye contact as he moves the ice slowly down my chest and over the front of my shirt. He pauses just over my right nipple as he slowly rubs the ice over the thin fabric of my tank top, soaking me through the material. With his free hand, he pulls at the flannel shirt he let me borrow, throwing it onto a nearby chair after getting it off me.

My breath catches in my throat as the cold from the ice reaches my skin through the fabric of my thin shirt and bra.

"Did you really think I wouldn't notice what you had on under there?" Jess asks in a low voice, continuing to rub me through my shirt with the ice, and a large wet spot is now forming on the gray material, revealing the dark-colored lace underneath.

"I didn't wear it for you, if that's what you're thinking," I say with a smirk, and think that unless he went through my bag, there's no way he would've ever seen it.

Honestly, I packed it by accident. I was in such a hurry when I'd packed that I grabbed the first black bra I could find and threw it into my duffel bag without even looking at it. I never imagined that I'd be in this situation with Jess again so soon, or ever again for that matter, so I'm glad I made the right call to wear it today.

"I think you're lying," Jess says as he presses the ice against me with more force, causing me to whimper at the sensation, and a smug look crosses his face. Jess runs a teasing finger underneath the strap of my shirt and bra and slowly pulls it down over my shoulder.

I feel like the asshole's got me right where he wants me, but I don't have the mental capacity to be annoyed with him at the moment.

*Two can play at that game.*

I grab Jess by the side of his neck and lean in before whispering in his ear. "Maybe if you're lucky, someday I'll show you what else I'm hiding under here, too," I say, biting the bottom of his earlobe, causing him to jump at the force of my teeth on his skin.

I gently pull on the sensitive skin with my teeth, and he groans into the crook of my neck, his grip on my waist growing tighter. A small shudder runs through my body at the feeling of his heavy hands on my skin. I think about how I fantasized about Jess's strong grip, and how his hands would feel if they gripped my waist like they're doing right now, and think that my imagination didn't do him justice at all.

Jess tosses away the ice he was holding, and I feel his arms as they wrap underneath my legs, lifting me so that I'm straddling his entire lap instead of just the one leg. He scoots forward in the chair again, so now I'm almost able to wrap my legs around his waist as I continue to straddle him.

He grips my thighs roughly, and the chair beneath us groans as we continue to grind into each other forcefully. I pull my body tightly against him, and I can feel his rock-hardness beneath me, making me wish there weren't several layers of fabric in between us at the moment.

"I thought teasing was off the table. Wasn't I a good boy for you earlier?" Jess says as he pants into my ear.

"Say that again," I say, nearly begging him.

"I wondered earlier if that would get you hot. Guess I was right," Jess says as he pulls away to look at me, and a sinful grin crosses his lips, like he's just discovered the secrets of the universe.

*So it was on purpose, then.*

"Say it, Jess. I want you to say it," I command as I grab behind his neck and stare into his eyes, and I'm half tempted to pull his head back by his hair.

Jess smirks at me. "I'll be a good boy for you, Ryan. Let me be your good boy," he says as our bodies continue to grind against each other.

"Oh fuckkk!" I gasp out, my back involuntarily arching hard as I come. Jess wraps his arms around my body tightly and holds me against him as I ride out the aftershocks of my orgasm, my head dizzy from my high.

Jess grabs my neck, pulling our foreheads together as we breathe hard against each other. "Ryan, I—" Jess leans in close, but before he can do anything, I reach down in between us and undo his belt. "Wait, Sam, what are you—"

"I thought you said you wanted to be my good boy?" I say, and Jess watches me with wide eyes as I undo the button of his jeans before unzipping them.

I'm barely able to slip my fingers under the waistband of his briefs, gently grazing the veins of his lower abdomen with my fingertips, when I hear car tires coming down the dirt trail toward our campsite. The sound causes me to snap my head up in the direction of the car.

"Don't worry, Ry, they're probably just lost. Once they see that they're... *interrupting* something, they'll leave," Jess says, still trying to catch his breath. "I guess we can always let them watch us, if you're into that," Jess jokes as he leans in, kissing my neck, and my fingers reflexively weave into his hair.

I lean into his touch one last time, not wanting this to end just yet. Even after what just happened, I feel my cheeks flame a bit at Jess's words. I'll admit that I do have a bit of an exhibitionist kink, but I feel like this really isn't the time or place, especially with my dad and brother in the vicinity.

"Sure, that is, unless you don't mind it being Rebecca who watches us," I say, and Jess immediately pulls back, staring at me with a look of confusion mixed with disgust.

"Ew, Ry. What the hell?" he says, pulling a face at me.

I buckle Jess's pants and zip up the zipper before climbing off him, my legs feeling a bit wobbly from how I was straddling him for so long.

Jess is still staring at me with a weird look on his face, so I explain my comment, forgetting that he wasn't here earlier when Rebecca left. "There's a ninety-eight percent chance that that car is Rebecca's Uber," I say, and nod to the car that just pulled up. "She left right after you guys did this morning."

"What is there even to do up here? I doubt there's anywhere for her to shop," Jess says and scoffs as he shakes his head.

"That's exactly what *I* said," I say and give an exhausted laugh as I rub my hands over my face.

My head is starting to clear, and a twinge of shame works its way through me. So much for talking about what happened last night before anything else happened… Jess is the one who started it this time, but why do I feel like I just took advantage of him again?

"Shit," I say, looking down, and notice the huge wet spot on my shirt that's right over my right nipple.

If Rebecca sees, there's no doubt she'll run her mouth about it to everyone, especially my dad. I'm not usually bothered by what others think of my sexual exploits, but since Jess supposedly has a girlfriend, that basically makes me a home wrecker, and that's not really a title I want to have.

*Should've thought of that earlier, you dirty whore.*

I put fighting my inner demons off until later as I look around for Jess's flannel so I can hurry and cover up. I quickly search all the chairs around the fire but come up empty. When I turn around to face Jess, he's standing behind me, already wearing the flannel shirt I was just looking for.

"Wait, what? When did you even get up?" I look over at the empty chair where he was just sitting a second ago. "Hey! Give me that back!" I say as I grab at the flannel, trying to get it off him.

"If you want to undress me so bad, just ask, I'd be happy to help return the favor," he says and winks at me.

I ignore him, still trying to get the flannel off his large frame. "Oh my god, Jess, why are you making this so difficult!" I ask as I grasp and pull at his shirt. "It's like trying to put a shoe on a fucking baby," I say, starting to get irritated with his noncompliance. Jess just raises a brow at me like he has no idea what I'm talking about, and the corners of his mouth twitch upward as I continue to jerk him around by the flannel.

"Also, I thought you were dizzy and couldn't stand up straight?" I ask, the flannel almost free from one of his arms as I continue pulling on the fabric.

"I guess I made a miraculous recovery. I've got a pretty great doctor," Jess says and winks.

"*Had* a great doctor," I say with my hands on my hips as I give up on trying to get the flannel back.

"You'd better be quick, I'll stall for as long as I can," he says as he winks again before straightening his shirt.

I watch as Jess walks off toward the car that just pulled up a few feet away, and I try to figure out what I'm going to do. I know it's not a life-or-death situation, but I really don't want to equip Rebecca with any more ammo to use against me later on.

I know I have an extra shirt in the tent, but then I'd have to walk past Rebecca and the car and decide that plan's no good. I spot the water bottle Jess left in the chair cupholder from when I gave him the ibuprofen earlier and go to grab it.

*Stupid Rebecca.*

I sigh as I grab the bottle before twisting the cap open. I turn away from the car, pretending to drink the water as I purposely spill it down the front of my chest, soaking most of my shirt.

*Gah, that's fucking cold.* A quick shiver runs through me, and I wonder how the water managed to stay freezing cold when the ice melted so fast.

I hear a car door open and turn to see Jess helping Rebecca out of a black Volvo as he offers her a hand. She looks momentarily panicked when she sees Jess back at the campsite, and I see her look around for Chris's Razor, probably wondering why the guys are back so early.

"Don't worry, they're not back yet, it's just me." I hear Jess say, and Rebecca watches him as he shuts the car door behind her. The driver doesn't waste a single second as they speed off back down the dirt path.

Rebecca eyes me up and down with a look of disgust, obviously noting my wet shirt. "What happened to *you?* Forget your bib or something?" she says and sneers at me.

*Seriously? This bitch is literally the worst.*

I shake my head, ready to fight her, but before she can shoot off any more snarky remarks, Jess cuts her off.

"Well, we would LOVE to stay and chat, but I'm sure that John will be back soon enough to keep you company. That way you can tell him allll about your fun day out," Jess says as he winks and brushes past her as he walks to stand next to me.

"*Hmm…*" he murmurs as he looks down at my bare feet.

*Damn.* I'd forgotten I wasn't wearing any shoes. As soon as I saw Jess with blood all over his face, I jumped out of the tent and ran straight over to him. I was so preoccupied with playing doctor that I can't believe I didn't realize I was barefoot that entire time.

Jess grabs my hand and gestures to one of the makeshift tree stump chairs next to the fire. "Up, up," he says, keeping hold of me so I don't fall as he turns around, his back facing me.

Rebecca stands across from us with her hands folded across her chest giving us the worst stink face imaginable.

"Tell the others not to wait up," Jess says to Rebecca as he drapes my arm around his neck. I quickly realize where he's going with the gesture and don't fight him on it.

Although I'm pretty sure that Jess shouldn't be carrying anyone, especially with a head injury, I refuse to let Rebecca see us bicker like children. I tell myself that as soon as we're out of eyesight, I'll jump down and make sure that he's all right.

Jess reaches back and taps my thighs with his hands. I gently hop onto his back, grabbing him around the neck with my arms as he grips onto my legs tightly with his hands.

Rebecca stands in front of us still, her hands now on her hips. "Where are you two going? What about dinner? You know that John is going to be hungry when he gets back—"

"Figure it out, Becky, he's your husband, not mine," I say, not caring to play nice with her for a second longer. I feel Jess trying to stifle a laugh from below me as I give Rebecca a condescending smile and try to hold back my own laughter.

A look of rage takes over her features, and she looks like she wants to smack me across the face, and she honestly might've had Jess not been there. "You f—"

"Like I said before," Jess says, interrupting her. "Don't wait up, *Becky*."

Jess carries me on his back as we walk past a fuming Rebecca. We barely make it past her before we both bust out laughing, neither one able to hold it in any longer.

# Chapter Thirteen

You're not seriously going to carry me the entire way, are you?" I ask from Jess's back, my legs still wrapped around his waist as I cling to him.

I struggle to get down but can't because of how tightly he's holding onto my thighs. "We're still like a mile away or something," I say as I push against him.

"You're such a drama queen. It's only five more minutes away, and you know that," he says as he shakes his head.

"For real, Jess, let me down. You almost passed out earlier, the last thing you should be doing right now is lugging my fat ass around," I say, still worried about him having a possible concussion.

"Well... I might've been exaggerating just a tad so you'd take care of me," he says. "And honestly, I wouldn't mind carrying you across the entire mountain if it meant I got to feel these bad boys wrapped around me." I feel his grip tighten as he gives my legs a small squeeze.

"You think you're so smooth, don't you?" I say.

"You didn't seem to mind it last night… or just barely, for that matter…" Jess says, and I can practically feel the confidence oozing off him.

I nervously clear my throat. "All right then, new subject," I say, glad he's unable to see the blush that's staining my cheeks at the moment. "How do you intend for us to swim with no bathing suits?" I ask.

"Easy, we skinny dip, just like when we were kids. Duh," he says.

"Yeah, you definitely remember that wrong. I've never skinny dipped out here before," I say.

A part of me wishes I were brave enough to try it out back then. Who knows if it would've changed anything between Jess and me, but maybe he would've seen me as more fun and adventurous.

"Okay, well maybe *you* didn't," he says.

"*Whatever*, you so did not sneak all the way out here to skinny dip by yourself," I say and scoff, wanting to call him out on his bullshit.

"Who says I was alone?" he asks, and I immediately regret bringing up the swimsuits.

"Do you remember the park ranger who brought his daughter along that one year?" Jess asks me as he trails off, like he's remembering a long-forgotten memory, and I can hear the smile in his voice.

Of course I remember the park ranger's daughter from that summer. How could I have forgotten her beautiful bright red hair and pretty baby blue eyes, or the fact that I had to watch Jess fall all over her the entire trip? I was such a jealous mess that week that it was the first time I can ever remember wanting to leave and go home early.

"Amber."

"Damn, was that her name? How did you remember that? *I* didn't even remember that," Jess says and laughs.

Like it's so hard to believe that I wouldn't remember the name of the girl Jess chose to be with over me that summer.

As if.

I take a breath and try not to let my anger get the best of me, but it proves to be difficult. Jess shakes his head and chuckles, the actions only fueling my jealousy.

"Ryan, it's kind of funny, but I never told you—"

"Put me down, Jess," I say flatly, and decide to interrupt him before he has a chance to say one more word about *Amber*.

"What? No, not a chance, we're almost there," he says, and I push against him with more force, trying to get him to let me down. "Did you forget that you still don't have any shoes on?" he says in disbelief, snorting.

"Jess, put me down," I say sternly. "Now."

He stops and crouches down slightly as he releases my legs and I quickly slide myself down off his back. "What? Are you mad now?" he asks, eyeing me as I crouch down to roll up my leggings.

"No, it's nothing. I just don't really want to relive one of the worst summers of my life, that's all," I say and straighten. "Plus, my arms were getting tired from hanging onto you like a monkey. I just need a break."

It's a blatant lie. I could hang onto Jess forever and never get tired of it.

I cross in front of him and slowly step into the stream that follows alongside the dirt trail. Jess was right, though. We're almost there, only a few hundred more feet before the stream opens up into the smaller hidden part of the lake.

When I dip my toes into the water, it's freezing cold, and I struggle to keep a straight face. I'm too proud to admit defeat and ask Jess to carry me again, so I force myself to wade into the water a little deeper, hoping I just need a minute to adjust to the temperature of the stream.

Even though the day is starting to cool off, the sun is still shining, and the rays feel amazing as they beam down onto my bare arms. I try to shake off the chill that's making its way up my calves, and wiggle my toes in the water, wishing I still had Jess's flannel shirt on to warm me up.

Jess stays silent as he follows alongside me as I wade through the stream. "Why'd you bring us out here, Jess?" I ask without turning to face him. "We both know it's too cold to swim today." I try not to let my irritation get the best of me, but the tone of my voice does little to hide it.

"I brought us out here because you promised me a walk by the lake, remember? Do you not want to do that anymore?" he asks, and I can feel his eyes on me. I stay silent as we continue walking, not really sure what to say.

Of course I want to be here with him, *he's* the one who wants to talk about another girl…

"I wish you would just tell me what you're thinking sometimes," Jess says, letting out a huge breath, and out of the corner of my eye, I watch as he runs his hands through his hair. "It really drives me crazy not knowing how you're feeling, Sam."

I stop in the water and turn to face him. Jess halts his steps as well and turns his body toward me, his eyes on my face as he waits for me to say something.

What I really want to say is that I'm thinking about how that was probably the worst summer of my entire life. It was the summer after the incident with my mom, so my entire family was a complete mess—myself included.

I couldn't wait to spend the summer with Jess since I was finally able to admit to myself that I had real feelings for him, and I desperately wanted to tell him how I felt. Only, instead of doing that, I almost drowned in the lake and had to watch as he chased around another girl who wasn't me, all the while having to pretend like none of it bothered me.

I'm thinking about how I wish it were anyone but Jess who'd pulled me out of the water that day. I'd have given anything to have him look at me the way he looked at Amber, but after my *accident*, he only looked at me like I was something that might break. I wanted him to look at me with longing and yearning, but instead, I felt like I only got his pity. A love confession from me after everything that'd happened only would've made things worse.

"I don't know what I'm feeling, and I don't know why I'm mad at you all of a sudden. Amber's ancient history, and it's not like I'm a stranger to the fact that you always have female friends around you," I say, and sigh as I look up at the sky, shaking my head. I don't wait to hear his reply before I turn away and keep walking toward the lake.

"*Had* female friends around. It's not like that anymore," Jess says from behind me, and I look back to raise a skeptical brow at him.

"Believe what you want, but it's the truth. I'm sorry though, I guess I didn't realize that it bothered you so much," Jess says with an apologetic look. He tucks his hands into his front pockets and continues to walk behind me slowly. "Plus, that girl, Amber… she was—"

"It *doesn't* bother me because it's none of my business. But since you're the one who brought it up, what about that girl from the grocery store? You mean to tell me that was just a coincidence, and that she's not a member of the Jess Cameron fan club?" I ask, looking over my shoulder at him again.

"I thought you just said it was none of your business who I'm friends with," Jess says, his tone much more serious than before.

"You're right, it's not any of my business, except that you made it my business last night if she actually is your girlfriend," I say, turning to Jess, hands on my hips.

"As I recall, you're the one who initiated that situation last night, not me," he says and shakes his head. I can tell that he's getting pretty upset from the way he keeps clenching his jaw, but I decide to keep pushing the subject anyway.

"Just answer the question, Jess, are you dating her or not?" I demand as I throw my hands in the air.

"It's complicated all right, and like I said before, it's none of your business, so just drop it, Sam," he says, definitely mad now.

Jess is right, he doesn't owe me an explanation. It's not like we're together or anything. What he does is *his* business, not mine. I lower my hands and shake my head as I turn away from him and try not to cry.

At first, I think that Jess decided to turn around, until I hear his boots silently crunching on the dirt trail as he continues to follow along behind me.

After a few minutes, we reach the base of our secret lake spot, and I wade over to a large flat rock near the edge and climb on top of it. I shiver as I pull my feet out of the frigid lake and hold my knees to my chest, glad to finally be out of the water for a minute.

Out of the corner of my eye, I see Jess take off his boots before he climbs onto the rock and sits next to me, our shoulders touching as we sit side by side.

We stay silent for a while, both just staring out over the sparkling water of the lake. It really is a beautiful day, and I feel bad for ruining the mood.

When I finally manage to muster up the courage to ask Jess about what's really been bothering me, my voice comes out small.

"Jess," I say, and I feel his eyes on me as he turns to face me. "Did last night... mean anything to you?" I ask quietly and turn to meet his gaze finally.

"Of course it did. Why would you even ask me that?" he says incredulously. "That is, unless it didn't mean anything to *you*," he says, and a hurt look crosses his face.

How am I supposed to tell him that it meant *everything* to me? Just having him hold me while I had my mental breakdown meant more than I could ever express to him. He made me feel safe and loved, but most of all, he made me feel wanted for once. I've never wanted anything more in my life than to be wanted by only him.

But because I'm a coward, I don't say any of that.

"If you really are dating that girl, how could what we did have meant anything?" I ask. I feel tears welling in my eyes, so I look back over the lake and hug my knees in tighter to my chest.

I wipe my eyes with the back of my hand and sniffle, waiting for Jess to say something. When he stays silent, I continue rambling, wanting to make things okay between us again, and regret ever asking him about last night.

"If I'm being honest, I thought there was a possibility that you were dating someone, but I took things too far anyway. It's like you said before, *I* was the one who put you in that weird situation last night," I say, and look over at him with tears in my eyes. "I think I might've ruined everything. I'm sorry, Jess," I say as a few tears spill over.

"Sam, do you have any idea how important you are to me?" Jess says as he holds my gaze intensely, and his eyes shine brightly from the reflection of the sunset on the water.

I don't want him to see me cry, so I try to turn away. Jess turns my head gently as he cups my cheeks in his hands, forcing me to look him in the face.

"Madison is not my girlfriend," he says, still holding my face. "I'm sorry that I got mad before, but I meant it when I said that it was complicated. Please believe me when I say that you're the last person I want to keep anything from, but this is something that I need to figure out on my own. Ryan, you've always been there for me, and I need you. You're one of the most important things in my life, and I can't lose that."

I've always longed for Jess to say things like this to me, and although I do believe that he's genuine in his words, the way he's looking at me makes my heart sink in my chest.

"As for last night... and today..." he says hesitantly as he removes his hands from my cheeks. Jess shakes his head lightly before turning to look out at the lake as my world starts to implode around me.

*At long last, here it is.*

The thing I've been dreading most in the world, the thing I told myself I would never let happen, *the one thing* I swore to avoid at all costs.

Friend-zoned by Jess Cameron, and it stings more than I ever imagined it could.

I interrupt him before he has a chance to finish his sentence, knowing I won't be able to bear the crushing blow he's about to deliver.

"It's okay, Jess, I understand," I say, trying to fake my best smile as I hold back the flood that's burning behind my eyes. He turns to look at me with an expression that I can't quite read, so I painfully drivel on with my words.

"You don't owe me an explanation. Your business is your own, I shouldn't have overstepped. What happened between us was a mistake, and I'm sorry I crossed the line last night and took advantage of you. I won't ever let it happen again," I say, trying to give him a reassuring smile. "Don't worry, I'll sleep in Chris's trailer tonight so that you can actually get some rest."

"Ry, you don't have to—" Jess starts, but I cut him off with my babbling, unable to stop the word vomit that continues to pour out of my mouth.

"I'm sorry if I've been an inconvenience to you lately, that wasn't my intention—" I nervously fidget with my hands in my lap, desperately trying to salvage what remaining relationship we might have.

"Where we haven't really talked in a few years, it was naïve of me to think that you'd just let me poke around in your personal life like that. I hope you'll still let me be here for you as your friend—because you're right—I'll always be here whenever you need me," I say through a small hiccup, unable to keep up the façade a second longer, hot tears already starting to stream down my cheeks.

"Sam," Jess says with a look of pity, and I dodge his touch when he tries to reach for me.

"Now, I don't know about you, but *I* came here to swim," I say through my tears and forced smile.

It takes all of my strength not to break down and ugly cry in front of him, so before Jess can say anything else, I launch myself off our rock and into the lake.

When I hit the water, the cold just about knocks all the air out of my lungs. I flail around for a few seconds before realizing that I was in fact not in my right mind when I went in. Not only is the water in the lake somehow colder than it felt in the stream, but it's kind of murky from all the snow runoff. So now, not only am I soaking wet and freezing, but I sort of smell, too.

Jess doesn't jump in with me, he just watches me from where he sits on the rock with a serious look on his face. After a few minutes of watching me shiver in the water, he pulls on his boots and offers me a hand out of the lake. I grab his hand, and he yanks me onto the shoreline next to him, and I try not to splash him when I lose my footing.

Jess saves me from falling back into the water and steadies me by grabbing my arm. We're so close that I can feel the heat radiating off his body, and I try to ignore the urge to grab hold of him.

The second our skin makes contact, my entire body starts scream-ing at me to pull him in and to tell him how much I love him, how much I *need* him. I want to beg and plead with him to choose me over Madison, over every other girl in the world, but I can't.

I quickly pull my hand away, already knowing how that scenario would play out. Jess releases me once I'm stable, now back on the trail, and I wrap my arms around my freezing body.

I stand there next to Jess, shivering from feeling the breeze against my wet clothes as they cling tightly to my body, and wish I had never jumped into the water in the first place.

I look up, and Jess keeps giving me that look, like I'm just another poor sucker who fell for him that he had to let down gently. I'll bet it's some-thing he's been through a million times already, so I'm sure that I'm just one of the many.

*You're not special, Sam. You're not anything.*

The more I think about it all, the lower my heart sinks into my stomach.

"The sun is gonna set soon, we'd better head back—" Jess says as he looks me up and down, eyeing my sopping form. "But there is no way I'm carrying you back like that," he says as he raises a brow at me, break-ing me out of my self-deprecating thoughts.

"Okay, well, what do you suggest I do? Let you carry me back naked?" I shiver as I look away. "No thanks. I can just walk, it's fine," I say, determined to prove that I don't need his help.

My stubbornness is short-lived when I make it all of five feet be-fore cutting my foot on a rock, and I don't have to turn around to know that Jess is already scoffing at me.

"Here, take this and lose the shirt, at least," Jess says, walking around the front of me as I examine the small cut on the side of my right foot. He holds out his green flannel, and I continue to stand there staring at him, my arms wrapped around my trembling body, my foot now starting to throb as well.

Jess is still holding the flannel out to me when he frowns and shakes it, gesturing for me to grab it. "Come on already, you're gonna catch a cold or something," he says impatiently.

"You know that's not how colds work, right?" I say, and he just continues to frown at me.

I look at the flannel in his outstretched hand and sigh. "*Fine*," I say as I take it from him, secretly desperate for the warmth I know it'll provide me.

I open my mouth, but before I can even ask him to, Jess covers his face with both of his hands, muffling his voice in the process. "I promise not to look," he says, and I crack a small smile. I'm still a little upset about earlier, but still madly in love with every cute thing he does.

I quickly take off my shirt and bra before wringing out the material, setting the half-soaked wad on a nearby rock. I pull my arms through the sleeves of the flannel and snap the buttons closed.

"Okay, let's go," I say, only half shivering now that I've removed the majority of my wet clothes.

"Are you sure it's safe? I don't wanna get smacked," Jess says, still covering his face.

"Yes, you big dope, now let's go," I say jokingly, pulling his hands away from his face. He smiles at me, and I'm glad to see that some of the weird tension between us is fading already.

Jess crouches down in front of me, and I hop onto his back before wrapping my arms around his neck. Although I do feel bad for getting him wet with my still-soaked leggings, I'm not about to let him carry me back to camp with no pants on. Talk about embarrassing, especially after just being rejected by him, and the last thing I want is to come off as desperate.

Jess grasps onto my legs tightly, and we start the walk back to our camp. We've barely gone a few feet, but I'm already starting to feel better, grateful for the heat that Jess's body is putting off.

"Hey, Ryan?" Jess says hesitantly.

"*Hmmm?*" I murmur as I tiredly rest my head against him.

"Look, I know I have no right to ask this, and you don't have to answer, but… Sophie says that you're seeing someone and that it's fairly serious. Is that… really true?" Jess asks, and I can hear the hesitation in his voice, like he wants to ask me something else.

I let out a deep breath and close my eyes. "Nope. I got dumped," I say, wondering why Sophie would feed Jess with such useless misinformation.

Jess doesn't say anything, and I feel him take a deep breath before he speaks. "I'm sorry, Sam."

"It's all right, it doesn't matter. None of it matters anymore," I say, and feel a few exhausted tears stream down my cheeks.

I quickly wipe my face on the sleeve of the flannel and try not to let the overwhelming thoughts of being tossed aside by Daniel and a rejection from Jess in the same week get me down.

"Are you sure you're all right? Like, with your head, I mean?" I ask from behind him, trying to change the subject as I clear my throat and shake my tears away.

I think that Jess can sense my discomfort at our previous conversation, so he quickly changes gears as we drop the subject.

"Yep, right as rain. Those questionable pocket pills you forced me to take really did the trick," he says and scoffs. "I think I just need some rest, then I'll be as good as new," he says, followed by a large yawn.

I notice that his breathing is a little more labored than it was before, which worries me. I shake my head and tell myself that he's a big boy, and that fussing over him like a girlfriend is only going to make things more awkward between us.

Jess carries me back to camp in silence, and I almost fall asleep on his back, my head resting gently against his. The light chirping of the crickets in the background is almost enough to lull me to sleep. I try to savor the warmth of his body and tell myself that this has to be the last time I let myself be so close to him like this. I already know that I'm never going to stop wanting more, so the sooner I'm able to distance myself from him again, the better.

When we get back to camp, the sun is almost set, and there's a chill in the air from the light breeze. My upper body is warm except for the exposed skin on my wrists and neck, but my leggings are still damp. The cold air is causing my legs to go numb, except in the places where Jess's arms come into contact with my thighs.

We make it to the entrance of our camp, and I see Chris's Razor parked next to his blue pickup truck.

I hear voices coming from around the fire as Jess makes his way over to the others. "Wait, Jess, just leave me at the tent so I can change and grab my shoes," I say, trying to jump down as we pass his tent.

"Let's get you warmed up a bit first, you're shivering so hard you're making *my* teeth rattle," Jess says and chuckles as he holds me tighter, making me unable to get down without looking like a flailing toddler.

"You guys catch anything good?" Jess calls to the others as we approach the fire pit, interrupting their chatter.

Everyone stops talking, and they all stare at us as Jess gently lets me down next to the fire. The heat of the flame feels amazing against my freezing skin, and I'm glad that Jess brought me here first instead of the tent.

Rebecca gives me a hard once-over as she sits up in her chair. "You two look like you had fun. What happened? Did you have another *accident*, Sam? John told me about—"

Before she can finish her snotty comment, Jess cuts her off mid-sentence. "You know, we sure did, didn't we, Ry?" Jess says, turning toward me. "But what about you, *Bec*? Enjoy your R&R time today?" he asks with a smile but gets no reply from Rebecca as she sneers at him.

"Poor thing got another migraine today. It's a good thing she was able to sleep it off for most of the day. Right, sweetie?" my dad says, wrapping his arm around Rebecca's shoulder as he rubs her arm lovingly. "I hope you at least checked on her, Sam," he says, giving me a stern look.

"*Another* migraine?" Jess asks, shaking his head with fake concern. "Well, at least you were able to rest, sounds very... relaxing," Jess says, winking at Rebecca as she gives him a death glare before folding her arms across her chest.

The guys would never have paid attention to such a thing, but I notice that the shade of Rebecca's nails is slightly different from the color they were yesterday. She notices me staring at her hands and quickly unfolds them before tucking them under her thighs.

*So, she* was *at a spa, then.*

I consider outing her to everyone, but don't, since I know it won't help anything. It'll just end up making my dad upset with me, and that's the last thing I want.

I feel my stomach grumble and realize that I never had any lunch today. I look around and notice that the fish cooler is nowhere in sight and raise my brows at my dad. "Where's all the fish you guys caught? Shouldn't we get cooking before it gets too late?" I ask, already dreading having to wash and gut the fish, especially now having to do it in the dark.

"Uh, well, this year they weren't really biting like they usually do," my dad says as he scratches his head nervously. Chris and Jess stay awkwardly silent, and I notice that neither of them will make eye contact with me—or with each other.

"Okay… so you didn't catch anything?" I ask, followed by silence. "Wait, like nothing at all?" I say, and I'm met only with more silence.

I think for a second, and I'm glad I brought a backup meal in case I accidentally messed up dinner one night. "Well, it won't be like a huge meal or anything, but I brought stuff to roast hot dogs if you guys are up for that instead?" I ask and shrug as I look between them all and notice a disgusted look on Rebecca's face.

"Sounds great!" my dad says as he stands, rubbing his hands together. "I'll go find the roasting sticks."

"I'll go get some more firewood," Chris grumbles as he sets down the beer can in his hand.

"I'll grab the dogs, then!" Jess calls after my dad as he follows him over to Betty.

I'm guessing that Rebecca put the hot dogs in the RV's fridge just to annoy me, that is, if she didn't decide to hide them instead. I remind myself to thank Jess later for not making me be the one to retrieve them. If only I'd known about Rebecca's little pork "intolerance" sooner, I would've purposely made sure not to buy the all-beef dogs like I usually do.

Seeing my dad jump up so fast to help makes me laugh to myself. The guys must really be hungry if they're voluntarily helping with dinner. Typical that they'd wait for me to get back before starting on any food though, but at least hot dogs aren't difficult. Honestly, this new plan sounds much better to me than the cleaning, gutting, battering, and frying that I knew was in store for me with the fish, so I definitely won't be complaining.

I don't move from my place by the fire as I wait for the guys to come back with the hot dogs and skewering sticks. I turn my body so that my frozen butt is facing the fire, and so that I don't have to look at Rebecca. I can feel her eyes burning a hole into the back of my head, but still don't turn around even when my legs start to feel like they're on fire.

"You two think you're so cute, don't you?" I hear her spit from behind me.

I take a deep breath before answering, not really wanting to deal with her bitchy comments at the moment. "I don't know what you're talking about." A smirk pulls at the corner of my mouth. "We're not the ones who lied about where they were today," I say, knowing that I'm just antagonizing her.

"Do you realize that once John and I are married, I'll be your—"

"Okay, *seriously*, that's enough," I say and spin around to face her. "Do you honestly think that makes a difference? I don't give a rat's ass about what you think of me, or the fact that you think you have any say in my life whatsoever. I've been trying to play nice with you for my dad's sake, but at this point, I really don't give a fuck anymore," I say and laugh, cutting off whatever words that are about to escape Rebecca's mouth.

"You don't think I know what you're doing with my dad? You must think I'm a complete fucking idiot if you think that I can't see straight through your perfect little fiancé act," I say, trying my best to keep my voice down so that my dad doesn't hear us.

"Do what you want with him, but just know that you're wrong if you think you have the upper hand. You're just his flavor of the month, and the second he gets bored with you, he'll get rid of you, just like he did with the rest," I say and walk off toward Jess's tent, leaving Rebecca behind me to pick her jaw up off the ground.

I know I should feel bad about what I said, but I honestly feel so much better now that I got it all out. I meant what I said about her trying to control me, but as far as her relationship with my dad goes, I feel like I might've been a tad too harsh with my words.

Sure, my dad's gone through his fair share of women over the last few years, but for whatever reason, he's chosen to hang onto Rebecca longer than the rest. I'm glad that, at least now, she knows that I'm not some spineless pushover that she can boss around. Daddy doesn't pay for my bills, so she wouldn't have much to hold over my head if they got married anyway.

I hurry over to Jess's tent, already missing the warm glow of the fire, and quickly change out of my clothes. Despite basically roasting myself alive by the fire, my pants and hair are still damp from the lake, and one whiff of my hair tells me I was right about smelling like a wet fish.

I want to ask Chris about what happened today on their fishing trip and possibly get the real story behind Jess's busted lip, but I doubt he'll actually tell me what happened. I know it's bad to assume things, but if Angry Chris showed up today on the boat, there's a good chance he had something to do with Jess's injuries.

Even with dry sweats on, I still feel cold and shiver from the chilly air that's blowing through the unzipped windows inside the tent. I decide to put Jess's flannel shirt on top of my thermal pajama top, not wanting to give it up just yet. I fight my tangled hair up into a bun and quickly pull my shoes on before heading into the woods behind our camp.

"Chris!" I call out into the darkness as I search the tree line for him with my flashlight.

"What do you want? I'm getting wood," he calls back, and his voice helps me pinpoint his location from within the trees.

"Wait up! I'll come help!" I call and head in the direction of his voice. I stumble around in the dark for a minute, still trying to find him, my tiny flashlight doing little to help me see more than two feet in front of my face.

"Hold these," Chris says from a few steps in front of me, and I try not to jump at his sudden appearance. When he turns around, his head-lamp shines into my eyes, and I look away before he unloads four huge logs into my arms.

"*Seriously?*" I grunt, almost dropping the wood as I momentarily lose my balance, not expecting them to be so heavy.

"You said you wanted to help, so quit your bitching," Chris says as he crouches down to grab another large piece of wood before lobbing it onto my pile. He turns around and continues his search for more firewood, and I struggle to keep up with him due to the weight that I'm trying to balance in my arms.

"Hey, what happened out there today? You guys always at least catch *something*. Did you forget the poles?" I joke.

"Why don't you ask your boyfriend?" Chris says before adding another log to the pile in my arms.

I stare at him, momentarily confused. "Are you talking about Jess? Chris, you know he's not my..."

"Literally, *I do not care,*" Chris says before turning away from me, obviously annoyed at something.

"What's your problem? I've barely said two words to you since I've been home, so why are you being such a jerk to me?" I say, still struggling to contain the heavy pile of firewood in my arms as I follow Chris through the dark.

Chris whips around and throws down the log he's holding in his hand and gets right in my face. I can smell the alcohol on his breath and stumble backward, almost losing my balance when I trip over the random forest debris under my feet. I try to save them on their way down, but a few logs fall to the ground with a heavy thud when I lose my footing.

"My *problem* is that asshole dumped the entire fish cooler along with all of our bait back into the lake, and now I'm going to be stuck eating fucking hot dogs for dinner instead of the fish that *I* caught!" Chris yells angrily at me.

"So, I'm guessing that means the ham sandwiches didn't work as bait then, either?" I ask sarcastically, not afraid of him even in his current state.

Chris's headlamp shines in my face, practically blinding me, but I'm still able to make out the death glare he's giving me from behind its brightness.

Even though my arms are full with the logs, I'm still holding my flashlight in one hand. Chris is still in my face, fuming mad, so when I tilt my light toward him, I'm able to catch a glimpse of his swollen face, my mind finally putting the pieces together.

Jess never mentioned anything about the fish, but he also refused to tell me anything about his injuries or what had happened, either.

"Get that shit out of my face," Chris says, turning away mad.

"Why do you have a black eye?" I ask, trying to keep up with him in the dark when he starts to pick up his pace.

"Hey, asshole, I'm talking to you!" I call after him.

"Give it a fucking rest already, Sam! You're not mom, so stop acting like it, it's fucking annoying," Chris barks without turning back to look at me.

*Dick. For all I care, he can carry all the firewood back on his own.*

I dump all the logs on the ground and brush the dirt and small pieces of bark off of myself before walking back toward our camp.

Luckily, we weren't too far away, so I can spot the soft glow of the fire pit in the distance. I don't hear Chris behind me, but don't look back to see if he's following me either. Once he cools off, he'll head back, but until then, it's probably better for everyone if he stays away for a little bit.

245

When I make it back, my dad and Rebecca are already roasting their hot dogs over the fire, and from the looks of it, my dad's already on his second dog. I grab a roasting stick and casually look around for Jess, unable to spot him, and wonder if he's still in my dad's RV.

"Chris need help with the firewood?" my dad asks through a mouthful of bread.

"Nope, I think he's got it handled," I say coolly and smile.

"You gonna roast a dog, Sam?" my dad asks, handing me the bag of buns from his side table.

"Thanks," I say as I take the bag from my dad. "But I think I'll wait for Jess," I say, looking around for him.

"Sorry, kid, he had to take off," my dad says as he finishes off the last bite of his hot dog.

"What do you mean? Like, he went into the woods to pee, or like, he *left* left?" I ask, looking around, and sure enough, the green Jeep is gone from its place next to Jess's tent.

"He got a phone call and said he had to go. He just asked that we drop his tent and gear over to Sophie's whenever we get back into town," my dad says much too calmly, and I try not to panic.

"It wasn't Aunt Judy, was it? Is she all right?" I ask frantically, my mind starting to run through worst-case scenarios as my heart pounds in my chest.

Judy is all that Jess has got besides Sophie, and if something bad were to happen to her, he'd be crushed. I know that Jess is aware of how important she is to me as well, so if something were really wrong, wouldn't he have come and gotten me?

*If anything were to happen to Aunt Judy, I don't know what I'd do…*

"No, nothing like that. I asked him the same thing. He said he'd heard from them earlier and that they were both fine," my dad says, and my anxiety eases a little at his words.

I let out a sigh of relief before sitting down in my camp chair next to the fire. "If it wasn't Judy, did he say why he had to leave so suddenly, and without saying goodbye, either?" I ask my dad.

"Nope, he didn't say, he just said that someone needed him and that he had to go," my dad says with a shrug, and I try not to jump to conclusions. I already know that if it wasn't Aunt Judy or Sophie who called him, then there's a good chance it was Madison. I fold my arms across my chest, and suddenly I don't feel like eating anymore.

I set the roasting stick back on the pile with the others and turn to leave. "I'm actually not feeling great, I think I'm gonna turn in early," I say to my dad, and Rebecca gives me a snotty look but doesn't say anything.

"Night, then," my dad calls after me as I walk away.

I'm almost back to the tent when I hear Chris's voice in the distance and think that he must've waited for me to leave to rejoin my dad and Rebecca. He's probably trying to avoid another interrogation—not that I would've tried again, though. He made it clear how he feels about me caring about his well-being. *Oh well.*

I take my shoes off and unzip the tent before stepping inside. I don't know why, but I half expect Jess to be inside waiting for me, just like he was yesterday. I try to shake the feeling of disappointment, but the more I think about how I wish Jess were here with me instead of rescuing Madison, the worse I feel.

He basically told me it wasn't going to happen between us and that he's involved with someone else, so the fact that I'm feeling jealous and abandoned doesn't really seem fair. Thinking about how Madison could be in trouble and here I am wishing Jess never left makes me feel guilty. Regardless of my feelings toward her, I really do hope she's all right.

247

I turn off the small lantern and curl up inside Jess's sleeping bag, which now feels enormous with only my body to occupy it. I wrap my arms around myself and cling to Jess's flannel shirt—which I'm still wearing. I try to hold it in for as long as I can, but eventually the dam breaks, and I cry until I finally drift off from the exhaustion of my tears.

~

I wake up just before dawn, and after a fitful night, I finally gave up on trying to get back to sleep by the time the sun started to rise. What little sleep I did manage was filled with weird dreams that only left me feeling anxious and uneasy.

My head's pounding, and I can already feel how puffy my eyes are from crying last night. I kick myself for letting some stupid guy make me feel this way, even if that guy does happen to be Jess.

*What a lousy trip this turned out to be.*

I lie on my back, staring at the ceiling of the tent, and hope that everyone will be up soon. The sooner everyone's awake, the sooner we can get the hell out of here.

Aside from the year with the lake incident, this is the first time I've actually wanted to go home early. I usually dread the end of the trip, because in the past, it normally meant that summer was almost over and that we'd all have to go back to our regular lives. Which also meant no more trampoline sleepovers with Sophie or hanging out in Grandpa Millard's basement with Jess.

I sigh and continue staring at the ceiling of the tent when a large mosquito lands on the tip of my nose. I swat it away and sit up immediately when I notice the small red bumps on my hands and wrists. They probably got in last night when I rushed out to help Jess. I was in such a hurry when I saw him that I forgot to zip up the tent behind me.

*Great, this is just great.*

I'm still wearing Jess's flannel shirt, so when I roll up the sleeves, I'm glad to see that the mosquitoes weren't able to get me through the thick material. I'm afraid to look at the rest of my body and tell myself it's all in my head when I feel my ankles start to itch.

The sun is just barely up, and I can hear birds chirping outside the tent windows, which would normally be soothing to me, but instead, today it just pisses me off.

I climb out of the sleeping bag before I start rolling it up, ready to get home already. The sooner we pack up all our shit, the sooner I can get home to a hot shower, a nap, and a pint of Denali Double Fudge Chocolate Explosion.

# Chapter Fourteen
## Jess

I hang up the phone and let out a long breath.

*Fuck.*

I really don't want to leave, but Madison said she had no one else to call, which definitely makes me feel guilty not wanting to go since I know she's telling the truth. Now that I know she's in trouble, it makes me feel responsible for her well-being, especially since I told her to call me if she ever needed my help.

When I'd answered the phone, John caught on to the fact that something was the matter pretty quickly and asked about Judy and Sophie. I reassured him that both Sophie and Judy were fine since I got a message from them earlier about the mad sunburn Judy got on her ski trip. I have no idea how I have decent enough cell reception to get messages and calls, but a promise is a promise, and I know I can't leave Madison hanging.

After my phone call with Madison, I leave John rummaging through the fridge in his bus for the hot dogs. I figure the least I can do is say goodbye to Sam before I go. I know she was upset at me earlier, but I don't feel right about just taking off without a word.

I let out a deep breath as I make my way closer to the fire pit and run a hand through my hair. I still have a lingering headache from earlier and my forehead throbs a little when I accidentally graze it with my hand. The painkillers that Sam gave me earlier definitely helped my headache, but my stressful conversation with Madison brought it right back.

I want to ask Sam to come with me, but after our weird conversation by the lake, it might just make things more complicated. I want to tell her everything that's been going on with me lately, but it never really feels like the right time. She did ask me about it, so maybe I'm just a coward.

Judging by how upset Sam was today, she was obviously bothered by what had happened between us. And maybe I'm just dense, but I can't decide if she's upset because she's in love with me or because she hates me for letting any of it happen in the first place. I'm hoping it's the former.

Her jealous attitude at the lake today definitely confirmed that she has some semblance of feelings for me, whether they're positive or negative, I'm still unsure, but at least it's something. I've been holding out hope for what feels like forever, and nothing ever seems to change between us, at least not in a real way, not until now, anyway.

When I get to the chairs around the fire pit, I notice that Sam is no longer standing by the fire warming herself up like she was five minutes ago.

"Where's Sam?" I ask Rebecca and look around, wondering if Sam went into the tent to change into some dry clothes.

"Sorry, can't help you. Migraine, remember?" Rebecca says and points to her head. I give her a look, and she folds her arms across her chest and closes her eyes before resting her head back against the chair, ignoring me.

I shake my head. *Whatever, I don't have time for this.*

"Look, if you're not going to tell me where she is, can you at least just tell Sam that I had to go take care of an emergency and that I'll call her in the morning?" I ask, hoping that Rebecca possesses a shred of empathy within her and will help me out.

"If a bear doesn't eat her in the woods and she manages to come back alive, I'll consider it," Rebecca says as she cracks an eye at me before she promptly goes back to ignoring me.

"Thank you, Rebecca," I say before heading off to check the tent for Sam before I leave. I notice that the zipper's half open and poke my head inside to look around. There's no sign of Sam, only her damp leggings in a heap next to her open bag on the floor.

I'm glad that she's at least out of her wet clothes. If she ends up getting a cold because of me I'll never forgive myself for my stupid swimming idea, especially when I didn't even get into the water with her.

I grab my duffel bag out of the tent before zipping it back up, not wanting Sam to have to deal with my clothes at least. Before I go, I make sure to leave any extra supplies that Sam might need outside next to the tent.

I know that John will tell her I had to leave for an emergency, and I'm hoping that Rebecca will actually relay my message as well, though doubtful. Now that I'm thinking about it, Sam will probably be upset when she finds out that I left, but I really need to get on the road. Even if I haul ass down the mountain, it's still going to take me a good two hours to get back.

I sigh and climb into my Jeep, shutting the door behind me with a slam. I ruffle my hands through my hair and take another deep breath, feeling like a jerk for not coming clean about things. I start the engine and pull out onto the dirt road that leads to the main highway after maneuvering out of our camp and the surrounding trees.

I crank my stereo and lean my head back against the seat, staring at the road ahead of me. I'd grabbed a handful of CDs from my collection at Sophie's, thinking that Sam would be impressed that I remembered her favorite album is Hot Fuss by The Killers, but she didn't even react when I'd put it on earlier.

Even after Bluetooth became a thing, CDs had always sort of been *our* thing, so the thought that she didn't even notice that I brought some today kind of makes me feel bad. I decide to listen to it again and click play on the CD changer instead of using my phone's Bluetooth.

As I'm driving down the road, listening to Mr. Brightside for the second time around, I think about last night, and it feels like it was some sort of fever dream. It took every ounce of self-control in me not to tear off Sam's ugly pajamas and plunge myself deep into her. Her skin felt so soft and warm in my hands, better than anything my imagination could've ever cooked up.

I know the only reason she was so confident is because she was half asleep when she first started grinding on me, but by the time things started to get hot and heavy, she was awake for real. Which means she was fully aware of what she was asking me for and still did it anyway. I thank my lucky stars that Sam was the one who made the first move, because if it were up to me, who knows if I ever would have.

Just thinking about the intimate moment we shared last night has my body warming up, and I crank the AC in my Jeep to help cool myself off. Now is not the time to be fantasizing about Sam and the perfect wet warmth between her legs last night, especially when I'm on my way to Madison.

253

I didn't correct Sam earlier when she basically friend-zoned herself, but I think it's best to leave it that way until I'm able to get my shit sorted out. I don't want to drag anyone else into my mess, least of all her. More than anything, I want to be able to tell her how I really feel, even if she doesn't end up feeling the same way. When that day comes and if she *actually* wants to be with me, I want to make sure nothing is standing in our way. And the way that things are with Madison right now makes that complicated.

I think subconsciously I've always loved Sam, I just didn't realize it until I almost lost her that summer. I thought about telling her how I felt, but it felt like bad timing since she was obviously going through some serious shit with her mom that year. I didn't want to come off as insensitive, so I told myself that I'd be there as a friend to her and then have that talk after things had sort of settled down.

The more time that went by, the closer we got to each other, and the less I wanted to mess that friendship up. Time came and went, and before I knew it, almost five years had passed, and she had a boyfriend.

After I get shit with Madison sorted out, I'll tell Sam how I really feel about her. I *have* to, because if I don't, I think it might actually kill me to keep it in another minute.

I know that Sam thinks that I brushed off what happened between us as some casual hookup, but I know that things can never go back to the way they were before, and I really don't want them to if I'm being honest. I can't just be friends with her anymore, and certainly not just friends with benefits either.

I want all of her.

~

"What do you mean you haven't spoken to her since then?" Aunt Judy says as she scolds me from her recliner by the window.

After I made it back to town and got things handled with Madison, I tried calling Sam, but it went straight to voicemail. I'd figured as much would happen since she didn't seem to be able to get very good reception earlier while I was with her.

I called her again the next morning, but the same thing happened, and I got her voicemail again. I told myself she probably just needed some space after what happened between us, so I tried not to overthink it.

At this point, though, it's clear she's obviously avoiding me, because that was five days ago.

"I've tried texting and calling her nonstop, but she won't answer me," I say, rubbing the back of my neck with my hand. Aunt Judy gives me a sweeping look, stopping on my feet.

"What? What's wrong?" I ask as I look down at my shoes, hoping I didn't track mud or dog shit into her room and onto her new rug.

"You seemed to walk in here just fine, so I'm just wondering if there's something wrong with your legs," Judy says as she frowns at me and crosses her stubby arms over her chest.

"Ha, very funny," I say and roll my eyes. "I just don't want to make Sam uncomfortable is all," I say and shrug. "She's obviously avoiding me for a reason. I think she just wants some space," I say, trailing off as I look toward Judy's open window.

"Strange. Now, why in the hell would Samantha need space from you?" Judy asks, narrowing her eyes at me. "What did you do?"

Worried that she might see right through me, I turn my body toward the window and tuck my hands into my pockets.

"Nothing," I say and shrug, still not making eye contact with her.

Instead of interrogating me any further, she just gives me a quiet *hmmm* in response.

"What?" I ask as I crook my head to the side and turn to look at her.

"Nothing, I didn't say a damn thing," Aunt Judy says, taking a sip of her tea before folding her hands neatly in her lap.

"Seriously? Of all times, now you decide you're gonna hold back?" I say and let out a breath.

"You're not ready to hear it. Come back later, and we'll see," she says and takes another sip of her tea before fluffing up her gray old-lady perm as she looks out the window, ignoring me.

*Stubborn as always.*

I sigh as I rub my forehead before taking a seat on the edge of Aunt Judy's bed.

"Jess, grab me that red blanket over there, would ya? I'm starting to catch a chill," Judy says, faking an exaggerated shiver as she gestures to the top of her dresser across the room.

*And still as bossy as ever, apparently.* I roll my eyes, expecting nothing less from her.

I walk over and as I pull the blanket off the dresser, something falls to the ground that was resting underneath it. I bend down to pick up the gray hoodie and notice that a few colorful rocks fall out of one of the pockets as they roll onto the ground. I pick up the hoodie and small stones and walk over to Judy as I hold it up between us.

"That sure as hell doesn't look like my blanket," she says.

"All right, cut the shit, Judy, why do you have Sam's hoodie?" I ask, not wanting to play her game.

"Because she came to see me and forgot it, that's why," Judy says, and blinks at me with an innocent expression on her face.

"So you let me babble on like an idiot that whole time, meanwhile, you'd already talked to her?" I ask, feeling kind of annoyed.

"You never asked if *I* had spoken to her, only that she wouldn't respond to *you*. You really are quite self-centered, you know," Judy says, giving me an attitude.

"Well, what did she say? What did she tell you? Did she mention if she was upset with me?" I ask, trying not to sound too desperate, but the urgency of my questions does little to hide that fact.

"Honestly, she didn't tell me much, but I'm still not convinced that you didn't do anything to her," Judy says, finally taking our conversation seriously.

I let out a breath and run my hands through my hair as I take a seat on the edge of the bed once again.

"I… *ah fuck*" I ruffle my hands through my hair roughly as I look down at the floor, unable to finish my sentence, not knowing how much Sam would be okay with me telling Aunt Judy.

"I knew it! So, you did do something!" Judy says, wagging a wrinkly finger at me. "I can't believe you!" she says as she flings one of the scones she was having with her tea right at my head.

"What the hell—you don't even know what I did!" I say, dodging the pastry as it crumbles to the floor behind me.

"You'd better go find her and fix this right now, Jess Cameron," Judy says angrily as she throws a hand toward me. "If you don't, you're gonna end up losing her for good, is that what you want?" Judy asks, raising her brows at me dramatically.

"No, of course not!" I say, rubbing my hands over my face before standing. "I'm just afraid that I seriously fucked things up," I say as I slump down in the padded chair across from Judy with a huff.

"Whatever you did, it couldn't be as bad as losing her. Do you really think she's gonna wait around forever for your sorry ass to finally make a move? *I swear,* Jess, I feel like I might die of old age waiting for you to grow a pair already!" Judy says, raising a brow, and now I'm sure that Sam didn't tell her what really happened between us.

"Damn, were you always this blunt about things?" I ask and chuckle at her direct words.

"Sure have, your thick head just never bothered listening to me before," Judy says, smiling as she tosses a small piece of her scone to hit me in the chest.

I laugh and thank her before kissing her on the forehead and rush out the door with Sam's hoodie in one hand and the small rocks clutched in the other.

# Chapter Fifteen

I let out a huff after closing my book a tad too aggressively, the cover slamming closed against the pages. Having read the same passage three separate times, I finally decide to give it a rest for the night.

My mind has been too all over the place to get any quality sleep, and during the day, I'm so exhausted from tossing and turning all night to be much good to anyone either.

*Not that they want to hang out with me anyway…*

I try not to sulk and think that maybe it really is just coincidentally bad timing that everyone seems so busy lately.

My dad's been spending a lot of time at the club this week, so I haven't really seen much of him since we got home from camping. And even though it's more than a year away, Rebecca's too busy with wedding preparations to put much energy into tormenting me at the moment, which I'm grateful for. I doubt she's actually doing any of the real work though, she's probably just using wedding prep as an excuse to flash her tacky ring off to anyone within a two-foot radius.

It's not really a surprise that Chris has been avoiding me since that seems to be the norm for us now. It makes me feel bad that we don't really have the greatest relationship, but I try not to dwell too much on it, knowing the harder I try to force anything between us, the more he'll just resent me for it later.

And as for Jess... I'm not *not* avoiding him, at least that's what I'd told Aunt Judy yesterday when I went to visit her. Right away, she knew that something was up. Judy was always pretty good at reading me that way, so I gave her the abridged version of what'd happened on the camping trip. I managed to leave out the steamy parts between Jess and me—and although she didn't press me on it—I'm pretty sure she could tell that something along those lines had definitely gone down.

I look at the clock and sigh. *Damn, it's only half past seven.*

I've already watched more TV than I can handle, and reading is out of the question. I'm feeling pretty exhausted and wonder if maybe I should just call it a night already, but after thinking about the restless night that's in store for me, I change my mind.

I still haven't had a chance to get together with Sophie like I wanted to, since she's been pretty busy with her internship these last few days. I texted her earlier today to hang out since we haven't gotten to properly celebrate yet, but she'd said that she had a long day and was going to turn in early. She promised we could hang on one of her lunch breaks next week, but if I don't get out of this house soon, I'm going to lose my mind.

I throw on some sweats after deciding to head over to Sophie's. It is Friday, after all, and even though she told me she still has to go into the office on Saturdays, it's not usually until after noon.

When I go to grab my gray hoodie, I can't find it anywhere and remember that I must've left it in Judy's room yesterday by accident. We'd made plans to get pedicures tomorrow afternoon, so I remind myself to get it then.

On my way to Sophie's, I stop at a convenience store to stock up on some junk food. I figure that if she's sleeping, I'll have to bribe her with an apology bag of Hot Cheetos and an energy drink to make it up to her.

I feel a bit selfish since she'd said she was tired and all, but I could really use some girl talk, even if she doesn't know that my problems are about Jess. Aside from my boy problems, there's so much I feel like we need to catch up on. I still haven't even told Sophie about what happened that day with Elliott and Jess, or about what happened with Daniel before I left to come home. Soph is usually one for some good boy drama herself, so I'm excited to hear more about what happened during her graduation week.

When I pull up the long gravel driveway to Grandpa Millard's old house, I feel a twinge of sadness when I think about him. We used to spend so much time here as kids, it feels so odd to be here without him now.

After he passed away last year, Sophie decided to keep the house even though she was away at school and said that she didn't have the heart to sell it. She wanted to keep it as a tribute to how Grandpa Millard always wanted to make sure that everyone always felt welcome, and like they had a place they could always go if things ever got rough.

I put my car in park and unbuckle my seatbelt with a click, and when I step out of my car, a thought suddenly occurs to me.

*Jess. How could I have forgotten he's staying with Soph?*

It's just after dusk, and it's hard to tell for sure, but I don't see his Jeep when I look around. I try not to think about where he is or *who* he's with at the moment and try to shake the thoughts from my head as I rush to get inside the house.

When I approach the house, I notice that all of the lights inside are off, including all of the porch lights, and wonder if Sophie really did turn in for the night.

I've been here so many times that I could find my way around with a blindfold on, so even in the dark, I'm able to find the key underneath the doormat to the side door of the house.

I slide the key into the lock of the door and slowly open it. I half expect the old thing to creak, but it doesn't. I also notice that the cracked shutters are fixed, and the side door looks like it's been recently painted as well.

*Looks like someone's been busy lately...*

Images of a sweaty Jess wearing a tool belt, doing manly chores has my face heating up, and I shake my head at the thought.

*Keep it together, Sam.*

I slip into the kitchen before shutting the door behind me, quietly locking it again.

I set the bag of snacks I brought with me onto the kitchen counter just as I hear a voice and notice a faint glow illuminating the hallway leading to the living room. I wonder if Sophie might've fallen asleep with the TV on, and I quietly pad down the hallway toward the living room to check.

I try to be quiet with my footsteps as I cross the floor of the hallway and tell myself that I'll probably just head home if she's actually asleep. I thought I wouldn't feel guilty about waking Sophie up, but now that I'm here, I don't think I can bring myself to do it, especially since it's purely for my own selfish reasons.

"Soph...?" I whisper as I peek around the corner to the living room, half expecting her to be sprawled out across the couch surrounded by junk food wrappers.

"What..."

My words catch in my throat, and my heart thunders in my ears as I try to take in what I'm seeing.

Chris sits on the living room couch in his underwear, and Sophie straddles his lap with her arms resting around his shoulders.

Aside from Chris's boxers, they're both naked, with random articles of clothing and playing cards strewn around them on the couch cushions and floor. They look up when I speak, surprised looks on both of their faces.

I look to my brother and then to my best friend and feel nauseous.

Sophie scrambles to cover herself with a blanket, and for what feels like the first time in forever, Chris gives me an apologetic look instead of his usual one of disdain.

"I-I... I have to go—" I say and turn around before I rush back down the hallway.

"Sam, wait!" Sophie calls after me. "WAIT!"

I'm halfway through the kitchen when I feel her grab the back of my arm to stop me, and I rip away from her hold as I turn to face her.

Words fail me as I just stare at my best friend, and I feel my features contort as I try not to cry. When Sophie doesn't say anything either, I turn to leave again.

"Stop! Sam, you don't understand," she says from behind me as she follows me to the door.

"*Understand what?*" I retort, my words finally finding me as I whip around to face her.

"That you lied to me?" I spit, and she flinches at the venom in my words, my almost tears now replaced with anger.

"Sam… I—" she starts, but also seems at a loss for words.

"You what? Are you going to tell me that you *love him* or something?" I say, and she flinches again as I mock her.

"N-no… I…" Sophie says as she looks around frantically, and her discomfort at my accusation is obvious.

"I can't believe you've been blowing me off all week for this," I say, gesturing down the hallway to where a fully clothed Chris is now lurking awkwardly in the shadows. We briefly make eye contact, and I just shake my head at him before I turn my attention back to Sophie.

"Look, I know I've been busy, I'm sorry I—"

"Too busy for me, but not too busy to screw my brother? Is that it?" I say as I sneer at her, completely uninterested in hearing her bullshit apology.

"Sam, I'm sorry you had to see us like that, but I promise it's not like that!" Sophie says, still fumbling at an apology as she tries to reach out to me.

"Jesus Christ! I couldn't give two shits about you fucking my brother!" I yell, pulling away from her, and Sophie gives me a confused look.

"I needed you, and you lied to me!" I say, and hope that Sophie can see the hurt in my eyes.

"About Chris, about being too busy to see me for the last week and a half—what else have you lied to me about?" I ask as I throw my hands in the air.

I can tell that she's obviously uncomfortable, and before I let her answer, I continue my angry rant. "Were you actually at your internship when you flaked out on camping, or were you just hooking up with other random guys like always?" I demand, still seething mad at her.

"*Is* there even an internship?" I ask.

"That's not fair, Sam," she says, her eyes glossy with tears.

"I always knew you were a slut, I just never thought you'd ditch me so that you could blow my brother." The words barely leave my lips before I feel Sophie's hand as it collides with my left cheek.

The sound of the slap echoes throughout the dark kitchen, and I stagger backward, momentarily stunned as I raise a hand to my burning cheek.

"*Fuck you*," I spit at her.

Sophie clutches the blanket around her as she stares at me with a look of shock on her face, as if realizing what she'd just done. We've definitely had our fair share of fights over the years, but it's never come to physical blows, so being slapped by her feels like another level of betrayal.

I grab my keys off the counter and pull open the kitchen side door to leave, not bothering with the snacks I'd brought with me. Just as I pull open the door, someone pushes it open from the other side, and I stumble backward a few steps from the force.

Jess stands in the doorway and gives me a stunned look for a split second before I watch as recognition flashes across his eyes. Jess smiles his perfect charming smile at me, and I can't help but admire how white his teeth are. My annoyance is already at an all-time high, especially after seeing his stupid sexy self looking fine as ever in his backwards ball cap and light green t-shirt.

*Dammit, could this night get any worse?*

"Howdy, Sam. Here for a late-night booty call?" Jess says, winking at me, obviously oblivious to what just went down in the kitchen.

I shake my head and let out an exasperated breath, looking down as I push past him.

"Hey, wait up, where're you going?" Jess calls after me. "Dude, where are your clothes?" I hear him ask Sophie, but I don't bother with trying to make out her response.

I was so preoccupied with Jess earlier that I didn't even notice Chris's stupid lifted truck right in the middle of Sophie's driveway, and I let out a frustrated groan. My shoes crunch loudly against the gravel of the driveway, and I will them to move as fast as they'll take me, wishing I could teleport away directly underneath a heavy rock.

"Hey, Ryan, wait! What's going on?" I hear Jess's voice calling from behind me, and he's closer now that I'm almost to my car.

I stop and turn to face him. "Why don't you ask your skank of a cousin," I say angrily, immediately regretting the words as soon as I say them.

"Hey now," he warns, giving me a look.

"*Shit.* I know, I'm sorry," I say with a sigh and rub my hands over my face.

Neither of us says anything, and a heavy silence falls between the two of us. I look up and watch as Jess nervously rubs the back of his neck with his hand.

"Look, Sam, this is obviously not the right time for this, but—"

"I'm sorry, I have to go," I say, turning to reach for the door handle of my car.

"You're avoiding me," he says, and I can hear the hurt in his voice. "It's obvious. I thought we left things okay between us at the lake, but your attitude toward me would say otherwise," Jess says with a nervous chuckle.

"You're right," I say, letting out a breath as I turn back to face him. "I *have* been avoiding you."

I knew I wouldn't be able to avoid him forever, and that the second I saw him again, any lingering anger would quickly dissipate, just like it always does whenever I'm in his presence.

"Ryan, how are we supposed to fix things if I can't ever get a hold of you and you're also never home?" Jess says, raising a brow as he calls me out.

"Okay, I'll admit to ignoring the calls and texts, but I've been home all week, and you haven't stopped by once," I say, my turn to call *him* out.

"Okay, I know, that one's on me," he says, putting his hands up defensively, and I notice the small brown paper bag that he's holding in his right hand along with his jacket.

"Is that what I think it is?" I say, stepping toward Jess before quickly snatching the bag out of his hand. "Midnight cookies, eh? Looks like I'm rubbing off on you," I joke, trying to lighten the mood.

"Well, technically it's only like nine thirty, so I don't think they're allowed to count as midnight cookies *just* yet," Jess says as he cracks a small smile. "They're actually for you…" Jess says sheepishly, rubbing another hand behind his neck before half tucking it in his front pocket.

"Yeah right, nice save," I say and roll my eyes as I open the bag and peek inside. The large cookies smell delicious, and I have to stop myself from taking a sample bite out of one.

"Believe what you want, Ryan, but I'm actually just coming back from John's house. The cute little hermit who lives there wasn't home, so I was going to save them until I could get a hold of her," he says, shrugging.

"Very funny," I say flatly before closing the bag after taking the tiniest bite from one of the cookies. Any treat from Leonard's Bakery always makes for a tasty breakfast, so my mouth waters at the thought.

"Wait, why were you bringing me cookies?" I ask Jess, eyeing him. "And, is that my hoodie?" I ask and gesture to the gray jacket in his other hand when I recognize the pink drawstrings.

"Judy asked me to give it back to you," Jess says as he hands the hoodie to me.

"Like I said, it's kind of hard to communicate with someone who won't ever pick up their phone," he says and gives me a crooked smile. "Besides, I feel like I kind of owed it to you, you know, after forcing you to ride down the mountain with John and the She Devil," Jess says with a shrug and gives me an apologetic smile.

"Surprisingly, it wasn't actually all that bad, I just blasted My Chemical Romance in my headphones while I channeled my angsty teenage years," I say, and Jess laughs as he gives me a full smile, causing my stomach to do a small flip.

"But I will say, you definitely owe me one for putting away that damn tent all alone," I say, and Jess tilts his head at me with a questioning smile.

"Do you mean to tell me that the all-knowing Sam Ryan couldn't figure out how to put away a simple tent?" he asks, trying to hold back his smile.

"I never said that I didn't know how," I say, putting my hands on my hips. "It was just a major pain in the ass, that's all."

I shake my head at the images that cross my mind of how ridiculous I must've looked fighting with that stupid tent and its four hundred poles. Especially after getting zero sleep that night, and without an ounce of caffeine in my system either.

"Well, next time I promise to be there, and then I can help you put it away," he counters.

"And, what makes you think there'll be a next time?" I ask, raising my brows. "This last trip was kind of a disaster, I don't know if I want a repeat of that," I say, scoffing lightly.

"Hmm, it's just a hunch I guess," Jess says with a shrug. "Especially since I know how much you enjoy tent camping," he says. Jess's voice is low, and I can feel his heavy gaze on me even in the dark.

I'm grateful that the porch light is still off, otherwise, he'd see my flaming cheeks, and I do an internal facepalm at my own stupidity. You'd think I'd be used to his flirting after all this time, but he still manages to get me flustered every time. I don't say anything, afraid the tone of my voice will betray how I'm feeling, so I just stare at him.

"See, wasn't that fast?" Jess says.

"What was?" I ask.

"You were avoiding me, and shit's still kind of weird, but look at how fast we got back to *us*," he says, and I can hear the soft smile in his voice.

And there he goes. Ruining it. *Us* as in Sam Ryan and Jess Cameron—platonic friends—not *us* as in *together* us.

"Goodnight, Jess," I say and give him a halfhearted smile. I pull on the handle of my car door, and he reaches out to stop it as he braces his hand on the top of the doorframe.

"I was serious about before. Let me make it up to you. Coffee, tomorrow. I'll pick you up at eleven. You should be up by then, right?" he teases.

I roll my eyes at him and pull on the door handle again. "Night, Jess," I say again. This time, he doesn't stop me when I try to open my door, and removes his hand from the car as he steps to the side so I can climb in.

"Think about it, okay, Ry?" he says. I shut the door and roll down the window with a *whirr*. "I'm not gonna go to sleep until you text me," Jess says with a pouty smile as he leans in toward me through the open window.

"*Goodnight*," I say, putting the car in reverse.

Jess steps away from the vehicle and calls after me as I back out of the driveway. "I'll even let you get an extra-large whatever the hell sugary drink with extra whipped cream and sprinkles!" he yells.

I smile to myself as I see Jess's dark silhouette waving after me in my rearview mirror.

It's kind of ironic that I was going to see Sophie to help get my mind off of Jess, but then *he* ended up being the one to get my mind off the shit show earlier with her and Chris.

I don't realize I'm grinning the entire drive home, momentarily forgetting about how upset with Sophie I am, and think about my coffee order for tomorrow.

My smile widens.

*What a chump. As if I'd ever pass up a free coffee.*

# Chapter Sixteen

I check my phone for the tenth time, and only one minute has passed since I last looked, even though it feels like it's been at least ten minutes since then. I'm sitting on my dad's living room couch waiting for Jess to pick me up, and I fidget anxiously with one of my rings.

Last night, after I got home—and after I'd devoured the cookies from Leonard's—I texted Jess to pick me up at eleven and to prepare his wallet for the coffee monstrosity I planned on ordering today. I wasn't able to sleep very well, which was no surprise after what had happened between Sophie and me earlier.

Apparently, getting absolutely no sleep is something that's slowly becoming a regular thing for me. I just hope that I don't get permanent bags under my eyes because of it.

I keep fiddling with my rings before I wipe my palms on my jeans for the hundredth time to dry the sweat that keeps accumulating there. I don't know why I'm nervous, it's not like it's a date or something, and the thought makes my heart drop a little. Jess doesn't see me in that way, he made that clear the other day. The whole "you're so important to me" speech should've made me happy, but instead it just made me feel worse.

I've kept my feelings for Jess up high on a shelf for so long that I'm having a hard time putting them back, especially after allowing myself to feel even the teeniest shred of hope the other day.

*Friends.* I tell myself. *Be content with that, Sam.*

I sigh and think about Sophie. I don't know how she's able to handle the no-strings-attached life. To be honest, even though my last relationship was that way, I'd always hoped for more with Daniel. I think that, for the most part, I don't *hate* those kinds of relationships. They're definitely less messy, at least until one of you starts to get attached.

I *was* upset about Daniel, but I think that this time feels different for me since it's Jess we're talking about. If I didn't have such a pathetic lifelong yearning for him, maybe I wouldn't be overthinking it so much.

In a typical scenario, we'd hook up, he'd tell me he didn't feel anything for me, we'd call it quits, and then both move on, no problem, easy peasy …if only it were that simple for me.

A knock on the door breaks my train of thought, and I stand to answer it. I already know who it is, but regardless, my heart still races a bit. When I open the door, Jess stands smiling on the front porch wearing his signature dark jeans, navy blue shirt, and black boots. His shoulder-length hair is perfectly tousled, like he just got out of the shower, and I can already smell his conditioner from where I'm standing.

"Morning," he says, smiling before giving me a once-over. "Should we go?" he asks and jerks his thumb behind him.

I grab my purse off the entryway table and walk past him out the door toward his Jeep. I catch the familiar scent of his woody cologne as I brush past him and inhale just enough not to make it obvious that I am indeed smelling him like some creepo.

"Hey, you took the top off," I say, noticing that the top and doors of the Jeep are gone, replaced with a mesh bikini top. "Looks good," I say as I step over the ledge and climb in before putting my seat belt on.

Jess smiles as he turns to look at me after climbing into the driver's seat. "I can't explain it, but I just love how free it makes me feel," he says.

It takes everything in me not to tell him that I know the feeling all too well, so I just smile at him instead and say nothing.

"Ready?" Jess asks, clicking in his own seatbelt, and I nod at him in response.

He puts his hand behind my headrest and looks behind us as we back out of the driveway. Jess let me pick where we're getting coffee from, so I chose the small café that he, Sophie, and I would frequent in high school.

We ride to the coffee shop in silence, the sound of the wind drowning out any chance of conversation. When we pull into the parking lot of the Blue Diamond Café, Jess puts the Jeep in park before looking over at me. A large smile crosses his face, and he lets out a huge belly laugh as he throws his head back against the headrest.

"What?" I ask, grabbing at the visor. From what I can see in the tiny mirror, my hair is sticking up all over the place, even with it all pulled back in its large clip. I frown and grumble to myself as I try to fix the unruly pieces that are standing up everywhere.

"Here, let me help. The mirrors in here are a joke, there's no way you're gonna get them all," Jess says as he softly grabs my wrist to stop me.

I turn to him, and he gently smooths down the remaining pieces of hair that managed to escape the clip. I watch his handsome face intently as he fixes my hair, and how he furrows his brows in concentration.

"May I?" he asks, and I wonder what he means until I feel his hand as it gently grasps the back of my hair clip.

I nod and feel him gently release the clip, causing my long hair to fall down over my shoulders.

"There, that's better," Jess says, his voice low as our eyes meet.

I find myself leaning in, and am slowly closing the small gap between our faces before Jess clears his throat and we both pull away. My cheeks feel warm, and I'm a little embarrassed that I let myself get caught up in the moment so easily. I unbuckle my seatbelt and turn to step out of the Jeep, a slight flush staining my cheeks.

*Damn, this friend thing is gonna be more difficult than I thought.*

"Hold on, let me get that for you," Jess says, already halfway out of the Jeep, before rushing around to my side. I watch as he quickly circles the vehicle and wonder what he means by that.

"Your Highness," he says as he grabs hold of an invisible door and pretends to open it for me. Jess smiles and does a half-bow as he holds his hand out for me to take.

"You're such a dork," I say, playfully rolling my eyes at him before grabbing his hand.

When I step out of the Jeep, Jess's hand lingers on mine for a second longer than normal as we walk, and I wonder if he's actually going to let me go or not.

To my disappointment, though, the moment is quickly over when we reach the door to the small café. Jess lets go of my hand as he gets the door for us, and gestures for me to go in ahead of him.

"Damn, you were not kidding, were you?" Jess says as he eyes my drink from his side of the booth.

I'm sure he thought he was being funny with his comment about getting an extra-large whipped cream whatever, but I did in fact take him up on that offer.

I take another sip of my drink and do a little happy dance at the sugar explosion that hits my tongue. I got an XL triple-M explosion: marshmallow, matcha, and mocha; extra whipped cream, heavy on the chocolate drizzle, with just a *tiny* bit of blue sprinkles on top.

"I can't believe they're still willing to make that for you after all this time," he says, eyeing my drink with a look of disgust.

"Only because I'm special," I say as I bat my eyelashes at him. "This is a Sam Ryan exclusive recipe. Only a select few are even privy to its existence, so you can keep counting yourself lucky," I say before taking another sip through my straw and do another little happy dance.

"Damn, an *exclusive*, you say? Who would've ever thought," Jess says teasingly.

I shrug at him from across the booth. "Don't you remember? You're actually the one who invented it," I say, thinking back to all the times we used to study here after class in high school.

"Did I really?" Jess asks with a crooked smile as he furrows his brows.

"Remember? We were sitting over there in the corner," I say and point across the café, ironically to where a small group of teenagers is sitting.

"I mean, that *was* our favorite table," Jess says, smiling at me. "Some of my best ideas came from sitting over in that booth."

I shake my head at the memory and can't believe that such a simple time feels like a lifetime ago.

"That day, I'd just bombed my trig test and you were trying to cheer me up. You'd made some joke about ordering all these crazy flavors mixed together so I actually tried it—though the chocolate drizzle was my idea. Pretty genius, right?" I ask and wag my brows up and down at him.

"It's definitely something…" Jess says with a smirk as he shakes his head at me. "It's good to see that your tastes are still the same—sugar with a side of sugar. Looks like some things never change," he says with a wink.

I give Jess a squinty-eyed look as I shake my head. "Here, just try some," I say, and slide my glass toward him.

"No thanks, I'll stick with what I have," Jess says, lifting the mug of black coffee to his lips before taking a sip.

I impulsively reach across the table to feel his forehead.

"Uh, what're you doing?" Jess asks as he tries to hold back a smile and I quickly pull my hand away.

"Just wondering if you're feeling all right?" I ask, observing his drink.

"Yeah, why?" Jess asks, raising a questioning brow at me as he sets down his mug.

"Well, unless that's decaf"—I nod to his coffee—"then there's something seriously wrong with you, Mr. No Caffeine," I say jokingly.

"Couldn't sleep, is all, figured I'd take a page out of your book, see what all the hype's about," he says with a shrug and a crooked smile.

"Well, if that's the case, then you're off to the wrong start. Here," I say and slide my glass toward him a second time.

I try not to think about how if both of our lips touch the same straw, it'll count as an indirect kiss. It wouldn't be the first time we've shared a drink, but now that I've felt those perfect full lips on my neck, I can't help but wonder what they'd feel like pressed to my mouth instead.

"One sip, just try it, and I promise you'll feel better," I say, nodding to the glass as I struggle to keep my mind out of the gutter.

"If this puts me into a sugar coma, I'm holding you personally responsible," Jess says before taking a hesitant sip through the straw.

"Well?" I ask, wagging my brows in anticipation.

"*Awful*," he says, trying to hold back his smile.

"Liar," I say, and watch as he takes another drink from the straw before sliding my glass back toward me.

"Okay, it's not terrible. It's definitely not as bad as it looks," he says, smiling.

"Not able to sleep then, huh?" I ask as I casually stir my drink with my straw. "Thinking about work?"

"I mean, sure, among other things," Jess says, staring at me with those eyes again.

"So…" I say, still trying not to think about Jess's lips as I change the subject. "You never told me why you're back in town. I thought your contract with the rig didn't end for a while?" I ask.

"Why, eager to get rid of me?" he asks with a smirk.

"Just curious, is all," I say and shrug.

"I guess I just felt like taking some time off. What good is having money if you don't ever spend any of it or go anywhere?" he says. Jess takes another drink of his coffee before making a face and sets the mug back down.

"True," I say. "Is that why the new Jeep, then?" I ask, wondering if he's planning on staying in town for a while since he bought a vehicle instead of just renting one for the time being.

"Yeah. Grandpa Millard's old Jeep finally kicked the bucket a few weeks after I got back into town," Jess says, shaking his head.

I smile to myself and remember how many times that old bucket of rust broke down with us in it. I used to pretend to be annoyed by it, but I always thanked the heavens if I managed to get stranded with Jess, always praying it just happened to be the two of us.

"I'm glad that this new Jeep is more reliable, but it just doesn't feel the same. I'm thinking I'll just restore Grandpa Millard's instead and use the green one for a backup," Jess says with a shrug, and I can't help but wonder if he's as fond of those times as I am.

"Well, if you need somebody to hold a flashlight or a wrench for you, I might know someone," I say nonchalantly, thinking that he's definitely planning on staying in town for a while if he's considering taking on a project like that.

"Really?" Jess says and lowers his eyebrows as he bites the corner of his lower lip. "I might just take you up on that," he says, and he gives me a look that makes my heart flutter.

*Don't do it, Sam. Don't do it.*

I can't help myself from picturing a mechanic Jess all greasy under the hood of that old Jeep ...or how said hood would be the perfect height for him to bend me over on...

I shake my head and take another sip of my drink. Jess gives me a questioning look but doesn't say anything. I nervously clear my throat and sit up straight, before trying to change the subject.

"In between running errands for my dad, it looks like Sophie's been keeping you busy around Grandpa Millard's house," I say, remembering the repaired shutters from last night.

"Surprisingly, she hasn't asked me to do anything," Jess says with a shrug.

"What about all the new paint everywhere?" I ask and raise a brow.

"I asked Soph about it too—since there's no way it was her—and she says that she got one of her new handyman boy toys to do it," Jess says with a chuckle, and we both smile at that. Sophie always did know how to get her way with things.

"So, if you haven't been fixing the house or working on the old Jeep, what have you been up to?" I ask curiously.

"Well, as you know, there's not much to do in this town, so I've been... sorta... painting again," Jess says shyly as he rubs the back of his neck with a hand.

"What? That's amazing! You have to show me what you've been working on," I say and smile widely at him.

It's been ages since I've seen any of Jess's work, probably since high school at least. Come to think of it, I did notice some painting supplies on the kitchen counter while I was at Sophie's, I just figured they were leftovers from whoever was painting the house.

"How long have you been painting again? When can I see it? What is it of this time?" I ask, and Jess just smiles at me from his side of the booth. "What?" I ask when he doesn't answer me.

"Nothing, I just didn't expect you to be so excited, is all," he says. "It's not like I'm a pro or anything. I know you know it's really just a hobby," he says and shrugs.

"Of course I'm excited, you're like, insanely talented, Jess," I say as I beam at him.

"You really think so?" he asks bashfully.

"Absolutely. I've always loved all of your work," I say and instinctively reach across the table to grab his hand. "I know how much you love it, so why did you ever stop?" I ask him.

"Guess I lost my inspiration," he says softly, and we hold each other's gazes, Jess's hand still in mine.

"*So…*" We both say at the same time, and I pull my hand away from his and place it in my lap, electricity buzzing through my fingertips at the brief contact we'd shared.

"Sorry, you go," I say.

"No, it's okay, you go," Jess counters.

"I was just gonna say that… that the weather's sure been nice lately, hasn't it? Usually this time of year—" I say, wanting to smack myself for chickening out.

"Cut the shit, Ryan, I know that's not what you were really gonna say," Jess says, and gives me a lopsided grin. I should've known he'd be able to see right through me.

I let out a small *humph*, and sigh. "And how do you know what I was gonna say, huh?" I ask, narrowing my eyes at him as I fold my arms across my chest. "For your information, I find weather patterns to be *quite* fascinating," I say, sticking my nose up in the air playfully.

"All right, fine, if you're not going to ask, then I'll just tell you," Jess says as he folds his arms and leans down against the table.

"Tell me what?" I ask, playing dumb as I take another sip of my drink.

"About why I had to run off the other night," he says, watching my reaction closely. "I know you're aware that things with Madison are a touchy subject with me, but you don't have anything to worry about."

"Why would I care about that?" I ask, and look away, trying to seem indifferent as I finish off the last of my drink. I loudly wiggle my straw across the bottom of the glass to get the last of the whipped cream from in between the melting ice cubes.

When Jess says nothing, I look up at him, and he furrows his brows as he studies my expression.

"*What?*" I ask defensively. "You basically told me that you'd never date me, so why should I care if Madison is your girlfriend or not?" I say and take a breath, trying to stop myself from getting too worked up. Jess gives me a serious look, and I think we both know I'm lying because if it didn't really bother me, I wouldn't have reacted like I did.

I let out a deep sigh. "Jess, it's none of my business, so why do you keep bringing it up? Is this really what you wanna talk about right now?" I ask, sitting back against the worn cushion of the booth.

"I didn't say that I'd never date you, I just said that things are complicated right now and I don't want to confuse you," he says, ignoring my questions.

"What a crock of shit!" I retort angrily. "You keep saying 'it's complicated' but then still don't explain anything!"

"You say that you don't want to *not* not date me and then shut me down, but then *still* flirt and make eyes at me every chance you get!" I say, throwing my hands in the air.

"You say you don't want to confuse me, but you're doing just that! *I don't know what you want from me!*" I say angrily, gesturing back at myself dramatically, and I notice that the other people in the café are starting to look our way.

"Look, Sam, I'm sorry. I'm just trying to protect you," Jess says with an exasperated sigh as he rubs his hands over his eyes.

Of all the places to talk about his "not" girlfriend, this isn't one that I'd like to have the memory tied to. I hate myself for the raging jealousy that burns through me at the mere mention of Madison's name.

*I want it to be me. Why can't it just be me?*

I look Jess in his beautiful eyes, and ache at the longing in my chest, feeling like the weight of it might suffocate me.

"The only thing I need protection from right now is *you*," I say, immediately regretting it after seeing the hurt look on his face.

Unable to take it back, I stand and rush out of the café, the bell on the door ringing as it slams shut behind me.

The moment I step outside, tears start to well in my eyes, blurring my vision as I try to orient myself. I rush over to the edge of the sidewalk trying to think of the quickest escape route. Half of the old buildings in downtown have been torn down and redeveloped, making everything look so different from when I'd seen it last.

"Ryan!" I hear Jess calling to me from the entrance of the café.

I know I can't talk to him right now. No matter how hard I try to put away my feelings for Jess, they just keep falling back down as if the shelf they were on is now made of paper or something.

At this rate, I'm never going to get over him. I need to get out of here, and not just *away*, but out of town.

Not knowing exactly where I'm going, I pick a direction and run down the street, turning and weaving through the alleyways of the businesses.

I stop and lean back against the brick wall behind a music store, trying to catch my breath, when I hear Jess calling my name. I duck behind a large dumpster, trying to hide from him, when I hear him stop at the mouth of the alleyway. He's still calling my name as he stops momentarily, and for a second, I think I've been found out.

I don't move as I hold my breath, still crouched behind the smelly dumpster. I hear the sound of Jess's voice again, followed by his heavy footsteps on the pavement as they slowly get farther and farther away.

I sigh and slump back against the brick wall next to the large dumpster as I try to catch my breath.

*What a shit summer this is turning out to be. I should've never even come home.*

I'm sure that no one will even notice if I pack up and head back to school, and it's still early enough in the day that after I see Aunt Judy later, I should still be able to make it back to my apartment before dark.

I peek around the side of the rusted green metal of the dumpster and check to see if the coast is clear. I stand and rub a hand over my forehead as I stare down the length of the alleyway toward the street.

I think that if I run back in the direction Jess just came from, I might be able to lose him completely. I'm still not entirely sure of where I am, and wonder if maybe I should just try to hail a cab before I end up getting myself more lost.

Just as I pull out my phone, I hear what sounds like a shoe gently crunching on broken glass when I feel someone grab me from behind. They snake one arm around my waist, roughly placing their other hand over my mouth.

For a split second, I think it's Jess and wonder how he was able to get behind me with only one way into the alley. Almost immediately after being grabbed, I recognize the smell of cheap cologne and cigarettes.

Elliott.

"Well, if this isn't my lucky day," he says, and I struggle as I try to get away from him, the smell of his rancid breath on my neck already making me want to puke.

"Let go of me!" I try to yell, my words coming out muffled from the pressure of his hand over my mouth.

"I don't think so, sweetheart. You—FUCK!" Elliott yells as I bite down hard on the fingers covering my mouth, causing him to release me momentarily.

"*JESS!*" I yell as I run away from Elliott, but I only make it a few feet before he grabs me again. Elliott drags me back down the alleyway as he twists my arm behind my back, and the pressure makes my eyes water.

"What the hell do you want?" I manage to rasp out as I claw at Elliott's other hand that's now threatening to crush my windpipe.

"*Shhhhh*, calm down, I just wanna talk," Elliott coos mockingly as I continue to struggle against him. "Last I recall, we had some unfinished business," he says, releasing my throat.

As if reading my mind, he gives me a warning by twisting my arm further behind my back, and the pain is almost unbearable.

"I know you like to play rough, but if you say a word, I won't hesitate to break it," Elliott whispers the words menacingly as he slowly runs his hand down the front of my body.

He gropes one of my breasts before cupping me through my jeans, and I struggle against him. He twists my arm further, and my body grows heavy, and I'm afraid that I might pass out from the pain that's now radiating from my wrist up through my elbow.

"Don't pretend you don't like this, he told me that you do," Elliott says before he bites my ear with a sinister chuckle.

I start to thrash against him, but stop myself, not wanting him to rip my ear off when I feel his teeth dig deeper into my skin the more I move. I pray that someone will walk by and see that I need help, but I didn't notice many people out on the streets today, and my heart drops in my chest.

"He told me all about the filthy things you two would do, all the sick and twisted ways that he'd get you off," Elliott says, releasing my ear from in between his teeth before licking up the side of my neck. The smell of the dumpster mixed with Elliott's rank saliva on my skin makes my skin crawl and I hold back a gag.

"Like, how you begged him to cut and bite you," Elliott whispers into my ear with a low chuckle. "You play innocent, but you love the pain, don't you? You sick fucker."

"*Shut your mouth!* Let go of me!" I say as I angrily thrash against him.

My mind flashes back to the last time I was in a similar situation with Elliott and how if Jess hadn't shown up right when he did... I try not to think about what would've happened then, or what might happen even now.

Elliott's still groping me as he pants heavily in my ear, when I notice the bulge in his pants pressing against me from behind.

*This can't be happening.*

I feel like I'm going to throw up, and panic starts to set in at the gravity of the situation. I fight harder to get away from him, and I throw my head back with all my force.

Elliott's nose collides with the back of my skull in a loud crunch, and he staggers back, temporarily stunned. I slam my foot down on top of his as hard as I can before pushing myself away from him and try to make a beeline for the street. I almost trip over my own feet from how shaky my legs have gotten, but I catch myself, knowing I can't afford to fall, not right now.

"Help! Someone help!" I scream, making it farther down the alleyway than I did the first time, when Elliott grabs hold of my arm again.

"I warned you not to scream, bitch," he snarls from behind me, his words sounding wet. I don't turn to face him, but I imagine it's from the bloody nose I just gave him, and even though the back of my head throbs, I wish I'd had the strength to hit him harder than I did.

Before I can scream again, I feel an intense pressure in my elbow and wrist, followed by a sharp pain up the length of my forearm, and I hear something snap. The pain is enough to take me down, and my legs buckle underneath me as I crash to the pavement on my knees. I put my left wrist out to catch me, but it's not enough to slow the momentum of my falling body as I smack face-first onto the dirty concrete.

"Hey now, stay with me," Elliott says mockingly as he grabs a fistful of my hair, forcing me to look up at him. Blood drips down his face and off his chin onto my shirt as he hovers above me, his hand still painfully woven into my hair. My entire skull hurts and I feel like I might pass out.

Excruciating pain throbs from my wrist up to my right bicep, and I try clutching my arm to my chest, but I'm unable to move it.

My knees throb, and the material of my jeans feels wet, along with the palm of my other hand. I'm afraid to look down at the state of my body, dreading that it looks as bad as it feels.

I sense my head getting heavy, and my vision starts to blur. "Wake up you dumb cunt, the fun's just getting started," Elliott says with a bloody smile as he slaps my face with his palm.

He squeezes my cheeks together in his hand, and shakes my head from side to side, trying to rouse me, but my eyes start to lose focus. The insides of my cheeks throb and I taste the metallic bite of my own blood from the soft skin digging into the sides of my teeth.

My vision starts getting splotchy, and I can hear the echo of Elliott's voice as he yells at me through the ringing in my ears. He's still slapping my face roughly from side to side when I see flashes of green through my staticky vision.

My mind envisions the deep green color of the leaves on a plant, freshly cut grass, the moss that clings to the rocks on the side of a stream, and then to the eyes of the boy that I love. All before everything fades to darkness.

# Chapter Seventeen

## Jess

### 6 Summers Ago

"That Amber girl is pretty cute, huh?" Sophie asks me as we continue peeling the potatoes for dinner.

"Who?" I ask.

"You know, that redhead who's been hanging around the ranger's station. I think she's his daughter or something," Sophie says casually, still peeling the same potato she was working on five minutes ago.

"Eh, she's all right. Not really my type," I say. I shrug as I toss my peeled potato into the container before grabbing another out of the bucket by our feet.

I briefly remember seeing someone with red hair yesterday when we passed by the station, but I'll admit that I wasn't really paying attention. Sam had decided to debut a new pink swimsuit, so I was having a hard time focusing on much else. The way the tight material clung to her body in all the right places was enough to keep me distracted for most of the day—and the night.

"Don't tell me you didn't notice her checking you out while we were at the lake yesterday, either?" Sophie says as she puts her hands on her hips and raises a brow at me.

"If you don't get to work, we're never going to eat," I say, ignoring her question as I gesture with my potato peeler for her to get back to it.

"Are all boys this dense? I mean, seriously," Sophie mutters to herself as she grabs another potato to peel.

"I dunno, Jess, she's got a pretty nice ra—"

"Drop it, Soph," I say, cutting her off. "I'm not interested, okay?" I say as I jokingly throw a potato peel at her.

Sophie puts her hands up in defense. "Jeez, *all right*. Hangry much?" she says as she flips her dark hair over her shoulder.

"Hey guys, how's it coming?" Sophie and I both turn our attention to Sam as she approaches us with a large container in her hands. She sets down the large plastic tub filled with fish onto our small work table and lets out a quick breath as she puts her hands on her hips.

"We'd be done by now if someone would stop their yapping already," Sophie says as she eyes me up and down.

Sam and I exchange looks before we both burst out laughing. "What?" Sophie says, emanating a high level of sass as she puts both hands on her hips.

Sam tries to stifle her laughter as she answers Sophie. "No offense, Soph, but you like sort of hold the reigning title of *yapper* in the group."

"For your information, having a regular conversation does not mean that I was *yapping*," Sophie says as she sets down her peeler before flipping her bouncy curls over her shoulder again. "Rude. You're both rude," she says, storming off with her nose in the air.

"Hey, wait, we still have like a hundred potatoes left! Get back here, you brat!" I call after her before she turns around and sticks her tongue out at me.

"Come on Fifi, don't be like that," I say, and she flips me off at the mention of the nickname she despises. Sophie sticks her tongue out at me again and stomps off, her tightly curled ringlets bouncing around her head as she walks.

"I swear that girl is fifty percent hair and fifty percent attitude," I say, chuckling to myself as I toss another potato into the bucket at my feet.

"Do you really have that many left?" Sam asks as she walks over to me and leans over the potato bucket, peeking inside. "I didn't even know we brought that many," she says as she raises a suspicious brow at me.

"Nah, I was exaggerating. We've got like five left," I say, shrugging. I smile back at Sam and notice her blush before she turns away, pretending to look busy. "Where's John? Isn't the fish usually *his* thing?" I ask and turn my head, trying to spot him.

"Oh, well… he said he was tired, so I volunteered to help," Sam says quietly as she looks down at the container of raw fish. "I will say though, gutting them was a lot grosser than I'd imagined it'd be," she says as she scrunches her nose.

"Wait, so he made you gut them, too?" I ask and raise a brow at her.

Sam gives me a halfhearted shrug. "It's all right, it was my choice to help out."

"And by *help out* you mean you pretty much did it all, didn't you?" I ask and shake my head with a *tsk* sound. "You should've come and got me, I would've been more than happy to help you," I say, trying to meet Sam's eyes.

"Really, Jess, it's okay, I don't mind. I guess it was bound to happen sooner or later…"

"What was?" I ask, already knowing what she's about to say.

"My dad giving me more responsibilities, you know, since everything that happened last year," she says, and I can hear the sadness in her voice. Sam gives me an apologetic smile and shakes her head as she looks off toward the trees, her mind obviously somewhere else right now.

"Sure, but that doesn't give him a free pass to not do shit anymore," I say, walking over to her.

"Are you... *defending* me?" Sam asks as she turns her gaze back toward me, raising her eyebrows. "Okay, where's the real Jess? Because you would never," she says as she squints her eyes at me suspiciously, and a small grin tugs at the corner of her mouth.

"Oh, shut up," I say, rolling my eyes at her. "Here, let me help," I say, gently pushing her to the side with my hip. "You take over the potatoes, and I'll fry the fish."

"Are you sure? I really don't mind—" she says as I hand her my potato peeler.

"Like I said, we've got... *eh*... maybe only about a hundred more or so until we're done, give or take a few," I say, winking at her. I watch as she blushes again before grabbing a potato out of the bucket.

It doesn't take long for us to finish prepping dinner, since the brunt of the work was cleaning and gutting the huge bucket of fish we caught earlier today.

Sam finishes peeling and slicing the potatoes around the same time that Sophie decided to put away some of her attitude and rejoin us, but she still refused to actually help with anything.

I put Sam in charge of cooking the potatoes while I finished battering and deep-frying the fish. Sophie's contribution was popping a few pans of Jiffy Pop over the fire, a "pre-meal appetizer" as she'd put it. I'd asked her to at least help prep dessert for later, and she promptly decided to ignore me and started throwing pieces of popcorn at my head instead.

"Would you stop that? You keep getting them in the oil," I say and laugh, trying to swat a piece of popcorn away before it lands in the hot pan.

"Sorry, can't," Sophie says after throwing another piece at me. "Your head's so giant, it'd be a waste not to use it as target practice," she says, and both she and Sam giggle as I frown at them.

After dodging what feels like a hundred pieces of popcorn to the head, I start trying to catch them in my mouth instead. A few keep landing in the fry oil, and I give up on trying to pick them out, figuring they'll just add some extra flavoring to the fish.

"One more, come on, one more," I say, egging Sam on to toss another piece at me. "I'll catch this one for real this time," I say and gesture for her to bring it on.

She throws a small handful of popcorn at my head, and I only manage to catch a few of the pieces with my mouth.

"What the hell?" I say, laughing as I munch on the popcorn. "That's cheating!"

Sam lets out a giggle as she smiles at me, and I feel like my chest might explode. "Sorry, I thought you were a pro." She steps toward me and brushes the popcorn out of my hair. "I guess you're all talk then, huh?" she says.

I watch as her cheeks flush again from our close proximity, and this time when our eyes meet, she doesn't look away. "There, all better," she says, brushing a stray piece off my shoulder, still not breaking eye contact with me.

"Okay, final round," Sophie says as she walks in between Sam and me to grab the popcorn bowl off of the table, inadvertently forcing us to break our intense eye contact.

"If you manage to catch all of these, we won't make you do the dishes. Deal?" Sophie asks, full sass with her hands on her hips.

"Um, well, seeing as though you haven't really helped much at all, I don't see how that's fair but okay...?" I say, giving her a look.

"Ready?" Sophie says with a mischievous glint in her eyes.

Before I can even ask, the girls exchange glances and giggle. "Rapid fire!" they both say in unison, laughing as they pelt me with the pieces of popcorn as fast as they can.

I'm barely able to catch any with how fast they're throwing them at me, most of them hitting me in the face, making it hard for me to see anything.

"You know that's like, super wasteful, right?" Chris says, taking a seat in one of the chairs as he cracks open a can of Mountain Dew. The second Chris joins us, the dark cloud he usually brings with him slowly takes over the space, drastically lowering the mood.

"Oh, lighten up, Chris," Sam says as she playfully throws a piece of popcorn at him.

He stares at her and watches the popcorn bounce off his arm with a flat expression. "Is dinner ready yet?" he asks.

"You're always welcome to help out if you think we're taking too long," I say, and the oil sizzles as I flip over another piece of fish in the frying pan.

Chris puts his hands behind his head as he leans back in the camp chair and settles in. "Pass. I'll just wait then," he says with an annoyed sigh.

"Then again, maybe it's best you don't, it might literally kill you to do something helpful for once," I say and Chris glares at me.

"Where's Dad?" Sam asks as she tosses another piece of popcorn his way, trying to get his attention when he doesn't answer her. Though she doesn't say as much, I'm sure she changes the subject to distract me and Chris from fighting.

Chris just looks down at where the piece of popcorn landed on his leg and flicks it off with a finger. "Don't know, I think he was trying to get cell reception or something."

Sam gives the potatoes in the dutch oven another stir as she looks down at them. "That's weird, why would he—"

"I literally don't know," Chris says and throws his hands in the air, obviously annoyed with Sam's question. "Who knows why he does half the shit he does these days?" Chris says, still refusing to look her way.

Sam says nothing, and I watch as the happy, playful Sam from a few minutes ago slowly disappears. The way her expression changes makes me want to punch Chris in the face, but Sophie tries to beat me to it.

"What's your damage, man? Chill the fuck out," Sophie says from her chair next to Chris, and for a second, I wonder if she's going to dump her drink in his lap.

"Whatever. Call me in five years when the food's ready," Chris says before standing, and then walks off in the direction of our tent.

I let out a breath and run one of my hands through my hair, and wonder if we'll ever get to see *normal* Chris again.

The worst part about all this is that he wasn't always this way. Chris has always been a lone wolf but never really a jerk, even with that short temper of his. Ever since last winter, everyone in the Ryan family has been having a pretty tough time adjusting to things, especially Chris. That's not to say that Sam's not having a difficult time either, I think she's just doing a better job at hiding it than he is.

Whenever Sam talks about her mom, she just gets really sad about it all. Chris, on the other hand, just gets angry and then shuts down, and in the last few months, things have only gotten worse with him. He's incredibly hotheaded, he's got next to no patience, and forget about having any kind of filter either. I think we're all trying to be understanding, but at this point, he's becoming sort of insufferable to even be around anymore.

Since Soph and I basically grew up with the Ryan family, seeing what Chris and Sam were going through really made me feel for them. Even though Chris and I weren't super close per se, I still wanted to let him know that I cared. So, right after their mom left, I tried talking to him about it. I tried to let Chris know that I was there for him if he needed it, and that I sort of had an understanding of how he was feeling—albeit not the same— but that I was able to empathize with him.

He told me there was no way I'd ever understand what he was going through since I'd never even had a mother to remember in the first place, so I promptly told him he could go fuck himself before I punched him square in the jaw. After that, things haven't been the same, and if anything, I think I might've only made things worse. Even though he's turning into a serious asshole, I'll still be here for him if he ever wants to talk for real.

Sam gives the potatoes another nervous stir as we take in the tense silence left by Chris's gloomy presence.

"He has a serious attitude problem," Sophie says, breaking the silence. Sam and I exchange glances but don't say anything, both of us smiling.

"What?" Sophie demands. "Don't you dare say anything!" she says, trying not to laugh herself, before throwing a few pieces of popcorn toward us. She throws the last few pieces into the air, catching them in her mouth, and we all cheer in unison.

After we finish cooking dinner, John eventually returns from wherever he was off to earlier.

"Thanks for getting things ready, son," John says, and claps me on the back as he passes behind my chair to grab himself a plate.

"No problem. Honestly, I didn't do much, Sam really did most of—"

"So, Jess, how's Judy been doing these days?" John says, cutting me off before I can finish my thought, and I notice that Sam deflates a little in her chair.

"Judy's good," I say hesitantly before glancing over at Sam, and I catch her sad gaze for a second. She gives me an apologetic shrug, and I clench my fists, my anger simmering at John.

*I hate it when he does this to her.*

"Good," John says before putting a few potatoes and a small piece of fish onto his plate. "Tomorrow's our last lake day, so make it count, kids," he says after taking a bite of the fish.

"Can we go out on the boat again?" Chris asks from his chair next to the fire.

"I don't see why not," John says, and I watch as he plays with his food before he eventually sets his plate down onto the small fold-up table that's attached to his chair.

Although I do like the fishing part of the trip, more than anything, I look forward to hanging out with Sophie and Sam on our lake days. We always swim out to the small floating dock in the middle of the lake and just hang out, at least one of us always getting sunburnt to the max— usually me. It's honestly my favorite part of the trip. Especially since if we go swimming tomorrow, I'll get to see Sam's pink swimsuit again.

"Since your official guy's fishing day was today, does that mean we can all go?" Sam asks. Her face lights up, and the excitement is evident in her voice.

"On second thought, maybe we shouldn't," John says before walking his plate over to the trash. "Wouldn't want to overfish a good spot," he says, giving Sam a half-assed smile.

"Oh, okay… yeah, you're probably right," she says as she fiddles with her hands in her lap, paired with an embarrassed look on her face.

"Well, I'll see you kids in the morning. Thanks again for the food," John says as he claps Chris on the shoulder before he turns and walks off toward his tent.

"I'm out," Chris says, standing. "Dinner was mid, as per fucking usual," Chris says and snickers as he turns to leave, obviously waiting for John to be out of earshot before being an asshole.

"Hey, Chris, I think you forgot something," Sophie says, and I watch in slow motion as she grabs the half-empty soda can Chris left in his cupholder and throws it at the back of his head.

Chris slowly turns around, and Sophie stands with her hands on her hips, ready to challenge him. His face is red with anger, and Sophie stares at him calmly before she nonchalantly picks at one of her nails.

"Oh, I'm sorry. Did you forget something *else?*" she asks, looking around innocently.

Chris looks like he might explode but just lets out an angry breath before storming off, a clear wet spot on the back of his shirt from where the soda can hit him.

"What the hell, Soph, do you want him to actually murder you?" Sam asks, eyes wide as she covers her mouth, trying not to laugh.

"Nice shot," I say, giving Sophie a nod of approval and a high five.

Sophie folds her arms across her chest and turns to Sam. "Look, Babe, someone's gotta put that douche in his place every once in a while, and I have no problem getting to be the one who does it."

Sophie helps clean up for about five minutes before she lets out a huge yawn and decides she's over the whole thing, but I don't really mind since there are only a few things left to wash at that point. Sam stayed behind to help me dry the rest of the dishes, and I'm glad for the extra company, especially since it's hers.

We stand next to each other as we wash the dishes, the sound of the crickets keeping us company as we clean.

I finish washing up the last pan in the folding table sink and hand it over to Sam to dry. "I'm sorry about John earlier," I say, leaning against the fold-up table as I watch Sam dry the last pan I'd just handed her.

"Why? It's not your fault," she says with a shrug. "You'd think I'd be used to being rejected by him by now. Maybe he was like this before and I just never noticed," she says, turning to me with sadness in her expression. "It's whatever." Sam shakes her head. "He's obviously not taking things well with my mom leaving and all, so I can't blame him for being a little distant lately."

"Being distant and being a dick are two different things," I say as I take a seat in the double camp chair next to the dying fire, hoping she'll decide to join me.

Sam lets out a breath and sits down beside me in the large chair. "I know," she says, and leans back before resting her head against my shoulder, looking up at the night sky above us.

There's a slight chill in the air, so the warmth of her body next to mine feels nice. I think about wrapping my arm around her, but don't, not wanting to make her feel uncomfortable.

"Jess?" she asks, her head still tilted toward the stars, and the small fire crackles and pops in the fire pit in front of us.

"Yeah?" I ask as I follow her gaze upward.

"Do you believe in destiny?"

"Hm?" I ask without asking.

"You know, like, that there's some big grand plan for everything that's supposed to happen in a person's life," Sam says, and I can feel her eyes on my face, her head still resting gently against me.

297

"Well… honestly, I don't know," I say, looking down, and she turns her head to the sky again before I'm able to meet her eyes.

"That's too bad," she says with an exhausted sigh.

"Why'd you say that?" I ask.

"It sure would be easier to imagine that the reason for all the bullshit in life was because it was all a part of something bigger," she says before sighing again.

I consider my response for a second and wonder if it will make Sam feel any better or if I should just keep my mouth shut.

"I don't know if I believe in destiny or fate or whatever, but I think that the people who are meant to be in our lives will always find a way back to us. Even if it ends up taking longer than we'd like it to," I say as I look down at her again, hoping she'll meet my eyes this time.

Sam sits up and turns toward me, and for a second, I think she's going to get up and leave. "Thank you, Jess," she says, and even with the dim light from the dying embers of the fire, I can see that her eyes are glossy.

"For what?" I ask, feeling bad for unintentionally making her cry.

"For always knowing exactly what I need to hear," she says, and a stray tear runs down her face as she blinks up at me. I don't say anything as I lean in and softly brush away her tear with the pad of my thumb.

"Always," I say, and the word is barely more than a whisper.

When our eyes meet, it's like time slows down, and I notice things about her that I never have before. Like the small flecks of brown that line the inner irises of her hazel eyes, and how her long eyelashes gently brush the tops of her cheeks when she blinks.

I lean in close to her, wanting to get a closer look and our noses brush slightly. I notice how the light freckles that usually pepper her nose and cheeks look darker and more spread out than usual, probably from the sun of the last few days.

Our lips are only mere centimeters away from touching, and I can feel Sam's soft breathing against my face. I'm unable to concentrate on anything but her, and don't think twice about any possible repercussions from what I'm about to do.

I lean in to close the gap between us when I feel the warmth of Sam's hand on my chest, stopping me from going any further.

She gives me a sad smile as she leans back, putting some distance in between us. "We should probably get some rest," she says before standing.

My mind is racing, and I don't want to let her go yet.

I've known for quite some time that my feelings for Sam were starting to turn into more than just that of a friend, but with all the shit that she's got going on in her life right now, I can't help but feel guilty about telling her. It seems selfish of me to spring something like this on her right now, like the timing is all wrong.

"Ryan, wait," I say, and I grab her hand when she turns to walk away. Sam says nothing as she turns to face me, and the sadness in her eyes makes my chest hurt. "How would you feel about hijacking John's boat in the morning?" I ask, not saying what I really wanted to.

"You wouldn't," she says with a scoff, and I'm glad to see that her tears are gone.

"Try me," I say, holding up the keys to John's boat. "If he doesn't like it, he should stop leaving these where anyone could just take them. Honestly, it's very irresponsible," I say, dangling the fish keychain in front of my face as Sam gives me a look.

"What? He left them in the cupholder," I say innocently as I point to the chair where John was sitting earlier.

"Let me take you out on the water tomorrow. We can bring some poles, and I think we still have some live bait that we didn't use either," I suggest, giving Sam a warm smile as I give her hand a light squeeze.

At first, she smiles brightly at me, but then her expression grows sad again and she turns away. "It's all right, I'm not really one for pity invites," Sam says as she looks down at the ground, no doubt thinking back to her conversation with John earlier.

Trying to get her attention, I give her arm a light shake, wanting her to look at me. "Who said anything about a pity invite? I think it'll be fun with just the two of us. What do you say?" I ask.

"I don't know, Jess. Maybe we shouldn't," she says.

"Come on, Ry," I say and shake her arm again lightly. "You know you want to," I say with a wink.

At first, she says nothing, so I wag my eyebrows up and down before giving her my best puppy dog eyes.

"Welll... okay," she says finally as she smiles down at me. "Let's do it."

"Just so you're aware, the best fishing days start at the crack of dawn. Are you sure you can handle that?" I ask, teasing her as I give her hand another shake.

"You kidding? And waste a perfectly good opportunity to piss my dad off? Not a chance," she says with a small smile.

I continue to hang onto Sam's hand, and we hold each other's gazes as she stands in front of me in the bright moonlight. I look up at her and can't help but admire how beautiful she looks right now and wish she wouldn't have stopped me from kissing her before.

"Night, Jess," she says slowly before turning around.

"Night," I say, and let her hand slip from mine as she turns and heads in the opposite direction from mine and Chris's tent.

The second she's out of eyeshot, I slump down into the chair and let out a breath as I smack myself in the face with my palms.

*Fuck me, what was that?*

My pulse is racing, and my body feels like it's on fire from the two seconds our skin touched just barely—not to mention how uncomfortably tight my pants have gotten…

I told myself I wasn't going to bring up my feelings to her until she was able to work through her family shit, and here I am literally about to lose it over a kiss that didn't even happen. I tell myself that I need to cool off, otherwise I'll never be able to get any sleep tonight.

I pour some water on the dying embers of the fire to make sure they're completely out for the night, and head down the small trail toward the upper part of the lake.

I decide that a quick dip in the cold water should be enough to cool me off for the time being. As long as Sam doesn't touch me again in the next week or so, I should be able to avoid spontaneous combustion—for a while at least.

The full moon's bright enough to illuminate the pathway to the lake, so I don't bother with bringing my flashlight. I stare up at the moon and stars as I walk and think about what Sam said earlier about destiny. She's right, it would be nice to know that all the shit things that have happened in the last few years were for a reason and not just because.

I try not to dwell on it, but I can't help thinking about the car accident I was in with my dad, and what bigger reason there could possibly be that called for his death, along with both of Sophie's parents.

I try to put it out of my head, and I let my mind wander as I continue down the trail toward the lake. My mind keeps going back to the look on Sam's face right before our almost kiss, and the slight flush of her cheeks. When I think about the warmth of her breath on my face and just how close she was to me, I feel my body heating up again, and I decide to pick up my pace.

When I reach the small hidden part of the lake, I take in the view before getting undressed. The water is as sleek as glass, perfectly reflecting

301

the night sky across its calm waters, and the tall grass surrounding the small pool sways gently in the breeze.

I kick my boots off and pull my shirt over my head as I strip down and set my clothes next to the shoreline. I figure I'm safe to go au natural since the likelihood of running into someone else is almost zero, especially since this part of the lake is less maintained, so not many people even know about its existence. That and there's no way anyone else would be crazy enough to swim in the freezing water this late at night.

Before I can give it a second thought, I dive off the bank, my body making a huge splash as it breaks the surface of the water. The second I hit the freezing lake, my entire body feels like it's being pricked with tiny needles, cooling me off almost immediately.

When I surface, I gasp for breath as I shake my hair out of my face and wipe my eyes. I bob up and down in the water, trying to catch my breath, and I notice steam radiating off my body from the difference in temperatures.

I float onto my back, looking up at the night sky, wishing Sam were with me right now. I know how much she loves looking at the stars and the thought makes me smile to myself, knowing how excited she'd be to see so many out on such a clear night like tonight. I think back to our conversation earlier and wish she would've been able to enjoy them instead of feeling bad because John was an asshole to her.

I'm still gazing at the twinkling sky above me, now trying not to think about Sam's pink bikini yesterday, when out of the corner of my eye I notice a flash of movement by the shore. I quickly submerge my body, and as I turn, I catch a glimpse of someone slowly making their way into the water.

Moonlight streams through the branches of the large tree on the opposite side of the small pool, illuminating the body, but only in streaks.

I quickly turn away once I realize they aren't wearing any clothes, and my mind starts to race.

I panic, thinking it might be Sam having followed me out here. I can't say I've never imagined her naked before, because I literally did just that this morning, but I don't know how I'd handle seeing the real thing right now. My pulse starts to quicken, and I can feel my body growing hot again despite the cool temperature of the water.

I hesitantly turn my gaze toward her again, and I can feel my plan to hold back my feelings about to go right out the window. My budding excitement is suddenly replaced with disappointment when I recognize the flaming red hair of the girl Sophie was talking about earlier. Her milky white skin is a drastic contrast to the bright color of her hair, and although she is beautiful, she's not my type. She could never be. It's not her fault, she's just not *Her*.

The girl stands in a shallower part of the lake, her body submerged just enough to cover her nipples as she looks over at me. Sophie was right about one thing though, the girl does have a pretty massive rack—that much I can tell, even with the darkness of the water surrounding her body. I look away from the girl with the red hair, trying to pretend she's not there, wishing she were someone else instead.

"Hi," she says coyly as she slowly swims toward me.

"*Um*, hi?" I say, making my way toward the shore, purposely trying to sound unfriendly so she'll take the hint.

*So much for my midnight swim.*

I'm grateful to have at least cooled off a bit, but I wish I could've enjoyed it a little longer. I'm not usually one to turn down a bit of fun, but right now I'm not in the mood—at least, not in the mood for a redhead.

Something about what happened tonight with Sam felt different. Sure, I flirt with her and tease her most of the time, but she usually just brushes me off and calls me annoying. I'll admit, it's usually just to get a rise out of her, but tonight... tonight was the first time it felt like something changed between us, like she was finally open to the idea of... *me*. I've teased her countless times, but she's never given me *that* look before.

I squint and search the shoreline, trying to remember where I put my clothes, knowing I've got to get out of here. If things actually are changing between Sam and me, I'm sure as hell not going to do anything to mess that up.

Even though there's not actually anything going on between us yet, Red over there couldn't be less subtle with her advances. It wouldn't sit right with me if someone saw us out here and decided to blab to the whole camp—word no doubt making it back to Sam—and the last thing I want is for her to think of me as some sort of man-whore.

"My name's Amber, what's yours?" Red asks, breaking my train of thought as she starts to get within a dangerously close range of me.

"*Uh...* it's Jess," I say reluctantly.

"Nice to meet you, Jess," she says as she gives me a once-over, and I feel like smacking myself for telling her my name.

"Okay, sure," I say, annoyed, mostly at myself now, as I finally spot my clothes and boots.

"It's a nice night, Jess, you should stay a while," she says as she treads water directly across from me, blocking the way to my clothes. "Since there's no one around, we might as well have some... *fun,*" she says innocently.

*That's it, I'm out.*

I say nothing as I shake my head and quickly swim past her before wading out of the water up to my waist. I can feel her eyes on me and try not to sound like a total douche when I tell her to stop staring at me so hard.

"Sorry, am I making you uncomfortable?" she says as she starts to wade out of the water before looking down at herself. "You're welcome to look. I guess it's only fair," she says as she continues to walk out of the water, revealing her bare chest to me.

"Oh my god! What the fuck are you doing?" I say, putting my hands up to shield her naked body from my vision.

I turn and hurry out of the water up the bank, one hand on my crotch as the other reaches for my pants. I snatch my clothes off the ground as fast as I can, still trying to keep myself covered, before I quickly scurry away.

"Oh, lighten up," she calls, and I can hear the echo of her cackling behind me.

I hurry down the trail butt ass naked until I find a big enough tree to hide behind before I pull my pants and boots back on. I know the girl already saw me, but I'd prefer not to change in front of a complete stranger, especially since I'm sure it wouldn't take much for her to get the wrong idea.

I lean against the tree, and my breath comes out foggy as I let out a heavy sigh. *What the hell even was that?* I'm guessing she probably knows all the secret spots around here if her dad really is the ranger.

I run a hand through my wet hair and decide to head back before a certain crazy redhead decides to follow me back to my tent. I peek around the tree but don't see her, so I hustle back down the trail as quickly as I can.

When I get back to our camp, I notice that all of my stuff has been dumped on the ground in front of the tent, my clothes and sleeping bag included. I guess Chris didn't like me calling him out earlier for not helping.

I curse under my breath as I pick up my things and try to brush off the majority of the dirt, grateful it's not mud instead, or some other questionable substance.

When I step inside the tent, I point my flashlight straight into Chris's face, not surprised to find him still awake. "You're an asshole, you know that?" I say, still shining the bright light at him.

Chris squints his eyes and waves a hand at me. "What the hell? Get that out of my face," he says, annoyed.

"Why the hell are you so sweaty?" I ask, raising a brow at him, and notice that his cheeks look flushed.

"Fuck you," he says before turning onto his side, pulling the top of his sleeping bag over his head.

I turn my light off and lay out my bedding before taking my pants off. I'm exhausted from the day and hope that Chris didn't pull any other dick moves that I don't know about yet. I climb into my sleeping bag and pass out as soon as my head hits the pillow.

~

I don't set an alarm, but I'm already wide awake just before dawn, the excitement of the day causing my body to get up on its own. I fold my arms behind my head as I stare up at the ceiling of the canvas of the tent. I smile to myself when I think about getting to spend the morning alone with Sam and can't wait to see her.

Even though one might take what happened last night as a rejection, I still don't mind. I know she's got a lot going on right now, so just getting to spend time with her is enough for me, even if it's just as a friend right now.

When I look over at Chris, he's sound asleep in his sleeping bag. He's snoring loud enough to wake a bear, and I'm surprised that he wasn't the reason I woke up so early. I consider smothering him with my pillow, but decide against it, figuring Sam probably wouldn't be too happy if I accidentally killed her only brother.

I throw on my last pair of clean pants and one of my shirts from the other day. I give the shirt a quick sniff—*eh, could be worse*—and shrug before pulling it over my head.

I unzip the tent and step outside before I pull on my boots and stretch my arms over my head with a yawn. I inhale the brisk, pine-scented morning air and let it fill my lungs as I take a deep, cleansing breath, excitement brewing beneath my skin.

I swat a bug away from my face and then smile to myself. Somewhere, I read that certain types of mosquitoes love the taste of sour blood, so I decide to leave the tent unzipped a few inches, hoping to give them a good breakfast.

I find myself unconsciously grinning widely as I walk, thinking about the way Sam smiled at me when she and Sophie were pelting me in the face with popcorn last night. I make my way to the small boat dock that's across from the ranger's station when I hear someone holler at me.

"Mornin'!"

When I look up, I see that Gary, the camp ranger, is waving me over. He's sporting his khaki-colored uniform, and I can't help but notice that his shorts are just a tad bit too short for a grown man.

I glance over to where John's boat is gently swaying in the water as it bumps against the rubber bumper of the dock. I don't notice Sam waiting for me yet, so I head over to where Gary is still waving at me from next to the tiny ranger's station.

*It's more like a shed than an actual station.* I scoff to myself at the thought. Looks like Gary got the short end of the stick being stuck with this area to manage.

"Morning. What can I do for you, sir?" I ask as he holds out a hand for me to shake, the other holding a speckled blue metal coffee mug.

"Josh, was it?" he asks, giving me a firm handshake.

"Jess, actually," I say, correcting him.

"Short for Jessie? Or James, I'm guessing?" he asks before casually taking a sip of his coffee.

"Nope, just Jess," I say, not really in the mood for small talk, and wonder what he's after.

"Is that a family name or—"

"Sir?" I ask and raise my brows in confusion.

Gary just shrugs before continuing, as if he forgot where he was going with the whole thing. "Right, well, I was wondering if you had a second to help me out with something," Gary says as he puts a hand on one of my shoulders and tries to steer me toward the tree line behind the station.

"Actually, sir, I've got plans this morning. I really need to get my boat ready to go if I want to have a chance at some decent fishing today," I say, trying not to sound rude as I turn myself out of his grasp.

"Ah, I see. I assume you're referring to Mr. Ryan's boat, then. Right?" he says, giving me a fake smile. "By the way, where is Mr. Ryan this morning? I haven't seen him out yet," Gary says as he cranes his neck to the side, pretending to look for John.

"What was it you needed help with, sir?" I ask, knowing he probably won't let me go until he gets what he wants.

"Glad you had a change of heart, son," he says, steering us deeper into the trees behind the station.

*Like I have a choice.*

I either go with and make Sam wait, or don't, and Gary'll nark to John that I'm *borrowing* his boat.

"Dendroctonus rufipennis," Gary says.

"I'm sorry?" I ask as I stare at Gary, and wonder if he might've added a little something extra to his coffee this morning.

"Spruce beetles, son," Gary says as he roughly pats me on the back and gives me a look like I should already know what the hell he's talking about.

"The damn bark beetles have been everywhere this year, wreaking all kinds of havoc on the trees in the area," Gary says as I follow him through the forest, getting farther and farther away from John's boat, and from Sam.

"Okay...?" I say. Gary gives me a sharp look, and I'm sure he can hear the impatience in my voice, but he continues with his story anyway.

"We've had quite a few trees falling in pedestrian areas over the last week or so," he says casually, like we're two old friends catching up with nowhere to be, and I roll my eyes.

"Now, usually it's nothing I can't handle myself, but last night we had quite a large one fall and now it's blocking the main road to the campsite directly above us," Gary drawls on as we stop in front of a massive tree that's blocking the small dirt road. "I just need a hand clearing it out of the way real quick," he continues, and rubs his Ned Flanders-style mustache contemplatively before he takes a sip of his coffee.

"Okay, well, aren't there people whose job is to remove fallen trees like this one?" I ask, raising my brows as I gesture to the large trunk in front of us.

"Sure are, you're looking at 'em," Gary says, gesturing to himself and then to me with his thumb.

"Whatever, let's just get this over with," I say as I roll my eyes, shaking my head.

We heave and grunt as we try pushing the tree off the small pathway—and by we, I mean *me*. Gary mostly just points and yells at me to push this way, or pull it that way, still holding that damned coffee mug in his hand.

I lean against the trunk with a huff, out of breath and sweaty from straining against the heavy wood. *So much for the clean clothes I put on earlier.*

"Seriously, Gary, can't you just cut it up with a chainsaw or something?" I ask, still trying to catch my breath.

He sets down his empty coffee mug on a nearby tree stump before folding his arms across his chest. He slowly rubs his mustache as he looks at the tree, considering what to do next.

Moving at the speed of a grandma snail, it's a wonder that the man manages to get anything done around here, and I roll my eyes at Gary's urgency.

"I s'pose that'd work. There's one in the shed next to the station," he says before turning to stare at me.

I shoot him a look that says, *Okay, and what do you want me to do about it?* Gary frowns at me before waving me off to get the chainsaw.

*This is ridiculous. Could this asshole be any lazier?*

After cursing Gary the entire way back to the shed, I decide that this is where my help ends. I'll bring him his stupid chainsaw, and the rest is on him. The longer Sam and I wait to "borrow" John's boat, the better the chances are of him catching us himself anyway.

I'm almost to the ranger's station when, across the lake, I spot Sam walking up the small dock toward John's boat. I quickly duck inside the small shed next to the station and search for the chainsaw, thinking the faster I can lug the stupid thing back to Gary, the quicker I'll be on the boat with Sam.

When I open the small door, I see that the tiny shed is full of junk inside, and I wonder how Gary is able to find anything in the mess. It's

mostly full of old tools and camping gear, all dusty and covered in cob-
webs. I move a few boxes around, and dust stirs in the air. I cough as I
wave my hand in front of my face, trying to clear some of the dust from
getting into my eyes.

"Whatcha doin'?" A high-pitched voice says from behind me,
causing me to jump, and I accidentally knock over a stack of boxes when
I bump into them.

I spin around and see that it's the girl from last night. She's wearing tiny white short shorts and a yellow spaghetti-strapped shirt that's
barely able to accommodate her chest size.

"Jesus Christ," I say, letting out a breath. "What are you doing in
here?" I ask as I rub my forehead with my hand, my heart rate slowly
getting back to normal.

"I asked you first," Red says, giving me a slow once-over.

"I'm looking for the chainsaw. Have you seen it?" I ask as I turn
around and sift through some more old junk. "Gary asked me to bring it
to him," I say, mostly to myself.

"I think I saw it outside somewhere," she says from beside me as
she pretends to help look. "I'd be more than happy to show you where,"
she says, and I jump when I feel a hand on my lower back.

"Okay, *that's* enough of that," I say, stepping away from her, and
notice that she's purposely blocking the small door.

"Sorry, did I do something wrong?" Red asks innocently as she
twirls a piece of her curly hair around one of her fingers.

"Look, I'm sorry, but I'm not interested, okay? So please stop
…*whatever*… it is that you're trying to do here," I say and gesture between
us with my hand.

Red gives me a confused look. "Wait, I—"

"Tell your dad I'm sorry. Something came up so he'll have to find someone else to help him," I say, and have to physically move her so that she'll get out of my way.

"Hey, wait!" she says as I step around her and leave the shed.

When I get outside, I look over at John's boat, trying to spot Sam again, and hope she doesn't think I blew her off, especially since I know how much that'd hurt her after the way John treated her yesterday. When I see her head pop up—her arms full of the docking ropes—I smile to myself and shake my head. Always the independent one, even when she has no idea what the hell she's doing.

I figure I'd better get over there fast to help Sam before she hurts herself, when Red tries to stop me. "Is it because of that other girl?" Red says from behind me, and I feel her grab hold of my right bicep.

"What?" I say, turning toward her.

"Is she your girlfriend or something?" Red asks, clearly annoyed. "I thought you were supposed to be single."

"*That* is none of your business," I say sternly as I grab her hand and remove it from its place on my arm.

Red looks like she's about to say something else when I hear a loud splash come from the water. I turn and look to the spot where Sam was standing just a second ago and search the length of the dock with my eyes when I notice that she's not there anymore.

"Sam?" I call as I glance around John's boat from across the water, trying to spot her. "Sam!" I call again with more urgency as I scan the dock again, and I can't help feeling like something is wrong.

I rush down the small hill over to the edge of the lake and notice a small ripple when I search the top of the water for her. I know that Sam's a strong swimmer, and figure that she'll resurface at any second.

I wait a breath, then another. Nothing.

I know that something doesn't feel right because she should've surfaced already. I try to stay calm as I sprint down the wooden dock toward John's boat, but before I'm able to make it there, panic grips me when I realize that the giant bundle of ropes Sam was carrying is nowhere to be found.

I rush to the side of the boat and notice that the anchor line is pulled taut from under the water. "Shit!" I yell, realizing a second too late what must've happened.

Without thinking, I dive straight into the water, clothes and all, and just as I'd suspected, through the murky water, I can see the boat anchor and docking lines tangled around one of Sam's legs, dragging her just below the edge of the surface. Her hands float weightlessly next to her body as her hair sways gently around her in the dark water.

I swim toward her through the murky water as fast as I can and grab onto her body as I pull at the heavy ropes around her leg, desperately trying to free her from the weight that's holding her under.

I quickly free Sam from the ropes, and just as I break the surface of the freezing water, Red is there, kneeling on the dock reaching toward us. She grabs hold of Sam's arms and helps me as we hoist her up before I pull myself out of the water and onto the dock next to Sam's lifeless body.

Water from my hair drips into my eyes as I try to check Sam for a pulse, and when I put my ear to her face, my deepest fear is all but confirmed when I realize that she's not breathing.

I pull Sam's chin up and squeeze her nose as I blow a breath into her mouth and watch her chest rise. "Come on, Sam, you can't," I say, starting chest compressions before blowing another breath into her mouth as I pinch her nose with my fingers.

"Oh shit, is she ...*dead?*" Red says as she starts to cry.

I snap my head toward her. "No, she's not *dead!*" I yell in Red's face before starting another round of CPR. "Don't do this, Sam, *please*

313

*don't do this,*" I say as I blow another breath into her mouth before continuing with chest compressions.

I curse John for insisting on using heavy old school hemp ropes instead of the newer nylon ones that float, thinking that if he weren't such a cheapskate that none of this would've ever happened.

"You can't, Sam, you can't!" I grit out through calm desperation as I fight to keep my hands steady.

My eyes burn as the dirty lake water continues to drip down my face and onto Sam's as I keep pushing down forcefully onto her chest with my palms. "You don't get to die, you can't," I say, still trying to keep a steady rhythm with my compressions.

The fact that Red is crying hysterically beside me has got me on my last nerve, and I explode angrily at her, the stress of the situation getting to me. "What the fuck are you still doing here? Go get help already!" I snap at her. Red flinches at my intensity but then gets up before running off toward the ranger's station.

*Great, a lot of help Gary's going to be.*

I feel a hopeless dread take over me when I realize that the CPR isn't working, and that if anything, I'm probably hurting Sam more than doing any good at this point.

"*Dammit,* Sam, you can't leave me!" I yell as I grip her shoulders, shaking them violently. My eyes are starting to sting, but this time, it's not from the lake water.

*Both of my parents, and now Sam… This can't be happening.*

My cracked voice comes out in a helpless sob as I slam my hands down onto the wood of the dock as I hover over her body.

"*Sam, please!*"

Her body suddenly jerks, and she coughs up what feels like a gallon of water straight onto my face and chest. Relief immediately floods through me, and I help her sit up and turn her onto her side. I rub her back gently as she lets out one wet cough after another, seeming like she managed to swallow half of the lake.

Sam's body heaves with each breath, like she still can't get enough oxygen. My hands shake from the adrenaline rushing through my system as I continue to rub her back, trying my best to soothe her as she trembles and coughs.

"*Jess,*" Sam croaks as she tries to look up at me. Her glossed-over hazel eyes struggle to focus, and I feel her hand grip the hem of my wet t-shirt sleeve as she turns toward me.

"Hey, it's all right, you're all right," I coo gently, rubbing her arm as I lean over and hug her body to mine. Sam frantically grips and pulls at my shirt, and I feel her let out a sob against me.

"Oh my god, is she okay?" Red says, appearing suddenly as she kneels down beside us, somehow still crying even though she's not the one in distress.

I turn to give her an annoyed glance but feel bad when I notice a look of genuine concern on her face. I turn my attention back to Sam and see that the expression on her face changes as she looks back and forth between Red and me.

I feel Sam's hand as it loosens its grip on my shirt, and her sad eyes start to roll. I want to tell her that Red means nothing to me and that I don't even know the bitch.

I want Sam to know that she's all I can see now, all that I'll *ever* be able to see, but before I have the chance to tell her that I love her, her body goes limp as she passes out in my arms.

# Chapter Eighteen

## Jess

"Sam!" I yell as I race down the street in the direction she ran off to. *Dammit. Why did she bolt like that?*

"Sam!" I call again before stopping at the mouth of an alleyway to catch my breath. I guess she really wasn't kidding about her cardio level.

I stare down the thin space in between the buildings but don't see any movement. I consider checking behind the stacks of crates and large dumpster, but don't, not wanting to waste any time if Sam is still running down the street. I turn and take off down the main road, calling her name still, quickly glancing down the alleyways and streets in between the buildings.

I search for an hour with no sign of her before heading back toward the café. I probably would've had more luck had I driven instead of running on foot all across downtown, but I feel like any chance of finding her now is probably gone at this point. I'm sure she took a cab home, otherwise, I feel like I would've seen her by now. I wonder if I should call Sophie to see if she's heard from Sam, but I decide not to when I remember their fight from yesterday.

After I saw Sam off last night, I made my way back up to the house before I noticed two silhouettes standing just outside the door. The small porch light illuminated their figures, and as I got closer, I realized it was Sophie and Chris.

At first, I thought my eyes were playing tricks on me when I saw their faces glued together with one of Chris's hands resting on Sophie's backside.

*Ahh, now Sam's comment about Sophie being a ho makes more sense.*

"What the fuck?" I say, almost wanting to laugh, not believing what I'm seeing.

By the time I make it to the house, Chris is walking past me to his truck as Sophie turns to go inside.

"Butt out, Jess, it's none of your concern," Sophie says rudely before trying to shut the door in my face.

"Whoa, hold on a second, I never said anything," I say, catching the door with my hand before it hits me in the nose. "I'm just surprised, is all."

I follow her into the house and close the door behind us before Sophie turns around to face me. "You didn't have to say anything, your face said it all," she says flatly. She folds her arms across her chest, and I'm glad to see that she ditched her blanket dress for some actual clothes.

I shrug as I put my hands up defensively and raise my brows. "Hey now, like I said, I was just surprised. I guess I never saw that coming."

"Shows how observant *you* are," Sophie says with a snort.

"I just don't think I've ever seen you have a regular conversation with the guy, that's all," I say, leaning back against the kitchen counter.

"So what? You're the only one who gets to pine after someone they can't have?" Sophie asks, raising a brow.

"And what is *that* supposed to mean?" I ask, folding my arms across my chest defensively.

"You know exactly what I mean," she says, pointing a finger in my face. "You and I both know that you've been carrying a torch for Sam ever since we were teenagers. When are you going to get over that, Jess?" Sophie says with a sympathetic look on her face.

"Okay, well you're one to talk then, aren't you?" I say, giving her a puzzled look.

"Things between Chris and me are... You wouldn't understand, okay?" Sophie says finally. "It's different, Sam doesn't feel that way about you, Jess. I've told you before," she says, trying to change the subject.

"Did Sam ever specifically say to you that she didn't have any feelings for me? Like, at all?" I press, not believing Sophie for a second. I might've in the past, but after everything that's happened recently, even if Sam didn't feel that way about me before, I don't think that's the case anymore. I try not to give myself any hope, but I can't help the electricity I feel in my chest when I think about Sam and me together.

"Yes, she said that you're like a brother to her," Sophie says, refusing to make eye contact with me.

"Liar," I say, staring her down.

"It's true, ask her," Sophie says, calling my bluff as she picks at her nails, still unwilling to meet my eyes.

"Holy shit," I say, realization hitting me.

"What?" she says, her eyes snapping up to meet mine.

I let out a deep breath and shake my head. "What?" Sophie demands.

"I'm such a fucking idiot," I say as I groan into my hands. "I can't believe I never noticed."

"I didn't see it before, but it was *you*, wasn't it?" I ask incredulously as I lift my face from my palms.

"What was me?" Sophie asks, clearly agitated by my unclear accusations.

"All this time, it was *you* who didn't want Sam and me to be together. That's why you tried to set me up with that random ass girl that year at the lake," I say, pointing a finger at her, and everything starts to make sense now.

"I don't know what you're talking about," Sophie says, starting to look uncomfortable as she tries to hold her ground.

"*You* were the one who told that girl I was alone that night, weren't you? *You're* the reason she followed me out to the lake and basically threw herself at me," I say, shaking my head in disbelief.

Sophie says nothing and stares at me with furrowed brows, her arms folded across her chest, and her silence all but confirms my suspicions.

"That wasn't the first time, though, was it!" I say, more to myself than to her. I put my hands on my head and pace around the kitchen, my wheels spinning in high gear as I put the pieces together.

"I was ready to ask Sam to prom when you told me that she already had a date, that's the only reason I agreed to play the away game with the baseball team! I wanted to take her, but she ended up going with that drunk asshole instead, all because you didn't want *me* to go with her!" I exclaim as I continue my accusations, and the look on Sophie's face reveals that I'm right about it all.

"What about graduation night? Did you know that Sam was in there with that guy?" I demand, my mind thinking back to all the times it seemed like we missed our chance to finally be together. All the times I almost confessed to Sam, but didn't, because I was told there was no way she'd return my sentiments.

"No, I swear! I didn't know Sam was bringing Brad to that party," Sophie says, shaking her head. "Don't you remember who dragged her out of there that night?" she asks as she puts a hand to her chest dramatically. "If I didn't get Sam out of there, you know what would've happened. Brad was a serious creep," she says, shaking her head at the memory.

Accusing Sophie of that last one feels like a stretch, but at this point, I wouldn't put anything past her. We were all supposed to meet up at a friend's house after graduation when Sam texted that she'd already hitched a ride with some guy from our class. Obviously, I wasn't happy about it, but it's not like she was my girlfriend or anything, so I had to just sit back and watch.

"Is this why you tried so hard to talk me out of going camping last weekend? You know how much that trip means to me, Soph!" I say, and watch the hurt that flashes across Sophie's eyes.

"Why, Soph?" I ask, my anger brimming at all of the lost time because of her elaborately orchestrated scheming. Sophie's expression softens, and I see tears start to well in her eyes. "No. Stop. You do not get to cry right now," I say sternly. "Explain yourself."

Sophie presses her body back against the fridge where she was standing and lets herself slide down its front before slumping to the floor on her butt. She lets out a breath and covers her face with her hands.

"Don't you understand, Jess? What would've happened between all of us if you two had gotten together back then?" she says, and her voice is barely audible through her hands. It's something she always has a habit of doing when she's embarrassed, and I feel bad even though I'm still mad at her.

I don't say anything as I watch her, waiting for her to continue. Sophie drops her hands away from her face, and tears stream down her cheeks as she looks up at me with bloodshot eyes.

"You two would've gone off all happy and in love, and you would've forgotten all about me. *I would've had no one!*" Sophie says angrily through her tears, and my heart softens a little at her words.

I sigh and move to sit beside her on the kitchen floor as I cross my legs in front of me. "Soph no—"

320

"Take your sympathy and shove it, Jess," Sophie spits before I can console her.

"I would've lost both of my best friends and been completely alone again. I was not going to let that happen. That's why I made damn sure that Sam always knew when you had a new girlfriend and that you knew your affections for her were wasted," Sophie says before she starts crying into her hands again.

Although I am angry with her, I do sympathize in a way. Had the roles been reversed, I might've felt the same way. Two of the most important people in my life leaving so they could be happy together, away from me.

I guess that's the difference between Sophie and me. Because I know what that sadness and loneliness feel like better than anyone, I never would've let her feel alone, not again, not after what happened with our parents. If anything, she should've trusted me since I'm possibly the only one who really knows exactly what she went through back then.

"How selfish are you that you took it this far for all these years?" I ask her, shaking my head.

"I know it was wrong, Jess. I'm sorry," Sophie says as she continues to cry into her hands.

"So apparently, the rules you set for everyone else don't apply to you, then?" I ask, and gesture to the door with my hand, referring to the little show I witnessed on the porch earlier between her and Chris.

She looks up at me, regret in her teary eyes. "I never intended to act on my feelings toward Chris. We've never actually been serious, I swear. I've made sure to keep it casual this entire time," she says, desperately trying to plead her case.

"I knew it wasn't fair after what I did to keep you and Sam apart all these years. But I just…" she says, her own teary hiccup cutting her off.

"Soph, I love you," I say softly, grabbing her hand. "Even if not by blood, you *are* my sister. I promise you could never lose me—or Sam—

*ever*. I think she loves you maybe even more than I do, if that's even possible," I say, and we both laugh softly at that.

"You should've trusted that even if things between Sam and me had changed, it would never have changed how we felt about you. It's always been us, Soph, it'll always be us. *All* of us. Even that asshole Chris," I say, letting out a small laugh as I rest my head back against the kitchen cabinets.

"*Jess*," Sophie says as she starts sobbing, and I pull her to my chest to hold her. "I'm sorry, *I'm so so sorry!*" she says, and I hold her while she cries, her tears soaking the front of my shirt as we sit on the kitchen floor. "She's never going to forgive me," Sophie says through her sobs.

"She will. I know she will," I say, stroking the back of Sophie's head gently as she continues to borderline wail like a big baby. "It's okay Soph, it's okay," I say, and try not to chuckle at how over the top she's being. "Just let it out."

Eventually, she stops crying, and after she calms down, I let out a breath I didn't realize I was even holding. I let go of Sophie and force her to look up at me. "Hey, let's order a pizza," I say.

"Extra pepperoni?" she asks, sniffling up at me with her big sage-colored doe eyes.

"*Extra pepperoni*," I say, and smile at her before kissing the top of her head.

I try to shake away my thoughts from last night and focus on the task at hand. After no luck with finding Sam, I decide to head to the retirement home, hoping Aunt Judy will have some sage words of advice for me. Either that or she's just going to smack me and then chew me out. Judy was the one who told me to apologize to Sam, and look at how well that turned out.

After I pull up to Judy's retirement home, my anxiety gets the best of me, and I decide to text Sophie anyway before going in.

Hey. Have you heard from
Sam lately?

No, she's still ignoring my
messages. Why?

No reason.

Wait, weren't you supposed
to be with her today?

…

Wtf Jess

It's fine. It's probably
nothing. I'm overthinking
things.

What happened?
What did you say to her?
Oh, shit, did she reject
you??
Damn, I did not see that
coming.

No, she didn't reject me.
Dick.

???

I just pulled into Judy's. I'll
fill you in later when I get
home.

323

k.

I sigh and slip my phone into my pocket as I head to Aunt Judy's room and knock on the door before letting myself in.

"Come in! It's about time! You're late—"

Aunt Judy meets me at the door. She gives me a disappointed look before turning back toward her recliner by the window. "Oh, it's just you," she says.

"Okay...? Hello to you too, I guess," I say, closing the door behind me.

Aunt Judy waves me off as she sits down in her chair. "I thought you were Samantha," she says disappointedly. "She's not with you, is she?" Judy asks, craning her neck to look behind me.

"Sorry, no," I say and sit down in the chair opposite her recliner. "I was with her earlier, but..."

Aunt Judy gives me a look like she might throw something at my head. "I thought I told you to make things better with Sam, not worse!" she says exasperatedly as she throws her hands in the air.

"I did," I say and shrug. "Before I could finish explaining myself, she took off," I say, putting my hands up defensively.

Judy gives me a disapproving grunt as she narrows her eyes at me.

"In truth, I sorta hoped that she'd be here with you, that's why I came by," I say, scratching my head.

Judy crosses her arms and throws her nose in the air. "Well, when you do see Samantha, be sure to let her know that I'm mad."

"Honestly, you'll probably have a better chance of seeing her before I do, but I'll be sure to tell her," I say and scrunch my brows together. "Wait, what'd she do to make you so mad?" I ask.

"She was supposed to be here an hour ago, and now we've missed our pedicure appointments. Do you have any idea what I had to do to get out of my poker game today so I could go to that appointment?" Judy asks me, raising her brows, and I shake my head in response.

"Well, I'll tell you. I had to bribe that old bitty, Blanche, with my dessert for the next two weeks," Judy says as she holds up two stubby fingers at me. "TWO WEEKS, JESS! Can you believe that?" she says before she throws her hands up in the air dramatically.

"Wait, what do you mean an hour ago?" I ask, trying not to jump to conclusions.

"*I mean*, we had plans to go out today, and Sam never showed up. She didn't call or anything, and now her phone keeps going to voicemail," Judy explains. "That's why I figured she was with you."

"I was prepared to forgive her since it probably meant that you two had patched things up," she says with a humph. "If you're sittin' here with me right now, you obviously didn't do somethin' right," Judy says and rolls her eyes at me.

I stand from my chair, almost knocking it over, and dial Sophie on my phone. Aunt Judy looks up at me, startled by my sudden movements. "What the hell's wrong with you, kid? You trying to give this old broad a heart attack?" she says angrily as she grasps at her chest.

"Sorry, Judy," I say and quickly kiss her on the head before rushing toward the door.

"Where are you going?" she calls after me, confused.

"To find Sam," I say over my shoulder just as Sophie picks up the phone, and I rush out the door to the parking lot.

"And you're sure that was her last location?" I ask Sophie as I speed down the road in my Jeep.

"For the tenth time, *yes*. Her shared location with me says the last place she was before she turned her phone off was at that record shop down on 6th," Sophie says, her voice echoing through the Bluetooth speakers of my Jeep.

"Dammit, why would she turn her phone off," I grumble, mostly to myself.

"Probably because you shot her down again and she wants nothing to do with you right now," Sophie says.

"First of all, that was a rhetorical question, and secondly, your smartass remarks aren't helping anything right now," I say, turning down 6th street.

"Sorry," Sophie says apologetically through the phone.

"Okay, I'm hanging up now, I just got here. Let me know if you hear anything from Sam," I say.

"Sure thing, let me know if you find her," Sophie says before hanging up the phone.

I park on the street right in front of the shop and see a new sign on the door that reads Retro Rhythm. I think back to the last time I was here, back when the shop was called Gil's. Grandpa Millard loved music and would bring me along sometimes when he'd shop for vinyls.

I hop out of my Jeep, and when I open the door to the small store, a bell rings as I walk in, alerting the worker behind the counter. The second I step into the old shop, my senses transport me back to when I was twelve or thirteen, sifting through the old crates with Grandpa Millard for the latest Chicago album. The shop still has the smell of a building of its age, and the floor creaks beneath my feet as I walk across the old wood.

The worker sitting behind the counter has long blonde hair and is wearing round tinted sunglasses—and if I had to guess, I'd say he was high as a kite right now judging by the expression on his face.

"Welcome in, my dude. What can I help you find today?" he asks with a friendly smile.

*Yeah, this guy is definitely stoned.*

I smile at him as I sift through one of the crates of vinyls on the table near the front of the shop. "I'm actually just looking for my girl. She was supposed to meet me next door, but I figured she might've wandered in here instead," I say, trying to sound more like a concerned boyfriend than a creepy stalker.

"Sorry, my guy, it's just been me in here this afternoon," the cashier says, looking around as if he'd just realized he's actually at work.

"Okay, no worries, man," I say casually and shrug. I give him a physical description of Sam, on the off chance that she walks into the store, though I'm sure that's unlikely at this point.

"Best of luck, my guy. I'll be sure to keep an eye out for your girl," he says, giving me a military salute as I nod and walk out the door.

*Shit.* I sigh and rub my eyes as I climb into my Jeep and feel my phone vibrate in my pocket.

Any luck?

Nope, no sign of her.

I'm sure she's at home. Just give her some space, she'll come around when she's ready to talk.

Yeah, maybe you're right.

Don't beat yourself up about it too hard.

I put my phone down and start the Jeep with a huff. I try calling Sam's phone one more time, and just as I'd expected, it goes straight to voicemail. I put my Jeep in reverse and head back to the main road.

I'm almost home when my mind starts to overthink things more than it already is. Okay, so Sam's obviously mad at me, but why miss her date with Aunt Judy? That just doesn't make any sense. It's so unlike Sam to pull something like this, especially to not even call Judy, either.

When we were growing up, Sam was always right there with her for *every single* old person activity that Aunt Judy wanted to go to. Sam was always the first to volunteer for anything having to do with Judy at all.

*So why is she messing with her streak now?*

I shake my head, trying to just forget about it, but I can't help the nagging feeling in my gut. I turn the Jeep around and head toward John's house instead, hoping that Sam's there.

I try to rationalize with myself as I speed down the street. *I'll just check in on her real quick, make sure she's safe, and then I'll give her all the space she needs...*

I try Sam's cell again, and it goes straight to voicemail. *Dammit, Sam.*

I pull into John's driveway and notice Chris standing in front of his pickup truck, a hose in one hand and a can of beer in the other. *Typical.* He stares at me as I put my Jeep in park and jump out.

"What are *you* doing here—" he asks, but I hurriedly cut him off.

"Sam, is she here?" I ask impatiently.

"What?" Chris scoffs. "You have a lovers' quarrel or something?" he mocks and turns back toward his truck. I watch as he sprays the passenger door with the hose before taking another swig of his beer.

I'm not in the mood to deal with his shit, so I walk right past him up to the front door. Most of the time I'm able to handle Chris's usual sour disposition, but not today of all days.

"Hey asshole, where do you think you're going? I asked you a question," he calls after me, and I suddenly feel water soaking into the back of my shirt.

"What the fuck, man? What's your problem?" I say angrily as I turn to face him.

"Sorry *bro*, it's just water. Lighten up," Chris says, laughing before finishing off the last of his can. He lets out a large belch and grabs another can out of the cooler next to his truck before cracking it open with a *hiss*.

I shake my head, reminding myself that I've got more important things to deal with right now instead of Chris. I turn back around and climb the porch steps to the house, and just before my hand can grasp the door handle, I feel water on my back again. This time, the water lingers on me longer than before, soaking my shirt completely.

*Fuck this.*

I let my temper get the best of me as I turn and dart off the porch. Chris is still laughing when I tackle him to the ground by his waist, and the hose and beer can fly from his hands as we tumble onto the grass.

"What is your damage, man?" I ask angrily as I straddle his waist, trying to pin him down.

"*You*, you asshole. I'm so damn sick of you! It's always Jess this, Jess that, *well fuck you, Jess*," Chris says before he takes a large swing, clocking me in the jaw.

The hit somewhat takes me by surprise, which Chris uses to his advantage. He roughly shoves me off of him and we switch places. Chris now straddles me instead, simmering mad above me.

"Ohhh, I get it, you're still mad about before, aren't you?" I say, out of breath with a smirk, realizing that he's still sore about what'd happened on the boat with the fish.

"You do realize that was your fault, right?" I grab Chris by his shirt and pull him toward me. "Or can you not remember?" I say with an angry scoff. "If you didn't spend that entire morning chugging beer cans until you were drunk off your ass, it never would've happened," I say, struggling to keep my anger at bay, especially since I know that he blamed me for the entire incident.

Chris's features twist angrily before he slams me down into the grass, putting the full force of his weight on me, making it hard for me to breathe. "You fucking asshole," he seethes, and before he can hit me, I reach up and grab him by his shirt before I throw him off me in a surge of adrenaline.

We roll around on the grass as we fight each other, each landing our fair share of punches and a few cheap shots along the way, including a sharp elbow to my ribs and a bite mark on Chris's ear. We eventually both end up on our feet, sweaty, covered in dirt and blood, still both ready to keep going. Chris waves at me to bring it on, and I'm just about to charge at him when John interrupts us.

"I think that's quite enough, boys," John says, and we both snap our heads up toward the house. John stands on the front porch with his arms folded across his chest; his face twisted into a frown.

John interrupting our fight was enough to temporarily calm my anger toward Chris, reminding me of what I'm even doing there in the first place. I rush over to John, out of breath.

"Sam, is she—"

I barely get the words out when my phone rings and I frantically move to check the caller ID. When I see that it's Madison, I hit decline and look back up at John, a look of worry now on his face.

"Jess, what's this about? What's going on?" he asks, eyeing me suspiciously.

I shake my head, still trying to catch my breath. "I was with Sam earlier, and now I can't get a hold of her. I was hoping she was here—"

"She's probably just ignoring you. We'll let her know you stopped by," Chris says, stepping toward John and me. "Or, maybe we won't," he says, and snickers.

I let out an exhausted breath and turn back to John and plead at him with my eyes. "Please just tell me she's here."

John's brows furrow together as he speaks. "Sorry, kid, I haven't seen her all day," he says, but I'm not totally convinced of that. He never pays Sam any mind, so how in the hell would he even know if she were home or not?

My phone rings again, and I hit decline.

"Shouldn't you get that?" John nods to the phone in my hand just as I'm about to hit decline for the fourth time in a row when my screen lights up again.

"It's nothing, it's not important," I say, shaking my head, remembering the last time that Madison called me like this.

"It doesn't seem like nothing," John says, narrowing his eyes at me.

I wait two seconds, and just as I predict, my phone lights up again with Madison's name. I pick up the phone and turn away from John and Chris.

"*What?* What, Madison? What the fuck do you want?" I hiss angrily into the phone at her, and I'm only met with silence.

"*Shit.*" I run a hand through my hair as I try to calm down. "Sorry," I say as I let out a breath. "What's up? Are you okay?" I ask more calmly than before.

"I've been trying to text you, Jess, but you haven't been responding," Madison whispers through the phone. "Jess, something's wrong," she says.

*She can't be serious right now.*

I sigh heavily as I look toward the sky, and place a hand over my face, rubbing my eyes. The girl is turning out to be such a pain in my ass, it makes me wonder just what she needs "rescuing" from this time.

"Are you okay? Are you hurt?" I ask. "Where are you? I'll come pick you up," I say and turn, walking toward my Jeep.

I decide that if Sam's not here at John's, then there's no sense in my staying any longer. I tell myself that as soon as I'm off my call with Madison, I'll call Soph again and see if Sam's location has updated at all.

*If Sam's not here, then where the hell could she be? Maybe she went to the retirement home after all. I'll check there on my way just to be safe...*

I'm barely paying attention to Madison on the other end of the line when she speaks.

"No, not me, Jess," she whispers. "There's another girl here, I think I recognize her from that day at the grocery store. She said her name was Sam, but I pretended not to know her."

Dread fills my body at Madison's words.

I stop in my tracks and turn back toward Chris and John, both still silently watching me from the front porch.

"Madison, where are you?" I ask sternly. Her voice sounds panicked through the phone, and I can hear what sounds like an echo, like she's in a bathroom or something.

"Jess, these guys are serious. You're gonna need backup," she says. "I'm not sure the name, but it's one of the old stores downtown," Madison says, her voice trailing off.

"Do they sell records there?" I ask her frantically.

It sounds like someone is banging on a door, and I can hear yelling on the other side of the phone. "*Maddy, hurry up in there, I've gotta take a piss!*"

"Jesus Christ, Elliott! Give me two seconds!" she yells back at him.

My blood runs cold, and I hope I'm just imagining it. Did she just say... *Elliott?*

"Madison, who are you there with?" I ask her, my voice still frantic.

"*Shit*, I have to go, Jess," she whispers quickly before the line goes dead.

"Madison? Madison!" I yell into the phone, trying not to pull my hair out in frustration.

"How typical, you say you're looking for my sister, but yet you've got girls calling you off the hook," Chris says, now standing at the base of the porch.

"What is that supposed to mean?" I ask angrily as I turn to face him.

"Nothing, just that it seems like you're the only one who doesn't seem to realize that Sam's in love with you like some fucking idiot," Chris says with a scoff.

I let my temper get the best of me a second time and charge Chris, tackling him to the grass again. Only this time, I don't give him a chance to land a single punch as I repeatedly smash my fist into his face over and over again.

I feel John's arms from behind me as he pulls me off of Chris. "That's enough! I will not tolerate this anymore, understand?" he says angrily from behind me. He tightens his hold on me, but I don't give him a response, wishing he'd let me go so I could pound in Chris's face some more.

Chris lies on the ground and grabs at his jaw. "*Son of a bitch*," he murmurs under his breath as he wiggles it from side to side, no doubt checking to see if it's broken or not.

"Why are you such a shitty brother, huh? Don't you see how much she cares about you?" I ask, out of breath from trying to free myself from John's grasp. "Either of you!" I add, trying to turn and look at John.

"I'm fine, dammit!" I say, jerking away from him when he hesitates to let me go.

Chris turns his head to the side and spits a mouthful of blood onto the grass before he glares up at me. "Why the fuck do you care so much? This isn't even your family," Chris says, still lying on the grass on his side, now propped up onto his forearm.

His words sting, and I think back to all the time I spent here as a child—with him, with John and Helena, and with Sam. I knew they weren't my blood relatives, but I really did feel like I had a family when I was with all of them. Judy did the best she could, but the time I spent with the Ryan family felt different—it felt… whole.

I think about all the summers with Sophie and Sam, all the time we spent together at this very house, and the thought of her makes my chest ache.

I think about her beautiful smile, and how when the light hits her hair just right, you can see streaks of auburn through the dark strands. I think about her sarcastic sense of humor, her wit, and the way that she makes me feel so alive just by being near her.

My best friend. My heart. *My* Sam.

"You might not feel like I'm family to you, but Sam is *my* family. She's everything to me. I… I love her," I say with an exhausted breath, though I'm sure Chris wasn't expecting a response.

"Chris, whatever your beef with me is, I need you to put it on hold for now," I say, walking over to where he's still lying on the grass and hold my hand out to him. "I need your help," I say, waiting for him to take it.

"Why in the hell would I help you when you just beat the living shit out of me?" he asks incredulously.

"Go find someone else," Chris says, turning onto his hands and knees before trying to stand, still refusing to take my outstretched hand.

I grab onto his right forearm, helping him up even though he tries to push me away. "You don't understand," I say. "Elliott has Sam."

John and Chris both exchange confused glances before asking in unison.

"*Who?*"

334

# Chapter Nineteen

When I open my eyes, a wave of vertigo hits me, and I feel like I might throw up. I sit up and try to look around, but the room spins. I catch a glimpse of a rainbow of colors before I have to shut my eyes again.

I take a few deep breaths before I'm finally able to look around, and I see a giant tie-dye sheet hanging on the wall across from me. The colors slowly stop moving as my dizziness eventually subsides, and I try to blink the residual blurriness from my vision.

*Where the hell am I? And, why does everything hurt?*

I feel a dull ache coming from my right arm, and when I try to move it, I groan as a sharp pain shoots from my wrist all the way up to my shoulder. My elbow is throbbing, and I hiss at the pain as I look down at my arm. The skin feels tight and swollen, and I can't be sure, but it feels like something is definitely broken.

I try wiggling a few fingers on my right hand, and another intense pang shoots up the length of my arm. The feeling is enough to make me double over the armrest of the leather couch I'm on, and bile rises in my throat. I try to hold back my vomit, and breathe slowly through my nose, desperately trying to ground myself, and when I look down, I'm even more confused.

I notice a dark orange color covering most of the floor and wonder who in the hell still has shag carpet these days.

I slowly glance around at my surroundings, grateful that my eyes have finally focused, and that the room is no longer spinning, but I'm beyond confused. I can't for the life of me recall how I got here, and the more I try to remember what happened, the worse my head throbs.

I push myself up and sit back against the couch cushions as I take in the space around me. The room is small, maybe the size of a living room or an office space. Given that I can see copper pipes and wooden support beams all across the ceiling, I think it's safe to assume that I'm in a basement. I sweep the room again with my eyes.

*What in the 1975?*

Dirty orange carpet covers the entire length of the area, with a smaller red rug toward the center of the room—both of which are made from the same ugly shag material.

The walls are covered in brightly designed mandala tapestries, with one more colorful than the next. Giant swirls and circles dance on them, each one intricately designed, and I find myself admiring their beauty despite the anxiety building in my chest.

There isn't much furniture in the room except for the small leather sofa and a matching loveseat. There are a few shelves littered with various books and vinyls, and a small coffee table in the center of the room next to a patchwork jean beanbag.

I sniff the air, trying to place the pungent odor that fills the room, and spot an incense holder on the coffee table in front of me, right next to a large ashtray and a giant bong.

*So, that would be the smell, then…*

I crinkle my nose at the strange mixture of scents and feel my headache coming on stronger now that I've actually placed the unpleasant aroma around me.

I look around, wondering what I'm doing all alone in a dank 70's-style basement with a jacked-up arm, and my brain continues to pound against my skull. Deep down, I know that something is off, and I feel my fight or flight instincts starting to kick in. Confused or not, I know for a fact that I've never been here before, and would be lying if I didn't admit to being scared out of my mind right now.

I stand from the couch, thinking it's high time to get the hell out of here, when my knees wobble and threaten to give out beneath me. Out of reflex, I try reaching out my arms to steady myself, but the connection with my brain is lost somewhere along the way when only one of them cooperates. I land hard on my left wrist, grunting as my body connects with the carpeted cement. I feel like I might've twisted it from the force of trying to catch my body weight.

I roll over onto my back, both wrists now throbbing as I stare at the ceiling above me. I notice that the wooden supports are painted a dirty brown color, and wonder if that was done on purpose or if it's just due to the age of the building.

I chuckle through the pain. *What a yucky color. It reminds me of Elliott's eyes…* Dread sets in full force as I remember what happened in the alleyway.

*Wait, what* did *happen?*

I panic, trying not to jump to conclusions, unable to remember what all happened before I passed out. The last thing I remember was Elliott groping me before he tried to twist my arm off.

I do a quick assessment of my body, and other than my wrists and arm—and aside from the pounding headache I have—no other parts of my body are sore.

*That doesn't mean he didn't touch me, though…*

I try not to think about Elliott's hands all over my unconscious body, and suddenly I feel nauseous again. I roll onto my left side, and I gag at the pain that shoots up my other arm. I breathe through the aching discomfort as I clutch my injured arm to my chest and sit up slowly, not wanting to make myself even more lightheaded than I already am.

I pull myself up off the sofa before standing, my legs less shaky this time around even though my knees throb, and I'm careful not to let myself fall again.

I stand still for a second, trying to gather my bearings before I dare move again, and glance around. I scan the room for a way out, and from what I can see, the only visible exit is a small metal staircase in the corner of the room.

I slowly make my way over to the stairs before grabbing onto the railing with my left hand. I only make it up a few steps when I hear several voices echoing from up above before the door at the top of the stairs swings open with a loud clang.

Fluorescent light streams down the dark stairway, and I put my good arm up to shield my eyes from its brightness. I stagger back and almost lose my footing before grabbing onto the railing, catching myself before I fall. My frame jerks, and I wince at the pain it causes to my right side, forcing me to take a step back down the stairs.

Though it's too bright to make out faces, I see three silhouettes at the top. One of them unmistakably a woman, her figure and heeled boots a dead giveaway.

"Thank god," I say up to the woman. "I need help, I was attacked by some psycho, and I think my arm is broken," I say as the figures make their way down the stairs toward me.

One of them closes the door behind them, cutting off the bright light, and I hear snickers from behind the woman from her companions.

"Some psycho, huh? Sounds dangerous," someone says, and more snickers come from the shadows. "*Oooo*, how scary."

They all laugh, and I hear a familiar voice mocking me. Unease runs through me as I recognize the voices, and I stumble backward off the last step of the stairs, falling onto my butt as I hit the hard ground.

"What? Don't tell me you're not happy to see me?" one of the voices asks mockingly.

"What are you doing here, Kyle?" I demand, looking up at my ex-boyfriend as he stands towering over me at the base of the stairs.

"Me?" he asks, looking around. "Why, this is my shop, of course. You're looking at the newest owner of Gil's, or as we like to call it now, *Retro Rhythm*," he says proudly. "The better question would be, what are *you* doing here, *baby*?" he asks with a mocking smile.

*As if he doesn't know.*

I try to scoot myself backward, wanting to get as far away from him as I possibly can.

"Owner? Yeah right," I say with a scoff. "And don't call me *baby*," I seethe at him.

"What? You don't think I'm smart enough to own my own business? Is that it?" Kyle asks, and the way he angrily takes a step toward me has me rethinking my choice of words.

"No, I never said that. Though I'm sure you acquired it by nefarious means, I don't really give a shit either way," I say, feeling like I might only be making things worse for myself by provoking him.

I scramble back awkwardly, only able to use one hand to help me as Kyle keeps moving closer. "Look, Kyle, I don't know what I'm doing here either, so please just let me leave," I say, trying not to let the desperation in my voice show. If he thinks he's got me cornered, he'll just keep pushing. It's how the sick bastard gets off.

Kyle shakes his head with an unfriendly smile. "I don't think so. I think we should do some catching up first, don't you, Elliott?" Kyle calls over his shoulder up toward the stairwell.

Elliott steps into the light of the room, followed by a beautiful brunette. I'm sure that my eyes are bugging out of my head by the look on Kyle's face before he turns to face the girl. And, unless Madison has a doppelgänger who is also named Madison, my information about her coming from Alaska with Jess was a load of shit.

I feel my cheeks burn. How many other things have I gotten wrong about Jess, about Madison, about *everything?*

"You two know each other?" Kyle asks, looking between us both as he raises a brow.

Madison flops herself down onto one of the ends of the leather sofa before giving me a judgmental once-over.

"Yeah right, does it look like we'd be friends?" she says with a scoff before looking down at her phone, and what little hope I had quickly turns to dread again.

I try not to take her comment personally, and wonder for a second if maybe she doesn't recognize me. Granted, we only met for a minute that day at the store, but now I'm wondering if maybe I should've been more friendly toward her.

I consider my options and figure it doesn't matter if Madison recognizes me or not. She's the only one who can get a message to Jess, and I pray that she'll help me.

"I need you to call Jess. Please, just tell him I'm here. Tell him Sam, is here," I say. The panic in my voice is becoming increasingly difficult to hide with every passing second, and I wonder if this situation couldn't get any worse.

"What is she talking about, Maddy?" Kyle asks as he turns to her, irritation clear in his voice.

"Hell if I know. I don't know anyone named Jessie," Madison says, scrolling through her phone with an annoyed look on her face. "Look at that huge bump on her head, she's obviously confused," Madison says as she nods toward me without looking up and pops her gum loudly against her teeth.

Reflexively, I reach my hand up to my head and wince at the tenderness—and sure enough—I feel a giant goose egg forming on the left side of my forehead. I pull my hand away to reveal a few small crusts of dried blood on my fingertips, wondering just how hard I fell, and figure that would explain my splitting headache.

I wonder if maybe Madison and Jess broke up, and that's why she's pretending not to know him. Granted, he did say things between them were pretty complicated. I try not to judge, but I'm having a hard time picturing Jess being involved with someone like Madison. I get it if she doesn't want to be besties or anything, but I feel like this has to be breaking some important girl code rule.

"Enough with your games, Kyle," I say finally, trying to keep my voice calm as I turn my attention back to him. "You don't even live in this town, so what are you really doing here?" I ask, trying to stall while I think of an escape plan.

Elliott sits down in the blue beanbag and lights the large bong before he takes a deep inhale and then passes it to Madison. We briefly make eye contact as she takes a hit from the bong, but then quickly goes back to looking at her phone. I watch as Elliott leans back and stretches out his legs as if getting ready for a show and smiles widely at me with his crooked teeth.

"No games here, baby," Kyle says, putting his hands up defensively. "The way you always talked about your *beloved* hometown made me want to check it out for myself," he says, mocking me.

Kyle knows I've never had a particular love for this place, only for the people here—but, I never told him that part.

"Turns out it's a nice little town. I might've decided to put down some roots here, who knows, maybe find a nice girl to settle down with," Kyle says, crouching down next to me so that our faces are almost at eye level. When he goes to reach for me, I flinch, causing his features to twist in anger.

Kyle reaches out and gently puts his hand around my throat, as if in warning. "Did you really think I was going to hit you?" he says, and I stare back at him silently, trying not to let my fear show.

When he finally releases me, instead of moving away, he inches even closer. Kyle puts a hand on my cheek, and I turn my head away. He pulls his hand back, pretending to be hurt by the gesture, but it doesn't reach his eyes.

"Sam, I did this for us," he says, barely above a whisper. I stare at him with confusion as he stands and turns away from me.

"What do you mean you did this for *us?*" I ask, thinking he must've lost his mind. Kyle sits on the small loveseat next to Elliott and his beanbag before crossing one of his ankles over his knee and sits back in the chair.

"Kyle, we're not together anymore, why would you say something like that?" I ask as I furrow my brows, wondering why I'm even bothering with trying to rationalize with an obvious crazy person.

"You're too good for me, Sam. I always knew that you were. That's why I wanted to prove to you that I could do something good for you, for *us*," Kyle says as he lights up a cigarette from the pack that was lying on the table. He takes a long drag as he sits back in the chair again. His words sound sincere, and I almost believe him for a second until I remember who I'm dealing with.

At one point in time, I thought I really loved him, but he quickly ruined that. I know there's no shortage of decent guys out there, but I think that subconsciously I just wanted to stop myself from thinking about Jess all the time. Guess that's why I picked the first guy to come along who was almost his polar opposite. I wanted to make sure that there was no way I would mistake any part of my new guy for Jess. So that's exactly what I found.

The day that Kyle walked into the campus bar, I let myself fall head over heels for him. He was of average height with a thin build, short blonde hair, and pretty light brown eyes that seemed to hold nothing but mischief in them.

Tattoos covered his pale body from his neck all the way to his fingertips, with almost every piercing under the sun to go along with—including some I had never even seen in real life before.

His dangerous aura reeled me in quickly, and looking back, I wish I'd have been more careful.

Even though we met at the campus bar, Kyle wasn't a student at my school. He was working for a maintenance company that came to repair the beer taps that would frequently break. Of course, me, working there as a bartender, and him, fixing said things behind the bar, we ended up spending a lot of time together.

343

The first time he asked me out, I basically shouted *"YES!"* before he was even able to get the question out. After that, we started seeing each other regularly outside of work, and at one point, we even almost moved in together.

But instead of using my intuition about his alluring red flag slash borderline threatening persona, I let myself be drawn to it. I got caught up in the fantasy of dating a "bad boy" and eventually started making excuses and justifying his toxic behavior, which included treating me poorly on the regular.

At first, it was thrilling and exciting. Kyle was fun and mysterious, and the sex was crazy and passionate. Kyle showed me a whole new world of pleasure that I never even knew was possible, especially after only dating high school boys.

When I started to expect more from Kyle beyond just the physical aspects of our relationship, he didn't like it.

Most nights, he would come over drunk, and I started to feel like he was just using me. We didn't talk about real things anymore, and I felt like I was only becoming a warm body to him. I didn't want to be alone, so for a while I put up with it and let him use me whenever and wherever he wanted to. At first, I was okay with it because I was sort of using him in my own way too, but I wanted more from him. I *needed* more.

Kyle would whisper sweet nothings into my ear and tell me how much he needed me, and I forced myself to believe his bullshit, even though I knew that his words were empty.

Eventually, I started to get sick of his disrespectful behavior, especially since it only seemed to get worse. I had been thinking about ending things with Kyle for some time, but when I caught him with another girl in his bed, that was the last straw for me. Part of me always hoped that things would change and go back to the way they were before when we first got together, but after witnessing what I did, it made me feel like he didn't think I was worth it.

I honestly thought he'd be relieved since I was giving him an easy out of our relationship. Though I *was* upset, I don't think I gave him the reaction he was looking for, and I wonder if that's one of the reasons why he was so furious with me. It wasn't like I didn't get upset when I caught them, I just knew that no matter how much crying and pleading was involved, he'd already made his decision, and I was obviously second choice. Even though I'd planned to break up with Kyle, seeing someone else in his bed made me feel like I'd probably never meant anything to him in the first place, and that thought stung like a bitch.

Kyle broke every dish in his apartment that day before begging me to stay with him. It took every ounce of self-respect I had in me when I told him it was over for real. Kyle then responded by punching a large hole in the kitchen wall. That was the first time I was ever truly afraid of him, and even though he let me leave that day, he still called after me from on his knees in the doorway when I walked out.

I felt so alone and worthless in that moment, that it took almost everything in me not to turn around and go back to him. Even knowing what was in store for me if I stayed with him, the fact that I didn't have to be alone anymore was almost enough to make me stay and bury my head in the sand.

Shortly after that, I met Daniel. He was quiet and nerdy and seemed like the last person in the world to throw a plate at me or to punch a hole in something, so I let myself start to fall for him instead. *I guess we know how that one turned out, though…*

"All right. Say I believe you," I say from my place on the orange rug as I snap myself back to reality.

I can see the hope that flashes across Kyle's eyes at my words. "Does that mean—" Kyle starts.

"First, answer me one thing," I say.

I have no intention of ever taking him back, especially since I'm already fairly certain of what his answer will be, but I need to hear it, nonetheless.

"How long were you seeing her?" I ask, and Kyle says nothing as he leans forward in his chair and I can't quite read his expression, so I repeat my question more clearly.

"Were you or were you not sleeping with another woman the entire fucking time we were together?" I say and this time, Kyle clenches his jaw and looks away from me, which only fuels my fire.

"Would you slip out in the night after you told me that you loved me to go and fuck her?" I ask through calm rage and feel myself getting riled up. I know there's nothing between us anymore, but the betrayal I felt by someone I thought I loved and trusted still lingers in my chest.

"Answer me, Kyle," I demand as I fume at him, unsure of why I'm so upset over someone I feel nothing for anymore.

I watch as Kyle's features quickly turn to anger as he meets my eyes again. He stands and grabs the ashtray off the coffee table before throwing it against the wall behind me, glass and cigarette butts flying everywhere as it shatters against the cement wall. My heart starts to race, and I cover my face to shield my eyes, but no one else even bats an eye at Kyle's angry outburst.

"Seriously, Kyle?" Madison says as she finally looks up from her phone, seeming more annoyed that her scrolling was disturbed than out of any actual fear of him.

Madison stands from the couch as she brushes off the cigarette ashes that landed in her hair and storms off toward the stairs in a huff. Neither Kyle nor Elliott pays her any attention as she leaves, her heeled boots clacking on the metal as she climbs, and the door slams shut behind her.

I turn my attention from Madison back to Kyle, my heart still racing from the shock of his violent outburst. I stare at him in silence, my anger still simmering at him.

"What do you want me to say, Sam? That I would picture your face while I was inside of her? That after you left, I wished it was your voice crying out my name instead of hers?" Kyle licks his lips as he gives me a sinister look, his voice dropping an octave as he continues.

"Do you want me to tell you that every time I felt her nails on my back, I wished that it was you who was digging deep into my flesh instead? Is that it?" Kyle says as he grabs at his crotch, and his eyes look wild. *"Because I did."*

I watch him with rage in my bones and feel like scratching his eyes out. "That's the worst apology I've ever heard," I say through gritted teeth.

"It's the truth," Kyle says as he looks at me with a half-lidded expression.

In the past, the tension of our fight combined with his dirty words would've been enough to make me want to screw his brains out right then and there, but now, they only make me want to murder him.

"You made me feel like complete trash, and now you think I'll take you back just because you tried to get me worked up with some mediocre dirty talk?" I ask in disbelief, still struggling to keep my anger at bay. "I felt worthless for *months* because of your lies and how you treated me."

Kyle gives me a blank stare as he takes another drag from his cigarette before tapping the ashes onto the floor.

"I can't believe I ever wasted my time on a fucking deadbeat loser like you," I say and shake my head with an exhausted sigh.

Kyle cracks a small smile at my words, and I'm feeling so angry that I want to cry. "Fuck you, Kyle," I say as I glare at him, trying not to give him the explosive reaction I know he was hoping for.

Kyle's cigarette sizzles as he puts it out against the wood of the coffee table. "Okay," he says darkly, biting his lip as he looks at me. "Elliott. Door," Kyle says without breaking eye contact with me. Elliott lets out a giddy laugh at Kyle's command and jumps up out of his beanbag.

347

"What do you think you're doing, Kyle?" I ask frantically through my anger. I know it's a stupid question that I'm sure I don't actually want the answer to, and I kick myself for playing right into his trap.

"I knew you'd take some convincing," he says, standing as he unzips his leather jacket before draping it over the back of the loveseat. "I figured I'd end up having to remind you of what you've been missing these last few months." Kyle swipes his tongue over his bottom lip, and his eyes darken as he steps toward me.

*Last few months?* This guy is delusional.

We haven't been together in over a year, and even during that last little bit, it was like we weren't even a real couple anymore, and he knows that.

The sound of Elliott's boots on the metal steps of the stairs snaps me back to reality, and I hear the heavy door as it groans open before someone calls down to him. "Yo, Elliott, you got a second?"

I try to yell for help, hoping someone upstairs will hear me, when Kyle bends down and grabs my head as he puts his hand over the lower half of my face, blocking both of my airways. He shakes a finger in my face as he makes a small *tsk* sound, and signals for me to keep quiet.

I used to think Kyle would never physically assault me, but now I'm not so sure. We used to get pretty rough before, but that was only ever during sex, and it was always consensual.

Kyle's got a look in his eye that I've never seen before, and I'm positive that he's on something right now. As far as I know, he was never using while we were together, but after finding out that he lied to me about plenty of other things, god only knows what else he was hiding from me.

The door closes behind Elliott as he leaves to go upstairs, and Kyle lets go of my mouth. I gasp for air, coughing as I try to get away from him. He grabs hold of my good arm, yanking me to my feet, and it sends pain up through my right torso from his roughness.

"Kyle, please," I beg as he pushes me toward the leather couch. He throws me down so roughly that my body bounces against the hard cushions, and I land on my injured arm. I let out a yelp and double over the front of the couch, my eyes watering as I dry heave from the pain.

Kyle pushes my shoulders back onto the couch so I'm splayed across its cushions, and tears stream down both of my cheeks. I try to stay strong, but the last of my bravery and any remaining physical strength I had are quickly running out.

"Not saying that I mind, but I thought it'd take you longer to beg for it," Kyle says into one of my ears as he rests his heavy body on top of mine, pinning me to the couch.

"Please, Kyle, if you ever loved me at all, let me go!" I say, and the desperation I was trying so hard to hide shines through me like a spotlight.

"Please just let me go," I sob, pleading with him as I press against his chest with my hand.

"Don't you worry, baby, I'm gonna show you just how much I love you," he says, trying to unbutton my pants, and I continue to cry as I struggle underneath the weight of Kyle's body. "Then you're not gonna want anything except for my c—"

"Ky, we've got customers," Elliott calls down from the top of the stairs, interrupting Kyle's vulgar words.

"Tell them to fuck off, I'm busy right now," Kyle says as he puts a hand over my mouth before I can scream for help. He's still fumbling with the zipper on my pants as I thrash my body wildly, trying to make it as difficult for him as I can.

I hear Elliott's footsteps on the metal stairs as he slowly walks down them, our eyes meeting when he gets to the bottom of the landing. He watches Kyle and me with a cruel smile on his face, and the look in his eyes makes me feel sick to my stomach.

Kyle whips his head up, momentarily halting his attempts at undressing me. "Either join in or get the fuck out," he says impatiently.

349

"I would love nothing more…" Elliott says slowly, eyeing us both up and down before continuing. "But unfortunately, like I said, Ky, we've got *customers*." And the way Elliott says the word makes me think he doesn't mean it's someone interested in buying some dusty old vinyls.

Kyle nods at him, finally understanding his meaning, and lets out a sigh of frustration. He looks down at me and then back to Elliott before nodding at the record cabinet in the corner of the room.

Elliott nods back at him and walks over to it before opening the lid. I watch as he pulls out a small paper sack from inside the cabinet and brings it over to Kyle. Elliott fishes out a small Ziplock bag from inside the paper sack that looks like it's filled with pink jelly beans.

Elliott hands a few over to Kyle, and at first, I'm confused when I watch Kyle pop the pills into his mouth, and I realize what's happening a second too late.

Kyle leans down and squeezes my face in his hand, kissing me roughly as he forces his tongue into my mouth. I try to resist, but before I realize it, the small pills dissolve in between our tongues, leaving a sour strawberry aftertaste mixed with the flavor of menthol cigarettes.

Kyle releases my face, and I turn my head to the side and cough as I try to catch my breath. Sheer terror runs through my entire body.

*No no no no no no no no! This can't be happening!*

"What did you give me, you asshole?" I spit through my tears, still coughing as I continue to push against Kyle's body on top of mine.

"Don't worry, baby, it'll help you relax," Kyle says with a lethal purr before bending down to kiss me again. I try to turn away, but he grabs my face with his hand and shoves his tongue in my mouth a second time.

I'm seething mad through my tears as I bite down hard. Kyle pulls back, flinching from the pain as he puts a hand to his mouth, and a small droplet of blood has formed on the corner of his lip.

"See, I knew you missed this," he says darkly as he winks at me before licking the blood away. "I'll bet you're wet as fuck down here right now, aren't you?" Kyle says as he cups my crotch over my jeans with his palm and I jerk my body beneath him, feeling disgusted by his touch.

"I'll be right back to check this sweet cunt for myself," Kyle purrs into my ear.

He finally climbs off me, and I roll onto my side and force my fingers down my throat, trying to make myself throw up. My eyes water, and I gag, but nothing comes out. "Sorry, baby, it's too late for that," Kyle scoffs before heading up the stairs with Elliott in tow behind him. I hear the metal door as it quickly slams behind them, followed by the sound of multiple locks engaging.

Though I don't want to believe it, I know that Kyle's right. Whatever he forced on me dissolved almost immediately, and I realize that any chance of being able to throw it up is unlikely.

As soon as they're gone, I quickly readjust my clothes the best that I can with the use of only one arm, and struggle to get up and pull myself off the couch. My body is already feeling heavy from whatever drug Kyle forced on me, and I start to feel woozy as I drag my feet across the shag carpet.

I try to make my way toward the stairwell and almost fall multiple times from how unsteady I've become. Once I get to the base of the stairs, I lift one foot and realize that there's no way I'll make it up the steps in my body's current state.

"Help! Can anyone hear me?" I call up the metal stairs, figuring my best bet is to try and get one of the customers to hear me. Here to buy drugs or not, I'm hoping they wouldn't just ignore the sound of someone trapped in a basement calling for help.

"*HELLO?*" I yell toward the ceiling, the volume of my own voice causing my head to throb, and I close my eyes from the pain.

I try to take a step up the stairs again, wanting to get myself just a little bit closer to the door, when I lose my footing. I try to steady myself as I stagger backward, but my knees lock and then buckle before I fall to the ground, landing flat on my ass.

I'm so lightheaded that the harder I try to get up, the more nauseous I feel and eventually can't hold the weight of my body upright any longer. I slowly lower myself down onto my back, thinking it's better that I do it now before I lose control completely and end up banging my head on something.

I know I should try to get up and leave, or at least yell for help again, but I can't seem to make my body do anything at all. My limbs have grown extremely tired, but the pain in my arm is slowly subsiding, and I can tell that whatever Kyle gave me is taking hold fast. I've only ever smoked weed before, so this experience is entirely new and definitely an unwelcome one at that.

I'm beyond queasy, and try to sit up, wanting to prop myself up against something so that I don't end up accidentally asphyxiating. I only make it about halfway before I sink back down onto the shag carpet. I roll onto my side and stare at the colorful tapestries on the walls, their designs now moving and swirling like a beautiful kaleidoscope all around me.

I hear footsteps upstairs, and then what sounds like chairs scuffing across the floor, and wonder if they're moving furniture around. Elliott did say they had customers up there, so now doesn't really seem like the right time for that.

*How unprofessional.* I'd scoff if I could feel my face.

My eyes lazily make their way around the room before finally landing on a purple lava lamp on one of the shelves in the corner. I watch as the swirls bounce up and down, the contents mixing and jiggling around against each other inside the glass.

*What a pretty lamp. Maybe I'll ask if I can take it home with me...*

More voices come from upstairs, and then a loud thud. I wonder if someone's moving a refrigerator or something, and for some reason, the thought makes me laugh. I clutch at my side as I continue to lie on the smelly carpet, my eyes now watering from how hard I'm laughing.

I hear the lock on the metal door disengaging and sigh to myself. "Back already?" I ask, even though no one's there yet, and my words come out slowly, each syllable drawn out sluggishly.

I want to ask if the customers at least got something good, but I can't seem to make the words come out. *Who would've thought anyone still even shops at this stinky old place?* I want to say. The words don't form, and I let out a belly laugh like it's the funniest thing I've ever heard, causing my eyes to water again.

The sound of the metal door slamming against the cement wall makes me jump a little, but I don't bother looking over, already anticipating who it is.

*Then there's the fact that I can't move my body to actually look.*

I giggle at the thought, wondering when my neck stopped working along with the rest of my extremities.

"Hey, Kyle, can I have that lava lamp?" I ask, still half-laughing, thinking it'd look real nice in Judy's room. I try to point at it with a finger, but I'm still unable to move either of my arms. I'm afraid to look up at Kyle—or worse, Elliott—so I let my eyes stay focused on the corner of the room, still mesmerized by the flowing goo of the hot lamp.

"Ryan!"

The use of my last name snaps me away from my trance as I look up at the person hovering above me.

"*Heyyy…*" I say, and my voice sounds like it's far away. I'm unbearably dizzy, and my head gets even heavier, white blotches now obstructing most of my vision. "Jess!" I say happily, trying to smile at him, but can't tell if I actually am or not.

Jess bends down next to me and looks over my body, stopping on my arm. A look of horror crosses his face, and I strain to look down as well and notice that my right arm is bent at an unnatural angle behind me.

*Maybe that's the reason I couldn't seem to move it.* And I want to laugh at the ridiculousness of it.

"Oh, yeah," I say with a heavy sigh. "Something bad happened."

I'm trying to hold back a laugh as Jess checks me to make sure nothing else is broken. He's careful with my arm even though I can't feel the pain anymore as he untwists it from behind me and gently rests it across my stomach instead.

Jess looks down at me with a furious expression on his face and I feel the faint sensation of my pants being zipped back up, presumably followed by the button.

"Are you mad, Jess?" I ask quietly as I stare up at him, feeling guilty for making him upset.

Jess quickly meets my eyes, and his angry look softens. "No, not at you," he says as he puts a hand to my cheek, and my chest eases a little at his words.

"Are you here to save me?" I ask, now barely able to keep my eyes open, and I notice my skin starting to warm, making me feel uncomfortably hot.

"Always," Jess says as he threads an arm under my knees and another behind my back. "Let's get you out of here," he says as he lifts me into his arms and stands.

"Jess, you smell really good," I say as I rest my head against him, and I can hear his heartbeat thundering through his chest. "Is there a drum in here?" I ask as I bump my head against his chest, trying to stifle the laugh I feel coming on.

"Sam, stop, don't do that. Stop moving around, you're going to hurt yourself," Jess says as we make our way up the dark stairwell.

His body is warm against mine, and when I nuzzle into him, I notice a tear across the front of his shirt. I try to get a better look at the source of the blood that's soaking the material, but my head is so heavy I can barely hold it up.

"Jess, did you have to fight a dragon to get to me?" I ask, no longer able to contain my giggles.

He lets out an exhausted laugh at that. "Sure did, now please stop moving," he says as he looks down, giving me a gentle smile. The small gesture makes my heart flutter, and even though he's smiling at me, I can see the nervousness behind his eyes.

"You're rescuing me," I state and start to cry even though I'm giggling uncontrollably. "Jess, let me kiss your mouth," I say through my hysterics as I reach a hand up to touch his hair.

I feel Jess tighten his arms around me. "Let's get you fixed up first, then you can kiss me all you want, okay?" Jess says, and his tone is serious. I continue pulling at his neck, wanting to thank him for saving me, but he resists, straightening so that I can't reach him with my mouth.

I hear a bell ring, followed by the feeling of the cool outside air on my skin as I continue to cling to him. My body is still burning up, so the sensation of the cool breeze feels nice on my burning skin. He carries me across the street and I inhale deeply, glad for some fresh air.

"Hang on, okay? I'm going to set you inside," Jess says as he tries to lower me into the back seat of his Jeep.

"N-no, Jess!" I say as I pull at his shirt and turn myself further into his chest when I see the missing doors.

"What? What's wrong?" he says, pulling me tighter into him as he frantically looks me over.

My voice is muffled as I press my face into his shirt. "If there are no doors, I might float away," I say, gripping the wet material of his shirt tighter in my fist.

Jess's body is still tense against me, but I feel him relax a little as he lets out a breath. "Baby, you're not going anywhere. I promise I won't let you go," he says gently, and I swear I can feel him kiss the top of my flaming head. "Now we've gotta go, all right?" he says, trying to put me into the Jeep again.

"Why are you moving around so much, Jess?" I ask, wondering why he's suddenly gotten so unstable.

Jess hesitates before answering. "Sam, that's you. Your body's shaking," he says calmly. "Let's get you in the back. I'm gonna sit with you, okay?" he says before yelling impatiently over his shoulder. "Chris! What's the holdup? Let's go, NOW!"

*Chris is here? I must've heard that wrong.*

"Jess, wait," I say, pushing against his chest with my hand, and I can feel my features twisting.

Jess realizes what I mean before I can put the feeling into words as he turns us away from the Jeep. I hang my head to the side as my body starts to jerk, my stomach emptying itself onto the pavement next to us.

I close my eyes, feeling dizzy all over again, and everything around me starts to wildly spin out of control. I hear Jess curse under his breath before calling out to someone, and I feel the cold sting of the asphalt through my clothes as he sets me down onto the sidewalk.

My ears start to ring, and I open my eyes to Jess's face hovering above me. I see him look over and yell to someone again but I can't hear what he's saying. Jess looks angry and keeps yelling at them before looking down at me again, and I feel the vague sensation of his hands on my cheeks. His face is wild with panic, and I can't help but admire those beautiful emerald eyes as they blaze down at me, content if they were the last thing I ever saw in this shit world.

My vision starts to blur, and I can feel my eyes starting to roll into the back of my head as I feel my body begin to convulse. I feel a strong

356

sense of déjà vu as my mind flashes back and forth from a seventeen-year-old Jess to the older version of him that's now hovering over me. In both versions of him, I can see him mouthing my name, yelling at me.

I can't hear anything over the sound of the ringing in my ears, and Jess's face is the last thing I see before my vision slowly fades completely, bright emeralds replaced with the darkness of a vast ocean.

# Chapter Twenty

## Jess

"Okay, remind me again who this Elliott guy is?" Chris asks from the passenger seat. He pulls out a wad of bloody toilet paper from one of his nostrils before throwing it out the side of the Jeep.

"Focus, Chris, I've already explained it all," I say, annoyed at his lack of listening skills as I race down the road, going forty over the speed limit.

"So, Elliott is her ex, then?" Chris asks, confused.

"*No, Chris,*" I say impatiently above the sound of the wind. I take the next turn a little too fast, and feel like we might've been on two wheels.

"Elliott is the one who attacked Sam that day she met your dad and Rebecca for dinner. The dinner *you* were supposed to be at, too, remember?" I say irritably as I practically yell at him.

Out of the corner of my eye, I see Chris's shoulders lower as he exhales deeply, and I turn to face him. "Look, man, I know it wasn't your fault, I'm not blaming you," I say apologetically over the sound of the wind.

Chris shakes his head. "No, you're right, but I probably should've been there at the very least."

I almost don't say anything, but I can't stop myself. "That night, were you with Sophie?" I ask, looking over at him.

Chris says nothing before turning his gaze back toward the road, and I shake my head. "A conversation for another time, then," I say, and shoot him a warning glare. Now's definitely not the time, but I've got a few things to say to him about his little arrangement with Sophie.

We ride the rest of the way in silence, except for the noise of the wind whipping around us in the open air of the Jeep. I skid us to a stop and park on a side street, not wanting Elliott to spot us before we devise a rescue plan.

"I'm glad you were there to protect Sam that night, Jess," Chris says as we both climb out of the Jeep. "I know that in the past I've been—"

"A complete dick?" I say and raise a brow at him.

Chris cuts me a sharp look before continuing. "Yeah. But that doesn't mean I want anything bad to happen to her."

"Look, Chris, she's just trying to look out for you. Cut her some slack for Christ's sake," I say, and Chris nods at me with a look that borders on regret.

"Let's check if they have a back door," Chris says as we head down the alleyway behind the shops. We stop in front of the metal door that reads Gil's, which tells me that the shop's name change was fairly recent. Chris pulls on the metal door handle several times, even though it's obviously locked.

I look around and realize that this is where I hesitated to look for Sam earlier today and kick myself. Just after she'd run out of the coffee shop, I thought she might've come down here, but I didn't want to waste any time, so I kept on running down the street. If I had just taken the two extra seconds to check, she'd be safe right now.

"Jess, look," Chris says, snapping me out of my thoughts, and I turn toward where he's crouched on the ground. He holds up a cracked cell phone, and we both immediately recognize the Polaroid photo of Sam and Sophie through the back of the clear case.

"That would explain why she wasn't answering, and why this was pinned as her last known location," I say, stating the obvious while Chris tries pulling on the locked door again.

"Shit, well now what?" he asks.

"Looks like it's time to shop for some vinyls," I say, and Chris follows me as I head back down the alleyway toward the front of the shop.

"Wait, hold on a second. If what you say is true and you really beat the snot out of this guy Elliott, isn't he going to recognize you the second you walk in there?" Chris asks from behind me.

"Probably, but when I came by earlier to look for Sam, there was only one guy running the place. I doubt Elliott will be attending to customers if he's in there with Sam..." I say, not wanting to finish my thought.

Chris claps his hands together behind me. "So we're settling this with fists, then," he says, and I can hear the menacing smile in his voice.

"As long as we get Sam back, that's just fine by me," I say, rounding the corner of the building as we head down the sidewalk toward the small row of shops.

I glance through the window of the music store and notice the same guy from earlier sitting on a stool in the corner behind the register. He's still sporting his round sunglasses, and still wearing the same expression on his face as before.

"Okay, we're good. Let's go," I say from beside Chris, and we both head into the store.

The bell on the door rings as we enter the shop, waking Stoney Baloney from his trance behind the counter. "Welcome in, my dudes— Oh, hey man!" he says, and I'm surprised he recognizes me from before. "Did you find your girl?" he asks with a friendly smile, and this time I notice the lanyard around his neck with a name tag that says *Carter*.

I return his smile. "I did actually, it was just a misunderstanding," I say, trying to keep my tone light.

"Right on, right on," he says, nodding at us. "So, what brings you gents in today?" he asks, nodding at Chris.

*Shit, now what?*

We hadn't really discussed a proper plan—mostly just get in, find Sam, kick some ass along the way if need be, and then get out. I'm still trying to formulate one when Chris speaks up.

"My man, we were wondering if you might be able to hook us up?" Chris asks.

"For sure, my dude, for sure," Carter says as he casually glances around the store. "We've got some classic Stones, we've got some Zep, or if you'd like—"

"Sorry bro, I think you've got me wrong," Chris says, smiling. "I heard that you guys have a private collection—very exclusive shit—only available for a *select few*, if you catch my drift," he says with confident charisma and I'm kind of surprised that he's capable of another mode besides raging asshole.

Chris gives Carter another look, raising his brows as if he couldn't make what he's looking for any more obvious.

"*Ohhhh*, I see," Carter says in understanding as he nods at us with a smile. "You must mean some of that *Strawberry Six*, then."

Chris smiles and nods back. "So you think you can help us out, then?" he asks.

"Give me uno momento, my dudes, I'll be right back," Carter says before turning down a long hallway near the back of the register.

"You think he's in on it?" Chris asks as he eyes Carter down the hallway.

"Doubt it, that guy is way too cooked," I say, trying to keep my voice down. "Also, what kind of an idiot would drag a kidnapped girl through the front door?" I ask.

Chris and I exchange glances before both silently acknowledging that it's very possible that Elliott did just that. If he's stupid enough to kidnap someone in broad daylight, he's obviously not someone who thinks things through very well, and I'm sure that Chris is thinking the same thing as I am.

I hear what sounds like a metal door as it groans open at the end of the hallway, and Carter calls to someone. "Yo, Elliott, you got a second?"

Chris and I exchange glances, and I quickly step to the side of the register, blocking myself from the view of the hallway. "I'll wait for your signal," I murmur quietly as I stand close to the wall, just out of view. Chris nods back at me before turning back toward Carter with a dangerously friendly smile on his face.

I hear another voice speak that isn't Carter's and recognize the nasally tone belonging to Elliott. "You got cash, then?" I hear him ask Chris impatiently.

"That depends," Chris answers back with just as much enthusiasm as Elliott.

"On what, dickweed? Are you seriously wasting my time right now?" Elliott says sharply, and I can see him leaning toward Chris over the counter like he's trying to intimidate him. The thought is almost laughable, since Chris is 6'5" on a bad day, whereas Elliott's pushing maybe 5'9".

From where I'm standing, I'm able to see Chris pull out his wallet before leaning over the counter, presumably showing Elliott his cash.

"It depends on whether you have what I'm looking for or not," Chris says with a touch of crazy in his friendly voice. "Now, get me what I'm asking for, or I'll take my money somewhere else, understand?" he says, and I wonder how much of it is really an act. It sure seems like he's done this before, and I try not to think about what kind of trouble Chris has been up to these past few years.

This time when Elliott speaks, he's much friendlier than before, and I wonder just how much cash Chris flashed him with. "Hey, guy, there's no issue, let me get the boss. He can show you what you really want to see," Elliott says, almost overdoing it with his friendliness. I'm able to catch a glimpse of a hand as it reaches across the counter trying to pat Chris's shoulder.

"You do that, then," Chris says coolly as he turns his body away, the hand just barely missing him.

I hear footsteps as Elliott walks away, and I'm guessing he's going back down the hall to the metal door where he came from earlier. I hear the door groan as it opens again, and Chris turns toward me giving me a look. I'm sure we're both thinking the same thing.

We were only accounting for the cashier and Elliott. Now, who knows how many others are here? A heads-up from Madison sure would've been nice. I run my hands through my hair in frustration.

*Things just got more complicated.*

I wonder where Madison is and hope that she got out of here like I texted her to earlier after I left John's house with Chris. If things go sideways, the last thing I want is another person getting hurt because of me. I also don't want to have to choose between saving Madison and saving Sam, since the choice is pretty obvious to me.

I pull my phone out and text Sophie instead, thinking that shit with Madison can wait until later. I let Sophie know that I think I've found Sam and tell her to call the police if she doesn't hear back from me in ten minutes. She immediately reads the message, and my phone lights up with her name when she tries calling me. The ringer sounds, and I try to silence it as quickly as I can, praying no one heard it.

> What the fuck Jess? Is she
> alright? What's going on??
>
> ANSWER MY CALL
> ASSHOLE

> Everything's gonna be fine.
> Can I count on you?

> Duh. But you owe me an
> explanation pronto.

I slide my phone back into my pocket just as I hear footsteps approaching the front counter. "Looks like you're in luck. The boss says he's got what you're looking for, if you can pay, that is," Elliott says to Chris.

"I thought we've been over this already," Chris snaps, and Elliott raises his hands defensively.

"Hey now, no need to get—" Elliott doesn't have a chance to finish his sentence before Chris grabs him by the front of his shirt and pulls him over the countertop onto the floor.

Elliott falls to the ground right in front of where I'm standing, leaving him temporarily stunned. Chris looks over at me before taking off his jacket and I give him an incredulous look.

"*What the fuck?* What about the signal?" I mouth to him.

"That was it," Chris says before he shrugs unapologetically. He turns away from me as he reaches down, pulling a dumbfounded Elliott up by the lapels of his leather jacket.

"What the hell, man?" Elliott grunts out as he frantically grasps at Chris's hands. "I thought we had a deal?"

"Turns out I've changed my mind. I'll settle for getting my sister back, and then maybe I won't end up wiping the floor with your ugly face," Chris says to Elliott, and after watching what he just did, I'm starting to wonder if he might actually be crazy.

"Who, Madison?" Elliott says in a panic. "Take her, take the bitch, she's annoying as fuck anyway," he says, putting his hands up defensively.

"Sam, you piece of shit! Where the fuck is Sam!" Chris yells into Elliott's face as he shakes him by his jacket.

Elliott chuckles lightly, some of his bravado finding him again. "Ohhh, I see. I should've known there'd be a line down the block for that sweet piece of ass. If you want a turn to fuck her, you're going to have to get in line," Elliott smirks as he laughs in Chris's face. His sick words infuriate me, and I think that if Chris doesn't kill him, then I happily will.

"You have a disgusting mouth," Chris says as he punches Elliott in the teeth forcefully. "Where the fuck is she?" he demands, shaking Elliott by his jacket.

Elliott flashes Chris a bloody smile. "Good luck, but you're too late," Elliott says before biting down onto Chris's hand that's still holding him up by his jacket.

Chris lets him go, momentarily stunned from being bitten. "*Argh*, dammit," Chris mutters angrily as he shakes his hand.

Elliott tries to scramble away as he crawls across the hardwood floor, before Chris quickly grabs onto one of his feet, dragging him backward.

"Get back here, you damn weasel," Chris says just as Elliott kicks him in the face, almost knocking him over.

365

I don't hesitate, hoping their fight serves as the distraction I need to locate Sam, thinking that this might be my only chance before some serious shit goes down.

While Chris is pummeling Elliott, I run down the long hallway behind the register. I know I heard a heavy door slam earlier, and if I were going to keep a hostage in this place, the basement would probably be it.

I know Elliott said he was going to get the "boss" but I didn't hear any other voices besides his and Carter's, so I think that maybe he was just bluffing. Either way, it doesn't matter—the sooner I find Sam and get the hell out of here, the better.

*Who knows what Elliott's done to her...*
The thought fuels my rage, and I stalk down the hallway even faster.

I spot a door at the end of the hall, and head straight for it, when something, or rather, someone, slams into me. They push me up against the wall from a small door on my left, crashing into me so hard it almost knocks the wind out of my lungs.

A pair of pale tatted hands reach up and grab my neck, pinning me to the wall, and I notice the words FUCK and YOU tattooed across his knuckles in faded black ink. I'm a little dazed from before, but quickly shake it off when his grip tightens around my throat, cutting off my air supply.

"Now, what do we have here?" he says slowly, and my eyes widen a little in recognition. "Come to raid our private stash I see?" he growls into my face as I pull at his wrists. "You'd better tell Theo that he fucked with the wrong guys. That is, if you can even speak when I'm through with you," he says menacingly as he tightens his hold on my throat.

"So, *you're* the 'boss' then? I've gotta say, I'm very underwhelmed," I rasp out through my constricted airway.

I slam my forehead into his nose and he staggers back, releasing my throat from his hands. "I don't know who the fuck Theo is, but I'll send him your regards," I say through my coughing as I try to catch my breath. Knuckles raises his lip in a snarl, and I lunge at him before he has the chance to pin me again.

We're almost evenly matched height-wise, but I've got a good forty pounds of muscle on him for sure, so I try to use that to my advantage.

I ram into him, trying to kick his feet out from under him, but he uses my momentum and weight against me to twist himself out of my grasp. I stumble past him into the opposite wall, catching myself quickly before whipping around to face him.

I'm ready to lunge at him again when I see him pull a small switchblade knife out of his back pocket. Knuckles clicks the knife open and smiles darkly at me. "Did you really think you could just waltz right in and no one would stop you?" he says, pointing the knife at me.

"More or less," I scoff and shrug, trying to stall as I quickly weigh my options.

The hallway is too small for me to be able to get past without taking him out, and if I don't incapacitate him completely and Sam's not actually downstairs, then I'll have trapped myself down there with no way out.

The likelihood of an old place like this having a basement exit is pretty slim, plus, that would leave Chris to fight off Elliott and Knuckles on his own. After witnessing Chris's intensity earlier, it's clear he could probably take them both on, but it's obvious that they don't fight fair, especially when there are weapons involved.

I shake my head, feeling like I've wasted too much time already, and figure I'll have to risk it.

*I just need to get downstairs… I just need to see that she's all right…*

"Nice tats," I say, trying to provoke him. "Who designed your ink, a preschooler?" I say, snickering as I nod to the dark ink covering both of his arms.

Knuckles curls his lip in a half snarl before lunging at me again, this time wielding the knife. He swipes it at my face, and I dodge it just before the tip of the blade cuts my cheek. I swing my fist into his stomach as hard as I can and watch as he doubles over.

The old floorboards creak beneath us before he turns and lunges at me again, and we both crash into the wall. Knuckles tries to plunge his knife into my ribcage and I grab his wrist, stopping him before he's able to stab me. I slam his forearm with my other hand, trying to disarm him, but the way he's gripping the knife so tightly makes it nearly impossible.

Knuckles rams one of his studded combat boots down onto my foot and tries to sweep my legs out from under me, but I sidestep him before he can. I shove him away with all the force I have, but he just comes right back, lunging at me again and again, and the sheer intensity of the guy makes me wonder just how many drugs he's on.

He comes at me with the knife again when I block his arm. I hit him with an uppercut to the chin, and feel the vibration of his teeth rattling against each other when my fist collides with his face.

His body slumps back against the floral wallpaper, and I'm about to punch his lights out with a final blow when I hear a muffled sound coming from behind the metal door.

I can't make out the words, but I'd know the sound of that voice anywhere, and for a second, I forget that I'm still in the middle of a knife fight. "Sam!" I call out and snap my head toward the door.

By the time I realize that I've let my guard down, it's too late. I see Knuckles moving out of the corner of my eye, and his swipe is as fast as lightning when I feel the cool metal of his blade as it slices across the skin of my chest and right pec muscle.

I stagger backward, my back slamming against the wall as I look down at the gaping wound across my chest, the blood already soaking through my shirt. *"Fuck,"* I gasp out, the pain from the deep cut a sensation I've never experienced before.

"And here I thought you were just another junkie looking to make a free score," Knuckles says, wiping the blood away from his mouth with the back of his hand.

"Sorry to disappoint, but she's not going anywhere," he says, slightly out of breath as he nods toward the metal door with a dark smile. "We've got plans later that don't involve you."

Knuckles touches the tip of his knife to one of his fingertips, the blade still fresh with my blood, and I watch as he slowly twists it with a sinister grin on his face. "Unless you wanna watch?"

Rage mixed with pure adrenaline consumes me, and I see red. The pain across my chest is no longer at the forefront of my mind at the thought of what the asshole has planned for Sam.

*"I don't share,"* I say through gritted teeth as I take two long strides, closing the gap between us as I catch my second wind.

I block the next slash of his knife before I grab his wrist and slam it into the wall, finally forcing him to drop it. The metal clangs to the ground, and I use my forehead to headbutt him as hard as I can, almost knocking myself out along with him.

"What is it with you sick fuckers and thinking you can just pass Sam around however you want," I say, furious at the thought of what's been said about using her.

Knuckles's hands fumble for the collar of my shirt as he tries reaching for my neck again when I grab the back of his head, pulling his torso down as his face collides with the top of my thigh in a wet crunch. I feel his nose break against my knee, and his body goes heavy.

369

I throw him to the ground in a heavy heap before kicking him in the stomach a few times. He coughs and spurts out a mouthful of blood across the hardwood flooring. He gasps, trying to catch his breath as he struggles to stand, but can't.

I pick up the bloody knife and put my knee on his chest. Knuckles groans as I simultaneously push down on his body with my leg and pull him up by the collar of his shirt, his will to fight seemingly gone now that I've got him pinned.

"Listen carefully, motherfucker, because I will not be repeating myself," I say as I press the knife up to his throat and I feel his body stiffen underneath me.

"I will not hesitate to end your life if you ever come near Sam again. You or any of your tweaker friends. Do you understand me?" I say, pressing the blade against his throat with more pressure, forcing him to look me in the eyes.

Knuckles stares up angrily at me. "Fuck you," he tries to spit at me through his swollen face, blood now flowing down out of his nose and mouth.

"*You're not getting it,*" I say, irate as I press the knife more forcefully into his throat, this time drawing blood as it starts to cut through his tattooed skin. "For your sake, she'd better be all right, otherwise, I'm going to hold you down while I let her carve you up with your own blade," I seethe at him through my teeth, slicing the knife deeper into his skin as he flinches.

"*Now* do you understand me?" I ask, pressing our foreheads together as I whisper the words, and hope I look as crazy as I feel inside.

I continue to stare wildly into his eyes, and the thought of Sam being in any pain because of this psychopath is testing my moral compass. One quick movement and he'd be out of the picture for good.

I seriously consider it for a second, but when the image of Sam's bright smile flashes across my mind, I immediately rethink my decision.

370

If I murder this dirtbag, I'll go to jail and I might not ever see Sam again, and that's not something I can live with.

Knuckles gives me a look of understanding, and I wonder if he finally realizes that I'm dead serious with my threats. He swallows hard and then nods at me before I toss the knife down the hall. He relaxes a little and lets out a labored breath just before I drive my right elbow into the side of his face, knocking him unconscious as his body slumps to the floor.

# Chapter Twenty-one
## Jess

I look down at the smooth rocks in my hand. The deep green of the smallest stone glimmers against the artificial lighting above me, and their smooth finishes clack together as I turn them over in my palm again. My heart aches as I continue to stare at the small stone, knowing exactly why she chose it.

"Ryan family?" I hear someone call from the double doors to the waiting room entrance, and I spring to my feet, sliding the small stones back into the pocket of my jeans.

"Yes, that's us," John says from beside me before I can speak up. Not that it would matter though, John and Chris are technically the "Ryan" family, not me.

"I'm Dr. Owens, I'd like to give you an update on Ms. Ryan's condition," the doctor says as she introduces herself and shakes John's hand before gesturing for him and Chris to follow her.

I go to sit back down in the waiting area when John turns to me. "No, son, you too," he says as he nods, motioning for me to follow the doctor along with them.

"But I—"

"What Chris said earlier was out of line." John shoots a dirty look at Chris, who then looks down at the floor uncomfortably.

"You're always welcome with our family, Jess. I hope you know that you *are* a part of it," John says, reaching a hand out to me. "No matter what happens between you and Sam, you always will be."

I stand and take his extended hand before we exchange a quick hug, and he claps me on the back before pulling away. We trade nods in a silent agreement and then follow the doctor down the long corridor toward the patient rooms as she begins to give us an update on Sam.

Dr. Owens walks us through Sam's injuries, and I have to fight to keep myself calm. The doctor tells us that Sam sustained a segmented spiral fracture to her right forearm with a partial tear of her UCL. Or, in layman's terms, her forearm was fractured in two places, along with a few small tears in the ligaments in her elbow joint as well, all likely from forced trauma. Meaning, it didn't happen by accident, and that someone forcibly twisted her arm past the point of its natural resistance, thus causing it to break like it did.

She had multiple scrapes on her knees and palms, along with a minor concussion and a scratch on her head. Nothing too deep to need stitches, but enough to leave a pretty big bump.

When it came to what drugs she might have in her system, they were still waiting on the full toxicology report from the lab to be sure. I'd mentioned the name 'Strawberry Six' earlier in the ER, and immediately everyone clammed up. From what they told me in the ambulance, it's still a relatively new drug, so they don't know much about it, just that it's some pretty hardcore shit. Supposedly, it has six different opioids in it—hence the name—but where it just hit the streets, not much is known other than that.

"As far as the possibility of an assault, that's something I'll discuss with Ms. Ryan when she wakes up," Dr. Owens says, and I'm sure she can sense the discomfort lingering in the air at the mention of a possible rape.

"Ms. Ryan's not intubated or anything, so she should wake up on her own here in a few hours after the grogginess from the anesthesia wears off. You're all welcome to wait in her room for her if you'd like," Dr. Owens says with a warm smile as she nods to the door we've now stopped in front of.

"So, what you're saying is that she's going to be fine then, right?" Chris asks the doctor, and it's clear that he didn't listen to a word she'd just said.

"Yes, I do think that Ms. Ryan will most likely make a full recovery, but until we know for sure what substances she could've potentially ingested, it's hard to know how her body might react. I'd like to keep her here under observation for a few days if that's all right with you," Dr. Owens says, looking at me.

I look to John and Chris. "Oh, I'm not—we're not—" I say, slightly uncomfortable before looking back at Dr. Owens.

"The emergency room staff told me you were the one who rode in the ambulance with Ms. Ryan earlier," she says, raising a brow.

"I did but…" I say, a little confused, thinking she must've gotten my name off my chart earlier when I was in the ER.

After we got to the hospital, they took Sam off on a stretcher and wouldn't let me see her until I let them bandage the cut on my chest. I gave those poor nurses a hell of a fight until they finally threatened to call security on me if I didn't calm down. By the time I was done getting my stitches, Sam was already in surgery for her arm, and I was told that I'd have to wait to see her until she was out of recovery.

"My apologies, Mr. Cameron," Dr. Owens says. "Since you're the one listed as Ms. Ryan's emergency contact, I had just assumed domestic partners. That was my mistake," she says, apologizing again before she turns toward John and repeats her questions about keeping Sam overnight.

*Me? Sam's emergency contact? Why not Sophie, or John?*

"There's a coffee machine down the hall, or a cafeteria on the second floor if you guys want to grab a bite to eat," Dr. Owens says, gesturing down the hallway to her right, before John shakes her hand and thanks her.

"Wait," I say, just before she walks away. "What about the seizure?" I ask the doctor.

"What seizure? You never mentioned a seizure," John says as he looks to me and then to Dr. Owens with concern in his voice. I feel bad, but in all the commotion of the last few hours, I'd forgotten to mention it to him.

"I brought it up to the EMTs when we were in the ambulance and then again when the nurses took Sam away, but in all the chaos, it must've slipped my mind," I say to John apologetically. He gives me an annoyed look but nods his head in understanding anyway.

"Like I said, until we have the full toxicology report back, it's hard to say what caused it, whether it be from the possible drugs in her system, an underlying condition she was unaware of, or simply from the stress of the situation on her body. Honestly, it could be a combination of multiple things," Dr. Owens says with a shrug. "I've requested a neuro consult just to be safe though, so Dr. Allensen should be up to speak with you all first thing in the morning," she says as she kindly pats me on the shoulder.

"You guys have had a long day, you should try and get some rest," Dr. Owens says as she looks between the three of us before closing

375

the file in her hands. John thanks her again, and she gives a slight nod before making her way over to the nurses' station.

The second I see Sam when we walk into her room, I feel my heart sink to the bottom of my stomach. Though she's sleeping, a look of pain is splayed across her delicate features, and the sight of her like that makes my chest ache.

My body fills with guilt as I look at her, tubes and wires all over the place, and I draw in a sharp breath, the air filled with a cold sterility as I take in the image of her lying in the hospital bed. Sam's right arm is covered in bandages from her wrist almost all the way up to her shoulder, and a large, bulky-looking sling holds her arm to her body. There's an IV drip connected to her other arm that's attached to multiple bags of solution that hang on a pole next to her bed, and I notice a clear oxygen tube that sits just beneath her nose as well.

*This is all my fault.*

If I had just done a better job at explaining myself, Sam never would've run off, and she'd never have been anywhere near Elliott or her psycho ex in the first place. This happened to her because of me—because of *my* self-centeredness. Why couldn't I have just been straightforward with her? Why didn't I just tell her the truth from the start?

I clench my fists at my sides, trying to hold back the rising anger from my thoughts. "I'll be back. I'm going to get a coffee," I say and turn around without waiting for a response from either John or Chris.

"If you're getting coffee, I'll take a—" Chris starts, but I round the corner of the doorway before he finishes. "Okay, that was rude! Asshole!" Chris calls after me. I hear John shush him, mentioning something about disrupting the other patients, and I roll my eyes and scoff to myself. *Like Chris would even care about that.*

I make my way down the hallway toward the coffee machine that Dr. Owens had mentioned earlier, and of course, it ends up being one of those old-timey ones that only accepts coins.

I reach into my pocket, and, by some miracle, I find a quarter. I insert it into the machine and press the button for a dark roast, but nothing happens. I try pushing the other buttons, and still, nothing.

"*Fuck,*" I say under my breath. I smash all of the buttons repeatedly, only realizing that I've started having a come-apart when I hear a voice to my left.

"Need a spot?"

I turn to see Dr. Owens standing next to me with a paper cup in her hand just after I angrily slam a fist down onto the top of the machine.

"Let me guess, old Gertie here stole your quarter?" she asks, raising a brow as she tenderly pats the top of the old hunk of metal.

"Yeah, sorry," I say with a huff and shake my head, feeling bad for taking my frustrations out on the antique.

"Here, have this one," Dr. Owens says, holding her cup of coffee out to me.

I look at her outstretched hand and politely try to wave her off. "No, I—"

"Don't worry about it, I've already had one too many cups today. And besides, you look like you could use it more than me," she says and smiles, giving my disheveled look a once-over before trying to hand me the paper cup a second time.

"Thank you," I say, taking it from her. "I honestly sort of hate coffee, I just needed to get out of that room…" I admit, looking down at the floor as I rub a hand behind my neck.

Silence falls between us, and I feel like an idiot for thinking that someone as busy as her would have the time—or even want—to listen to me gripe about my personal problems. I'm just about to thank her again and walk away when she speaks.

"I didn't know if you'd want me to mention it before with those other two around, but you should know that when we were prepping Ms. Ryan for surgery earlier, she was calling out for you," Dr. Owens says as she leans against the wall next to the coffee machine.

"But how? I thought that Ryan—I mean, Sam, was unconscious," I say, staring at her in disbelief.

"Initially, when we brought her back, she was, but right before we were about to put her under, she regained consciousness. She seemed very disoriented and frightened, but I mean, given the circumstances, who could blame her?" Dr. Owens says, shrugging before putting her hands in the front pockets of her long white lab coat.

"She repeatedly called for you and even tried ripping out her own IV," she says, and I meet her eyes with a look of concern.

"Don't worry, she was about to go under general anesthesia anyway for the surgery, so we sedated her before she was able to hurt herself," Dr. Owens says, trying to reassure me, and I just stare at her, unsure of what to say.

"I'm sure this is very hard for you, Mr. Cameron, seeing Ms. Ryan like this, I mean," she says, giving me an apologetic smile.

"It's Jess, call me Jess," I say.

"Jess." She nods and gives me a half smile. "Well, *Jess*, it's obviously not my place to assume things, but it sounds like you mean a lot to Ms. Ryan. I'm sure she'll be very pleased to see you here when she wakes up," Dr. Owens says, still smiling warmly at me. She gives me a pat on the arm as she walks past me and heads down the opposite hallway.

"Hey, thanks again," I say as I turn and call after her. "For the coffee, I mean," I say, raising the paper cup in the air. "And for …everything else." She gives me a small smile and nods before turning around and continues on down the long hallway.

I make my way back to Sam's room, stopping in front of the door as I read the small whiteboard on the wall just outside her room.

### Room 304

*Samantha Jo Ryan*
*Attending Physician: Dr. Gloria Owens*

It's weird for me to see her full name written out like that. I hardly ever call her Sam, let alone Samantha. Come to think of it, I've probably only called her that maybe once or twice ever. Originally, I'd started calling her Ryan because I knew it annoyed her, but I think somewhere along the way, it started to grow on her. It was like this special thing we had between the two of us, and I liked that. No one else was allowed to call her that. No one but me.

I think about that day I was with Madison when we ran into Sam at the store. I didn't mean to seem cold; I just wasn't expecting to see her there. I'd called her Samantha because I didn't want Madison to think we were close. I know it was wrong, but where Madison is prone to getting into trouble, I just didn't want Sam to end up getting roped into any of it. Even though I didn't intend for them to meet—at least for a while—I'm glad they did. If it weren't for Madison, who knows how long it would've taken me to find Sam today.

I take a deep breath and try to steady myself before entering Sam's hospital room, not wanting to see her in pain, even if she *is* asleep.

When I walk into the room, Sam is sound asleep in her bed with the look of discomfort still on her face. John and Chris sit in the chairs by the large window as Chris fiddles with the TV remote as he flips through the channels, looking for a sports channel, I'm sure.

"Here," I say, handing the cup of coffee to John.

He eagerly takes it from me before taking a sip. "This is cold," he says, trying to hand it back to me, but I walk away before he can.

I take a seat in the chair next to Sam's hospital bed and shrug when I look at John. "What can I say, the machine was broken."

"Where's *my* coffee?" Chris asks as he reluctantly looks away from the TV, having finally settled on a basketball game.

I lean back in my chair and fold my arms across my chest. "You know where the coffee machine is," I say as I pretend to watch the game.

Chris half stands and looks like he's about to fight me when John shoots him a warning glare, making Chris sit back down in his chair.

"Where's Sophie, by the way? Shouldn't she be here?" John asks and makes a face after taking another sip of his cold coffee.

"I told her it might be best to wait until Sam wakes up before she comes by," I say.

The room is honestly pretty small, and it's already a little too crowded for my liking. I don't want Sam to feel overwhelmed when she wakes up, so I think it'd be best to keep visitors to a minimum for now.

"Besides, Sophie's gonna bring Judy along with her since it's too late to check her out of the retirement home tonight anyway. They'll probably swing by sometime in the morning," I say, answering John's question through a yawn as I lean back in my chair.

"What about Rebecca? Where's she at?" I ask John, but not because I really care, or even want her here for that matter. Regardless of Rebecca's feelings toward Sam, I figured she'd be here to support John at the very least.

John shifts in his chair and crosses one leg over the other knee before he takes another sip of his coffee. "Hospitals make her uncomfortable, so I told her she didn't have to come," he says before setting the cup on the side table in between him and Chris.

I shake my head and am just about to give John a piece of my mind when he puts up a hand to silence me. "Whatever you're going to say, don't. I've tried to be patient with you all, but don't think I haven't noticed the attitude you guys keep giving Rebecca," John says and then looks to Chris, who raises his hands defensively.

"Jess, what I said earlier will always stand, but neither you, nor anyone else, has any say in who I choose to be with, so I don't want to ever hear another word about any of it. Is that understood?" John asks sternly as he looks between Chris and me.

Chris and I exchange looks before both giving John a "yes, sir" in unison. John nods in acknowledgement, and I go back to pretending to watch the game on the TV. I definitely didn't expect that from him, at least not at a time like this. I guess I should've probably known better than to have asked John about Rebecca though, especially since I'm sure he can guess that I'm Team Sam over Team Becky.

We sit in silence for a few hours, with Chris flipping through random TV channels, trying to find something to keep us entertained. The only things on at this hour are reruns of Little House on the Prairie and M.A.S.H., neither of which is my cup of tea, but to be honest, I'm not really even watching. I'm too busy checking on Sam every five seconds to pay any attention to much else. Every time she stirs, I think she's going to wake up, but she never actually does.

When Sam's nurse comes by to check her vitals, I ask them why she still isn't awake yet and why she looks like she's in so much discomfort. They tell me not to worry, and that some people take a lot longer than others to wake up after surgery, and that Sam's probably not in any pain because of all the medicines they gave her through her IV while she was in recovery.

The nurse looks at me like I'm seriously overreacting, but if I find out that Sam was in pain this entire time when she wakes up, there'll be hell to pay.

Sam's nurse tells us she's leaving for the night and I'm glad, hoping that the next one to come on shift knows what the hell they're doing.

I look at the expression on Sam's face and wonder if she's not in pain, then maybe it's because she's having bad dreams instead, and I'm not sure which is worse.

It starts to get pretty late, and I notice that John's head keeps dipping like he's about to nod off at any second.

I try to keep my voice down, but he still jumps anyway. "You should head home for the night," I say. "Maybe try and get some sleep."

"No, it's all right, I can stay," John says through a large yawn as he rubs his tired eyes.

I look at my watch and then over to Sam. She's still out cold, and the expression on her face has softened a little, but she still looks uncomfortable as hell. The thought sends another pang of guilt through my chest, making me wish I could do something more to help her besides just sitting here.

"It's getting pretty late, and the nurses did say it could still take her a good few hours to wake up. I'll call when she's up," I say, nodding toward the door. "Don't worry, I've got this."

"I know you do," John says as he stands to leave, apparently not having to be told twice. "All right then, call me if anything happens," he says, yawning again.

John bends down and shakes a slumped-over Chris in his chair, trying to wake him. He blinks up at John sleepily as he sits up and wipes the drool off his chin with the back of his hand.

"Time to go home, son, we'll be back in the morning," John says, and Chris stands, ready to leave as well.

They're halfway out the door before John turns around. "You sure you'll be all right? You could use some rest as well," he says, gesturing to my chest.

"Yeah, I'm sure. I'll be fine," I say, giving him a reassuring look. "If anything happens, I am in a hospital after all," I joke.

"Well then, I'll see you in the morning," he says before he turns to leave.

I sit down in my chair, resting my head back against the hard cushion as I let out a deep breath.

"Hey, Jess?" John says from the doorway, having stepped halfway back into the room, and I look over at him. "I don't think I thanked you properly for today."

"Don't mention it, I'm just glad she's safe," I say as I look over at Sam, a dull ache still lingering in my chest at the sight of her.

I turn back to John and wonder if he's going to leave, but then he stares down at the ground awkwardly as he continues to speak. "I'm sure you've noticed that these last few years haven't been the easiest for our family, so thank you for always being there for her when I wasn't," he says, and the sincerity behind his eyes catches me off guard.

"I promise I always will." I reach for Sam's hand and hold it in my own as I stare at the small freckles that pepper her nose and cheeks. "For as long as she'll let me, I promise I'll always do my best to protect her," I say, turning back to meet John's eyes. He gives me a nod before turning around and gently shuts the door behind him as he leaves the room.

I sigh and lean back in my uncomfortable chair, still holding Sam's hand in mine, hoping that she'll wake up soon.

I don't know at what point I fall asleep, only that my heart feels like it's beating a mile a minute when my body jolts me awake roughly. I wake up in a sweaty panic, and images of Sam convulsing on the pavement while I couldn't do anything but watch, linger at the forefront of my mind. I check the large digital clock hanging over the door and I let out a deep sigh. 3 a.m.

I glance over at Sam and watch as her chest rises and falls as she breathes easefully, her expression finally peaceful at last. The machines around her beep lightly in the background, and the faint glow of their screens is the only light in the dark room.

I stare at Sam through the dimly lit room and wonder how I let myself get here. I've had so many chances to tell her my true feelings but I always wuss out at the last second.

I rub my thumb against the back of Sam's hand and let out a deep sigh.

*You're a fucking coward, Jess Cameron.*

I pull myself out of the uncomfortable chair before stretching my arms above my head, yawning. *This is going to be a long night.*

I decide to take a lap around the nurses' station to stretch my legs and use the bathroom. I'm hoping to clear my head enough to try and get at least a few more hours of sleep, knowing I'm definitely going to feel it in the morning if I don't, especially since now I know that caffeine only makes me feel like shit instead of actually helping me any.

I do my lap around the nurses' station and head to raid the vending machine I passed on the way after I feel my stomach growl. I'm not really in the mood for processed junk food at this hour—or really any hour for that matter—but I haven't eaten since yesterday when I was at the diner with Sam, and even then, we'd only managed to order drinks before she took off.

The more I think about it, the more I can't believe that was only yesterday. I shake my head to myself and wonder how it's even possible that so much can happen in less than 24 hours.

When I make it down the hall, just like the coffee machine from earlier, the vending machine in front of me looks like it's straight out of 1985, and of course, it only takes cash.

I pull out my wallet, hoping I have some change, and curse the hospital for not updating their vending machines with card readers like the rest of the modern world has. I fish out a five and insert it before it gets spit back out at me. I sigh, my patience already non-existent.

*Typical.*

I check my wallet for another small bill, but I only have a fifty. I let out an annoyed breath at the sign on the glass that reads, *Sorry, no bills over $10.* I try the five again, reinserting it face up, face down, and then backward—the bill reader spitting it back out each time. I grumble as I try straightening out the paper using the edge of the machine before trying it a few more times.

"Yes!" I throw my fist in the air triumphantly as the reader finally accepts my cash.

I click the numbers for a bag of Doritos, watching as the giant spring slowly turns, only for it to stop halfway before it can actually drop the bag.

I sigh in defeat, deciding to settle on hunger for the time being as I catch my forehead in my hand, and figure that I'll probably have better luck down in the cafeteria in the morning.

I click the coin return to collect my change, and to my surprise—no coins. I angrily press the coin return before I silently throw a quick tantrum, endeavoring to hold in my frustrations, but just end up looking like a crazy person, I'm sure.

I run my hands through my hair and let out a breath before looking around, hoping no one saw me making a scene in the hallway.

*Damn ancient vending machines.*

I grumble to myself as I make my way back down the hall toward Sam's room. I guess I should've seen that coming. *Fool me twice, right...*

I'm about halfway back to Sam's room when I see a red light blinking above one of the doors, and it only takes me about half a second to realize whose room it is. My heart starts pounding, and I sprint down the hallway.

"Ms. Ryan, you need to calm down! Please!" I hear multiple voices yelling the closer I get.

"No, let me go! I need to leave!" I hear Sam's voice as I swing the door open, trying to enter the room. I faceplant into the back of a rather large male nurse, causing him to turn around almost immediately.

"Ry—"

Before I can finish calling out to her, the nurse pushes me straight out of the room and into the hallway as he closes the door behind him.

"You can't be here, visiting hours are over. Who let you in?" he asks, releasing me with a little more force than necessary, and I stumble back a few steps and try not to trip over my own feet.

I take one look at his uniform and realize that he's more of a security guard than an actual nurse, which would explain the poor bedside manner.

"Yeah, no shit visiting hours are over, it's three in the goddamned morning," I say sarcastically.

"No one *let me in*, I've been here all night," I say, annoyed, as I try to push past him. I reach for the door handle before he steps in front of me. "Let me through. I need to get in there," I say angrily, still trying to get around him.

"Ms. Ryan, please, you need to get back in your bed, you're going to hurt yourself!" I hear someone say through the door just before a loud clang sounds, like something just got knocked over.

"You don't understand! I need to help! He's hurt! I need to help him! Please, you have to let me go!" I can hear the pleading tears in Sam's voice as she fights the nurses.

At first, I wonder if she might still be loopy from the anesthesia, but then I realize who she's talking about. The last thing Sam saw before she passed out, was me carrying her with a bloody gash across my chest.

I'm sure the only reason she didn't freak out in that moment was because of the drugs.

The security guard pushes me backward roughly a second time and stands in the door defensively as he mad-dogs me with his arms folded across his chest. The man has no doubt let what small amount of power he thinks he has go straight to his head, and I want to laugh at the arrogant expression on his face.

"Enough. Just let me through already, I can help," I say, my patience waning as I try to push the man aside. He grabs me, twisting one of my arms behind me before putting me into a tight headlock.

"*Let me go, you fucking mall cop,*" I rasp out, my airways restricted from the tight hold he has me in.

"Sir, I'm gonna need you to calm down," he says with a condescending satisfaction.

"What the fuck are you restraining *me* for? Aren't you supposed to be helping the nurses?" I say incredulously, wondering why he's bothering with me instead of doing his actual job, and I hear another loud clang come from behind the door.

"They've got everything under control in there. You can see her after you've both calmed down," he says, tightening his grip on me as I continue to struggle. "Or maybe you should just come back in the morning," he says with a snicker as he tries to walk us away from the room.

"Seriously? You're literally the fucking worst," I say under my breath as I try to pry myself out of his hold. I twist and turn myself under his arm when pain erupts around my chest, and suddenly my shirt feels wet.

"Bree, get the sedative," I hear someone say from behind the door.

"NO! LET ME GO! HE WAS BLEEDING! I NEED TO HELP HIM!" I can hear the frantic tears in Sam's voice, and I want more than anything to be able to go to her.

"JESS!" she screams, and the sound of her voice echoes through the door loudly. "JESSSS!"

"SAM!" I call out to her to let her know that I'm all right. "I'M HERE! SAM, I'M RIGHT HERE!" I try, but my voice doesn't come out at the volume I need it to.

"Dammit, let me go!" I say as I fight against the guard.

I'm getting seriously ticked off and have no doubt that I could kick the rent-a-cop's ass, but I know that the second I show any actual signs of aggression, I'll probably be removed from the premises for good.

"She's calling for ME, asshole! Let me help her for Christ's sake!" I say and momentarily stop struggling against him.

"That's my girl in there, *please*," I say calmly as I try to catch my breath, pleading with him to let me go to her as I raise my hands in surrender.

The guard hesitates before he reluctantly releases his hold on me. "Don't make me regret this," he says as he lets me go.

I burst into the room just in time to see an elderly nurse emptying a large syringe into Sam's left bicep, the other nurse trying to hold Sam steady without touching her injured arm. They both look up at me, surprised by the sudden intrusion.

I watch as Sam's body gets heavy and she starts to stagger, before bumping into the hospital bed. I rush to her and catch her just before her body falls and slides off the bed onto the floor. The nurses try to help the best they can, but they're clearly worn out from trying to catch her earlier.

Sam looks at me with heavy eyes, still fighting to stay awake, before she places her left hand on my chest. Realization hits us both at the same time when Sam reaches her hand up to her face. Her fingertips are wet with my blood, and tears flood her eyes as she looks up at me and whispers the words "*I'm sorry*" before her body goes limp and she loses consciousness.

The nurses help me as I gently hoist Sam back into her hospital bed, and I'm careful not to get any more of my blood on her in the process. When the security guard pokes his head in the room and asks the nurses if everything is all right, they wave him off, telling him they've got it handled. He frowns at me when I chuckle to myself at the nurses' dismissive attitude toward him before he leaves the room.

When I look around the small room, I wonder how Sam was able to do so much damage in the five minutes I was gone. The small table next to the bed, and the chair I was sitting in earlier are both tipped over, along with a small lamp that was resting on the bedside table. Both nurses are disheveled and look exhausted, like Sam put up a pretty good fight while they were trying to restrain her.

I fix the table and place the lamp back where it belongs as one of the nurses picks up the IV pole that was lying across the floor before standing it upright next to Sam's hospital bed. Before I'm able to do anything else, the elderly of the two nurses instructs me to sit and stay put while she gathers some supplies, obviously noticing the large bloodstain on my chest.

I shake my head when I look down, wondering how many more shirts I'm going to ruin today, knowing that I got lucky with the random one I'm wearing that happened to be in the ER lost and found. It's a little too tight for my liking, and honestly, it borders on being a crop top, but now that it's ruined, at least I don't have to wear it anymore.

The nurse returns with an armful of sealed packages and a box of gloves before she introduces herself as Lynda. She dumps all of her supplies onto the foot of Sam's bed and asks me to lift my shirt so she can examine the injury on my chest. I brush her off, trying to convince her that I'm fine, even though the blood soaking through the light gray material would suggest otherwise. She gives me a look, and I reluctantly lift the fabric, revealing the square bandage that's taped to my chest, and how it's almost completely saturated with blood.

As Lynda tends to my cut, the other nurse, Bree, tasks herself with reattaching Sam to all of her machines and IV. Because of the way Sam tore the needle out, Bree tells me that her veins are probably bruised, so she has to place the IV through a vein on the top of Sam's left hand instead.

389

I watch the nurse as she fishes around Sam's hand for a vein with the IV needle, and I have to look away. Even though I know Sam's unconscious and can't feel it, I can't bring myself to watch. The thought of something causing her any more pain than what she's already had to endure is almost too much for me to handle.

"Squeamish?" Bree asks when she notices me look away.

"Something like that," I answer.

I sit patiently in my chair while I watch Lynda scrub her hands at the small sink in the corner of the room before putting on a pair of bright blue gloves. She motions for me to lose my shirt, and I don't argue, figuring I don't really have another choice. Any other time, and I might've flexed my pecs to try and embarrass her, but the muscles in my chest hurt so damn bad that I don't even try.

Lynda gently grabs a corner of the bandage and slowly starts to peel it away from my skin. I try to hold still, but the sensation of the tape being removed so slowly makes me itchy all over. She scolds me to keep still, but instead, I reach up and rip the bandage off with one swift pull.

I let out a sigh of relief. "There. Better?" I ask, smiling innocently at her as she takes the soiled bandage from my hand and rolls her eyes.

"No wonder these ripped, you're too rough," Lynda says as she nods to my chest before shaking her head disapprovingly.

I smirk at her. "Sorry," I say, and shrug.

"This is one nasty cut," Lynda says as she starts to clean up my wound, and I see that some of the blood is now starting to dry around the edges.

When I look down at my chest, it's pretty gnarly looking, and as it turns out, I ripped about half of the stitches. I guess that's what happens when you wrestle with security, go figure.

I don't say anything as I continue to watch Lynda prep the supplies to restitch me with. She opens another sterile package with a needle in it and sees me eyeing the syringe in her hand. "What is it now?" she asks flatly as she raises a brow at me.

"No offense, but are you qualified to do this?" I ask, nodding to the suture supplies she placed on the small rolling table next to Sam's bed. "Aren't stitches... like a doctor thing?" I ask and raise a brow at her.

Lynda frowns and waves a gloved finger at me. "For your information, I've been working at this hospital since before you were even alive, so the answer is, *yes*, I'm qualified to do this," she says as she puts the sterile cap back on the needle before setting it down on the table.

"You're always welcome to go back down to the ER. I'm sure they'd love to see you again," Lynda says, giving me a look that suggests that word must've gotten around about my rampage from earlier.

I shut my mouth and shake my head, not wanting to leave Sam again, afraid they won't let me back upstairs if I do. "Good, now hold still already!" Lynda says, wagging her finger at me again, and I feel like she and Judy would get along great. The thought makes me smile to myself and I say nothing when Lynda gives me a questioning look.

I sit quietly and watch as she gives me a small injection into the muscle of my right pec just above my cut, numbing the area before she removes the old stitches. I don't feel much pain, only a slight tugging sensation as she cuts and removes the half-torn sutures from my skin.

By the time Lynda starts stitching, my chest is almost completely numb, and I hardly notice when she inserts the needle over and over again as she closes up the large cut for the second time.

"Now, I don't know what kind of trouble you two've gotten yourselves into, but..." she says, pausing as she pokes me with the needle again. "I hope you get it all sorted out. You seem like good kids," she says, and I let out a small grunt and wince, really feeling it with that last prick of the needle. I sense the string pulling again, and I watch Lynda reach for the thin scissors on the table before she snips the end of the suture thread and looks up at me.

I get the feeling she wants to ask me more about what happened, but when I don't provide her with any details, she doesn't press. Lynda gives me a quick pat on the knee before she stands and gathers up the used supplies. She disinfects the table and washes her hands after she disposes of the soiled wipes and bandages into the red biohazard container underneath the sink.

Since my shirt is ruined, I put on the black hoodie that Chris had left behind earlier and zip it up halfway. I'm grateful that I don't have to wear something from the lost and found like earlier, and I remind myself to text Sophie to bring me a clean shirt in the morning.

The other nurse, Bree, finishes up with Sam around the same time Lynda is done with me, and I thank them both for their help before they leave. Of course, they gave me the standard, "no problem, you're welcome, it's our job" spiel, but I could just tell by the looks on their faces that they were both pooped.

I look up at the digital clock on the wall and see that it's now almost 5 a.m., and if I had to guess, I'd bet they've both been here close to twelve hours already. I let out a yawn and wonder how nurses do it, feeling like they've got to have some sort of superpower to be able to do what they do every day.

I sit back in my chair, yawning again, and decide to scoot myself as close to the bed as possible. I know myself, and there's a good chance I'll fall asleep again before Sam wakes up, especially since she was just sedated for the second time. I was tired before, but I'm definitely feeling it now, largely from my almost wrestling match with Paul Blart in the hallway earlier.

It upsets me that I wasn't here when Sam woke up last time, knowing she had to have been scared and confused when she woke up all alone, and probably in a considerable amount of discomfort at that. The nurse, Bree, said that the sedative they gave Sam earlier would slowly wear off after a few hours and that she should wake up calmer than when she went out. I'm skeptical about that, but at least I'll be here next time since there's no way in hell that I'm leaving this room again until she wakes up.

I gently hold Sam's hand in mine, noting the huge IV that's now taped to the top of her hand, and see that the skin is already starting to look bruised. I know that the nurse didn't do it on purpose, but I still don't like the fact that it's probably going to hurt like a bitch when Sam wakes up.

I scoot my chair closer to Sam and gently press a kiss to the top of her hand before resting my head on the edge of the bed. I take a deep breath and feel my eyes growing heavy with each passing second before I inevitably fall asleep, my hand wrapped firmly around Sam's.

# Chapter Twenty-two

"Looks like lover boy got more than he bargained for," Elliott says as he laughs into my ear with his sour breath.

"No! Don't!" I yell, struggling to break free from the constraints of his arms. "Kyle, no!" I plead with him.

"Sorry, doll, but he asked for this. Anyone who gets involved with you will always end up the same," Kyle says, and Jess crashes down hard onto his knees as Kyle kicks his legs out from under him.

"It's inevitable," he says as he pulls Jess's head up by the back of his hair, forcing Jess to look him in the eyes.

Kyle slaps Jess on the cheek, trying to rouse him from the brink of unconsciousness. "Wake up, handsome. Things are just getting tasty. Let's have a little more fun," Kyle purrs as he runs the edge of his blade along Jess's right cheek, causing blood to trickle down his face. As the thin metal slices into his skin, Jess flinches, recoiling from the pain. He tries to fight back but can't, his body completely devoid of any strength at this point.

Kyle tilts Jess's head toward me, now forcing him to look in my direction. "This…" Kyle gestures to Jess with his blade, before pointing it at me. "Is all your fault, Samantha," he says through a menacing smile as he roughly jerks Jess's head again. I watch as Jess winces in pain from the force of Kyle's grip in his hair as he reaches up and grasps at the hand fisted in his hair, but he's too weak to pry it away.

I try to break free only to be yanked backward by Elliott. "No, I didn't mean—"

"She's not worth it," Kyle says as he crouches down beside Jess, and he whispers in his ear as they both look at me. "Deep down, we all know it. She's not worth anything at all," Kyle says with a mocking smile. "Look at what she did to you. She doesn't love you, she doesn't love anyone. She can't," he says into Jess's ear.

"Y-you…" Jess's breath catches in his throat as he chokes on his words. "*You* did this to me." Jess's words come out ragged through the broken skin of his mouth, and the look of betrayal in his beautiful eyes cracks my heart in two as his gaze burns into me.

"No! Jess, I didn't mean for this to happen!" I say, hiccupping through my tears.

"*Sam*—" Jess says with a wet cough as blood drips out of the corner of his mouth.

"*NO!* I'm sorry, Jess. Please, I'm so sorry!" I cry, snot and tears running down my desperate face, and the joints in my shoulders and wrists strain painfully the harder I try to get away from Elliott. I try to step on his foot, but my body won't cooperate as Elliott continues to laugh into my ear.

Kyle gives me a cruel smile before he grabs hold of Jess by the head before kneeing him in the stomach. Jess lets out a painful cough as he doubles over from the force of the blow, gasping for air through his broken lips.

"*Causing pain.* That's all you'll ever be good for, Samantha," Kyle says mockingly as Jess continues to cough, blood coming out of his mouth in a crimson spray, staining the hardwood floor beneath him.

"Can't you see?" Elliott whispers into my ear, and I try to elbow him in the ribs but can't move, my body still feeling like it's frozen in place. "Nobody wants this. Nobody wants *you*."

Elliott's words sting, and my eyes continue to burn as I watch the scene in front of me unfolding.

Kyle's other hand is still tightly wrapped in Jess's hair as he pulls his body upright by his head, before pressing his blade against Jess's skin. Jess cries out and tries to stop the hand that's wielding the knife, but can't, and the thin metal continues to pierce through his skin. I watch as Kyle torturously carves a long, deep cut across the muscle of Jess's chest and I scream.

"JESS! NO!"

Blood pours out of the deep gouge caused by Kyle's blade, and I sob as I see the light drain from Jess's eyes, the vibrant emerald color behind them slowly fading to a dull gray.

I'm crying hysterically as I watch as Jess's body slumps onto itself, and Kyle throws him down into the growing pool of his own blood.

"I'm sorry, I'm sorry," I say over and over, my eyes fountains of tears as I sob, watching the life fade from Jess's body.

Kyle and Elliott laugh, and their cruel taunts echo throughout the room as the walls start to blur and spin around me.

"Ms. Ryan, you need to calm down! Please!" someone says as they grab at me. When I blink and look around, I see wires and cables connecting my body to various machines around a small hospital bed.

*What am I doing here? No, this is all wrong.* I frantically search for an exit to escape through.

*I have to find him.*

"No, let me go! I need to leave," I say, ripping my arm from the woman's grasp as I pull at the cords, my skin stinging as I tear the adhesive of several small wires from my chest.

"Ms. Ryan, please, you need to get back in your bed, you're going to hurt yourself," a short, gray-haired nurse says as she tries grabbing me. I realize that I'm not actually seeing double, and that there are two nurses, both trying their best to corner me in the small room.

I move to sidestep one of them, but don't make it far when I realize I'm connected to an IV pole. I try to pull at the tube that's inserted into my left arm and realize that I only have use of one of my arms. I grasp the tube and turn my body roughly, violently trying to rip it away, causing the metal pole to fall as it crashes to the ground, knocking a lamp onto the floor with it on its way down.

"You don't understand! I need to help! He's hurt! I need to help him! *Please*, you have to let me go!" I yell at them.

I feel the warmth of something dripping down off my pinky and ring finger and realize that I'm bleeding from where I tore the needle out of my arm. Part of me knows it should hurt, but I can't feel anything except for urgency and despair, praying that I can still get to him before it's too late.

*You did this to me...* Jess's words echo in my mind. My face feels wet with tears as I continue to plead with my captors, feeling like I'm running out of time.

Jess was right, this was all my fault; the look of betrayal in his eyes as he blamed me for everything, the gaping cut across his chest *...and all that blood...*

*I have to help him, he can't die... he can't... I need him...*

I turn and dodge another hand that's grasping at me and run for the door. I'm only halfway there when I hear one nurse say to the other, "Bree, get the sedative."

I frantically reach for the door handle, trying to get away one last time. "No, please!" I say, crying, before they catch me and drag me back toward the bed, and I continue to fight and thrash against them.

"NO! LET ME GO! HE WAS BLEEDING, I NEED TO HELP HIM!" I yell frantically. "*JESS!*" I scream, my throat hurting from how hard I'm straining.

I almost manage to get away from the nurses a second time before they corner me again. "*JESSSS!*" I scream again, the high pitch of my shriek hurting my ears, before I feel a sharp pain in my left bicep and look down at a large syringe of clear liquid being emptied into my arm.

Images of Jess bleeding out and in pain overtake my vision as I stumble backward, my legs about to give way beneath me. I back into the bed but can't seem to get my body to cooperate, and I'm unable to stand upright or sit myself down on the mattress, either. I fight against the sedative, willing myself to stay awake.

My head starts to spin, and I can feel myself sliding down toward the floor.

*No, no, no. I'm not going to be able to get to him in time...*

Both nurses are out of breath as they try to maneuver me back up onto the bed when I feel someone catch me, stopping me before I hit the ground. When I look up through my blurry vision, I recognize the dark green eyes and breathtakingly handsome face looking down at me.

A wave of relief suddenly washes over my body, followed by dread when I feel a warm wetness. I raise my hand to my face, and even through my cloudy vision, I'm able to make out the bright crimson color that coats my fingertips, and I can't tell if this is actually real or not.

My eyes burn with tears, and I feel like I'm in a never-ending nightmare. I speak, but I'm unable to hear my own voice, and at this point, I'm not sure if I've actually said the words out loud or not.

"There you go, sweetie, just relax now. Everything's all right," a woman says, the words a faint echo as I will myself to focus on maintaining consciousness.

I try to hold onto him, desperately wanting to stay awake but my head grows unbelievably heavy before my vision is lost once again.

∼

The next time I open my eyes, the inside of my mouth feels like the Sahara Desert and my body feels like it's been run over by a truck. I look around the dark room, and my eyes struggle to focus on anything. The room has a strong smell of antiseptic, which immediately grounds me in a hospital setting.

I try to move, but both of my arms are heavy. My body feels like it's been tied down in every direction, and I vaguely remember fighting some nurses, and wonder if someone finally decided to put my arms in restraints so that I couldn't escape.

I pull harder against the restraints and realize that my right arm isn't actually tied down like I thought it was, it's just extremely heavy. My eyes are still trying to adjust to the dark room, and it takes me a second to realize that my right arm is almost entirely wrapped in bandages. I don't try moving it again, now keenly aware of a sore numbness that runs from my wrist up to my shoulder. I tug at my other arm, and staticky tingles shoot all the way up to my neck, making me wince at the discomfort of the sensation.

My eyes finally focus on my surroundings, and I see that there's a body half draped over my left arm, sitting in a wooden chair beside my bed. The room is completely dark except for the faint glow of the machines beeping around me, but I don't need to see to be able to recognize the familiar scent of the body in the chair.

Jess.

I calmly look down at his sleeping form and wonder how it's even possible that he's here with me. I try to recount the last few hours of my life, but everything comes back in jumbled images: Elliott, Kyle, a nurse yelling at me, orange carpet, and a lava lamp.

And Jess, bleeding out on the floor in front of me…

My head throbs, and I'm unable to differentiate between what was real and what wasn't, and the pain in my head only worsens the harder I try to remember what actually happened. I decide that if this *is* another dream, I'll let myself enjoy it for a second longer. I'm glad to see Jess sleeping peacefully beside me, even if it isn't real.

I watch as Jess's torso rises and falls with each deep breath that he takes, and I'm beyond grateful that he's alive in this reality. The last time I saw him, he was being sliced apart, and rage fills my body as I think about Kyle's taunting laughter.

*I'll make Kyle pay for what he did.*

The room is silent except for the quiet beeping of my heart rate on the small monitor to my right. I feel a gentle puff of air into my nose and realize that I must be wearing oxygen.

I mentally curse my own mind, though, wishing my subconscious had made this dream a little more exciting if it were going to involve Jess… I have a million other scenarios I'd rather play out with him that don't involve me being in a hospital bed—at least not one where I can't maneuver.

I hear a gentle knock before the door opens, and I look up as a soft fluorescent glow peeks through the crack in the doorway. "Well, I'll be damned, you're awake," an elderly lady in scrubs says quietly, noting the sleeping body half draped across my bed. "You're not going to make me sedate you again, are you?" she asks, wagging a finger at me, and I shake my head lightly, careful not to make myself dizzy.

"Okay then, good. That was too much excitement for this old lady anyhow," she says. "I'll be back in a little to recheck your vitals. Press the button if you need me before then, all right?" I say nothing as I nod at her, and she gently closes the door behind her, darkness filling the room once again.

I look down at Jess, his shoulders still rising and falling steadily with each deep breath that he takes. I gradually drag my tingling arm out from under his torso and watch as he stirs lightly. I wiggle my fingers until the feeling slowly starts to return and notice the sting of an IV needle taped to the top of my hand.

Once the feeling is back, I gently run my hand through Jess's dark hair. I let my fingers play with his silky waves, thinking that I'll never be able to do this in real life, so I'd better savor the moment while I can.

Jess's body suddenly stirs and jerks as he sits up, inhaling sharply as he looks around in a panic.

"Good morning," I say, my voice still groggy from just having woken up myself.

"Ryan, you're awake! Are you all right? How are you feeling? Should I get a nurse? Are you okay?" Jess asks me frantically as he reaches over to the bedside table before flipping on a small lamp. He shifts and hovers above his chair, and I can faintly see a crazed look in his eye, like he can't decide if he should sit back down or run for help.

"You know, now that I can see you with a little bit of light, I think that real-life Jess is much more handsome than dream-land Jess." I rest my head back against my pillow and fluff it up with my free hand, the feeling now back in my arm as well.

"No offense," I say, trying to shrug, but only one of my shoulders cooperates, the other still numb and completely useless.

"What?" he asks me in disbelief, brows furrowed so hard they're almost touching each other.

"Look, I know, I'm sorry, but there's no way you could compete with the real thing," I say with another half-shrug. "Though you are *quite* the specimen," I say teasingly as I reach for his bicep.

Jess watches blankly as I reach over and gently squeeze the muscle of his arm before staring back at me.

"Wh—Sam, this *is* real life. You're not dreaming," he says, and I can hear the worry in his voice.

I scoff. "Yeah right. Prove it," I say, challenging him. I don't give him a chance to answer before continuing. "Exactly, that's what I thought, you can't, because none of this is real," I say as I wave my hand around the room, continuing with my rant. "First of all, real Jess is much more handsome—as I had previously mentioned. Secondly, the last time I—"

My words are cut off as Jess leans in toward me and gently presses his lips to mine. The kiss is soft and warm, but I can feel the tension in his body, like he's holding himself back.

Jess breaks the kiss and rests his forehead lightly against mine, and I try to lean into him again.

"How was that? Real enough for you?" he asks, his voice low and gravelly.

Our lips are inches away from touching again, and I almost don't hear him from how loud my heart is beating in my ears.

*Now this is what I'm talking about, maybe this dream* won't *be so bad after all.*

"You proved nothing, real Jess would never," I say breathlessly as I grab a fistful of his jacket and roughly pull him back toward me.

*If this is all I'll ever be able to get, then I want it all.*

I crash his lips to mine, desperate to feel him again. Jess kisses me deeper than before and I feel his tongue as it swipes over my bottom lip. I feel a whimper leave his lips and his body flinches when my fist collides with his chest, the fabric of his hoodie twisted in my hand as I pull him tightly toward me.

I pull away and see a grimace of pain on his face, and watch as he breathes heavily as he stares at me, studying my expression. "I…" I stammer, trying to get my hazy thoughts straight. "*Dammit*, is this real life or not?" I say in frustration, more to myself than to him.

Through the low lighting, I watch as Jess's eyes soften as he reaches for my hand. "It's okay, you didn't hurt me, it's just a little sore, is all," he says with a crooked smile.

Tears start to well in my eyes, blurring my vision again. "I don't understand, I saw him cut you. I saw you bleeding out. I… I saw you…"

I can't bring myself to finish the sentence, and my body starts to shake. "But, you're *there* and I'm *here*. How? How are you here?" I say, gesturing to my hospital bed and then to his chair as I start to cry harder.

"Hey hey hey, it's all right, Ryan. Don't cry, I'm here," Jess says, shushing me gently as he gives my hand a light squeeze, careful not to disturb my IV.

"I'm not hurt. I'm all right, okay? Everything's okay," he says gently as he reaches for my face, catching a tear with his thumb as he cups my cheek in his palm. I lean into his touch and close my eyes. "You can't get rid of me that easily," he says, and I can hear a small smile in his voice.

"Jess," I croak and open my eyes, the tears still flowing out of me like a river. "It's all my fault. Everything's my fault," I say through a hiccup, unable to catch my breath, making my chest hurt.

"It's okay, everything's okay," he says, pulling my face against him as he rubs the back of my head gently. "It's not your fault, please don't say that," he says as I grip the collar of his hoodie, trying not to sob.

Jess attempts to pull me to his chest, but I resist, pushing against his shoulder with my hand. "No, I can't," I say, trying to fight against him.

"You're not going to hurt me, I promise," he says softly as he puts a hand over mine.

403

I cry even harder, trying to sort through the memories of the last few hours, and it's not until then that I consider that maybe it hasn't only been a few hours.

Who knows how long I've been here? *Days? Weeks, even?*

"Jess, tell me that you're actually here, tell me that you're okay, and I'm not just imagining this," I plead, and I'm sure that my eyes are wide with desperation. "I need you to be okay, please tell me that you're okay," I say, sobbing now, and feel like I might be on the verge of hyperventilation.

I'm hysterical as I grab at his hoodie, worried that I might stretch it out, but just as afraid to let him go again.

"I'm here, okay. I promise I'm here," Jess says, trying to reassure me as he brings my hand to his mouth, kissing my palm.

Jess puts both of his hands on either of my cheeks, forcing me to look him in the eyes. "Ryan, I need you to breathe, okay? You're going to pass out if you don't calm down," he says, looking into my eyes intensely as he tries to settle me down. I know he's right, because I can hear the beeping of the machines going off around us as my heart hammers against my ribcage.

Jess holds my face in his hands as he forces me to breathe with him. I follow him in taking a few deep breaths, my body still trembling from how hard I was crying, and the beeping on the monitor by my bed slowly returns to normal after a few minutes.

"Everything is all right, okay? I'm here, and you're here, and we're both safe," Jess says calmly with a nod. "Say it back to me now, everything is all right," he says again, and I repeat the words back to him before he releases my face from in between his warm hands.

My voice comes out small and cracked as I reach for the hem of his sleeve as he stands. "*Wait*—"

"Don't worry, baby, I'm not going anywhere," Jess says gently, and I quickly catch on as I watch him take his boots off.

It's tricky with the IV in my hand, but I scoot myself as far to the right of the bed as the plastic guardrail will allow without disturbing the bandages on my other arm. There's honestly not much room in the small bed, which I don't mind, and I'm glad when I see that it doesn't seem to bother Jess either.

After taking off his boots, Jess carefully lifts my IV tube up and around so it's out of the way before lowering himself down on the bed beside me. He's barely made it onto the uncomfortable mattress before I angle myself toward him, desperately wishing I had use of both arms to wrap around him.

He places one of his arms around my waist the best that he can with the awkward angle of the bed and my hurt arm and interlaces the fingers of our other hands together as he rests them in between us.

"Come here," he says quietly, and I nuzzle into him, trying to use the faint aroma coming off his skin to calm myself down with. I take deep, steadying breaths and try not to get hysterical again, terrified that he might disappear at any second.

I'm careful not to move too much, not wanting to hurt him, but Jess pulls me in tighter when I resist, and I finally rest my head against him. I'm not sure how much time passes. The longer we stay that way, the more my anxiety subsides, the comfort of being beside Jess regulating my nervous system almost immediately.

Just as my eyes start to feel heavy and I think I might drift off again, I feel Jess whisper something against me before kissing me on the head.

Finally at peace, I let myself fall asleep to the gentle thumps of Jess's heartbeat and his warm, strong hand in mine.

# Chapter Twenty-three

This time when I wake up, I feel like myself again. There's no worry or fear, and no nightmares to jolt me awake in a frenzied panic. When I open my eyes, I see sunlight shining through the curtains near the window, and I can hear the birds twittering just outside.

I look over and see that Jess is still right beside me, fast asleep with one arm still lazily draped across my hips. Our bodies are sandwiched together in the small hospital bed, and our hands are still interlaced down in between us. I yawn and try to stretch out the arm that's wedged in between mine and Jess's bodies without letting go of his hand, and notice the complete soreness of my entire body when I do.

I lean my head back against the bed and blink the sleep out of my eyes as I draw in a sharp breath and yawn again. A lot of the haze has cleared, and I'm able to remember most of what happened with Kyle and Elliott, along with last night, but not much else in between. I look down at

Jess's body and see that his tall frame is barely able to fit next to me on the bed, his feet almost hanging off the edge, and I smile to myself at the sight.

I think back to last night and decide that what happened between Jess and me was most definitely not a dream. I mean, I've had some pretty real dreams before, but never a kiss that felt like *that*.

The thought has my face warming up, followed by the rest of my body. My heart rate starts to pick up when I realize just how tightly our bodies are pressed up against each other, our legs seemingly more inter-twined than they were last night.

A pain shoots up my left side as I shift my weight and try to adjust my broken arm. The way I'm lying is causing a cramp in my shoulder and up into my neck, and I strain to carefully reposition myself. My body feels hot, and I want to take the blanket off, but I don't bother even trying to since I can see that it's wedged tightly underneath Jess's sleeping form.

Jess sits up in alarm. "Ryan, I'm here!" he says as he looks around the room quickly, like he half expects me to be on the run, or something.

I let go of his hand and reach up, trying to pat down the mess of waves on one side of his head. "You seriously have the cutest bed head," I say, making fun of him as I let out a small laugh.

Jess blinks at me with big sleepy doe-eyes. When they meet mine, the tired haziness behind them clears, and they soften when he realizes that nothing's awry.

His eyes are half-lidded as he looks down at me before tucking a stray piece of hair behind one of my ears. "That's *my* line," he says with his gravelly morning voice and gives me a crooked smile. I blush and turn away, removing my hand from his head, and place it back in my lap in between us.

"Jess, about last night…" I start, unable to look him in the eyes, and he stays silent, giving me the chance to gather my thoughts.

"Thank you, Jess …or more like, *sorry*, I mean…" I say and shake my head. "I was acting like a crazy person, so I get that you had to snap me out of it somehow," I say, now barely able to shrug my good shoulder from the pain that's radiating up from my other side. I'm feeling embarrassed about everything, and I wait for him to reply as I continue to avoid his eyes.

Jess places a finger under my chin, tilting my face up to look at him. "You didn't force me to do anything, if that's what you're thinking," he says softly. "If anything, I should be the one apologizing to *you*. God knows what you went through, and I forced myself on you with that kiss. I'm so sorry, Sam," he says with a look of regret on his face, and I can see the weight of it behind his eyes.

Before either of us has a chance to say another word, the door swings open, interrupting the building tension between us.

"*Girl*, I could kill you for scaring me like that!" Sophie says, entering the room with Aunt Judy in tow behind her.

"What's all this now?" Sophie asks, giving us a coy smile at the fact that Jess is in the hospital bed with me. Aunt Judy takes one look at our bodies pressed up against each other and says nothing as she stands next to Sophie. She gives us a smug grin and places her hands on her hips.

"What?" Jess says as he raises his brows at Judy. "You got something to say, old lady?" Jess asks, challenging her.

Sophie and I exchange glances before she puts her hands up and steps back, gesturing in front of her for Judy to go on ahead with Jess's beating.

"Listen here, you punk," Aunt Judy says as she grabs Jess by the ear, pulling him out of the bed next to me. "Why in the hell didn't you come get me last night? Do you have any idea how angry I am?"

"Whoa whoa whoa, wait a second, ow ow ow! I'm sorry, I'm sorry, let go!" Jess says, putting his hands up in surrender. "I didn't want you to worry, and I knew they wouldn't have let me check you out so late!" he says, trying to defend himself.

"Well, a lot of good it did, numbnuts!" Judy says, scolding him as she finally releases his ear. "You ever heard of a prison break for cryin' out loud?" she asks, waving her hands at him. Jess says nothing as he frowns and rubs at his ear.

"Next time something happens, you'd better be prepared to come break me out, otherwise, the nurses at the home will be the least of your worries!" Judy says, wagging a finger at Jess as he pulls his boots on from where he left them on the floor next to the bed.

"All right, you have my word that next time something happens, Operation 'Prison Break the Wrinkly Old Hag Out of Her Home' is a go," Jess says, backing toward the door as Aunt Judy looks around the room for something to throw at him.

"You guys look like you could use a coffee," Jess says to us through a smile as he backs himself closer to the door. "Need anything else while I'm out? Denture cream? Maybe some adult diapers? The home did call to let me know that you're out again already." Jess lets out a disapproving *tsk* and waves a finger at Judy with a mischievous grin across his face.

"You little shit," she says as she takes off her sandal and hucks it across the room toward Jess's head. He's too quick for her though, and ducks out behind the door, laughing as the sandal bounces off the wooden paneling of the door before falling to the floor.

"And, I don't wear diapers!" Judy yells after him angrily.

"Everything okay in here?" a voice asks from just outside the door. A head slowly pops into the room as if trying to be wary of any other potential flying objects, and I recognize that it's the elderly nurse from earlier.

Aunt Judy waves her off as she walks over to where her shoe bounced off the door and slips it back on her foot. "Yeah, sorry about the ruckus, you can blame that knucklehead who just left," Judy says, waving a hand toward the door dramatically. The nurse gives her a look and nods, like she's fully aware of just how much of a handful that Jess is, and I wonder to myself what I missed while I was out.

Judy makes her way over to the chair beside my bed and sits down with a huff. Once Judy gets riled up, it doesn't take much to set her off a second time. We all watch and try our best not to laugh, knowing it wouldn't make the situation any better. Sophie looks at me like she might combust from holding in her giggles, so I clear my throat and look over at the nurse as she types something into the computer station attached to the wall in the far corner of the room.

"Not that I'm trying to get rid of you or anything, but what are you still doing here? You must've worked at least twelve hours already. I'll bet you're exhausted," I ask the nurse, trying to make some small talk.

"Fourteen, actually. We've been short-staffed the last few nights, so I've had to stay on a little longer than usual," the nurse says and turns toward me with an exhausted smile.

She walks over to the window and opens up the curtains, letting more sunlight into the bleak room. When she walks back past my bed, I notice that the name on her badge matches the name on the small patient information whiteboard hanging on the wall across from my bed.

My nurse, Lynda, returns to the small computer cabinet after quickly taking my vitals and closes the door with a click, folding the small computer back up into its compartment.

"Aside from the obvious, how are you feeling today? Are you having any pain anywhere?" Lynda asks before grabbing my hand, checking the bruised skin around the IV needle.

"Well, my left arm and shoulder are a little sore, but I think it's mostly from sleeping crooked. Other than that, I think I'm doing much better than before," I say, feeling bad if I gave her a hard time while I was out of it. "My head was a serious mess yesterday. Do you think that could be from the drugs?" I ask, and notice as Judy shifts uncomfortably in her seat.

Lynda shrugs, and tugs on both ends of the stethoscope around her neck with her hands as she pulls a thinking face. "Well, I'm not a doctor, but I can say that I've seen drugs do some pretty crazy things to people over the years," she says before continuing. "I did notice that you have a sleep condition listed in your chart called Elpenor Syndrome," Lynda says, and I just give her a blank stare.

*Sleep condition? What the hell?*

"So, I take it you weren't aware of it?" she asks, and I shake my head. "It's sometimes called Confusional Arousal, and it's known to cause confusion and disorientation when waking up sometimes," Lynda explains.

"Does it say in my chart how long I've had this for?" I ask, trying not to overreact, wondering why no one bothered to tell me about this sooner.

"While it can sometimes carry over into adulthood, it's usually most common in infants and babies up until around five years old," Lynda says. "But, it usually resolves itself with time," she says quickly, no doubt trying to backtrack after seeing the look on my face.

"I don't think you have anything to worry about. Sometimes it can be triggered by certain things, and in your case, I think it was a combination of multiple things. I read the notes in your chart, and it looks like your body was under a considerable amount of stress yesterday," she says. "I'd be happy to do some more research on it if you're concerned, though. There's a sleep clinic up on the fifth floor, I can ask if—"

"No, no, it's okay. Thank you, anyway. I was mostly just curious. I guess I've always known something was up with my sleep, I just didn't know I had an actual condition," I say, and find myself unconsciously trying to shrug.

"Honestly though, this morning when I woke up, I felt great. I wasn't confused or anything. I thought for sure I'd be a mess after that sedative," I say, turning to Sophie.

"Sedative?" Sophie mouths at me, her eyebrows raised, and I give her a look that says, *I'll tell you later*.

"If neither of you is going to say it, then I will," Judy says, looking between Sophie and Lynda.

"Say what?" I ask.

"Sam, honey, don't you find it funny that you've had trouble sleeping your entire life, and then—even after a traumatic life event—you woke up feeling great?" Judy asks, raising her eyebrows. I just stare at her, unsure of what to say. She puts her hands up and looks around, as if it's obvious that we should all know what she's talking about.

Judy lets out an annoyed breath before rolling her eyes dramatically. "Well, it's because of that numbskull—"

Aunt Judy is unable to finish her sentence when a knock at the door sounds before it opens slowly. A hand shoots through the crack in the door, holding up a white paper bag.

"I come in peace with coffee and bagels. Please don't throw any shoes at me," Jess says from behind the door, and I can hear the smile in his voice. "I promise to behave... at least until we're done eating," he teases as he walks through the door, holding a drink carrier with four large coffees in one hand and the paper bag in the other.

"Well, you've got about five seconds to hand over one of those coffees or I'll make sure to find something a lot bigger than a shoe to throw at you," Judy says, scolding him.

"*I'd like to see you try...*" I hear Jess say under his breath as he hands one of the cups to Aunt Judy after setting the bag of bagels down onto the rolling table next to my bed.

"I'm sorry, what was that?" she asks him flatly.

"Nothing. I just said that you look beautiful today, Judith, that's all," he says, giving her his signature all-too-charming Jess smile before handing Sophie and me each a cup.

"*Mmm hmm,*" Judy grumbles as she takes a sip of her coffee, which seemingly puts her in a better mood almost instantly, and I laugh to myself.

"Well, Ms. Ryan, I'm sure you haven't seen the last of me just yet, but I'm going to head home for the night," Lynda says as she checks the watch on her wrist. "My relief should be here any minute, so I'll send them in to check on you later," she says before giving us all a wave as she makes her way to the door.

"Hold up, Lynda. *This* is for you," Jess says, handing the last coffee cup to her. "It's decaf, so you're able to sleep," he explains with a smile as she takes the paper cup from him.

"Thank you, but... what's this for?" Lynda asks, eyeing him suspiciously.

"I just wanted to say thanks, for last night, that is. I'll admit, I am a little sore, so thank you for being so gentle with me," he says with a wink, and Lynda's entire face turns redder than a tomato.

"Okay, *what* is he talking about?" Sophie asks, turning to me with her brows raised in confusion.

"I have no idea," I say, and we both start to laugh.

"Obviously, I'm talking about my stitches. Perverts," Jess says innocently.

"All right, it's time for me to leave now," Lynda says, still a little flustered from Jess's comment. "I'll see you soon, Ms. Ryan, and you..." she says, pointing to Jess. "Don't go getting into any more fights, at least not until I get back, okay?"

"You got it boss," Jess says with a wink before Lynda leaves the room, shutting the door behind her.

"Fights?" I ask.

"Stitches?" Sophie asks, and we both turn to each other.

"It's nothing, it's really just a scratch," Jess says, shrugging. "Did you bring my shirt like I asked?" Jess turns to Sophie before catching the black shirt she throws toward his face.

"I also brought your crusty-ass sketchbook too, like you asked," Sophie says and pulls a small leather notebook out of her purse before Jess quickly snatches it out of her hand.

"Thanks," Jess says, and tucks the small notebook into his back pocket before unzipping his hoodie, revealing his bare chest underneath. In all the fuss of the last few hours, I hadn't even noticed that he wasn't wearing a shirt underneath the hoodie—which was probably for the best. Even though I'm injured, that does little to distract me from the fact that Jess has a near-perfect body. A near-perfect body that spent the night pressed up against mine...

The room goes uncomfortably silent as we all watch Jess change, revealing the large white bandage taped across the right side of his chest. Guilt swells through me when I see the bandage. I know my nightmare last night was just that, but I'm positive that the cut on Jess's chest is from Kyle.

Judy lets out a growl of disapproval. "I thought I told you to stay out of trouble!" she says, already on her feet, reaching up toward Jess's ear again.

"I told you it's nothing," Jess says, brushing her off, dodging her tiny stature as he pulls the t-shirt down over his body.

"You know what?" Judy says through gritted teeth, standing across from Jess with her fists raised, looking like she's about to drop-kick him. She's clearly not intimidated by him, even though he towers at least two feet above her.

"What? What're you gonna do, you old grouch?" Jess counters with his hands on his hips as he leans down toward her.

Judy lets out another annoyed grumble, and it looks like they're squaring up for a fight, which might've even made me laugh if the circumstances were different.

"It's my fault," I say quietly, and quickly feel everyone's eyes on me.

"What do you mean, Sam?" Judy asks as she jumps to reach Jess's ear before he swats her hand away without looking at her, his eyes now fixed on my face.

"It's because of me. It's all because of me. Jess never would've gotten hurt… *if it weren't for me*," I say, trying to hold back the tears brimming behind my eyes.

"You know that's not what happened, Sam," Jess says, anger and frustration in his voice as he looks at me while still trying to dodge Judy's small hands.

"Now look what you did! You made my Samantha cry!" Judy says as she swats Jess on the arm before she makes her way over to my bedside.

Judy takes my hand as she sits down in the chair next to my bed and looks me in the eyes, and there's a softness there that I don't often see from her. "Now, why would you say that, Sam, honey?"

"Because it's the truth, Judy," I say as I look at her, hoping she can see the regret in my eyes. "Jess never would've gotten hurt if it wasn't for me. You told me to look out for him, but I didn't. The situation I was involved in had nothing to do with him and he got hurt because of it, *because of me*," I say through a half-hiccup.

"I'm really sorry," I say softly, and a few tears manage to escape my throbbing eyes.

When I look over at Jess, his face is serious, and his brows are furrowed together in anger. "*Ryan—*"

"What's important is that you're alive, *both* of you," Judy says, interrupting him as she shoots a glare in Jess's direction. I give her hand a squeeze as she leans in to give me a gentle hug, careful not to disturb my arm. I hug her back as tightly as I'm able, and reign in my tears, deciding that I've cried enough in the last few days to last me a lifetime.

After a few minutes, my new nurse, Adam, rechecks my vitals before bringing me a breakfast tray. I don't have much of an appetite after eating the bagel and coffee Jess brought, especially after seeing the dressing on his chest. He says he's fine, but the thought of him being in any pain still bothers me.

I eat a few pieces of the fruit off my breakfast tray and offer the rest of the food to Jess, noticing that he didn't get a bagel and coffee for himself earlier. He politely declines and goes back to staring out one of the windows.

Sophie climbs onto the bed with me, and we find some juicy daytime soap opera to watch, and Judy settles in beside us in her chair.

Lunch comes and goes, and Adam brings extra food for me to share with my guests, for which I'm grateful. Jess takes a few bites of a sandwich I offer him, but only because I practically force him to eat before he gives the rest to Sophie. I notice that he's kind of in a mood, but I figure it's probably just from exhaustion and try not to take it personally.

After another hour of trashy TV, Aunt Judy is falling asleep in her chair, and Sophie is starting to doze off as well, when we hear a knock at the door. I holler at them to come in, and my dad enters the room first with Chris following along behind him, holding a small bouquet of flowers in one hand.

"Damn, did hell freeze over or something?" I ask, raising a surprised brow at him.

"Yeah, yeah, I'm glad you're not dead," Chris says, rolling his eyes as he sets the flowers down on the counter next to the sink. I watch as he steals a quick glance at Sophie and wonder if she's the real reason that he's here.

Sophie stirs next to me, and sits up in the bed, no doubt from hearing the sound of Chris's voice. She looks over at him, and they stare longingly at each other, and I wonder if this is new, or if I've just never paid attention to it before.

"How you feeling, kid?" my dad asks. He stands at the foot of the bed, giving my bandaged arm a once-over, and pulls his phone out of his pocket when it dings.

"I'm okay, just a little sore. They said they'd let me out tomorrow if I behave," I joke and give him a small smile, but he doesn't look up as he continues to fervently type into his phone.

"Good," he says as he pats me on the leg, one eye still glued to his screen. "Judy, always a pleasure to see you," my dad says to her, the sound of his voice waking her up.

Judy clears her throat and pretends not to have been startled by my dad's deep voice as she sits up and straightens in her chair. "Say, John, you wouldn't mind giving me a ride home, would ya?" she asks as she stands and stretches her hands over her head.

"Sure thing," he says and smiles politely at her before finally putting his phone back into his pocket.

"I'm glad you're safe and sound," Judy says, leaning over to kiss me on the forehead. "When you're feeling up to it, let me know, and we can reschedule our date," she says, winking at me.

I nod. "I'd like that," I say and smile at her.

"And *you*…" Judy says as she points a wrinkly finger at Jess before making an angry face at him. "We'll talk about this later," she says, no doubt referring to his injury.

"Byeee Judyyy," Jess drawls from his seat by the window. He'd been so quiet this whole time, I'd almost forgotten he was even there. After lunch, he just sat in his chair with his arms folded, never breaking his gaze from the window. I figured that he'd at least pull out his sketchbook if he were bored, but he never did.

"I'll make sure to have the home bill you twice this month on account of that diaper comment," Judy says to him before turning to walk out the door.

"Loveee youuu," Jess calls after her before she flips him off over her shoulder, the action making everyone in the room smile.

"I guess I'm going to take Judy back to the home now. Let me know if you need anything, all right? I'll swing by tomorrow morning to check on you again," my dad says before following Judy to the door.

"Okay," I say, giving him a small smile.

Part of me wishes he'd stay a little longer, but I tell myself to be happy with the fact that he even came by at all. Adam said that my dad was supposed to meet with my doctors earlier today, but he never came by. I tell myself that it's okay though, and that he's probably got a lot on his mind and just forgot. I sigh, knowing deep down that I'm just making excuses for him like I always do.

I notice that Chris is still hovering by the small sink with his hands in his pockets, looking uncomfortable and out of place. Sophie hasn't said a word to him, but the tension radiating between them is so thick I could cut it with a knife.

"You know, Soph, I'm actually getting a little tired. I might just try to sleep for a little while. Do you mind?" I ask, letting out a fake yawn that slowly turns itself into a real one.

She gives me a grateful look, knowing that I'm probably only telling a half-truth, before hugging me the best that she can. "I love you, Babe," she says as she pulls back to face me. "Let's talk when you get out, okay? I've got some things I need to apologize for," she says before hugging me again.

"Okay," I say, giving her a nod, knowing that I've got my fair share of apologizing to do as well.

"Can I catch a ride with you?" Sophie asks Chris as she climbs out of my bed and walks over to stand in front of him. It surprises me that she didn't flat-out tell him that he was giving her a ride instead of asking him for one.

"Sure," he says a little too quickly, and I wonder how long they've actually been seeing each other if she still gets him this flustered. I've never seen him act this way since he never dated anyone in high school, and now I'm wondering if this is the reason why.

Chris and Sophie both wave their goodbyes before heading out the door, and I shake my head. "That's going to take some getting used to," I say, mostly to myself.

I yawn again, this time for real, and glance up at the time, and see that it's only four o'clock in the afternoon.

"Are you sure you don't want to go home and get some rest? As far as I know, you've been here since at least yesterday," I say before yawning again. "Aren't you tired?" I ask through my yawn, glancing over at Jess. He's still sitting by the window, his arms folded across his chest, and with a serious expression on his face.

"Hey, are you okay?" I ask, wondering why he's acting so weird.

"Why did you list me as your emergency contact?" he asks, the emotion in his voice difficult to read.

"What do you mean?" I ask, confused, feeling like his question came out of nowhere.

"Earlier yesterday, when the doctor was giving us an update after your surgery, she said that you had me listed as your emergency contact. She thought we were... *together*," he says, and his expression is still hard to read, especially with the serious tone of his voice.

"*Oh*," I say nervously, unsure of what else to say.

"Why not put your dad, or Sophie?" Jess asks. "Why put me?"

I let out a small chuckle and shake my head. "You don't remember, do you?" I ask, and he raises a questioning brow at me. "Do you remember that last party we all went to together, the one on graduation night?"

"Sure, I remember you blowing Soph and me off to hook up with that douche, Brad," Jess says, and I sense a hint of jealousy in his voice.

"Right, well, then you'd remember that on our way out of the party, I fell because I was wearing a pair of Sophie's six-inch heels. I thought I'd broken my ankle when I fell and twisted it, so you guys brought me to the ER," I say, and Jess gives me a look like he only has a faint recollection of that night. When he doesn't say anything, I continue with my story.

"Even though I had just turned eighteen, I was still so scared of my dad finding out that I was drinking at that party. So, when you and Soph brought me to the hospital, you suggested we put your name down as my emergency contact instead of my dad's. Why we didn't just put down your number with his name, I'm not sure," I say with a half shrug.

I watch as Jess shakes his head and leans forward, resting his forearms on his thighs. "That's right, I remember now. God, we were all pretty trashed that night, weren't we?" he says as he rubs a hand over his face. None of us wanted to drive after the party, so we took a cab to the hospital instead. Honestly, the entire night was a mess from start to finish.

"Not that it really matters now, but for the record, I never hooked up with Brad," I say, trying to meet Jess's eyes. He stays silent for a moment, even though I know it's killing him to ask me more about it.

"What happened? Seemed like you two really hit it off," Jess asks, trying to sound nonchalant. The sour expression on his face suggests that it's still bothering him, even after all this time. He sits back, folding his arms across his chest as he glances out the window again.

"I don't know about you, but I think that most guys don't particularly like being called by someone else's name during a hookup," I say hesitantly as I watch Jess's expression closely.

"Well that's a dick move," he says with a scoff, and I blink at him, waiting for him to understand.

Jess slowly turns to meet my eyes, and his expression changes as realization sets in.

# Chapter Twenty-four

I can feel my cheeks starting to heat up, but I refuse to be the one to break eye contact first, not this time. Yesterday, I thought I was going to die, and then Jess kissed me. If I don't tell him how I really feel now, I might not ever.

"If it's all right with you, I'll leave you as my emergency contact, for now, at least," I say.

"Ryan, whose name did you say that night?" he asks, and I can see the intensity slowly starting to build in his eyes.

"You already know," I say, daring him to look away first this time, when a small sound knocks at the door, and I scream internally in frustration. It seems like every time we try to have a serious conversation, someone or something constantly interrupts us before we can.

"Come in," I say when no one enters the room, still holding Jess's smoldering gaze with my own. He looks just as annoyed as I feel, like he's ready to kick whoever it is out of the room so we can finish our discussion for once.

"Hi," a voice says, before stepping out from behind the door hesitantly. I immediately recognize Madison's beautiful face, her makeup and silky brown hair looking perfect today—as predicted—and I roll my eyes.

*Where the hell does she get off coming here?*

It feels kind of weird to see her here. Especially since the *last* time I saw her, she pretended not to know me, and now she's visiting me in the hospital?

"Hi…?" I say. I scrunch my brows in confusion, and when she doesn't say anything, I blurt out the first thing that comes to my mind without thinking. "No offense, but what are you doing here?" I ask.

*That is… unless she's actually here for him instead of me.*

I look over to Jess, who's still sitting in his chair by the window, now looking toward where Madison stands in the doorway.

*Has he been waiting for her this entire time? Is she here to pick him up or something?*

Jealousy burns through me at the thought of Jess leaving me here to go spend time with her.

Madison turns back toward the door. "Should I leave?" she asks Jess, clearly sensing the hostile vibes emanating off me.

"No, it's all right, Maddy. You don't have to go," Jess tells her. I turn and shoot him a dirty look, but it doesn't seem to faze him at all.

"Jess was just saying how tired he is, maybe you should give him a ride home," I say, the bitterness obvious in my voice. I could kick myself for suggesting he leave with her, but I'm just so mad I don't know what I'm doing.

JESS CAMERON, I LOVE YOU

"*Umm*, okay. That's fine with me…" Madison looks to Jess before turning her gaze back toward me uncomfortably. "I just wanted to stop by and see how you were doing, is all…"

*Yeah right. She's obviously here for him.*

I turn to Jess again, and I'm about two seconds away from kicking him out of my room as well, not wanting either of them to see me cry. I can feel the angry tears about to start flowing when Jess speaks.

"Sam, Madison is the one who told me where you were yesterday," Jess says as he unfolds his arms and sits up in his chair, his tone serious.

"What?" I ask, looking between Jess and Madison. She still looks uneasy as she holds onto the strap of her purse with both hands, still hesitating in the doorway, like she'd literally rather be anywhere but here right now.

"How else do you think I was able to find you?" Jess asks.

Honestly, I hadn't really thought about that. I know I have my location shared with Sophie, but even then, I remember dropping my phone when Elliott grabbed me. Even if Jess had checked that back alleyway, he'd have no reason to believe I was locked in the basement of that specific store. I have no doubt he wouldn't have given up on looking for me, but who knows how long it would have taken him to actually pinpoint my location.

"Yesterday, when I was at your dad's house looking for you, Madison called me and said that you were in trouble. She said that she thought she'd recognized you from the other day, and that you'd asked her for help," he explains. "If she hadn't called me when she did…" Jess's voice trails off, and I can tell he's running worst-case scenarios through his mind.

I look over when I hear Madison speak up. "I'm sorry if it seemed like I didn't want to help you. I was just afraid that if I'd said that I knew you, they'd try to stop me from calling Jess," she says nervously, still obviously uncomfortable. "I'm really happy that you're okay. The last time

423

they did something like this, there wasn't much I could do…" Madison says as she looks down at the floor.

*The last time?*

I try not to think about how many ex-girlfriends Kyle has kidnapped and assaulted, and wonder why in the hell she's still friends with people like them if there was a *last time?*

I guess I'm one to talk, though, I literally dated one of them.

I let out a breath and rub my forehead with my hand, feeling like the world's biggest asshole. "No, don't be sorry. I should be the one apologizing. I had no idea," I say, shaking my head at my own ignorance. "I'm sorry for being so rude," I say, giving her a small smile, trying to ease some of the awkward tension that's built up in the room.

"Thank you, Madison, you saved my life yesterday," I say, hoping she can tell that I'm actually being sincere.

"I'm just glad you're okay," she says, repeating herself before grabbing the metal door handle to leave. "I'll see ya around," she says, giving me a nervous smile before looking over at Jess.

"Thanks for stopping by, Maddy. I'll call you later, okay?" he says, smiling back at her before nodding. She gives a small wave before leaving the room, and the latch on the door clicks shut as it closes behind her.

I shake my head and let out an exhausted breath. "Unfucking believable," I say as I stare at the ceiling and let out a humorless laugh.

"She was just trying to be nice, no need to be an ass about it," Jess says sharply.

"This is so typical. Sooo *Jess*," I say angrily, turning toward him.

"What are you talking about?" he asks, annoyed.

"I swear, my life is just like one big shitty round of déjà vu," I say as I let out another exhausted breath.

"Seriously, Sam, what are you talking about?" Jess asks, clear aggravation in his voice.

"Nothing." I sigh and turn away from him, wishing I could lie on my side so that I could face away from him completely. "I'm just tired, that's all. You should go home and get some rest," I say without looking at him. "I'll be fine here on my own."

"Are you really trying to kick me out right now?" he asks.

"No, you've just been here for like two days, so you're starting to smell," I lie.

"I'll leave, but I doubt that's what you really want," Jess says as he takes a seat in the chair next to my bed. He folds his arms across his chest as he sits back and stares at me.

"And how would you know what I want?" I say and scoff, now forced to look at him.

"Because I know you, and pretty well, I'd say," he says with a smirk as he slowly gives me a once-over.

"Just go, Jess. I'm too exhausted to play this game right now," I say, letting out another exasperated breath.

"What game?" he asks.

"This back-and-forth bullshit we always do," I say. "It's exhausting, and I just... *can't*... right now."

"Are you referring to us *talking?* Because that's something that normal people do, they *talk* to each other," he says, raising a brow at me, and I feel like ripping my hair out.

*Is he seriously this dense?*

"Do I literally have to spell it out for you?" I ask, raising my brows.

"Apparently," he says, and his flirtatious tone has now grown serious again. "I don't know why you're so mad all of a sudden when you were the one who was being a jerk to Mad—"

"*Maddy?* Right," I say with an angry scoff as I shake my head as I look toward the dimly illuminated window. The room is much darker now as the sun continues to move lower into the sky.

I'm so not in the mood to be doing this right now, but in the end, waiting will only slowly make me lose my sanity.

*Might as well just get it over with already, just like ripping off a band-aid.*

"Whenever I think I've got a read on things between us, there's always some other girl there waiting for you. *Every. Time.*" I say, not looking at him, my gaze fixed on the far wall of the room.

Jess stays silent for a moment before answering. "You've got it all wrong, Ryan," he says and lets out a small laugh, but there's no actual humor behind it.

"There's always someone else. Don't you see, Jess? There will *always* be someone else," I say angrily as I snap my head toward him to meet his eyes.

"What are you talking about?" he asks, his tone much sharper than before.

"What don't you understand?" I ask angrily as I throw my hand in the air and try my hardest to fight back my tears. "It's never going to be me!"

"There *is* no one else, Ryan. There never was!" Jess says, standing so abruptly that he almost knocks his chair over.

"But there is! Do you have any idea how it felt to see you with that dumb redhead when you were supposed to be with me all those years ago? Why do you think I tripped into the water? *I saw you with her, Jess!* I saw you two coming out of that shed together," I say, unable to delay the waterworks any longer, and my face feels wet.

"No! You've got it all wrong!" Jess says, trying to grab my hand, but I pull it away from him dramatically.

"I was waiting for you like some fucking idiot, and all the while you were probably banging her in there! You never wanted to be with me, you just felt sorry for me, that's the only reason you invited me out that morning!" I cry angrily at him. "You just feel bad for me, even now! That's why you're here, admit it!" I spit through my tears. "And now it's happening all over again," I say as I fling my hand toward the door, gesturing to where Madison was standing just a second ago.

"No, that's not it!" Jess says, his brows furrowed as he frantically tries to reach for me again and I shake my head as I look away. "You don't understand, Ryan."

"Understand what? That I'm *important* to you, but not in *that* way?" I say, still refusing to look him in the eye.

"Ryan, I promised myself the day you almost drowned that even if you didn't want me to, even if you didn't want... *me*, I was always going to protect you. Always. But I didn't... I *couldn't*," he says, the intensity of his gaze softening as his glossy eyes meet mine when I turn to face him again.

I stare at him, but don't say anything, afraid that I might break down completely if I try to talk right now.

"I wasn't able to protect you then, and I wasn't able to protect you from those scumbags yesterday either, and look at what happened!" Jess says, and the fire in his eyes returns as he leans away from me and gestures to my arm. "I don't want to protect you because I feel bad for you, I just... I..." he says, shaking his head as he clenches his jaw.

Anger momentarily overtakes my sadness, and I snap at him. "Stop. I don't want any more of your sympathy," I say, trying to calm myself down before my monitors alert the nurses.

"I want you to want to be with me because that's what *you* want, not because you feel sorry for me or because you think I need protecting like some stupid kid! *Oh, poor little Samantha, always needing to be looked after. She's so pathetic that not even her own family wants her*," I say, mocking myself, the tears still falling as I cover my face with my hand.

I feel embarrassed beyond words and don't know how I'll ever face him after this. I'd always imagined how it would go if I told Jess how I felt, and this isn't exactly how I pictured it playing out. Especially since I didn't even confess any real feelings other than those of jealousy and resentment.

I hear Jess laughing gently and I look up in surprise as I pull my hand away from my face. I watch as he sits back down in the chair next to my bed before running his hands through his dark hair.

Jess lets out a long breath before speaking. "You've got it *so* backward, Sam," he says, sounding as equally exhausted as I am.

"I never wanted any of those other girls," he says, meeting my gaze intensely. "I invited you out on John's boat that morning because I wanted to be with YOU, and *only* you. That whole thing with that Amber girl was a setup. Sophie planned the entire thing," Jess says, shaking his head as he looks away.

"What—"

"No," Jess says sternly as he meets my eyes again. "Let me finish first."

I don't say anything as I continue to stare at him, waiting for him to speak as he stands and starts pacing around the room.

"I was planning on telling you everything while we were out on the water that morning. I figured there'd be no distractions and no one to interrupt us, but things didn't really go as I'd hoped they would." Jess runs a hand through his hair again as he looks down at the floor, and my heart starts to race at his words.

Jess halts his nervous pacing and looks up at me, meeting my eyes. "I've only wanted to be with you, Sam. For as long as I can remember, that's all I've ever wanted. No other girl has ever meant anything to me, not like you do. They couldn't have."

My head spins, and my heart starts to beat even faster.
*Is he saying what I think he's saying?*

"B-but you mean as like… a *friend*… r-right?" I ask, praying I'm wrong.

Jess shakes his head. "No. Not as a friend. Never as just a friend," he says as he stares at me intensely. "I've never looked at anyone the way I look at you, Sam," he says softly as he holds my eyes with his.

"I-I don't understand," I say quietly, still waiting for him to finish.

"Ry, I don't know how many times I've tried to tell you over the years, but you always manage to stop me before I can get the words out," he says with an exhausted sigh.

Jess moves to the foot of my bed and places his hands on the footboard. The plastic groans under the weight of his body as he leans toward me, and I blink up at him, partially in shock.

Silence fills the room as I wait to hear the words I've only ever dreamed of hearing him say.

His eyes are holding a fiery intensity that I've never seen before, and I feel like he's staring straight into the depths of my heart.

"Samantha. Sam. *My Sam.*"

My heart is pounding against my ribcage, and I feel like I've forgotten how to breathe.

"I am *so* in love with you, Sam Ryan," Jess says, his beautiful emerald eyes sparkling at me as he says the words.

I watch his shoulders soften, as if a huge weight had just been lifted off them. My heart swells at his words, and we hold each other's gazes intently, neither saying a word.

"Why didn't you ever say anything?" I ask, my voice coming out small as I break the silence between us.

"Because." Jess runs his hands through his hair again. "It just never felt like the right time," he says exasperatedly as he starts to pace around the room again.

When I think about it, he is partially right about that. There were a lot of times when things could've changed between us, but it felt like there was always something that would get in the way. Then again, there were plenty of times when the timing felt like it couldn't have been more perfect, and neither of us did anything about it. Now, I'm wondering if I'm the one to blame for that...

Jess looks at me as if he can read my mind. "I was scared. I should've told you how I felt that night," he says.

I think back to how we almost kissed under the stars, the night before we were supposed to go out on my dad's boat. Looking back, I was the one who pushed Jess away, not the other way around. I was always so afraid of being rejected by him that I never realized that I've been the one doing it to him this entire time.

*I can't believe that this whole time, it's been me.* It's no wonder he thought I didn't have any feelings for him all these years.

"I was afraid, and I was a coward. I knew that if I'd told you and you didn't feel the same way, I'd lose you. I was content just watching you from afar if it meant I still got to have you in my life at all," Jess says from his place by the window, and I can hear the pain in his voice.

"But, then I almost lost you anyway!" he says, getting himself riled up again. "If I had just told you how I felt, then you wouldn't be in this situation right now!" he says, gesturing to the bandages covering my right arm. "Everything that happened to you, all of your injuries, it's all on me!" Jess says, looking me up and down before stopping on my arm again with a pained look on his face.

"But you didn't lose me, Jess," I say gently, trying not to upset him more. "Really, I'm fine, it's not a big deal—"

"You're not though! Why do you always do that? Why do you think so low of yourself? It's like you don't think your life has any value! Sam, you are *everything*, why can't you see that already?" Jess says as he stalks back over to me, his intensity somehow even more heightened, and I'm at a loss for words seeing him like this.

"You don't understand, Sam. If you had drowned that day at the lake…" he says, shaking his head before continuing. "If anything had happened yesterday before I was able to get to you… I would have lost everything. *My entire world* would've been destroyed."

Jess braces his hands on both sides of the plastic bed frame as he leans down toward me, our faces now only a few inches apart.

"I know you think that what happened between us that night in the tent didn't mean anything, but it did," he says, his gaze fiery as he holds my eyes.

"It took everything in me not to rip every single piece of clothing off you and make you mine right then and there," he says, his eyes darkening as he says the words. "Even if it meant that you only wanted me for the night, I still would've done it anyway," Jess says, and I can feel my breathing starting to pick up at the memory of that night in the tent with him.

"All I need is one night—*one real night*—and you'll never question my feelings toward you ever again." Jess whispers the words in my ear, his voice dropping an octave as he leans in closer, and I swallow hard. The sensation of his breath on my ear sends chills through my entire body, and it takes all of my willpower not to pull him into me.

Jess sighs as he leans back and steps away before I can grab him. He puts a fair amount of distance in between us, and his expression changes as if he'd suddenly remembered where we are.

He turns around and starts pacing the length of the small room again.

"And, as for Madison," he says, pausing before rubbing his eyes with his hands.

"She's my sister."

# Chapter Twenty-five

"Your what?" I ask. "But, you don't have any siblings," I say as I state the obvious, and Jess just shakes his head. "How is that even possible?" I ask as Jess continues with his pacing around the small room.

Jess's mom died after having complications with his birth, so unless she had Madison *before* she had Jess…

"Apparently, my mom was really young when it happened, so not a lot of people even knew about the pregnancy," he explains.

"What about your dad? Do you think he knew?" I ask.

"As far as I know, he had no idea about any of it since it happened way before they were even together," Jess says before continuing. "I assume that Grandpa Millard knew about it, but since he isn't around to ask anymore, I'm not sure. Not that it would make much of a difference," Jess says with a shrug.

"Okay, but what if it did? Do you even know that she's actually who she says she is? What if she's lying to get money or something?" I ask, and feel kind of like a jerk for accusing someone I hardly know.

"She's not lying, because at first, I thought the same thing, I figured she was just some scammer. As it turns out though, when I asked Aunt Judy about it, she was reluctant to tell me anything at first, but in the end, she was able to validate the whole story," he says.

"So, Judy knew you had a sister this whole time and never said anything about it?" I ask, trying to keep my voice level even though I'm starting to get upset.

"Why would she keep that from you?" I ask, feeling a strange sense of betrayal even though the situation hasn't really got anything to do with me personally.

Jess shrugs. "Judy wasn't really around when it all happened, and the only reason she even knew was because Grandpa Millard told her about it. I guess she was sworn to secrecy or some shit," Jess says. "I'm not mad at Judy, though, and you shouldn't be, either," Jess says, probably noting my sour expression. "She was just keeping a promise that she'd made to her brother," he says with a sigh.

"After I got back to town, Judy gave me an old box of papers that belonged to Grandpa Millard, and I found a copy of the original birth certificate that matches the one that Madison has," Jess explains, and my head is reeling as I try to process everything that he's telling me.

"Hold up, then why the fuck did you let me think she was your girlfriend? Why not just tell me the truth?" I ask angrily.

"I told you repeatedly that she wasn't my girlfriend, *you* were the one who just kept assuming," Jess says and shakes his head. "Plus, I wanted to be sure it was all true before I told you and Soph," he says with a heavy sigh as he sits himself down in the chair next to my bed.

"Wait, so you didn't tell Sophie either?" I ask in disbelief.

"Do you seriously even have to ask that? She'd yap to half the town even if I told her it was an FBI secret," Jess says with a laugh.

"That's a fair point, I guess," I say, agreeing with him, knowing that secrecy isn't Sophie's strong suit. "But that still doesn't explain why you were being so sus about everything," I say, trying to call him out.

"Do you really think that it's a coincidence that Madison just so happens to be friends with people like Elliott and Kyle?" Jess asks, raising his brows at me.

"I don't know… I guess I hadn't really thought about it," I say.

"I know she seems like she's fine, but she's not." Jess rubs his hand over his face as he lets out a heavy breath. "She's an addict," he says, and I can see the weight of it behind his eyes when he finally looks up at me.

"She somehow found me through my mom's medical records. How she even got her hands on the information, I'm not sure, probably through one of her shady friends, I'm guessing," he says with a sigh.

"Apparently, Madison was born with a heart condition. She told me she wanted to find out more about her family tree, and maybe see if it was hereditary or something. At least that's what she claimed," Jess says, sitting back in his chair as he stares up toward the stained ceiling tiles.

"Damn, Jess, this is some heavy shit," I say, trying to imagine what he's been going through, and all alone, at that.

"Initially, I didn't really want anything to do with her, but after Aunt Judy pointed out that she's the spitting image of my mother, I couldn't help but want a relationship with her. Is that stupid?" Jess asks, looking at me with sad eyes.

"No, not at all. I don't blame you for wanting to get to know her, especially since both of your parents are gone. It sounds like you might be all each other has," I say, looking down at my hands folded in my lap.

"After everything I just confessed to you, do you really believe that's true?" he asks me softly, and I feel like an idiot for making him think I'm downplaying his confession to me earlier. Jess sighs and looks away when I don't answer him. "I dunno, Ryan, this whole thing just feels like a giant mess."

"You said she's an addict, like, as in present tense? Or, that she's in recovery?" I ask.

"Addict, as in present tense," Jess says as he rubs his hands over his face, and I realize just how exhausted he must be.

"When we had first started talking, obviously I had no idea, so when I told her that she could always reach out to me if she ever needed anything, I didn't expect it to escalate so quickly. That's why I had to leave our camping trip so suddenly. She called me from a party after she'd just taken something and was certain that someone was after her. She'd said it was an emergency and I was just trying to do the right thing—the *brotherly* thing—but it turns out that getting trashed at parties is something she does on a regular basis.

"That night when I went to pick her up, she was with Kyle," Jess says, and I feel an anxiousness in my chest at the simple mention of his name.

"If she was at a party with *Kyle*, then…" I say, realizing that her issues probably run a lot deeper than either Jess or I know.

Jess gives me an exhausted look laced with worry. "I know what you're thinking, and you're right. She was seriously zonked out of her mind when I found her, which was in that tatted asshole's bed, ironically," Jess says and rubs his hands over his eyes in frustration.

"Obviously, I didn't know who he was at the time, just some asshole who Madison says she parties with from time to time, and evidently also sleeps with," Jess says with a shrug and an exhausted sigh. "When I went to find you yesterday, he didn't recognize me, but I almost wish that he had. It would've made it that much more satisfying when I beat his ass to a pulp," Jess says with a smirk.

Jess kicking Kyle's ass? Now that's something I would've liked to have seen. But, I instantly take back the thought when I remember how Jess got hurt in the process.

"So, he let you drag her out of his bed, and didn't try to kill you or anything?" I ask, still amazed every day by the sheer amount of bravery and confidence that Jess possesses.

"Honestly, he was so high himself that he didn't even notice. He was too busy with the other bodies that were in the bed with them," Jess says with a disgusted look on his face before shaking his head.

I shift uncomfortably in my bed, wondering if Jess is more disgusted by the fact that he basically found his sister in the middle of an orgy, or the fact that it was Kyle whom she slept with. I can't help thinking that Jess might be disgusted with me as well since I used to date Kyle. I try not to let it get to me, but the thought lingers, making me feel selfish for letting my own insecurities intrude on Jess's story.

Jess continues, and I force myself to focus on his words.

"After Madison reached out to me, I decided to take some time off to get to know her and to see if she was actually telling the truth. That's the real reason I'm back in town. I was just about to book a flight back to Alaska when Sophie let it slip that you were planning on coming home, so I stuck around because I wanted to see you. I thought that if I got to at least see you one more time, that would be enough, and that I'd finally be able to let you go. I had no idea what to expect, and the thought crossed my mind that you might bring someone home with you. I told myself that if you were happy and, in a relationship, I'd take that as my sign from the universe to move on already. I'd be lying if I said I wasn't relieved when you showed up alone, though.

"I meant to tell you everything yesterday while we were at the Blue Diamond, but where things got out of control so quickly, I wasn't able to," Jess says apologetically, and I immediately regret overreacting like I did.

"I'm sorry I didn't tell you. I just wanted to keep you safe, and after I learned about Madison's substance abuse issues, introducing her to my family seemed like more than I was ready for. I guess I just didn't know how to handle it all," Jess says with a shrug.

I think about how I wanted to bring Daniel back home with me to meet everyone, and I'm beyond grateful that things between us didn't work out in the end. Not only that, but Jess was going through some seriously heavy stuff, and all alone no less. My stupid drama with Daniel was definitely nothing in comparison to the weight of everything Jess had been carrying, which not only makes me feel like the worst friend in the world, but also the most self-absorbed.

"Shit, Jess," I say, shaking my head at my own stupidity. "I'm so sorry about everything. I claim to always be here for you, but I wasn't even there for you when you needed it most," I say and look down, feeling ashamed. Even if he couldn't tell me what was going on with Madison, I still could've been there for him in other ways.

"After behaving like a pouty child, I definitely didn't deserve any of the nice things you've said to me today," I say, and look up to meet his eyes.

"You know that's not true," Jess says as he smiles at me. "But honestly, I expected nothing less from you," Jess says and smirks before he reaches over and pinches my nose playfully.

I laugh and swat my hand at him. "Okay, well, I promise that from now on, I'll let you finish telling me things *before* I overreact," I say, and both of us laugh at that.

"Deal," Jess says, smiling widely at me, and my heart does a somersault in my chest at the way he looks at me.

After Jess tells me about Madison, Adam comes in to recheck my vitals. Apparently, my heart rate monitor alerted him, and he came in to see why my pulse was still elevated. I tell him it was nothing and that I had been feeling sick earlier, but that I was feeling better now.

Adam looks between Jess and me before he rolls his eyes. "Honey, please, the hospital is no place to get freaky, at least not during the day while there are so many people on staff," he says before checking my machines and IV before leaving again.

My face feels hot, and I'm sure the color is beet red, and a tense silence starts to settle around us before Jess speaks up.

"I meant what I said earlier, Sam," Jess says, and I can feel his eyes on my face. I turn to meet his gaze, my cheeks still unbearably warm. "I'm sorry to spring all that on you so suddenly, I just needed you to know. All of it." Jess leans in toward me and cups my face in one hand as he gently presses our foreheads together.

I desperately want to tell him how I feel, but I'm suddenly out of breath and lightheaded. "Jess, I—"

"I think it's best we put a lid on things between us for now, at least until you're healed. Is that all right with you?" Jess asks with a hesitant look as he pulls away from me.

"Sure." I give him a reassuring smile, trying my best not to seem too disappointed.

I guess it's not like I really have much of a choice, though. As much as I'd love to jump his bones right now, there's not much I can do in a hospital bed with a broken arm. And, Adam is right, there'd be too many witnesses around right now...

After my talk with Jess, things seem to go back to normal between us, which surprises me since I was sure there'd be some lingering weirdness, but there's not. After all, he did just confess to me... It's something I've wanted to hear from him my entire life, and when the moment came,

I didn't even know how to react. I wish I had said it back, but I think that some twisted part of me is still a little bit scared.

Jess turns on the TV, and we sit and watch *10 Things I Hate About You*. I'm sure I've made him watch that movie with me at least ten times over by now, but he still insists, knowing it's my favorite.

By the time the movie is almost over, some officers come by to take my statement. At first, Jess tries shooing them off, telling them that it's too soon and that I still need to rest. I reassured him that it was all right since I would rather get it over with sooner rather than later. I tell the officers what happened, or at least what I'm able to remember, before listening to Jess as he gives them his statement as well.

Hearing Jess give the officers the details of his knife fight with Kyle has me feeling uneasy, to say the least. Like hearing about it somehow makes me feel like I'm reliving it, even though I wasn't even there.

"Looks like we've got everything we need. We appreciate your time," one of the officers says before putting away his small notepad and pen.

"What's going to happen to them? Elliott and Kyle, I mean," I ask as both officers head toward the door to leave.

"I'm not sure of the scope of your previous relationship with either of them, but it's no secret that they both have extensive criminal backgrounds, and what happened yesterday only adds to that," one of the officers says and gives me a sympathetic look, no doubt able to read my nervousness. "If you're worried about seeing them again, you shouldn't be, we got them on multiple charges yesterday, plus an outstanding warrant for one of them," he says, trying to reassure me.

I say nothing as I nod at the officer's words, hoping that what he's saying is true and that I won't ever have to see either Kyle or Elliott again.

"Let us know if you guys remember anything else," one of them says before handing Jess a card with his name and number on it.

"Thanks," Jess says as he stands to shake the officer's hand after taking the card from him.

439

After they both leave, Jess takes a seat back in his chair by my bed. "I know what you're thinking," he says, looking over at me.

"*Hmm...* that I could really go for a chocolate shake right about now?" I say, putting a finger to my chin. "How'd you guess?" I ask and smile at him, trying to shake off my discomfort from our conversation with the officers.

Jess gives me a small smile and lets out a chuckle before shaking his head. "Look, I know you're worried about..." he trails off, probably just as sick of saying Kyle and Elliott's names as I am. "But you shouldn't be. I'm not going to let them hurt you again. I promise," he says, and I can feel the intensity behind his beautiful eyes as he looks at me.

"What, are you gonna keep me by your side 24/7?" I ask with a scoff as I lay my head back against my pillow and let out a breath. Not that I'd mind, of course, but that seems sort of unrealistic.

"Sure, if that's what it takes," Jess says with a wink. "*Or...* we could just brush up on a few seasons of WWE, refresh your mind on some of the holds," he says before pretending to elbow slam my thigh. "Then you'll be all set to *really* kick some ass," he says teasingly.

"Oh, so *now* you're okay with me using wrestling moves," I ask and raise a brow at him.

"On second thought, maybe I'll have you save those for special occasions," Jess says through half-lidded eyes as he bites the corner of his bottom lip.

I feel my cheeks flush slightly. "What happened to keeping a lid on things?" I ask, suddenly feeling out of breath.

"Sorry, I guess I just can't help myself sometimes," Jess says as he nudges my good arm with his elbow. "You're just too fun to tease," he says, giving me that smile that makes my heart skip a beat.

"Whatever," I say and roll my eyes, trying to hide my excitement at hearing his words. "I wasn't kidding earlier though about a chocolate milkshake," I say. "Would you mind checking the cafeteria?" I ask sweetly as I bat my lashes at him.

Jess shakes his head and lets out a breath, and I watch as his eyes darken. "Anything else, Your Majesty?" he asks.

"That's all... *for now*," I say as I give him a slow once-over.

If he insists on teasing me, I think it's only fair I get to do the same.

# Chapter Twenty-six
## Jess

I click the down arrow on the wall next to the elevator. I watch as the small button lights up, and I wait for the doors in front of me to open.

I haven't really wanted to leave Sam alone, but she seems like she'll be all right for a few minutes. She is getting discharged in the morning, so I tell myself that I should probably stop being so clingy already.

I ride the elevator down one floor and follow the signs toward the cafeteria, and decide that I might get something for myself to eat as well. They've been pretty good about bringing Sam her food at mealtimes, and from the looks of it, it doesn't seem half bad either. Every time they bring her food, she tries to get me to eat some of it, which I usually decline, except for the ham sandwich she practically forced me to gag down earlier today. I haven't really had an appetite, not after last night.

I knew I needed to come clean with Sam, or it was going to eat me alive, especially after seeing how she reacted when she saw me take my shirt off. Remorse wasn't exactly the reaction I'd wanted her to have after seeing me shirtless.

I'm glad I finally put it all out there, but I'm still nervous about it. I'm relatively certain of Sam's feelings toward me, but I want to give her some time to think things through. It's easy to get caught up in the moment, and I don't want to pressure her into saying something she isn't ready to.

When I walk into the cafeteria, an elderly man in a volunteer's vest greets me before letting me know that the kitchen closes in five minutes.

*Typical, it's not even that late.*

I thank him for the heads-up and decide to check the deli fridge by the cash register and see that it's pretty picked over for the night. There's only one sad-looking tuna sandwich or an egg salad on rye left. I scrunch my nose and decide to pass on both.

*The milkshake.* I groan to myself as I rub my forehead, thinking I might just have one delivered.

"Not a fan?" I hear a voice say from behind me.

"Dr. Owens, hi," I say, turning around as I recognize the voice. "Do you ever go home? It seems like you live here," I say, joking.

"I could say the same thing about you, Mr. Cameron," she says, smiling, still refusing to call me Jess instead of Mr. Cameron.

I notice she has two cans of soda in her hand as she nods over her shoulder at me. "Why don't you come with me," she says, turning around.

"I don't know, I really should get back…"

"Come on, trust me," she says, nodding over her shoulder again.

I contemplate for a second before following her out of the cafeteria and then down a long hallway, my curiosity getting the best of me.

"You're not taking me somewhere scary, are you?" I ask, feeling a little suspicious.

"Of course not," she says with a small laugh, and I watch as Dr. Owens scans her badge on a card reader next to a door and hear a click as the lock opens.

"After you," she says, holding the door open for me before I walk through it. She pulls the large door shut behind us after following me into the room, and the lock beeps as it reengages.

Several plush sofas surround the large room, along with multiple flat-screen TVs that line opposite walls. I notice a few white lab coats just like the one Dr. Owens is wearing, hanging on a rack by the door, and wonder if this is the doctors' lounge.

"Pretty nice, eh?" she asks as if reading my mind.

"Not too shabby," I admit as I look around the room.

Toward the back corner, I notice a large kitchen area, baskets of fruit and snacks covering the lengthy countertop. I wonder to myself if maybe all the shitty vending machines in the hospital are because all the funds go to this fancy room. I scoff to myself as I shake my head.

I watch as Dr. Owens walks over to the fridge and opens one of the large doors. "*Hmm...* today it looks like we've got... roast beef, ham, turkey, or... veggie," she says, poking her head around in the fridge as she sorts through the sandwiches. "Take your pick," she says before turning to face me.

"Are you sure about this? Am I even allowed in here?" I ask, looking around at the other doctors in the lounge. They all seem so zoned out, I wonder if they even noticed when we walked in.

"Well, seeing as I'm one of the attending physicians, yes, you're allowed in here," she says, putting her hands in her lab coat pockets. "Just don't tell anyone, wouldn't want the nurses to get jealous," she says with a wink.

*I'm starting to like this doctor.*

"Turkey then," I say, and Dr. Owens grabs two sandwiches and shuts the fridge door with her foot.

She swipes a few bags of chips out of one of the baskets on the countertop, and even though her hands are full, she doesn't let me help. She gathers up the sandwiches and sodas, holding the corner of one of the bags of chips in between her teeth. She nods over her shoulder again before pushing open a small door next to the fridge.

I follow Dr. Owens out onto a small balcony that's furnished with a few small metal tables. The balcony overlooks the mountains behind the hospital, and even though it's just after sunset, I can still make out Cedar Hills Reservoir in the distance.

"It's beautiful out here," I say, taking a seat in one of the metal chairs across from Dr. Owens.

"It's nice to get some fresh air every once in a while. I love coming out here," she says, unwrapping her sandwich before taking a huge bite. "It gets so stuffy being inside all day."

"Is it difficult?" I ask, and she pauses her chewing. "Seeing all the suffering that you do, being a doctor and all," I ask, and she quickly finishes her bite before answering me.

"Sometimes," she says with a shrug. "Why'd you ask?"

"It just seems like shitty things always happen to good people. I think that after a while, I wouldn't be able to handle it all," I say and take a bite of my own sandwich, not realizing just how hungry I was until I opened up the wrapper.

"Thanks," I say as she hands me one of the cans of soda, and I realize that this was probably her plan all along. I don't usually drink sugary drinks, but I don't want to be rude, so I open the can and take a sip.

"Well, I guess to answer your question, even though I see bad things happening almost every day, I just have to remind myself to stay strong. Not just for the patients, but for their families too, you know?" she says. "It's the only way I'm able to continue on living, otherwise, the weight of it all would probably bury me alive."

I nod at Dr. Owens before taking another bite of my sandwich and smile to myself. I think back to the similar advice Sam's mom gave me all those years ago and how it still applies to the shit I'm going through right now.

We don't say much as we eat and watch the sunset, and I'm grateful to Dr. Owens for that. Just being outside for a minute already has me feeling a million times better. The last few days have been stressful to say the least, even with the weight of my confession now off my shoulders.

"So, did you tell her?" Dr. Owens asks through a mouthful of sandwich, and I choke on my soda.

"What?" I ask, coughing.

"Ms. Ryan. Did you tell her you were going to be a minute getting back, or was she resting?" Dr. Owens asks, gesturing to our little picnic.

"Oh, no, I didn't text her, but maybe I should," I say, grabbing my phone from my pocket, but then I remember that Sam doesn't have a working phone at the moment. The thought makes me panic for a second, just now realizing that she has no way of contacting me.

"Dr. Owens, can I ask you something?" I say, having a thought and she looks up from her sandwich before I continue. "Are you married?"

Dr. Owens looks like she's contemplating for a second and I quickly backtrack. "Wait, never mind. I shouldn't be asking you for advice," I say and rub my hands over my eyes. "Sorry if that was inappropriate."

Dr. Owens takes a quick sip of her soda to wash down her sandwich and gives me a friendly smile. "Well, I'm no expert, but I'll try my best. What's on your mind?" she asks.

I let out a sigh and look off over the small balcony toward the orange sunset in the distance. "Do you ever feel like just when things start to go okay, they can turn to shit just as quickly?"

"What do you mean by that? Are things not okay?" Dr. Owens raises a concerned brow at me.

"I mean not necessarily, it's not on my radar anytime soon, but, it just seems like the moment after I feel like I've finally got my footing, the rug always gets pulled out from under me. I guess I just want to prevent that from happening," I say with another heavy sigh.

"Well, I've been married going on ten years now, and I'll tell you that it isn't easy, not by a long shot. As long as you remember to fight for each other, at the end of the day that's all that really matters, I honestly believe it's that simple. That might be naïve of me to say, but I really do believe it."

I don't say anything as I take in Dr. Owens' words and give her a small smile and a nod in understanding.

"Do you wanna know what I think?" Dr. Owens asks before setting her can of soda back on the metal table.

"I have a feeling you're gonna tell me anyway," I say, giving her a smirk.

"Right, well, I think that Ms. Ryan's snagged herself a good one," Dr. Owens says with a warm smile.

"It's honestly the other way around," I say, figuring she can already see right through me, so denying it won't do any good.

"You'd better get back then, wouldn't want her to worry," Dr. Owens says, still smiling warmly at me.

I finish off my sandwich in two big bites before dumping the rest of the chips into my mouth, making a mess of crumbs all over myself in the process.

"Thanks again," I say, standing as I brush the crumbs off my shirt.

"Anytime," she says and winks at me.

I turn to leave but then have an idea. "Hey, Doc, do you mind?" I ask, gesturing back toward the lounge.

"No, by all means, help yourself," she says, nodding, and I thank her again before heading back inside.

I stop at the large refrigerator and open the freezer door. Just as I'd predicted, the entire freezer is packed from top to bottom with frozen treats. I dig around and find a pint of a chocolate explosion something or other, and figure it'll have to do. I grab the ice cream and a plastic spoon from one of the baskets on the counter and head back to Sam's room, hoping that I didn't leave her alone for too long.

# Chapter Twenty-seven

"You sure you don't want any?" I ask Jess as I dig out another huge spoonful of chocolate ice cream and shovel it into my mouth.

"Yeah, no thanks," he says, giving me a look of disgust. "How can you eat that? It looks like it's nothing but chocolate on chocolate," he says, still pulling a face at me.

"*Exactly*," I say before taking another huge spoonful. "Who would've thought they'd have entire pints of ice cream in the cafeteria," I say through my mouthfuls.

"Guess it pays to have connections," Jess says with a wink.

I roll my eyes and don't ask. Jess has always had a way with people, so I have no doubt that he's telling the truth.

I set the ice cream down on the small rolling table next to my bed. "Jess, thank you," I say, not sure why I'm feeling nervous all of a sudden.

"Don't mention it, Dr. Owens actually—"

"Not about the ice cream. I mean about yesterday, and today too,

I guess," I say, attempting not to let my nerves betray me. "Honestly, for everything. Thank you for rescuing me, and…" I hesitate as I look around the room before settling on Jess's face once again.

"What is it, Ry?" Jess asks, his tone gentle as he waits intently for my words.

"I'm sure you'd much rather be doing something else with your time. So…"—I awkwardly fidget with my hands in my lap as I fight the urge to look away from him—"thank you for not leaving me here all alone."

I still feel like the simple words aren't enough to express my true gratitude, especially after everything he's done for me these past few days.

Jess shakes his head. "I'm right where I need to be," he says warmly, giving me that smile that I love so much.

My heart skips a beat, and I feel a little flutter in my stomach at the way he's looking at me. He's given me that smile a hundred times before, but there's something different about it now. Knowing the feelings behind it lets me imagine a future that I never even let myself dream of before.

After I finish the rest of my ice cream, we watch some more TV. At this point, we're both bored as hell, but it's really all there is to do. Every time the door opens, I perk up. I secretly hope it's my dad, but of course, it never is. It's usually just Adam doing his rounds.

Around ten thirty, and after our third cheesy Hallmark movie, I start to feel my head getting heavy with sleep. I look over at Jess in his chair and notice that he's struggling to keep his eyes open as well.

I let out a huge yawn and snap my head up toward the door when I hear it opening again, but let out a sigh when I see that it's just Adam.

He checks my IV and lets me know that he'll be leaving for the night, but that Lynda should be here soon to take over for him. He gets me some Tylenol for my arm since I'm trying to stay away from any hard narcotics, especially after what happened yesterday. The last thing I want is for my head to get all muddled again.

Jess and I both thank Adam, and he tells us goodbye for the night before leaving.

"He's an idiot," Jess says, breaking my concentration away from the TV.

"Don't let him hear you say that, or his zesty ass will kick you straight outta here," I say and laugh.

Jess shakes his head before answering. "Not Adam. John," he says. "That's who you've been hoping is at the door every time, isn't it?" he asks, and I could kick myself for being so easy to read.

I sigh as I lay my head back against my uncomfortably flat pillow and look up at the white ceiling tiles above me. "Shit, is it really that obvious?"

"I know I'm all grown up now, but I guess I figured he'd be more concerned about me. You'd think I'd be used to it by now," I say with a sigh. "How lame that I still want daddy to worry about me," I say, and laugh at myself as I rub my forehead with my hand.

"It's not lame. You're right, he *should* be more worried about you. It makes me mad the way he disregards you all the time," Jess says, and I give him a questioning look.

Jess sits back in his chair, uncrossing his arms as he looks at me. "I always felt like it wasn't my place to say anything to your dad, and I didn't want to overstep and make you feel uncomfortable. You know, typical possessive asshole boyfriend behavior, only, I wasn't even your boyfriend," Jess says with a shrug. "Neither really seemed fair to you, but regardless, I still regret not saying anything," he says, shaking his head.

"Hmm, possessive asshole boyfriend behavior…" I put a finger to my chin. "Doesn't sound so bad when you say it," I joke, and his face grows serious.

"You shouldn't have to get used to being mistreated, not by anyone, least of all by your own father," Jess says, ignoring my joke.

"You deserve so much more than you let yourself have, Sam," he says, and I can see the sadness behind his bright eyes.

451

"I know," I say, and feel my eyes starting to get teary. Even though I agree with him, I sometimes feel like it couldn't be further from the truth.

"Are you tired?" I ask Jess as he reaches over and wipes a single tear away from my cheek with his thumb.

"Shouldn't I be the one asking you that?" he says softly.

"Truthfully, I'm beat, but I'm not the one who doesn't have a bed," I say teasingly as I sniffle.

"I guess you've got a point there," Jess says with a laugh as he pulls his hand away from my cheek.

"Hey, Jess?" I say hesitantly after a breath.

"*Hmm*?" he hums, gazing at me intently as he tucks a small strand of hair behind my ear.

"You're not planning on leaving tonight... right?" I ask quietly.

Jess's gaze is still fixed on me as he lightly shakes his head from side to side as he gives me a small smile.

"In that case, you know, it really is cold in here," I say, glancing around the room. "Aren't you cold?" I ask, and shiver dramatically.

"I can always go ask the nurses for an extra blanket..." Jess says, giving me a sly grin as he gestures to the door like he might get up and leave.

"Gee, you know I would ask you to, but I really don't want to bother Lynda already, you know, since she just barely got here and all," I say, my nervousness all but gone at the return of our familiar feeling banter.

"Right, of course," Jess says, and I can see him trying to hold back the large smile tugging at the corners of his mouth.

"Would you mind?" I ask, looking down at the space in between my body and the railing of the bed. "That is, if it's not an inconvenience to you," I say innocently.

"Not at all," he says, still trying to hold back his smile.

I watch as Jess takes off his boots before climbing into the bed with me, just like he did last night. I'm slowly trying to scoot my body over with my good arm when I feel a stark pain across my collarbone and down my other arm. I wince, and Jess stops moving, immediately backing himself away from me.

"Shit, are you okay?" he asks, looking me up and down frantically. "Forget about it. This is a bad idea, I'll just stay in my chair," he says, trying to move away from me before I grab a fistful of his shirt in my hand.

"No, it's fine. I'm fine," I say, looking up at him, and I'm careful not to touch anywhere near his injury as I grip the material. "I'll feel worse if I have to watch you sleep sitting up," I say with a small laugh, trying to picture his large frame attempting to get comfortable in such a small chair.

Jess gives me a serious look, and all of his playfulness from earlier is now gone. "No. I don't want to hurt you," he says, shaking his head, trying to pull away again.

"You won't," I say, refusing to let go of him.

I try not to sound too desperate even though I am. "*Please*," I say, pleading with him, and my voice comes out barely above a whisper.

I watch as Jess's eyes soften and he gently relaxes back toward me onto the bed, careful not to touch me any more than necessary. I snuggle myself up next to him and rest my head against his shoulder, not bothering with personal space since it's already too small of a hospital bed for one person, let alone two.

Getting to be pressed up against Jess for a second night in a row has me feeling like the luckiest person in the world right now, especially since I get to blame the lack of space in between us on the small bedframe.

Jess's body relaxes next to mine, and I watch as he gently drapes one of his hands across my body.

"Feeling warmer now?" Jess asks from beside me and I can feel the vibration of his deep voice through his chest.

"If you wouldn't mind, my hand is still a little cold," I say. I feel Jess's warm hand clasp around my own, and I sense him chuckle lightly against me.

"Better?" he asks as he gives my fingers a light squeeze.

"Better," I say and give his hand a small squeeze in return.

I let out a breath as I close my eyes, already starting to feel unbelievably relaxed lying next to him. I feel my head start to get heavy, and just before I drift off, I swear I sense him kiss the top of my head just like he did yesterday. Jess says something to me, but my mind drifts off before I'm able to catch it.

~

When I wake up the next morning, Jess is gone, and I notice that his boots and hoodie are missing from the back of his chair as well. I rub my eyes and try to sit up all the way, causing a significant amount of pain to shoot down my right arm and shoulder.

"*Dammit,*" I mutter under my breath as I gently slump back against the bed. It seems like whatever strong stuff they gave me after my surgery is all but worn off now from the way my entire right side is throbbing.

The nurses have been wanting to give me stronger narcotics, but I refused since I didn't want to risk a bad reaction. I remember the uneasy feeling that I got from the pain pills after I got my wisdom teeth out in high school, and I would prefer to bypass that this time around.

I click the nurse call button and figure that I'll ask Lynda if she can get me some Tylenol to take with my breakfast today, figuring that the longer I wait, the worse the pain is going to get.

The soreness in my forearm is more noticeable today, and my fingers feel a bit swollen when I try to move them. According to

Dr. Owens, I'll be in this stupid cast for the next six weeks if everything heals okay and there's no infection from the surgery.

I was concerned with how much mobility I would have once my arm has healed, but when she came by yesterday, Dr. Owens told me that as long as I do all the physical therapy like I'm supposed to, I should heal and be back to normal in no time.

"Mornin'," Lynda says as she enters the room with a small tray of food in one hand and a water bottle in the other. "You able to get any sleep last night?" she asks, giving me a wink as she sets the tray down on the small table next to the bed.

She rolls the table over my lap, and I try to push myself up, wincing again at the pain that rips across my shoulder and down my arm from the effort. "Yep, slept like a baby," I grit through my teeth at the discomfort as Lynda tries to help me situate my body so that I'm able to sit up properly.

"Get something in your stomach and then take these," Lynda says as she fluffs up my pillow and then gestures to a tiny shot glass on the tray with a few small white pills in it. "They'll have you feelin' better in no time," she says with a wink.

I thank her for reading my mind and don't question her instructions before I take a few bites from the large bowl of oatmeal on my tray. Calling it oatmeal is a bit of a stretch; it's more like a watery bowl of cold Elmer's glue with a few frozen berries on top. I force myself to swallow the spoonful in my mouth before dumping the contents of the plastic shot glass onto my tongue, swallowing the pills down with one giant gulp of water.

"I had a feeling you might be sore this morning," Lynda says, and I don't say anything as I take another swig of water, trying to wash down the residual oat glue as I raise a questioning brow at her.

"I checked in on you a little earlier, and you two looked mighty cozy yet somehow extremely uncomfortable all at the same time," she says, and I try not to blush at her words. "Finish up your breakfast, and I'll help you get dressed when you're ready," Lynda says before turning to the metal box on the wall, pulling down the computer.

"Wait, what do you mean? Lynda, are you giving me the boot?" I joke.

She's busy typing away on the computer before she folds it back up into the wall and then turns around to face me. "I just finished up your discharge papers. The doctor cleared you just now," she says, gesturing to the door, and I can faintly hear voices just outside the room.

"No offense, Lynda, but shouldn't Dr. Owens have come to talk to me before sending me home?" I ask and raise a brow at her.

"Sorry, honey, I thought you'd be all right with it. Your friend is out there right now talking to the doctor on your behalf," Lynda says, giving me a knowing smile.

"*Oh*," I say and try to shake off the slight flush now staining my cheeks.

I try not to show my excitement, but a part of me is all giddy inside at the thought of Jess talking to the doctor for me. It almost makes it feel like we're *together*. I know I'd probably be kicking my feet and giggling if I were actually able to move like that right now.

I smile to myself and notice Lynda staring at me. "What?" I ask as I fail to hold back the gigantic grin on my face.

"Nothing," she says, trying to hide her smile. "Call me when you're ready and I'll take this out," she says after unhooking the tube from the IV needle taped to the top of my hand.

I finish my breakfast the best I can, all the while, smiling like some love-sick dummy. I try swallowing down another spoonful of glue before finally opting for the banana muffin and the small cup of fruit instead. Oatmeal is definitely not one of my favorites by any means, it's up there with the likes of Brussels sprouts and canned peas, but then again—so is most fruit.

After I finish eating, I call Lynda back in to help me change into the sparkly iridescent blue zip-up tube top that Sophie brought me yesterday, along with a pair of comfy pink sweatpants. It was something that I thought was uncharacteristically thoughtful of her, but Jess confessed to asking her to get me some clothes when she had brought his shirt yesterday. The top Sophie picked out for me is definitely a little flashy for a hospital, but I'm grateful that it was so easy to get on with all the bandages on my arm.

Just about the time I finish getting dressed and Lynda removes the IV from my hand, Jess comes back from talking with Dr. Owens in the hallway.

"Good morning," he says, giving me that signature Jess smile. I can't help it when my heart starts to beat a little faster, and I'm grateful that the beeping machines are no longer able to betray me now that I'm disconnected from everything.

"What'd she say? Am I going to live?" I ask him with a smile.

"I'm sorry if I overstepped," Jess says as he jabs a thumb behind him toward the door. "I just wanted to make sure that we talked to the doc before you were discharged. I didn't think you'd mind, and I felt bad waking you up," Jess says nervously as he rubs the back of his neck.

I shake my head at him. "No, not at all. I'm glad you were able to talk with her," I say, giving Jess a grateful smile, and my heart flutters just thinking about the way he said the word "we."

Jess takes a seat in his chair next to the bed before filling me in on his conversation with Dr. Owens.

Aside from all the follow-up appointments I'll be needing to make in the next few weeks, she says I should be just fine. Dr. Owens said that she also went over my case with the head of the neurology department, and because I don't have a history of Epilepsy—and have only ever had the one seizure—it was most likely caused by extreme stress mixed with the hard drugs in my system. Jess called it a *psychogenic non-epileptic seizure* and said that Dr. Owens suggested we could follow up with a neuro specialist if we were concerned or had any further questions.

My arm—as I'd predicted—needs to stay in a cast for the next few weeks and then on to physical therapy thereafter for the foreseeable future.

She also said that due to the nature of the Strawberry Six drug, by now, it should be completely out of my system. Jess said she told him it's one of those drugs meant to give you a quick high and then your body metabolizes it out of your system pretty quickly after.

Other than that, Dr. Owens gave me a clean bill of health and said there was no reason to keep me at the hospital any longer.

Yesterday, when Dr. Owens came by in between one of our movie breaks, I got the feeling that she wanted to talk to me alone, but Jess wasn't about to budge even when she'd asked us for some privacy. In the end, it was because she was concerned about what possible sexual assault I might've dealt with while I was being held hostage. Jess looked pretty upset throughout the entire conversation, so I made it pretty brief when telling Dr. Owens that, although there was a close call, nothing had happened.

We say our goodbyes to Lynda and thank her for everything before Jess rolls me out to the parking lot in a wheelchair. I told him I was fine walking on my own, but he insisted, saying it was either the wheelchair or his arms that were going to carry me out.

"Your choice, Ry," he'd said, but still tried to pick me up anyway. I'd swatted him off and sat myself down in the stupid wheelchair. Even though being wheeled out to the parking lot is embarrassing, I didn't want him to hurt himself if he actually ended up carrying me instead.

"Really, I can walk from here, you don't need to push me all the way there," I say, fidgeting in the wheelchair.

"Chill out, Ryan, we're almost to the car," Jess says, still walking us at the high speed of a sloth as we cross the parking lot.

"Car?" I ask. "You don't own a car," I say, looking around for his Jeep.

"Technically, no, but I had Soph leave her Dart yesterday when she rode home with Chris.

"Why?" I ask, confused as to why he'd switch vehicles with Sophie.

"Wouldn't want you to float away," Jess says with a wink.

# Chapter Twenty-eight

After I was discharged from the hospital, things more or less went back to normal. My dad spent all of one day helping Sophie nurse me back to health before he returned to his regularly scheduled program of hanging out at the club all day long, combined with him staying over at Rebecca's place for days at a time. I guess I shouldn't be complaining though, because at least I don't have to deal with her for the moment. I'm sure that Rebecca would do everything in her power to make me as miserable as possible, even if I am still recovering from an injury.

In the beginning, after I was first discharged, Sophie insisted on staying over even though I told her I'd be fine on my own. We had a long talk after I got home, and we both apologized for what happened between us that night in her kitchen.

Along with Sophie's apologies for the weirdness with Chris, she also confessed to meddling with things between Jess and me. Apparently, she's been doing it most of our lives, saying that she didn't want to lose us, which is ironic because she's the one who's been bailing on *me* for years.

I get where she's coming from, but I definitely think she went about it all wrong. Instead of orchestrating all of these elaborate schemes, she should've just been honest and told us about how she was feeling. I'm still trying not to let it bother me, but to be frank, the whole thing with Jess bothers me more than when I found her and Chris together on the couch half-naked.

Lately, I've been able to convince her to only check on me for a few minutes during her lunch break. Sophie still insists on coming over after her internship most nights, but I always try to send her home after too long, since my dad is usually home by then.

*Usually.*

Not that he pays me much mind any more than he did before my accident, though.

I tell myself just to let it go since I know he's not going to change, and I don't want to waste all of my time and energy waiting for him to give a shit about me. I keep thinking about what Jess said to me at the hospital about accepting way less than I deserve from people. At first, I thought he was just saying it to be nice, but the more that I think about it, the more I'm starting to see what he meant by that.

On a good note, though, I'm grateful that Chris has been in a better mood lately, and I attribute that largely to Sophie. She hasn't said much, and I haven't pressed her on it, figuring she'll tell me when she's ready, but from the looks of it, things are starting to get pretty serious between the two of them. Sure, at first, I was a little upset about it all, but it was mostly just because she had lied to me about it, not because of some stupid girl code rule or whatever. I genuinely want them both to be happy, and if that means that they're together, then I'll definitely support them.

Sophie tried making me dinner tonight, but I sent her home, insisting that I was fine with warming up my leftovers on my own. I have to keep reminding her that I do indeed have another working arm that I can use. Some things are tricky, but I'm glad that my dominant arm isn't the one that's broken, otherwise, I really would've been screwed.

It's been about a month since my accident, and I've been dying to get my stupid cast off. Not only is it itchy as hell, but it's sooo not cute. Whoever decided to wrap me up after surgery didn't bother thinking about how nasty a white cast was going to look after only a few weeks. I've barely done anything besides leave the house for my doctor's appointments, and it's already starting to look pretty gnarly.

At my appointment yesterday, the orthopedic doctor told me that I should be able to get the cast off in the next few weeks. Normally, it would've come off already, but since I had to have surgery to set the bones in my arm and to reattach a torn ligament, they wanted to leave it on a little longer, just to be safe.

A few weeks ago, the police contacted me again to let me know that I might be called as a witness in Elliott's court case, but I ended up not having to testify. It sounds like there are plenty of other witnesses the police are going to use to put him away with for a few years due to crimes unrelated to my kidnapping. I'm glad that I don't have to testify, not that I would've minded helping the police get him, I'd just rather not ever see his psychotic ass again.

My phone rings as I walk into the kitchen, and I see Sophie's photo lighting up the screen. "Hey, what's up?" I say as I try to balance my phone in between my shoulder and ear as I scrape some pasta into a glass bowl from its plastic to-go container.

"Okay, Babe, so, hear me out. You put some pants on and come out with Chris and me tonight," she says, and I can hear Chris saying something in the background, probably grumbling at the idea of having to come back and pick me up.

*Not that I'd even agree to go, that is…*

"No way, you've been living on my dad's couch with me for the last four weeks." I stand up straight as I pull my phone from its place in between my cheek and shoulder. "You deserve a night out that doesn't involve me," I say with a small laugh.

"Do you want us to bring you back something, then? We're going to some new place—what was it called again, Chris?" she says, her voice sounding far away as she asks Chris where they're going, and I can hear him mumbling in the background again.

"Really, Soph, it's fine. Don't worry about it. I'll just eat my leftovers," I say and click a few buttons on the microwave, watching my pasta through the glass as it spins around. "You guys have fun, okay?"

"All right… but only if you're sure, because I can turn this car around right now," Sophie jokes in her dad voice.

"I'm hanging up now," I say teasingly. "Just make sure to get something really expensive if you're making my brother pay tonight," I say and scoff to myself as I lean back against the kitchen counter.

"I heard that," Chris says on the other end of the phone, and Sophie and I both laugh.

She asks me one more time if I'm sure before I force myself to decline, afraid that I might actually take her up on her offer if she asks again. The last thing I want is to crash their date, even though I don't really want to be alone. I sigh and watch my pasta as it spins on the glass turntable inside the microwave.

A few days ago, after I'd sent Sophie home for the night, I wanted to do something nice for my dad for dinner. Since I still don't have complete use of my right arm just yet, I was only able to chop about half an onion before I started having pain in my wrist just from holding it in place. I had then decided to order us takeout from an Italian restaurant in town and had told my dad not to eat before coming home from the club. I was hoping he'd get the hint that I had something planned before he could ditch me to go hang out with Rebecca for the evening.

When my dad got home that night, he told me that he got my text too late and had already eaten at the club with "the guys." That seemed highly unlikely since I'd texted him around 4:30 and he didn't get home until after 8 p.m.

He was home for all of five minutes before he grabbed a change of clothes and took his ass straight to Rebecca's place for the night, just as predicted. He thanked me for the gesture and had said "Sorry kid, maybe another night" while on his way out the front door.

I tried to hold it in, but I eventually ended up crying before I debated throwing all of the food into the trash. In the end, I didn't have the heart to waste anything, so I put it in the fridge for later and went to bed hungry.

Thus, the leftovers currently in the microwave.

I know that I'm not really injured anymore, besides the stupid cast on my arm. The rest of my bumps and bruises are all healed, but I can't help but want my dad to at least pretend he cares about me, injured or not.

After everything that happened, especially between Jess and me, I've been feeling pretty down. I know I should be happy since I finally heard those three magical words come out of Jess's mouth, but I can't help but wonder if he only got caught up in the moment or something.

Sophie hasn't said much about him when I ask, and every time I text him, he's only responded to my messages in short, clipped answers. I texted him a few times asking if he wanted to come over and watch a movie or something, but he's always got some excuse, saying that he's busy with a project, or that Aunt Judy needs him for this or that. Eventually, I stopped messaging him altogether because I felt like I was just bothering him.

The timer beeps, and I click the button before taking my bowl out of the microwave. I take a seat on one of the barstools at the counter, not wanting to eat another meal on the couch again for the thousandth time this week.

I'm ready to dig straight into my chicken alfredo, but just as I take my seat at the bar, I get a notification from the Ring camera that there's someone out front. I finally was able to get my dad to share access with me since I'm home alone most nights after Sophie leaves, Chris either leaving with her or with one of his friends. My dad's house is in a relatively quiet neighborhood, but it still makes me feel better being able to see who's at the door, even though it's usually just delivery drivers or the mailman.

I check the Ring app on my phone, but don't see anything. I've noticed that sometimes when the neighbor pulls into their garage or takes their trash cans out, it triggers a notification that there's someone at the door.

I put my phone down and twirl my fork into the pasta, my mouth already watering before I take a bite of the cheesy noodles. I hop off the barstool and go to put my bowl back in the microwave when I realize that the noodles in the middle are still a little cold. Even though they're warmed over, they're still just as tasty today, and I can't wait to devour the entire bowl.

Just as I click the microwave open, I hear someone pounding aggressively on the front door, and it's enough to make me jump. Startled, the bowl slips out of my hands and onto the countertop, the glass shattering as noodles and alfredo sauce splat all over the granite and onto the floor.

All of the blood drains from my face, and my heart beats frantically in my chest as I grab my phone to check the Ring camera again. My heart drops to the bottom of my stomach when I pull up the camera access and see that the screen is black. I rewind the footage to see what happened to the feed, but I only catch a small glimpse of a shadow before the camera lens is covered. I turn the volume all the way up on my phone to see if I can hear anything, but I can only make out someone quietly laughing in the background.

Immediately, my mind starts racing, and I'm afraid it's Elliott or Kyle, back to finish what they started. My heart starts thumping harder in my chest, and I feel like I can't breathe as my body starts to tremble.

I hear more banging on the door and jump again, this time dropping my phone onto the kitchen tile. I crouch down and scramble to grab it as the banging continues.

*Shit shit shit.*

I'm trying not to panic, but my hands are shaking so hard that I'm barely able to unlock the screen. I fumble with my phone in my hand before dropping it again. *Dammit.* I pick my phone up and hold it tightly with both hands as I rush to call the first person that comes to my mind.

I click on Jess's picture and wait for him to pick up. I listen to the dial tone, and for a second, I think that it might go to voicemail, but on the fourth ring, he finally answers.

"Well, well, well—"

My voice comes out shaky. "Jess, do you think you can—"

"Sam, what's wrong? Are you hurt?" he asks, and I can sense the urgency in his voice, the lighthearted tone from when he answered the phone already long gone.

"I'm not hurt… but there's someone banging on the door and they've blocked the camera," I say frantically. "I'm sorry to bother you, I'm just… *scared*," I say through my tears, and wonder at what point I started crying.

"Stay where you are, I'm coming," he says calmly. "Do you need me to stay on the line with you until I get there?" he asks, and I hear the engine of his Jeep turn over in the background.

"No, it's okay," I say through a sniffle as I peek around the corner of the kitchen island from where I'm still crouched on the floor. "I think I'll be okay until you get here."

"Okay, I'll be right there, don't move," he says before hanging up.

I stay sitting on the kitchen floor, huddled in between the sink and the island cabinets, and hug my knees to my chest, desperately trying to get my breathing under control. The pounding on the door has stopped, but every creak and sound of the house sends me into a mild panic.

It feels like forever, but it's only about ten minutes before the front door unlocks, and I hear footsteps as they cross the floor of the living room and into the kitchen.

"Ryan? Where are you?" I hear Jess call, and the sound of his voice makes it feel like I can finally breathe again.

"Here," I say from my place on the floor. "I'm here."

Jess rushes over and crouches down next to me. "Are you okay? What happened?" he says as he puts his hands on either side of my head and quickly looks me up and down, checking for any injury.

I take in Jess's appearance in the low kitchen light, and he looks like I disrupted a relaxing evening at home judging by his gray sweatpants and backwards ball cap.

"How did you get in?" I ask through my tears, swearing to myself that I'd deadbolted the door earlier after Sophie and Chris had left.

"I took Sophie's key," Jess says, staring into my eyes intensely. I had forgotten that I had made Sophie a key, it was so long ago that I figured she'd either lost it or gotten rid of it by now.

I don't say anything as I grab onto Jess's shirt. "C'mere," he says as he sits on the floor and pulls me onto his lap before wrapping his arms around me after gathering me into his chest.

467

The warmth of his body and the strength of his arms make it easy to let go of my fear. I inhale the faint scent of his cologne—woody and warm—grounding myself, reminding me that I'm safe with him.

"Hey, it's okay, don't cry anymore," he says as he rubs my back, trying to soothe me, and I bury my face into the crook of his neck.

I feel Jess's arms tighten around me, and I cling to his chest, letting the scent of his soft cologne envelop me. I can feel the steady thump of his heart through the thin fabric of his shirt and the sensation soothes me. Even though we were cramped up in a tiny hospital bed, I'll admit that I missed feeling him hold me like this, and I realize that I had forgotten just how comforting his embrace is to me.

Jess hugs me tightly, and I feel my breathing slowly return to normal before I pull away to face him.

"What happened, Ryan?" he asks, wiping a stray tear from my cheek.

I stare into his eyes as they continue to search mine with concern before I speak. "Someone started banging on the door, but the camera was blocked, so I couldn't see who it was. They just kept banging and banging, and the only thing I could catch from the camera was laughing," I say through a hiccup. "I panicked because I thought… I thought…" I struggle to speak as my body continues to tremble.

"You thought it was *them*," Jess states, his eyes somehow still soft while also lined with an intense fire. He caresses the back of my head with his hand, and I don't say anything as I look at him, already feeling like such a loser for calling him and panicking like I did.

"I'm gonna go check things out," he says as he goes to move me off him and tries to stand us both up. "You stay here, okay?"

I cling to the front of his navy shirt. "Wait, no! You can't go out there!" I say, trying not to sound as panicked as I feel.

I know I called him for help, but I can't stomach the thought of him getting hurt again on my account. Not that I think he couldn't take whoever's out there, because I have no doubt that Jess could seriously kick their asses—no matter who they are—I just don't want it to end up like last time.

"Ryan, it's okay, don't worry. Did you forget that I came in through the front door?" he says with a small laugh as he gently pries his shirt from my hands. "I'll be right back, I'm just gonna take a look around the house. Just wait here," he says, giving me a signature Jess smile, and my heart would sing if it weren't so anxious right now.

I watch as Jess crosses the kitchen to the living room and then heads out the front door before closing it behind him. I don't hear anything as I wait for him to come back, and try not to envision worst-case scenarios. I kick myself for not making him take some kind of weapon with him at least, even if it was just one of my dad's golf clubs.

About ten minutes pass before I hear the door open and watch as Jess crosses back into the kitchen before coming over to me, calm and collected as always.

"Everything's all right," he says as I look him up and down, searching for any sign of a struggle. "Sam, I'm fine," he says with a chuckle. Jess grabs my hands, stopping them from their poking and prodding, and holds them to his chest as he looks me in the eyes.

"It wasn't them," he says, and I look up at him with questioning eyes.

"But, then—"

"It was just some neighbor kids playing a prank on you," Jess says, giving me a warm smile before holding up a small piece of duct tape that he pulls out of his front pocket.

"What the hell?" I ask, looking from the tape to his face.

"I caught them a few houses down," he says. "It looks like they're trying to prank the neighbors with the old burning bag of dog shit on the porch prank, only, I think that someone forgot to tell them that they need to light the bag on fire for the prank to actually be a prank," he explains with a smirk before shaking his head.

"The only one who fell for it was Old Man Larsen a few houses down," Jess says, chuckling to himself. "It seems that man will never learn," he says, shaking his head.

"I gave the kids a few tips on the condition that they never bother this house again," Jess says with a mischievous smile.

"*What?*" I ask again, even though I heard what he'd just said.

"I watched and they only go for the houses with a side porch that doesn't have a railing, that way one of them can reach around and tape off the Ring camera without anyone seeing who it was," he explains. "Or, in Mr. Larsen's case, they just rang the regular bell since he's apparently not one with the times yet," Jess says, still smirking to himself.

I shake my head at my own stupidity. "So, you're saying that I'm just crazy and it wasn't Kyle?" I ask and let out a huge sigh of relief.

I look down and feel Jess's hand still on mine as he drops them down in between us, still holding onto me firmly. He peers down at me, and I meet his gaze. Even in the low lighting of the kitchen, the sparkles of his emerald eyes threaten to take me out.

"You're not crazy. Anyone would be a little freaked after what's happened," he says with a reassuring smile as he gives my arm a small shake.

"I'm sorry for making you come all this way for nothing," I say, feeling embarrassed.

"No biggie, I happened to be in the neighborhood anyway," he says with a shrug before reaching up to tuck a small piece of hair behind my ear with his other hand.

I playfully smack him on the arm. "Liar."

"Okay, so maybe I wasn't, but I'm glad you called. I've missed having someone to call me out on my bullshit all the time," Jess teases, and I smack him on the arm again, and this time we both laugh.

"Isn't that what Judy's for?" I ask and smile.

"Not lately. She's been too busy with being *Don Judy* of her retirement home," Jess says with a laugh.

"You're kidding?" I ask with a giggle.

"Swear to god, she and Phil are the top dogs around there now," he says, laughing again.

"Damn, Judy, what a fucking legend," I say, shaking my head as we both laugh at the absurdity of it.

Jess looks behind me at the spilled pasta and broken glass on the kitchen floor. "Have you not eaten yet?" he asks, raising a brow at me. "It's pretty late."

"I know." I nod and sigh. "My clumsy ass dropped the bowl when those *youths* started banging on the door," I say, leaning back against the countertop as Jess finally lets go of my hand.

I really couldn't care less about the bowl, but I'm pretty sure that it was one of Rebecca's newest additions to my dad's kitchen, so I'm sure I'll get an earful from her later about it.

Jess helps me clean up the mess of broken glass and noodles but insists on disposing of the evidence outside just in case Rebecca notices the shards of glass in the kitchen trash. I tell him that it's unlikely since she hasn't really been around for a few weeks anyway—thank god for that. Eventually, I'll have to face her, but at least for now, I don't have to worry about it.

"You've literally got nothing in this fridge. What have you been eating? Sauces?" Jess asks, peeking around the open fridge door at me before he continues to rifle through the million bottles in the fridge.

"Hey, having a large variety of sauces and condiments is an important staple in any American household," I say, and he just gives me an annoyed look before shutting the fridge doors.

"Takeout?" Jess suggests with a shrug.

"No, it's all right. It's pretty late. I'm sure that most places are closed now anyway," I say as I take a seat at the bar.

"Well, you need to eat *something*," he says.

Jess makes a *hmmm* sound like he's got an idea, before he turns around and opens the fridge back up, as if different ingredients are just going to magically spawn that weren't there two seconds ago.

"Allow me to showcase my skills, then," Jess says, and kisses his fingers like an Italian chef.

At this point, I don't bother resisting the urge to picture Jess in an apron cooking for me... in *only* an apron.

My breathing hitches at the thought.

"If you're going to cook in my kitchen there are rules then," I say with mock authority and fold my arms across my chest.

Jess turns to face me with raised brows before shutting the fridge door again, giving me a *Let's hear it* face.

"Well, first, you have to wear an apron," I say and shrug at him.

"Okay... and second?" he asks with a mischievous grin and puts his hands on his hips.

"Secondly, while shirts and pants are allowed, they're usually discouraged," I say casually and pretend to pick at my nails.

Jess drapes a kitchen towel over his shoulder before leaning against the countertop with his palms.

"Isn't that sort of dangerous for a kitchen?" he asks with a squinty-eyed look and a smirk.

"Sorry, I don't make the rules," I say with a shrug, honestly surprised at my own boldness.

"*Hmmm.*" Jess gives me a grin that's laced with trouble. "I guess it's a good thing you don't have any actual food for me to cook then, right?" he says with a shrug.

"Wouldn't want you to get a nosebleed or something just from watching me," Jess teases with a wicked smirk and a wink as he lifts his shirt before flexing his ab muscles at me.

I let out a dramatic breath and an *ugh* as I spin around on the barstool, trying to hide how flustered I am, knowing that I'm the one who started it. I should've known better than to try and outflirt Jess.

"Fine then, but if you insist on making me eat, please just don't make me any of your healthy old man food," I say, and he gives me a disbelieving look before rolling his eyes.

"What? You saw what I was going to eat earlier, not a single vegetable in sight," I say, raising my hands defensively. Not that I mind vegetables, I just don't think they deserve a place anywhere near noodles and cheese.

"That doesn't leave me with much to work with," Jess says as he leans back against the countertop with his arms folded across his chest.

He is right though, the fridge is pretty empty. I've been meaning to pick up some groceries, but I haven't really felt like leaving the house. Sophie volunteered to go with me, but I told her that I'd probably just have some delivered, since shopping with her is like shopping with a teenager. All she would've grabbed would've been junk food and energy drinks.

Jess goes over to the pantry and opens the door before he starts rifling through the shelves of dry storage.

"What are you looking for in there?" I ask as I strain my neck to see what he's doing. "Please tell me you found a chocolate pie," I say, still trying to see over his shoulder into the pantry.

"Better," Jess says, turning around with a box of cereal in each hand.

I nod slowly at him. "Okay, interesting choice."

"Obviously, this one"—he says before setting down a box of Bran Flakes—"is for me. And this one"—he says as he sets down a box of Fruity Pebbles—"is for the Sugar Queen," he says with a wink.

"So that's what I've been the queen of this entire time? Sugar?" I ask incredulously as I laugh.

"If the shoe fits…" Jess jokes, laughing with me as he pulls two plastic bowls out of the cupboard. "Just to be safe," he says when he notices me staring at the bowls.

"Right," I say sarcastically.

Jess takes the milk out of the fridge and sits next to me at the bar before pouring me a bowl of cereal and then one for himself.

"Sorry, but we're out of hippie milk at the moment," I tease, gesturing to the gallon of whole milk that Jess had just pulled out of the fridge.

"I'll have you know that I find your judgmental assumptions very offensive," he says, sticking his nose up in the air playfully. "Oat milk is just as tasty as regular milk, and for the record, I prefer whole anyway."

Jess pours the milk over his Bran Flakes and bumps into me playfully with his shoulder before looking down at my arm. "When's the bumper come off?" he asks, before eating a spoonful of his cereal.

I shrug at him. "Hopefully in a couple of weeks. The doctor says at this point it's more of a precaution because of the surgery," I say through a mouthful of cereal and milk.

"You know, if there really were anyone at the door, you could've just bopped them on the head with that, and you probably could've taken them down pretty easily," Jess says as he looks down at my cast.

"Care to test that theory?" I ask, swiveling my chair toward him.

"Maybe later," he says, his eyes darkening.

I feel my cheeks start to flush, and I decide to quickly change the subject. "Here, have a bite of this. I doubt you even know what they taste like," I say, holding up a spoonful of my cereal for Jess to try.

"Processed sugar, that's what it tastes like," he says, dodging my spoon as I try to choo-choo it into his mouth. "But, only if you take a bite of my old man cereal," he says, holding out a spoonful of his bran for me to try.

"So, you're finally willing to admit to eating a geriatric diet?" I ask, laughing.

"Your words, not mine," Jess says playfully.

"On second thought, you're right, you've tasted one sugary processed cereal, you've tasted them all," I say before eating the spoonful that was meant for Jess.

"Uh huh," he says, squinting his eyes at me. "You do know that eating something healthy every once in a while won't kill you, right?" he asks.

"Better safe than sorry," I say, shrugging, and he just laughs as he shakes his head at me.

After we finish eating our cereal, Jess puts the milk back in the fridge and the cereal in the pantry.

"Thanks for coming over tonight, Jess," I say as I lean against the sink after putting our bowls and spoons into the dishwasher.

"Why does it sound like you're kicking me out?" he asks and folds his arms across his chest from where he's leaning back against the kitchen island next to me.

"I'm not, I just figured you'd wanna leave since it's getting late," I say defensively, and he gives me another look. "I'm *not* kicking you out," I insist and laugh as I playfully punch him in the arm.

"How's about I take you up on your movie offer?" he asks.

"Sure, but only if we can watch *Twilight*," I tease as we both head toward the living room.

"Obviously, I was going to suggest *Twilight*. I mean, have you *seen* Jacob? So handsome," Jess says jokingly as he sits down on the large leather sofa across from the TV.

"I assume Soph is with Chris, but what about your dad? Shouldn't he be home?" Jess asks from the couch as I sift through the DVDs in the TV cabinet.

"Well, let's see… today's Tuesday, so he and Becky should be halfway to Macao by now," I say, still searching through my dad's extensive movie collection.

"Seriously?" Jess asks, and I hear him let out an annoyed breath.

475

"In my dad's defense, he did offer to cancel his cruise. Of course, that was after letting me know that everything was already paid for months and months in advance, and *of course*, none of it was refundable, including flights, hotel, and blah blah blah," I say with a sigh. "I told him just to go since it's not like I need a babysitter. There's no way he would've stayed home with me anyway, even if he hadn't gone on the trip," I say, shrugging.

Before Jess can say anything, I grab the movie *Inception* from the pile and hold it up to him, before raising my brows in question.

"Are you sure you wanna choose that one? There are sooo many other Leo classics, you know," he says, gesturing to the movie in my hand.

"You just wanna see Claire Danes, don't you?" I ask, squinting my eyes at him.

"She's hot. Sue me," Jess says, smiling as he leans back against the couch, manspreading as he puts his hands behind his head.

"Fine," I say, rolling my eyes as I turn back to the movie cabinet, and search the DVDs for *Romeo + Juliet*.

"The only reason I'm letting you pick is because you're the guest. The next one's my choice," I say, nodding as I hold up *The Silence of the Lambs*.

"Deal," he says with a smile.

I insert the DVD into the player and turn off the lights before I grab a blanket and plop down on the couch next to Jess. As the previews start, I can feel Jess's eyes on me already. I turn to look at him, and the faint glow of the TV illuminates his handsome, angular face in the dark.

"What?" I ask as he continues to stare at me.

"I'm sorry about your dad," Jess says before grabbing my hand. "That was kind of shitty of him to just leave like that," he says before giving my fingers a light squeeze.

"It's not like I'm seriously injured and need a nurse or anything, so it's not really a big deal," I say and shrug as I look at the TV. "Honestly, every time my dad does shit like this, the less it fazes me, so it hurts a little less than it did before. It's like I almost expect it now, ya know?" I say, trying to brush it off as I turn to face him.

Jess lets out a heavy breath. "Look, Sam, I'm sorry I haven't been coming to see you. I just—I wanted you to rest and heal, and I figured that me being here might've only made that harder for you," he says apologetically.

"It's okay. I know you're busy," I say, and I give him a halfhearted shrug as I gently pull my hand from his.

"No, don't do that," Jess says, and I can see him starting to get riled up. "You can make bullshit excuses for your dad and Chris, but not for me."

Jess sighs and removes his hat before running a hand through his hair. He quickly replaces it before he leans back against the couch, staring up at the living room ceiling.

"I wanted to give you space to think... I didn't want you to feel pressured by what I'd said to you. I know I dumped a lot on you that day, and I'm sorry for that."

Jess sits up and shakes his head before turning away for a second. "Regardless—I should've come by sooner to talk to you about it all," he says, meeting my gaze once again, and I can see a flicker of nervousness behind his eyes, even through the dark.

"Well..." I say, thinking for a second. "I guess you'll just have to make it up to me then, won't you?" I say and smile, having an idea. Jess just gives me a look like he's unsure of why I'm not angrier with him.

"Didn't you take first place one year in that state art competition Aunt Judy made you enter?" I ask.

"Second place, but only because that shit was rigged," he says as he shakes his head with a *tsk*. "Why'd you ask?"

I smile widely at him. "Hang on, I'll be right back," I say as I hop off the couch and run up the stairs to my room.

477

"Okay, here," I say, out of breath from running up and then down the stairs so quickly, and set down an array of colored permanent markers in front of Jess on the couch.

"And, *what* are we doing with markers…?" he asks, raising a brow at me.

I give him a coy smile. "Draw me like one of your French girls?" I ask and give him my most sultry stare as I bat my lashes.

"My *what?*" Jess asks in disbelief, laughing. "Okay, you are wayyy too big of a Leo fan for your own good," he says as he playfully rolls his eyes at me.

"What?" I ask defensively and try to hold in my giggles. "It was a joke, obviously," I say and smile innocently at him.

Jess just shakes his head at me. "I mean, Sharpies won't do, but I think that something can definitely be arranged if that's the kind of drawing you want…" he says, giving me a mischievous grin before lightly running a finger under the strap of my tank top. The action sends chills down my spine, and I struggle to keep my mind out of the gutter, wishing he'd take those fingers elsewhere.

I clear my throat nervously, trying to hide my excitement at his words. "Well then, I guess in the meantime, I would like to commission one Jess Cameron marker original, if you please," I say, holding up my blank cast in between us.

"You do realize I won the contest with a watercolor painting, right?" Jess says and raises a brow.

"*Almost* won," I tease, and he rolls his eyes at me.

"How am I supposed to watch the movie then?" Jess whines as he gestures dramatically to the TV with his hands.

"One thing. Draw me *one thing*, and I'll forgive you for abandoning me," I say as I fold my arms across my chest, not willing to budge until he agrees.

"Damn, that's harsh, Ryan," Jess says as he shakes his head.

The opening credits are still rolling, and I grab the remote before pressing pause. "Look, I'll even pause the movie so you don't miss anything good," I say, waving the DVD player remote around.

"How is it that you always end up getting your way?" he asks as he tilts his head with a crooked smile on his gorgeous face.

"I'm cute, that's why," I say, batting my eyelashes at him again.

"*Hmm*," he responds, giving me a quick squinty-eyed once-over before standing to turn the lights on.

Jess takes a seat in front of me as he sits cross-legged on the floor and grabs a marker before pulling the cap off with his teeth. I sit quietly and watch him, unable to see what he's drawing.

"Jess, can I ask you about something? There's something I've been wondering about," I say, and Jess just grunts in response as he continues to focus on what he's doing.

"When we were up on the mountain... that time with the... *ice cube*..." I clear my throat, a little embarrassed to actually be saying it out loud. "Did you actually know that I had my lacy bra on underneath my tank top, or was it just a lucky guess?" I ask. Jess slowly looks up from his drawing with a sly grin tugging at the corners of his mouth.

"Did you go through my bag?" I ask with a disbelieving laugh.

Jess pulls a face before shrugging. "Yeah, sorry," he says as he lets out a small breath. "I couldn't resist."

"Okay? And why is that?" I ask, raising a brow at him.

Jess shrugs again before going back to his drawing. "I wanted a memento from the trip, to remind me of you," he says nonchalantly as he puts down a pink Sharpie before grabbing a purple one.

My cheeks flame hotter than the sun at his words, remembering that I was missing a pair of underwear when I did my laundry after the trip. I just chalked it up to having been eaten by whatever dryer monster always seems to steal half of the socks out of my laundry.

479

Jess doesn't look up, but I see him smirk to himself, probably already guessing the effect his words had on me.

I clear my throat nervously and try to look at what he's drawing, but he covers it with his hand when I do.

"Hey, no peeking. You're not allowed to look at it until the movie's over," he says before continuing his drawing, his large hand still shielding it from me.

"What! *The whole movie?*" I protest. "Come on! Lemme see!" I whine, still trying to see what's underneath his hand.

"No way, it's a surprise. You're just gonna have to wait," Jess says with a smile, and his gaze is still intently focused on whatever it is that he's drawing.

"Okay, fine, but you'd better make it something nice. The last thing I need is to roll up to my next doctor's appointment with a wiener on my arm or something," I say with a laugh. Jess looks up from my cast and gives me a devilish grin before continuing his drawing.

"You didn't!" I exclaim, trying to pull my arm away to see.

"Stop, you'll mess it up!" Jess says through his laughs, trying to hold my arm still while I attempt to pry it away from him.

"You jerk, let me see already!" I say, laughing, still yanking at my arm.

"Sorry, no can do," he says before grabbing onto my bicep, stopping me from pulling my arm away from him.

We're both too busy laughing that it's not until I meet his eyes, that I realize just how close our faces are to each other.

Our noses are only mere inches apart, and when I try to lean back, Jess tightens his grip on my arm so that I can't. Our laughing quickly subsides, and we silently stare at each other in the quiet living room.

Jess longingly searches my eyes with his before he removes the hand that was covering his drawing, and I glance down. Small pink, and purple daisies litter the top of my cast, and right in the middle is a big red heart, the letters J+R written inside in black.

Jess's voice comes out low when he finally speaks. "Have you thought about what I said the other day at the hospital?" he asks.

I meet his eyes, and I try to think of the right words to express what I'm feeling. "I have," I say at last.

"And?" Jess counters, his eyes blazing into mine.

"And..." I hesitate for a second, not wanting to mess this up.

"Do you promise that you meant everything you said that day?" I ask, holding his gaze intently.

Jess reaches up to tuck a stray piece of hair behind my ear and speaks with a gentle intensity. "I swear on my life."

Hearing Jess say that is a relief, my insecure ass was sure that he'd changed his mind, especially where he hasn't tried to come over since he'd told me how he felt.

"Why didn't you come over to see me then? Really?" I ask, holding his gaze.

"I wasn't lying when I said I wanted to make sure you had time to heal..." Jess hesitates before answering completely, his eyes softening as he continues to look up at me.

His voice comes out low and gravelly as he continues. "*And...*" I watch as the muscles in Jess's jaw clench. "Because I knew the second you told me you felt the same... I wouldn't be able to hold myself back anymore."

My heart thunders in my ears.

"Then don't," I dare him.

# Chapter Twenty-nine

Jess doesn't hesitate before he captures my mouth with his in a fervent passion. I lean down toward him, needing our bodies to be as close as possible before Jess pulls me onto his lap. I straddle his waist on the floor in front of the couch and fist my hands tightly in his shirt, pulling him against me.

He kisses me like no one ever has before, and I understand now that I've been settling for mediocre kisses all this time and didn't even know it. Jess moves his mouth with such a deep yearning that it makes me realize that such a thing doesn't only exist in the movies.

Jess's hands grip onto my waist, his fingertips digging into my skin, and I rock my hips back and forth against him. I feel his lips part as he teases my bottom lip with his tongue, and I kiss and suck at his lips, desperate for more as I toss his hat to the ground and weave my hands deep into his soft hair.

"W-wait, stop," he says, trying to pull away from me, and the words come out muffled from our kiss.

I'm left breathless as our faces break. "What's wrong?" I ask, panting as I search his eyes.

"Nothing, I just…" Jess shakes his head and looks away. "I know that before, I said that even if you only wanted me—*in that way*… that I'd be okay with it." He hesitates, clearly struggling to get the words out. "And I am, I really am. If that's what you want, I'll be that for you. But, I just need to know."

Jess finally looks up, and I meet his eyes. "What is it that you want, Sam?" Jess's eyes glimmer, and I can see him yearning for me to say the words just as much as I had from him before.

I pause for a moment and raise my hand to the side of his face. I cup his warm cheek in my palm, and he leans into my touch.

I think back over the years to everything that's led up to this moment—all the memories and time we've spent together, the hardships and misunderstandings, the learning and growth. But, most important of all, the laughter and genuine love we've shared. Jess has always been there, and I don't know why it took me so long to see it. He's truly my best friend, and there's no one I'd rather have spent my life with than him.

He's my everything.

I don't falter, finally finding the voice to tell him what's enduringly been in my heart all these years.

"You've always been my world, Jess. Now, let me be that for you too." Our eyes burn into each other, and the air between us feels electric.

"You're my one, Jess," I breathe, and watch as the intense look on his face softens into a relieved smile, and notice that his eyes have grown shiny.

"Sam Ryan does that mean you'll be my girlfriend?" he asks, giving me a coy smile through half-lidded eyes.

"More like you'll be *my* boyfriend," I say before crushing our mouths back together, this time with more urgency from us both.

Jess grasps my ass firmly in both of his hands as he pulls me against him, and I tug at his shirt, trying to get it over his head.

Jess nips at the sensitive skin of my neck and I don't have the mental capacity to respond in words, so a small groan escapes my lips as I grasp at his strong arms around me.

"You sure don't waste any time," he says, and I can feel him smirking against the skin of my neck. "I *so knew* you had a thing for my arms," he says, smirking still as my fingertips dig into his biceps.

"Shut up and get naked, you've made me wait long enough already," I tease, out of breath, smiling as I continue to pull and rip at his clothes.

"Not here," Jess whispers into my ear and scoops me up into his arms, before walking us toward the stairs.

"Wait, what—"

"I've waited what feels like a lifetime for this moment, so there's no way in hell that I'm letting it happen on your dad's living room couch," Jess says as he chuckles darkly against me.

Jess's voice drops low as he whispers against my ear. "It's a good thing you ate earlier, because we won't be leaving your room for a few days at the very least," he says, his words causing my stomach to flutter with anticipation.

When we get to the top of the stairs, Jess sets me down and our mouths connect once again as we back into my bedroom. The kiss starts off slow and gentle, and I feel my body immediately starting to open up for him again with each pass of his perfect lips on mine.

My sense of urgency returns at the mere taste of him, and I pull at his shirt, desperately trying to get it off him. Jess quickly helps me pull the thin material over his head before he throws it onto the floor next to us.

I move my eyes from his face to his chest and broad shoulders, still half trying to wrap my head around the fact that this is real life and not just a figment of my imagination. No matter how many times I've seen

484

Jess without a shirt on, it'll never compare to how I'm seeing him now.

Finally, mine, at last.

Jess flexes his stomach as I run my hands down across his chest as I admire the sculpted lines of his hard muscles. Jess's breathing hitches the lower I move my hands, and I wonder if the anticipation is killing him as much as it is me.

Actually seeing him up close and finally touching him like this feels like a dream, and I can hardly wait to see and feel the rest of him.

I move to take my own shirt off, and Jess grabs my hands, stopping me before I can. "No," he says before lifting the hem of my shirt a few inches, lightly grazing my skin with his fingertips. Jess leans in and kisses down the side of my neck and across my collarbone before grasping the bottom of my shirt.

"Let me," he says before pulling away, his eyes ablaze with desire as he holds my gaze, like he's about to devour me whole.

I raise my arms and watch him with heavy eyes as he slowly pulls my tank top over my head before he tosses it to the floor.

I stand in front of him, my chest heaving lightly, breasts already fully exposed since I didn't bother with wearing a bra today.

Jess sweeps his eyes across my bare chest, and he bites his lip as he takes in my topless form, my nipples already peaked from the slight chill in the air.

He kneels down in front of me and stares up at me through his dark lashes. "*Ryan,*" he says breathlessly before grabbing me by my waist again. This time he leaves a trail of wet kisses across my stomach and ribs, and I thread my fingers through his soft hair, needing to touch him.

I think about the last time I felt his palms on my bare skin, and how I'd wanted more than anything in that moment for him to take control of me, body and all.

485

Jess stops his kisses and peers up at me through his dark lashes again before slowly tugging at the waistband of my black leggings, taunting the top of my hip bone with his mouth and nose.

I stare down at him, wanting to eat him alive already, but tell myself to be patient, wanting to savor every single second that I have with him.

He gently pushes me back until my legs meet the bed, and guides me to sit down. Jess kneels down in front of me and wedges his body in between my thighs as I widen my legs to make room for him.

Jess grips my hips, and I eagerly lean in toward him as he kisses my neck. I let out a small whimper when I feel his teeth gently sink into the top of my shoulder, and I lace my fingers into his hair and pull gently as I continue to moan out his name.

I can feel the tension in his body, like he wasn't lying earlier about waiting what felt like a lifetime for this moment, and I couldn't agree more with that thought. I don't know how many times I've dreamed about this moment, only ever waking up to be left alone and unsatisfied.

With one hand on the small of my back and the other on my waist, he gently floats me farther up the bed, my body now resting on a pile of pillows.

I look down at Jess and feel like he's taking everything so agonizingly slow that I feel like I could die. I watch as he peppers small kisses down my chest, stopping as he licks small circles around my left nipple before blowing on it, and I arch my back at the feeling.

Jess slowly makes his way down my abdomen before stopping just above the waistline of my leggings. He looks up at me as his fingertips trace just barely beneath the fabric. My mind is delirious from the feeling of his warm hands on my body, and if he's looking for permission, I'm not able to answer him with words.

He starts to pull at my leggings, and I lift my hips, desperate for him to remove them, wishing that he'd just shred the material already.

Jess leans back and pulls my pants off, along with my underwear in one smooth motion before tossing them to the ground next to our other clothes.

I spread my knees wide and expose myself to Jess, wanting him to see just how wet he's made me already. My heart continues to pound in my chest, and I feel like the anticipation might kill me if I have to wait a second longer.

His fiery gaze meets my own as he kneels back down on the floor, placing one hand on the bed next to me and the other on the outside of my thigh.

Jess sweeps his eyes down across my body, before landing right in between my legs. He hums in approval as his hand roams up and down the outside of my leg, before gripping onto my ass.

The feeling of his strong fingers digging into my soft skin lights a fire within my belly and I want to beg him to never let me go.

He leans in and kisses down the inside of my leg before lifting my ankle over his shoulder.

"You are fucking perfect," he says, his gravelly voice muffled as he continues to kiss down my leg while holding my eyes with his.

"Can I?" he asks, and his eyes lock onto mine as he gently bites down into the sensitive skin of my inner thigh.

I wince at the pain, but the sound that escapes my mouth betrays me, and I feel Jess smirk against me as he slowly kisses his way farther down the inside of my thigh.

He stops when he gets to my lower belly before looking up at me again, and I can feel his hot breath on me as he hovers just above where I want him.

"*Jess*," I beg through a breathy gasp and thread my fingers into his hair again.

"Put your tongue on me. *Please*," I say, tightening my grip.

Jess chuckles darkly before nuzzling his nose into the side of my thigh again before giving me a gentler bite than before. He makes his way down my leg, dragging his lips and the tip of his tongue over my skin as he moves.

I feel his breath and then his warm tongue on my most sensitive area, and my back involuntarily arches up off the bed. Jess's hands hold my hips firmly in his grasp, the only things keeping me from floating off into space.

Jess swirls his tongue in slow wet circles around my clit, the sensation driving me almost to insanity. His hands grope at my sides, pulling my body tightly against his face as I drape my legs over his shoulders and dig my heels into his back.

The wet sounds of my slickness on Jess's face echo throughout the room along with our gaspy moans, and I think that it might be the most erotic sound I've ever heard.

His warm, wet mouth feels amazing on me, and I feel like I won't ever be able to get enough of him. The thought of us ever going back to the way things were between us makes me realize that I'm never going to let that happen.

"Jess," I breathe out as I tug on his hair, trying to force him to look up. Jess peers up through his dark lashes, a wicked glint in his eyes as he flattens his tongue and slowly licks up my wet folds while maintaining eye contact with me.

"I—*oh fuck!*" I cry out. The feeling of Jess's warm tongue sliding deep inside of me cuts me off as he buries his face back into my pussy, somehow already knowing exactly what I wanted him to do.

Jess glides his tongue in and out of me in slow movements, circling and massaging with each long stroke. The way his nose rubs up against me is enough to drive me wild, and I pray that at some point he'll let me sit on his perfect face.

The thought of riding Jess's face into oblivion, combined with the sensation of his hot tongue moving in and out of me, brings me that much closer to my edge, and I feel like I might go over already. I grasp and pull at Jess's hair, trying not to crush his skull with my thighs as my climax nears.

Jess releases his hold on one of my hips before he reaches up, cupping one of my breasts in his hand before kneading it in his firm grip. I can feel small vibrations against my skin as Jess moans into my pussy, still sliding his tongue in and out, and I shudder with satisfaction at the thought of him enjoying this as much as I am.

I grab onto the hand that's gripping my chest. "*Harder, Jess, pinch me h-harder*," I moan out, and I feel a chuckle against my skin as he quickly follows my instructions.

He pinches my nipple between his fingers just enough to hurt a little, and the feeling sends me straight over the edge. I arch my back and clamp my legs down around Jess's head as I cry out his name and pull at his hair, one hand still tightly wound in his soft curls.

Jess waits for me to stop trembling before he lets go and removes his tongue from inside me, causing my body to jerk at the sensitivity. I'm delirious and can barely keep my eyes open as I watch Jess stand in front of me with a smug grin on his face.

His chest rises and falls heavily as he pants, now trying to catch his breath after basically being smothered by my pussy. I watch through heavy eyes as he wipes the corner of his mouth with one of his thumbs.

"So sweet," Jess murmurs as he licks his lips before climbing onto the bed with me. His body hovers over mine, and I grab behind his neck and pull his face down toward me.

I lick and suck at his mouth, desperate to taste his lips on mine— to taste *myself* on him.

"What a naughty girl," Jess says with a smirk, breaking our kiss momentarily before he pulls me back in with more intensity than before.

He kisses me wildly, any tenderness and hesitation now replaced with an impassioned urgency.

Jess's body is still hovering above mine, and I reach a hand down the front of his sweatpants, stroking his rock-hard length with my hand.

He groans into my mouth as I grip him hard and slowly slide my hand up and down. I run my thumb over the head of his dick, and I feel Jess's body tremble against me before his breathing hitches.

"*Fuck*," he groans out as he drops his head to my shoulder before biting me lightly.

Jess is breathless as he grabs onto my waist and scoots me up the bed, resting me farther into the pile of pillows before pulling away from me. I lean forward, trying to keep him close, but he gently forces me back against the pillows, causing me to whimper in protest as I continue to reach for him.

Jess backs up and stands at the foot of the bed, breathing heavily as he stares at me, and I can see his erection straining against the material of his gray sweatpants.

"Open those legs for me," he says, his eyes filled with desire as they sweep down over my body.

I slowly spread my knees apart, and run my left hand across my chest, my casted wrist resting at my side on the bed. I can feel the slickness down in between my thighs from when I came earlier, and the cold air on my exposed body sends a shiver down my spine.

I watch as Jess pulls on the drawstring tie of his sweatpants, before they drop to the floor and he steps out of them, at last revealing himself to me.

I swallow hard in anticipation as I take in his impressive size with my eyes. We're both breathing heavily as we watch each other in silence, and the building tension makes the air feel thick.

I don't know how many times I've envisioned this scenario in my mind, only now I'm filled with an incredible satisfaction that I'm here doing this with Jess instead of just my imagination.

Slowly, I snake my hand down the front of my chest, stopping to squeeze my breast before pinching my nipple in between my fingers, causing my breath to catch, and I let out a small moan.

Jess stands watching me with dark eyes as I trail my hand farther down, tracing my fingertips lower, stopping just above my left hip as I let my hand linger there.

"Do you want me to keep going?" I ask as I continue to drag my fingertips across my skin, amazed at the restraint that Jess is showing.

He gives me a slight nod, and I feel his eyes as they bore into me.

I tease small circles around my lower belly before dropping my hand lower, my fingers eagerly landing on my clit.

"Jess, do you have any idea how many times I wished this was your hand instead of my own?" I say, out of breath and lightheaded from trying to hold myself back from going over a second time.

"Show me," he says, the sound of his sultry voice a song to my ears.

I make a few small circles with my fingers before inserting one of them into myself and then add another. Jess doesn't say anything as I hold his gaze, fingering myself through half-lidded eyes, and watch as he fists himself with his hand.

Jess slowly pumps his cock up and down as he watches me, his hand now slick with precum.

I remove my hand from in between my legs and bring my fingers to my mouth, and Jess's eyes darken as he watches me lick them clean.

I spread my legs a little wider in invitation, seconds away from begging him to fuck me.

"Fill me, Jess," I say breathlessly, and Jess lets out a small growl before pouncing on me.

The second our bodies collide, I feel his cock sliding across my wetness before he slams into me as he lifts my hips to meet his body.

Jess gives me no time to adjust to his size, and I feel the delicious burn of his thickness as it stretches me out.

The sensation takes my breath away and I throw my head back against the soft pillows beneath me. I snake my arms around Jess's torso, clawing at the muscles of his back as I cling to him, and what was left of my lingering sanity is now long gone.

Jess grinds himself into me, pushing me farther into the pillows with each thrust of his hips. His motions are slow and deep, and we both pant and moan as our bodies move together.

Jess groans my name into my ear, and I bite at his shoulder, a familiar pressure already building at the bottom of my spine.

"I love you, Jess," I breathe into the crook of his neck.

"*Fuck me*," he says, and I feel his dick quiver inside of me. "Again," he says through his breathy moans. "*Again*—please," he begs desperately.

I lick and bite at his earlobe, my head starting to feel hazy as my orgasm approaches. "*I love you*," I whisper into his ear as I cling to him.

After hearing my words, Jess throws his head back and roars as his orgasm tears through him. I feel his dick twitching as he empties himself inside of me, and I arch my back as my own climax takes over.

Jess keeps moving us, and I scratch and claw at his back, never wanting our union to end. Though the sensation is overwhelming, I grind myself against him harder, riding my orgasm through the aching sensitivity.

We both collapse onto the bed, and Jess wraps his arms tightly around my waist, firmly holding me to his body. I rest my head on his chest and feel his heart thundering in his ribcage, like it might jump out of his chest at any minute.

"Never stop saying that," he says in between pants, and I can hear the smile in his voice as he tries to catch his breath.

"I love you I love you I love you I love you," I say, small giggles escaping me as I peck kisses all over his neck and chest, taking extra care to kiss the small birthmark on his neck that I love so much.

Jess rolls on top of me and groans into the crook of my neck as he holds me tightly against him, and I instinctively wrap my legs around his body. I feel him start to bite and suck on the already tender skin there, and even though I know he'll probably end up leaving a mark, I don't mind. If he does, it'll say: Jess Cameron finally belongs to me, Sam Ryan.

Jess continues to kiss my neck as his hands start to roam across my body, stopping to grab a handful of my ass.

"Wait, Jess, how are you still—" I say, all words leaving my brain the second he starts to move us again. I feel him starting to get hard again, his length still deep inside of me.

"You have no idea how long I've waited to hear you say those words," Jess says into my neck before kissing up my jaw and then over to my mouth. Jess swirls his tongue around with mine and I'm left wanting and breathless as he pulls away.

"You really thought I was gonna let you go after just one round?" he asks after breaking our kiss, a devilish look on his face when I meet his eyes.

"I want you in every angle, every position, and all over every square inch of this fucking room." Jess flips us over, and suddenly I'm straddling his waist. "Ride me," he says as he looks at me through his dark lashes, his tone more commanding than before.

My eyes start to roll, and I struggle to keep them open as Jess begins to move beneath me. My body arches from the pleasure of how fully I'm able to feel him like this, his cock hitting the perfect spot deep inside of me.

Jess grips my thighs hard enough to bruise as I start to rock and grind, matching his rhythm as he moves underneath me.

"Oh fuck, Jess. *Yesss*..." I moan out, grinding down on him roughly, and I have to close my eyes to curb my dizziness.

493

"That's it, baby, ride me hard," he says, edging me along with his words. "I wanna see you c-come again," Jess breathes out, and I can see that he's already starting to come undone himself.

Our bodies pound together, and the sounds of flesh-on-flesh echo throughout the room along with our gasps and groans.

"Jess, I-I'm—I'm g-gonna…" I'm unable to finish my words as my eyes roll all the way back into my skull, and my ears ring from the force of my orgasm.

Jess lets out a low groan and keeps moving me as his release crashes through him, and I feel him grip tightly onto my thighs. My entire body is tingling, and I collapse onto his chest. I'm panting so hard that I feel like I might actually pass out this time, but I'm too sated to care.

I'm trembling from the aftershocks, and Jess holds me firmly against his body as he wraps his arms around me. He gently flips us over so that he's hovering above me and slides himself out, and my body involuntarily jerks at the sudden emptiness left by him.

"You…are…*everything*," he says as he leaves a small trail of kisses along my neck and collarbone, and I slide my fingers into his hair.

"I can't believe you've been holding out on me all these years, I feel like I just experienced an exorcism or something," I say and laugh, still panting. I open my eyes as the world slowly stops spinning to look at Jess.

"Looks like we'd better make up for lost time then, shouldn't we?" he says, and I can feel him smile against my skin as he continues to kiss all over my body.

Jess brings his face up to mine and gives me a quick peck on the lips. "Be right back," he says with a giddy smile on his face before quickly scurrying off the bed.

"Wait, where are you going?" I sit up and call after him. Any other time, and I'd probably chase after him, but where my legs feel like they're now made of Jell-O, I know I should probably keep away from any stairs or open windows for the time being.

I hear Jess's heavy footsteps on the wooden stairs, before hearing the front door close just as quickly as it was opened. More heavy footsteps sound on the echoey flooring before Jess closes my bedroom door behind him.

"What in the world?" I ask, smiling.

In all his naked glory, holding a brown paper bag in one hand and two small cartons of milk in the other, Jess smiles widely before jumping onto the bed beside me. He hands me the small bag, and I don't even need to open it to know where it's from.

"Are you happy?" he asks with a cheesy grin.

I open the bag and take a whiff of the sweet cookies inside. "*Mmmm*, how did you manage to pull this off?" I ask as I inhale the sugary scent once again.

"Let's just say I have connections," he says with a wink.

Shaking my head at him, I gently lace a finger under his gold chain, pulling his face toward mine. "You really are something else, Jess Cameron," I say and let out a small laugh before pulling his lips to meet mine.

We only make it two more rounds before my growling stomach keeps interrupting us, and we decide to take a break. Jess helps me clean up and makes me drink some water before we sit on the bed and share the cookies from Leonard's.

"You think of everything, don't you?" I ask after taking a bite out of my peanut butter cookie.

"Obviously, because I'm like, the man," Jess says, bragging, and laughs before taking a bite of his oatmeal raisin cookie. I roll my eyes and take a drink of my milk before setting the carton down on my nightstand next to Jess's.

Jess shrugs halfheartedly. "I just knew that if I'd ordered real food, you probably wouldn't eat it—but if I ordered something sugary—there's no way you'd be able to resist," he says and smiles at me before he leans over to kiss me on the mouth. "That, and I knew you were gonna need your strength," he says with a cheeky smirk before trying to kiss me again.

I put a hand on his chest to stop him. "For your information, sugar is not the only food that I like," I say and laugh.

Jess leans in toward me, and I push at his chest playfully. "I guess you're right. For one, I know you *really* like meat," he says, still trying to reach my lips with his.

"You did not just say that! Straight to jail!" I say, laughing, trying to swat his hand away from where it's grabbing at my waist. I reach around and grab a large pillow and try to smack him over the head with it. Jess dodges the pillow effortlessly before swatting it out of the way while he continues to laugh.

"You think you're so funny, don't you?" I say before I quickly lean in and take a bite out of the cookie that he's holding in his hand.

"What—hey!" he says, unable to move out of the way in time, still distracted by laughing at his own joke.

I try not to choke on the cookie as I laugh. "Call it the cringe tax," I say, smiling at him.

"Whatever, you so know I'm right," Jess says before leaning toward me, and this time I let him kiss me.

After we'd finished the cookies, Jess drew us a bath. We tied my cast off with tape and plastic wrap to keep the water out, but I still haven't trusted myself to let it in the water, so I rest it awkwardly on the ledge of the tub.

I'm sure I'll definitely be feeling it more in the morning, but the hot water feels nice on my already sore muscles. I don't even remember the last time I went five rounds with someone, let alone with someone who made sure that I came every single time. Which was honestly fantastic, but I feel downright exhausted.

I know I shouldn't be thinking about it, but I can't help but be jealous of all the other girls that Jess has ever been with. I think about how they probably had no idea how lucky they were to be with someone like him, and not just because of the sex, but because he really is an amazing guy. He's thoughtful and kind, and always puts the needs of others before his own. Honestly, I don't really feel like I deserve to be with someone like him.

Jess squeezes the water out of a washcloth before rubbing it across my back and then plants a kiss on my shoulder. "What's wrong? You're uncharacteristically quiet for a Sam right about now," he says.

I let out a breath and bring my knees to my chest as I wrap my arms around them. We'd both agreed at the hospital that we'd be better at communicating our feelings from now on. It's clear that a lot of damage in the last few weeks could've been avoided if we had just talked to each other about what was bothering us.

"I'm just thinking about all the other girls you've been with in the past," I say, wanting to be honest with him for once, but can't help the envy that creeps into my voice.

I feel him run the soapy washcloth across my back again. "Why? Why would you torture yourself like that?" Jess asks softly.

I feel my cheeks heat as I say the words. "Because I'm jealous," I say, and hang my head in my hands, knowing it won't do much good to try and hide my embarrassment.

Jess takes the washcloth down the side of my left arm this time after wringing the soapy water out. "You shouldn't be. Honestly, the list isn't as long as you probably think it is," Jess says before kissing me lightly on the shoulder.

Hearing Jess talk about his potentially low body count doesn't make me feel any better; if anything, it only makes me feel worse, and now I'm wishing I'd never said anything at all.

"I know…" I let out an annoyed huff at myself. "It's stupid of me to think that a grown man, especially a charming, good-looking one, wouldn't have had a sex life," I say, and rest my chin on my arms as I fold them across the tops of my knees.

"*Hmm…* so you think I'm charming *and* handsome?" he asks, and I can hear the smirk in his voice. Jess leaves gentle kisses across my back and shoulders as I continue to pout unfairly, feeling too embarrassed to face him.

When I don't answer, Jess grabs onto my waist, and I can feel him trying to turn me around. I stubbornly hold onto the sides of the tub and hear him chuckle under his breath.

"Sam, look at me," he says, and I shake my head, refusing to turn around.

"*Please*, Ryan?" he asks softly, and I finally cave at the use of his special nickname for me and let go of the tub. Jess turns me around to face him, and I move my thighs to straddle his waist. I'm sure embarrassment is prevalent on my face as my cheeks flame, and I look away from him.

"Sam, I know it might bother you that I've had relationships in the past, but so have you," Jess says gently. "I don't like the idea of any other man besides me seeing you like this—or touching your body for that matter—any more than you do about some other girl touching *me*," he says, and I see the cool fire behind his eyes returning when I finally meet his stare.

Hearing him put it that way makes me feel guilty for being jealous over something that I have no right to be. He's right; just like I didn't have a say in who he dated in the past, he didn't have a say in who *I* dated either. For years, both of us have had to watch each other be with someone else who wasn't us. Feels kind of shitty no matter how you look at it.

"You're right, I'm sorry," I say, and look down, feeling ashamed.

Jess lightly puts a finger under my chin, forcing me to meet his eyes. "Sam, of all the girls I've ever dated, you're the first one I've ever said those words to."

*He must be joking.* There's no way he's never told someone he loved them. *Right?*

Jess must notice the skepticism in my eyes. "I'm serious," he says. "You're the only one I ever wanted to say them to. You're it, Sam. You always have been," Jess says, and his beautiful green eyes captivate mine with their intensity.

"I don't ever want to be with anyone else but you," he says, and the butterflies inside my stomach dance at his words.

I can feel tears starting to well in my eyes. "You're the only person in the entire universe I've ever wanted to hear that from," I say, and rest my hands on his shoulders.

"Hey, why are you crying?" Jess coos softly as he cups my cheek in his palm. "Shouldn't you be happy, then?" he asks with a look of worry on his face.

I run my left hand down his torso and stop at the faint scar across his chest from Kyle's blade. My fingers gently trace the raised skin, scar tissue present where it should be smooth.

I hesitate before answering, not sure how to put what I'm feeling into words. "Jess, when I thought you had—" I let out a labored breath as I force myself to say the word. "—died... after the nightmares I had in the hospital, I was so scared." I pause, remembering the vivid dream I had. I grab onto Jess's shoulders again and stare into his eyes. His face is frozen in a half-pained expression, and his eyebrows are furrowed together, as if remembering his own bad memories from my time in the hospital.

"If something had really happened to you, if you had actually..." I trail off, unable to make myself repeat the word.

"*Oh, Sam,*" Jess says quietly, his gaze glossy as he watches me with pain in his eyes.

"I know it's cliché as hell to say this... but I don't want to live in a world that doesn't have you in it," I say and let out a humorless laugh.

"Please don't ever leave me alone, Jess," I say, and I let the tears fall as I grasp at his neck and shoulders.

"I won't, I promise I won't," he says as he pulls my body toward his before wrapping me tightly in his embrace. I take several deep breaths, trying to stop my crying before it turns hysterical, not wanting to ruin the night even more than I already have.

"Let's run away, just me and you. Somewhere far," Jess says, and I pull away, meeting his eyes as I sniffle. "Somewhere where no one will ever find us."

"You make it sound like we're teenagers on the run or something," I say and laugh lightly as I sniffle again.

"It definitely sounds more exciting when you put it that way," he says, shrugging. "We can go anywhere, *anywhere* in the world that you want." Jess tucks a strand of hair behind my ear and holds my gaze intently as he waits for me to answer.

"But, what about our families? What about Judy?" I ask, feeling slightly guilty for not actually worrying about those things at all.

"Soph has Chris, your dad is getting married soon, and Madison… I don't know about Madison," Jess says, shaking his head.

"And, as for Aunt Judy, she's got a boy toy and her poker league to keep her occupied," Jess says and gives me a crooked smile before shrugging again. "We don't owe anyone anything, Sam. Plus, I'm done sharing you with everyone else," he says, winking, and I give him a squinty look and shake my head at him in mock disapproval.

"Don't get me wrong, I'll miss them, well, *most* of them… but you're the only family I need right now," he says, holding my gaze. I feel a smile slowly creep over my face and then watch as Jess mirrors it back to me.

"Does that mean yes?" he asks excitedly, and I feel his hands tighten around my waist as he beams at me with his perfect smile.

"But, where would we even go? What about my classes? What about your work contract?" I say, not really concerned with any of that either. I know we'll figure it out, and wherever we go, so long as Jess is there, I will be too.

"We can go wherever My Highness wants to." Jess smiles as he lifts my hand and kisses the top of it before winking at me.

"You really are too charming for your own good, you know that?" I say as I shake my head at him, both of us smiling from ear to ear.

My heart feels so full, and I don't think that I've ever been happier than I am in this moment. Nothing else mattering except for the two of us, together. Right here. Right now.

"Well, that would be because I'm *your* Prince Charming, eh? eh?" he says, wagging his brows up and down.

"Cringe tax, right now!" I say, laughing as I splash him with the bathwater.

Jess laughs and turns away, a few droplets hitting him in the face. "I guess since we ate all the cookies, I'll have to find some other way to make it up to you," he says, his eyes darkening as he sweeps his gaze down over my half-exposed body.

"Guess so," I say, and he pulls my waist firmly against his body, the water in the tub sloshing loudly around us.

# Chapter Thirty

We end up spending the next four days fucking like bunnies, only ever leaving my bedroom to pick up our food deliveries at the front door—or to get it on in the shower.

Since Jess is staying with Sophie at the moment and because my dad is out of town for a few weeks, we'd decided to take advantage of the empty house.

*If only teenage me could see us now...*

I was sure to let Sophie know that Jess and I had made things official and that it was in Chris's best interest to stay away for a few days. Of course, when I'd told her, she'd said she was ecstatic that we'd finally gotten our timing right, but a part of me questions her sincerity after all that Jess has told me about her meddling.

When we'd talked before, Sophie even confessed to a few things that I had no idea she was even capable of. And, honestly, I wish I'd never found out about those. Even after Sophie's confessions and apologies, a part of me knows that I should just forgive her since things ended up working out between Jess and me in the end, but I can't help but feel a little sore about it all.

Sophie tried to keep Jess and me apart for all this time so that she wouldn't be alone, but in the end, she's the one who left us both to go do her own thing. I'd like to think that eventually Jess and I would've ended up together anyway, regardless of Sophie's actions, but that thought only *slightly* lessens my irritation toward her.

Chris texted me last night, asking if Jess and I could stop behaving like animals so that he could come home and get some fresh clothes. He'd said that he didn't want to be scarred for life if he found Jess and me in a precarious situation on the couch, which is funny, because it'd be Chris's perfect karma for what he made me witness at Sophie's house.

This morning, after I basically forced Jess out of my bed, he agreed to go home and pack a bag to take to my place for a few days. My apartment lease ends at the end of the month, and I haven't renewed it yet since I wasn't sure if I was sticking around for the entire summer or not. "Running away" with Jess couldn't have come at a better time, and I smile at the thought of getting to spend more time alone with just the two of us.

After Jess left, I texted Chris that the coast was clear and decided to do some laundry in the meantime. Since neither Jess nor I has been wearing any clothes these last few days, the only real laundry I needed to take care of was my bedding, so I threw my sheets and a few blankets in the wash.

I pack up most of what I'd brought with me, plus a few of my newest additions I'd picked up at the crystal shop, along with a few other small things from my room, and hop in the shower to get ready. I try to hurry before Jess comes back and decides not to let me shower alone. I'll admit that the idea sounds pretty nice, but I'd feel bad telling Chris it was safe just for him to come home to Jess and me moaning in the shower.

The thought of seeing Jess all wet and soapy again makes me smile, and I remind myself to ask if he'd be willing to recreate the dream I had about him.

Just as I'm stepping out of the shower, my phone dings with a text message from Jess. I wrap my towel around myself and pick my phone up off the counter with a wet hand, anxious to see what he sent.

> Just stopping at Aunt
> Judy's to fill her in. Don't
> miss me too much while I'm
> gone.
>
> I love you.

*He said he loves me.*
My heart swells as I re-read the words.

I giggle and feel giddy just thinking about hearing him say them out loud the next time we're together, and can't wait to say them right back to him.

I finish up the laundry and get myself ready for the day before I put the rest of my packed bags next to the front door. I'm waiting for Jess to show up when I decide to kill some time and rid the fridge of our leftovers from the last few days. I'm putting a new bag in the kitchen trash can when I hear the front door open and close, and hear the sound of a bag being dropped on the floor.

I round the corner to the entryway. "Hey, Chris, if you want any of this leftover pizza—"

"Hey, kid," my dad says from where he stands in the living room, and I notice that his speech is slurred. His eyes are bloodshot, and he gives me a forced smile as he drops his suitcase onto the floor next to his duffel bag.

"Dad, you're home early. Are you all right?" I ask, eyeing him, guessing from his state that he isn't all right at all. My dad never comes home early from a trip, and this time, it's by a whole week, which is definitely concerning to me.

"Yeahhhh, I'm fineeee," he drawls and waves a hand at me, his intoxication becoming more apparent.

I hate to ask because I'm sure it'll open up a can of worms I have no interest in talking about, but I do it anyway.

I let out a breath. "Where's Rebecca? Didn't you ride back together?" I ask, figuring she'd be with him since it seems like my dad is unable to leave her side for more than five minutes at a time.

I fold my arms across my chest and watch my dad as he sways slightly from where he's standing.

"Rebecca's... not here," he says, looking around. "She's not here, is she?" he states, his eyes starting to gloss over.

I let out a heavy sigh. *Here we go.*

It's the same old story every time he breaks up with one of his girlfriends. He'll get beyond drunk and cause a scene—usually at the country club or somewhere public. Then he'll get upset and break things, and follow that by mistaking me for my mother. And then he'll just expect me to clean up the mess he'll have made of everything.

Looking at him now though, I don't think I've ever seen him this bad before, so it makes me think that maybe he wasn't the one who did the dumping this time.

"Bec's not here, but that's okay, right…?" my dad says, like he's trying to convince himself of the words as he staggers into the house, almost falling. I help catch him by his arm and try to steady him as I steer him toward one of the couches, not wanting him to fall and hurt himself.

"Because I have you to take care of me, right, Sammie?" my dad continues cheerfully through his tears as he lets himself collapse onto the couch.

I stand in front of my dad with my insides feeling torn apart. Seeing him like this has always been painful for me, and that's why I always give in. I'm forever the one left to clean him up and pull him out of his destructive patterns. Only then, after everything is all said and done and he's feeling great again, do I get left in the dirt.

Always the one taking care of others, but never the one getting taken care of. Always tossed aside, always disregarded.

Every. Time.

I think about Jess, especially our last few days together. He's always told me that I accept less than what I deserve from people, and I think that now I'm finally willing to admit that truth to myself.

I look at my dad with a dull ache in my chest.

*Not again. Not this time.*

I say nothing as I continue to struggle internally with what to say next, when I notice my dad lazily eyeing my bags at the door next to his.

"You going somewhere, kid?" he asks, barely able to keep his head up, and I wonder how he even managed to get home in this condition, especially if he was by himself.

"Um, yeah, actually I am," I say hesitantly.

"Noooo, don't gooo, Sammie, your brother and I need you," my dad says, giving me a large smile. The ache in my chest deepens since I don't know the last time he ever smiled at me like that, which only makes it that much worse now that he's only doing it because he's been drinking.

I know what needs to be said, but it's difficult for me to do, knowing deep in my heart that I can't let myself go back on my words. "I'm sorry, Dad. I-I can't stay here anymore," I say after taking a deep breath as tears start to burn behind my eyes. "You're… gonna have to find someone *else*… to take care of you," I say, desperately trying to maintain my composure as I fight against myself.

"Whataya mean, Sammie?" he says with a laugh. "You can't go. Let's watch a movie! Pizza too!" he slurs, aimlessly reaching around the cushions for the TV remote.

Hearing him say that only makes things more difficult for me since that's all I've wanted from him for the last eight years. It kills me not to give in and say yes to him, to help get him cleaned up and take care of him like I always do.

Jess's words keep echoing in my head, and the way his green eyes seem to pierce straight into me—as if he's able to really see me. Jess looks at me like I'm worth something. He always has. The thought makes my chest ache when I realize that he's never made me feel the way that my dad does.

Worthless—only until it's decided that I'm of value.

I know my dad won't remember any of what I'm saying tomorrow, but regardless, I feel like I need to get it out—if not for him, then for myself.

"Dad—" I try, but he's still fumbling around with his hands for the TV remote. "Dad, *listen*," I say more assertively, and he finally looks toward me, and I can see that he's struggling to keep his head up.

"Dad, I love you, but I can't help you this time," I say, and I clench my hands into fists at my sides to stop their trembling. I watch my dad as he struggles to sit up, obviously still drunk off his ass but at least aware that this is something important.

"But, Sam—" he says, trying to stand, his playful demeanor from earlier gone.

"No, Dad. Stop, please," I say firmly, forcing myself to stay strong as I push my tears back down. "I'm done being your emotional crutch. I should never have to be that for you. You always expect that from me, but when I need you, *when I really need you*, you disregard me and brush off my feelings like they don't mean anything at all," I say, my voice slowly starting to rise with each freeing word that leaves my mouth.

"Did you ever stop to think that maybe you weren't the only one affected by Mom's leaving? Did it ever occur to you that I was hurting just as much as *you* were hurting? The only ones who were actually there for me were not even people in my own family. Do you have any idea how that felt?" I say, now starting to get angry, and wish he wasn't drunk so that he'd remember the words I needed him to finally hear from me.

My dad only stares at me from the couch. I take a steadying breath, trying to calm myself down before speaking again, knowing it won't do anyone any good if I go and lose my shit.

"I know that you tried your best, and I'm grateful for all that you've done for Chris and me over the years. I've got my own life to live now, and I refuse to be used and tossed aside by you anymore," I say, and watch as tears stream down my dad's scruffy face. He sits back against the couch, no longer trying to stand.

"I can't keep letting you drag me back into your bullshit just because it's convenient for you that I'm the only one here," I say calmly, and we stare at each other in silence.

"Sam—"

Two knocks break us both out of it before Jess bursts through the door, a huge grin on his face.

"HONEY, I'M HO—"

He stops short, his eyes locking onto mine as his smile vanishes, immediately sensing that something is wrong. Jess rushes over to me, gently cradling my face in between his warm hands.

"Are you all right? What's wrong? You're shaking," he says, and I break his gaze and turn to look at where my dad is still slumped back against the couch cushions.

"What did you do?" Jess demands as he looks over at my dad, who stays silent from his place in the living room. Jess shifts his stance defensively and gathers me in toward his chest protectively. I close my eyes as I lean into Jess's touch before letting out a deep breath.

"Hey, didn't you hear me? What the fuck did you do—"

"Let's go," I say, cutting him off before opening my eyes as I meet his.

His concerned eyes search mine for a beat before he shoots a glare at my dad and then nods at me before taking my hand. I follow along behind him as he grabs my bags from by the front door on our way out of the house.

"Jess," I hear my dad call, and turn to see him by the archway of the living room. He's standing, eyes incredibly bloodshot, face wet with tears as he leans against the wall for stability.

Jess turns to look at my dad, and even though he doesn't say a word, his defensive body language says he'd be ready for a fight at the drop of a pin.

My dad's eyes are sad as they meet mine before looking to Jess. "Take care of her."

"Always," Jess answers, the tension in his body language relaxing a bit before pulling me along behind him through the open door.

When we get outside, Jess tosses my bags into the back seat of his Jeep before pulling me to his chest. He hugs me tightly, and I try my hardest to hold back the waterworks, not wanting to ruin the makeup I'd worked so hard on this morning.

"What happened?" he asks against me as he gently strokes the back of my head.

I continue to cling to him as I tell him about what was said between my dad and me, and he holds me even tighter. When I finish telling Jess what happened, my story drawn out by my failed attempts at keeping my tears in, he pulls away, forcing me to meet his eyes.

"I am so proud of you, Sam," he says as he gently wipes the tears from my cheeks with the pads of his thumbs.

"But why?" I ask, my voice coming out shaky, and I continue to hiccup even though I've stopped crying.

"You deserve the world, Sam—nothing less, not from anyone. Not from me. Not from your dad or Chris. And, most importantly, not from yourself," Jess says, holding my gaze intensely.

Jess gives me a soft peck on the lips before pulling away to look at me. "You *are* worth it, Sam. Understand?" he says, and I nod at him reluctantly, trying to force myself to believe in his words.

"Good," he says, smiling before he pulls me back to his chest in a tight embrace. "I know you don't really believe it, but I promise always to be here to remind you."

"Okay?" he asks when I don't respond, and I nod against his chest.

"Now let's get the hell out of here, yeah?" Jess says and kisses me on the head, before pulling away again. "You hungry?" he asks before offering me a hand to climb into his Jeep.

He rounds over to the driver's side and hops in, shutting the door behind him. I smile and look over at Jess, beyond grateful for him.

"How could I not be after all that cardio this morning?" I tease and sniffle as I wipe my tears away with the back of my hand, still trying not to smear my mascara.

Jess reaches over the center console and grabs my hand before planting a kiss on the back of it. "You'd better get used to it," he says with a wink. "We've still got a lot of time to make up for."

My stomach flips in anticipation just thinking about what he could be planning.

On our way out of town, we stop at one of Jess's favorite Mexican restaurants to get lunch. Even though I'm feeling a bit sad about what happened with my dad, somehow, I feel a little bit lighter about the whole situation. It's like a weight was lifted off my shoulders that I forgot I was even carrying because it had been there for so long. Even if my dad doesn't remember any of what was said, *I* will, and I'm proud of myself for finally saying what I needed to.

I let out a cleansing breath and try to shake the thoughts away before I take a sip of my pineapple drink. I watch as Jess smiles at the waiter and thanks him after leaving our food at the table.

I smile to myself, remembering what Sophie had told me about Jess being flirty with other guys. Before, I definitely believed it, but now, knowing what I do, I'm sure that Sophie was just making things up.

Jess turns to smile at me, and I just about swoon right into my enchiladas. "What?" he asks, raising a questioning brow at me.

"Nothing," I say, trying to hide my grin, and figure I'll tell him about what Sophie said later.

"Seriously, what?" Jess asks as he lets out a small laugh, obviously able to see right through me.

I take one look at Jess's biceps in his gray compression shirt and shrug as I bite my bottom lip.

Jess looks down at himself and then back at me. "Are you seriously objectifying my body right now? *And while I'm eating?* How dare you," he says, pretending to be embarrassed before he flexes an arm and gives me a wink.

I don't try to hide my blush as I take another sip of my drink and smile at him.

Jess is acting his usual charming self, only now it feels different between us—no, not different, *better*. I feel like a whole new world has opened up between us, and I can't fathom the thought of ever going back to how it was before. If I thought I needed him badly before, it's nothing compared to how I feel about him now.

I know we've only been officially together for a few days, but just being around Jess and the way he always brings me so high, has me feeling like the luckiest person on the planet. He makes me feel like I could ask for the world and I just might get it—with myself being the only thing standing in the way.

A thought suddenly hits me. "Holy shit."

"What?" Jess asks through a mouthful of his burrito and raises his brows in question at me.

I can feel the goofy grin that spreads across my face as I say the words out loud. "Is this our first official date?"

"My god, you're right," he says, smiling back, and I feel all giddy inside at the thought. "I'll tell you what, though, I promise you a do-over," Jess says, setting down his burrito.

I shake my head at him. "But why? This is sort of perfect already," I say, still smiling at him from ear to ear.

Jess shakes his head playfully. "No way, I owe you a proper, real-life first date. Dinner and a movie, maybe even some mini golf, and possibly... if we're lucky... a suuuper awkward kiss at the end of the night," he says, and we both laugh at that.

"Deal," I say, holding out one of my pinkies before Jess hooks one of his onto mine.

Jess's eyes sparkle as he stares at me longingly. "Deal," he says.

The second we get on the road, my head starts to bob, and I threaten to pass out. I'm exhausted from the little to no sleep of the last few nights, and I definitely overate at the restaurant, which really doesn't help my tiredness. Jess was just about to pay our check when the waiter offered us fried ice cream. Not only did I finish my half, but I also finished Jess's.

*Big shocker there, I know.*

Jess's warm hand around mine and the white noise of the wind gently blowing against the Jeep windows lulls me to sleep in a matter of minutes. Though it's summer, I'm grateful that Jess put the top and doors back on, at least for this trip, so we wouldn't have to drive two hours with the wind of the freeway whipping us around.

Before we left the restaurant, Jess made sure to get the address to my apartment on the off chance that I accidentally fell asleep on the drive there. It shouldn't surprise me that he'd assume that. I guess I must just be that predictable.

After a few hours, the slowing momentum of the Jeep wakes me. "Hey, we're here," Jess says quietly, and I feel him kiss the top of my hand as he gently tries to rouse me. He squeezes my hand gently, and I yawn before looking over at him.

"Hi," I say, and give him a dopey smile as I wipe the drool from the corner of my mouth, still trying to blink the sleep out of my eyes. "What?" I ask when I notice him staring at me.

"Nothing, you're just so damn adorable when you first wake up. You're like a cute little woodland creature or something," Jess says, and I just roll my eyes. He gives me a lopsided smile, and I try not to blush at the way he looks at me.

"C'mon, let's go in," he says and kisses the back of my hand again before opening his door.

Jess opens my door for me and helps me carry one of my smaller bags inside along with his. When we reach the small lobby, I stop to check my mail and send Jess on ahead of me up the stairs.

"I haven't seen you around in a while," a voice says from behind me. "Are you okay?" she asks, and I turn to see my downstairs neighbor standing in her doorway, multiple brown paper grocery bags in her arms.

"Oh, hi, Mrs. Ashley," I say, and help her catch one of her bags before it falls. I wonder what she means, but then I notice that she's looking at the cast on my arm. "Oh, this? Yeah, I'm all right. Thanks for asking," I say and give her a warm smile.

"No, thank *you*," she says, nodding to the grocery bag full of vegetables I'd saved from the ground.

"No problem," I say with a smile as I hand her the grocery bag. "It was nice to see you."

Mrs. Ashley smiles and nods at me before stepping through the threshold of her apartment, and I move to head up the stairs.

"Oh, and Sam," she calls over her shoulder, and I turn from my place on the staircase to face her, having only made it up a few steps. "There's been a guy poking around looking for you lately," she says, fiddling with her house key as she tries to get it out of the lock.

I feel all the blood drain from my face as a bolt of hot panic sears through my body.

"Guy? What guy?" I ask, my heart pounding fiercely behind my ears. "What did he look like? Did he have dark hair? Did he have tattoos?" I ask frantically, and the look on Mrs. Ashley's face tells me that I'm starting to freak her out.

"No... actually, he's that skinny blonde guy, the one who was coming around for a while," she answers. "You sure you're okay, Sam?" she asks hesitantly as she gives me a worried look.

I let out a relieved breath as I try to calm myself down.

*Daniel, she's talking about Daniel.*

I remind myself to check if he left anything behind when I start packing things up, which is honestly doubtful since he didn't even want to leave a toothbrush at my place, let alone any articles of clothing.

"Yeah, I'm fine," I say, and try to give her a reassuring smile. "Thank you for letting me know," I say before turning around, not really caring to explain my freak out to her.

I head up the stairs and stop in front of my apartment, watching silently as Jess struggles with the lock on the door. I can tell he's getting aggravated by the way he's mumbling profanities under his breath, and I try not to laugh at how cute he is when he's flustered.

"Need a little help there?" I ask, trying not to antagonize him.

"No, it's okay... I almost... got it..." he says, still struggling, and I pray that he doesn't break the key since it's the only copy that I have.

"Seriously, how in the fuck—A-HA! Got it!" he says before turning around. "See, it wasn't that hard," Jess says with a smirk, and I give him an encouraging nod and say nothing as I try to hold back a giggle.

"Pretty sweet digs, eh?" I say, showing Jess into the kitchen after he opens the door for me. I say kitchen, but it also just so happens to be the living room *and* the bedroom.

Jess sets our bags down on the floor and scratches his head with one hand, the other half tucked in his front pocket.

"What?" I ask as I set my keys and mail down onto the kitchen counter.

"Don't take this the wrong way, Ry... but this place is a total dump," Jess says hesitantly, glancing from the leaky kitchen faucet to the large crack in the far wall.

"Okay, rude," I say. "Do you have a problem with my humble living space?" I ask teasingly, already knowing he doesn't really mean anything by it.

Growing up, Aunt Judy always lived quite frugally. I'm guessing she wasn't anticipating that her retirement funds would end up going toward raising Jess and Sophie. That's not to say she was poor or anything; she just lived a little below her means in case of an emergency. Which, in the end, ended up working out when she fell and broke her hip.

Judy's old house never bothered me, honestly, I thought it was really nice. It had a sense of home that I rarely felt at my own house.

"You know full well, that of all people, I do not," Jess says and smiles at me, knowing I'm joking. "I guess I just figured you'd have a little nicer of a place. You know, with *daddy's money*, and all," he says, teasing me as he pokes me in the side with his finger.

"For your information, *daddy* doesn't pay for this place, nor does he pay for any of my other bills, my tuition included," I say and put my hands on my hips defensively.

"Is that so?" Jess asks quizzically, and I squint and give him a questioning look.

"Uh-huh," I say with a nod and smirk, giving him all the sass. "So, I guess what I'm saying is that you're welcome to stay home and be a good little housewife for me, and I'll go ahead and bring home the dough."

"Thanks for the offer, but that's not going to work for me," Jess says, his eyes darkening as he gives me a once-over. "Although I do like the sound of you taking charge... of some things, at least," Jess says, his voice dropping an octave as he steps closer to me.

"Ah, I see, so you want me to boss you around then, is that it?" I sweep my eyes down over Jess's perfect form and bite my lip. "I think that can be arranged," I say and hold my ground as Jess moves closer, looking like a predator who's about to devour its prey.

A knock at the front door startles me before Jess is able to pounce on me, and I jump at the sound. Almost instantly, my heart starts to race, and I feel my breathing catch in my throat.

Jess takes one look at my reaction and gently grabs me by the shoulders. "Hey, it's all right. Breathe, Sam, just breathe," he says, rubbing my arms. "I'm not going to let anything hurt you, okay?" he says, holding my eyes with his, the hot desire that was there only seconds ago, now replaced with protective reassurance. "I'll go see who it is, okay?" he says, and I nod at him as he gives me an understanding smile.

Having Jess here with me definitely helps my anxiety, and even though I'm still freaked out, I don't feel as scared knowing that he'll always try his best to keep me safe. Even though it's been a hot minute since my accident, I'm beginning to think that maybe I need to talk to a therapist or something about everything that's happened. I'm finding that I don't like the ominous feeling of terror and panic that I experience every time someone is at the door. The more time that goes by has me realizing that it's probably not going to go away on its own.

I hover in the kitchen and watch as Jess unlatches the multiple locks down the back of the old wooden door before opening it. "Can I help you?" Jess asks, his voice deep and commanding.

"Doubt it," the voice says with a snort. "Where's Samantha?"

When I recognize the voice as Daniel's, I let out a breath of relief and lean back against the kitchen sink, trying to slow my heart rate back down now that I know there's no real threat of danger.

"Sorry, she's not taking visitors right now," Jess says as he stands towering in the doorway. He's got one hand on the open door, the other bracing the doorframe, blocking anyone from entering without having to go through him first.

"What the hell is that supposed to mean? Is she here or not?" Daniel asks, his voice sounding annoyed.

Jess's body stiffens as he steps to block the front door even more, and the action makes me wonder if Daniel had just tried to sidestep Jess to get inside.

"Hey, what's your damage, man? What, are you like supposed to be her new *boyfriend* or something?" Daniel asks in a mocking tone.

"Not that it's any of your business, but yes. And we were right in the middle of something too, so if you don't mind—" Jess says as he tries to shut the door.

I can't help it when my heart does a little flip in my chest at Jess's attitude toward Daniel. I'd obviously be lying if I said I wasn't the jealous type—because I totally am—but, there's something about hearing Jess sound so possessive over me that's starting to get me worked up.

I hear what sounds like palms smacking on wood and watch as Jess shifts his stance more defensively as Daniel forcefully tries to push open the door.

"Sorry to break it to you, *guy*, but Samantha doesn't date. Why don't you do us all a favor and get lost before you end up getting your feelings hurt," Daniel says with an angry scoff.

Is this guy for real? All I tried to do *was* date him, but he's the one who always kept me at arm's length no matter what I did to try and get close to him.

A month ago, I would have given anything to see Daniel acting all jealous over me, but now, I can hardly even remember why I insisted on wasting so much of my energy on him.

I can feel the calm rage as it radiates off Jess's body all the way from where I'm standing by the kitchen sink, and wonder if maybe I should intervene. When I go to move, my legs feel a little wobbly from my almost panic attack a second ago, so I decide to just let Jess handle it.

"You're right, she doesn't date, at least not shits like you," Jess says, his tone sharp. "She told me about you, you know," Jess says, and I see him raise his hand and wiggle his pinky at Daniel with a snicker before putting his hand back on the door frame.

"And sorry to break it to you, but not only did you lose any chance you had with her, but you never really had one to begin with," Jess says in a condescending tone.

I watch as he removes his hand from blocking the door and folds both of his arms across his chest, as if challenging Daniel to try something.

"Now I think it's best that *you* get lost, before I get angry," Jess says, his body oozing possessive confidence.

I hear Daniel let out an annoyed breath. "If you're not going to let me in, at least tell her I stopped by."

"Nope," Jess replies flatly, firmly shutting the door in Daniel's face before he has the chance to say another word.

Silence falls between us for a second, and I can feel the hostile waves coming off Jess's body as he stays facing the door, one hand still firmly gripping the wobbly handle.

"Hey, I'm sorry about that…" I say nervously.

I never told Jess anything about Daniel, but with the meddling Sophie's been up to, I'm sure she already told Jess all about my new "boyfriend."

519

"I'm not," Jess replies as he turns around, a fire blazing behind his green eyes. "I'm glad he came over," he says, and I give him a questioning look.

"I'd love the chance to tell every man that you've ever been with to fuck right off. I want them all to know that not only should they have worshipped the ground you walked on, but they should've savored every sweet touch of your skin because they'd be longing for it someday," Jess says, and his intense words take me by surprise.

I didn't expect this sort of reaction from him, so I stand half-stunned by the kitchen sink, unsure of what to say.

When I don't say anything, Jess just stares at me with a lethal look in his eyes before continuing. "I want to make sure they all know that they'll never have you again. No one will," Jess says, and his intensity sends electric sparks through my entire body.

Jess's breathing looks labored as he sweeps his heavy gaze up and down my body, and I feel a wave of heat surging between my legs when I remember what we had almost started earlier before Daniel had interrupted us.

"Is that so?" I ask him through a half-lidded gaze.

Jess nods slowly at me, his eyes fountains of desire as he continues to undress me with the dark emeralds. "Because you're mine now, Sam Ryan."

I know most guys will say they aren't the jealous type—but then again, I think that's what they all say—and for the most part, I never thought that Jess was either. The thought of him being jealous of the other guys I've dated in the past gives me a small sense of satisfaction—as toxic as that may be—knowing that I'm not the only jealous one.

With my eyes locked onto Jess's, I walk over to the large window next to the couch and draw up the blinds, filling the room with the soft afternoon light.

Jess watches me with a curious look through his hungry gaze, and I know that he'll catch on quickly. I slowly pull my dress straps down over my shoulders and let the material drop to the floor around my ankles.

Jess watches me from his corner of the room, his eyes flooding with passionate wanting. "What are you doing? Someone will see," he says sounding almost breathless, a wicked glint in his eyes.

"If I'm yours, then show everyone who I belong to," I say as I glance toward the window before meeting his eyes again.

With equal parts desire and shock, Jess holds my gaze as I stare at him through half-lidded eyes.

I slowly run my hands down the front of my body.
"Fuck me where they can all see."

Jess quickly pulls his shirt off over his head and crosses the room toward me in two long strides, his fiery confidence from earlier still blazing hot through his skin.

I meet him halfway, and our bodies collide, our mouths crushing together in urgency as we grab and pull at each other. He backs me against the window, and one hand roughly grips my waist while the other gently works its way into my hair.

I pull at the clasp of his belt, trying to get his pants undone, and our tongues both fight for control. I wildly grasp at Jess's hair, desperately trying to free it of its hair tie so that I can thread my fingers through his soft waves.

Jess bites and sucks on my bottom lip before shoving his tongue deep into my mouth, and I savor the taste of him, knowing that I could never get enough.

I feel like I might suffocate from the intensity of the kiss but decide that I couldn't care less.

Removing his hand from its grasp within my hair, Jess reaches behind me to unclasp my lacey bra. He quickly spins me around, and I brace myself against the window with my palms.

Jess presses me up against the glass before I feel him lower and bite down on one of my asscheeks. I let out a whimper, the pleasure mixing with the pain. I feel him ripping the fabric of my thong before I glance back to see him quickly toss it over his shoulder behind us.

He bites down on my ass again, this time much harder than before, and I whimper again, "*Yes.*" I can tell it's going to leave a bruise, but I want him to do it again anyway. I want him to mark my whole body with his hands and mouth, to lay claim to my entire being, body and soul, and I long to do the same to him.

I hear Jess chuckle under his breath as he gives me a gentle kiss in the spot where he unquestionably left teeth marks. I feel Jess's warm mouth against my already burning skin as he slowly drags his lips up the length of my spine. The action sends goosebumps up my back, and I arch at the feeling.

Jess gently kisses my neck, and I push back into him with my hips, trying to create any sort of friction in between our bodies.

"You're extra greedy today, baby," Jess smirks against my skin as he wraps his arms around me. He grabs onto my breasts roughly as he kneads them both in his hands. "God, I fucking love this, I fucking love *these*," he mumbles under his breath as he continues to grab at me before biting down onto my shoulder.

"You say I'm greedy?" I pause, breathless as I place my hands over his. "Only greedy for what's mine," I say finally, leaning back into him.

The words send Jess into overdrive, and I feel him move behind me as he finishes undoing his jeans before pushing them to the floor. He grips onto my hips, and without warning, he presses into me deeply.

"*Ah! Jess*," I gasp out and throw my head back against his shoulder as I feel him start to move, surprised by the sudden intrusion.

"*That's right*," Jess growls into my ear as he presses me up against the glass of the window, harder and deeper with each thrust of his hips against mine. "This cock is all yours now, just like this pussy's mine," he says as he licks at my earlobe before biting down on it just enough to lightly sting.

Jess thrusts in and out of me, my eyes rolling back a little more each time his length hits that sweet spot deep inside. Pants and the sounds of our bodies slapping against each other fill the small space, the erotic sounds echoing off the walls all around us.

"*Jess*," I breathe out. "Touch me here," I say as I try to move one of his hands off my hips. Jess releases me, but instead of placing it directly where I want it, I bring his hand to my mouth and suck on two of his fingers, wishing they were something else instead.

"*Fuck, you're such a filthy girl for me*," Jess groans into my neck as I continue to gag on his fingers, and I feel his dick twitch inside of me.

I pull his hand from my lips. "Now. *Touch me now, Jess*," I say, and tug his hand down in between my thighs as he continues to ruthlessly pound into me from behind.

I arch my back into him harder as he starts to trace circles around my clit, increasing the pressure with each noise that I make.

"Wait, Jess—" I say, breathless, trying to turn around to face him. "I wanna see your face when you come."

He doesn't wait for me to ask again before he quickly slides himself out and flips me around to face him. Jess pulls our faces in together for another sloppy kiss, and this time I bite his lip before pulling away, forcing him to look at me.

Jess's eyes search mine, and their intensity continues to burn through me. "Tell me I'm yours, Sam. Only. Yours."

I don't hesitate, wishing he only knew the depth of my scorching love for him. "You're mine, Jess," I say, and bring my hands to either side of his face. *"You're mine."*

Jess lifts me, and I wrap my legs around his waist as he slowly walks us over to the bed. He lays us both down on the soft bedding, and we hold each other's gazes. I gently tangle my fingers through his hair again and pull his face down toward mine, stopping just before our mouths connect. The yearning I feel for him is almost painful as I peer up at his brilliant green eyes, wishing I could stare into them for eternity.

I spread my legs for him, and Jess slowly presses into me, both of us letting out breathy groans at the feeling. I wrap my legs around his waist, pulling his body tightly against mine, and slowly start to move my hips from underneath him.

We grind against each other, still holding eye contact while we breathe deeply together.

"Don't ever let me go," he whispers to me, and I can feel my eyes starting to burn.

I tighten my grip around Jess's waist with my legs and pull his neck down so that our noses are almost touching.

*"Never,"* I breathe, pulling our faces together into a gentle kiss.

Jess kisses me with reckless abandon as our bodies continue to throb and tremble in unison with one another.

As Jess pushes into me slow and deep, I can feel the pressure of my orgasm building deep from within my belly, and my body hums with electricity.

Jess's dick throbs hot inside of me and I can tell that he's close to his release as well. I can feel my walls tensing around him and he lets out a low groan at the feeling, and a few more deep thrusts of his hips have us both falling over the edge together.

Jess grasps onto my body tightly as he buries his face into the crook of my neck and gently bites down to stifle his low moan. My body pulsates with pleasure as it arches, and I tremble and shake in Jess's strong arms as he holds me tightly against him.

My head is in a pleasure-filled haze, and all I can think about is how I wish that this moment would never end, wanting to stay like this with him always.

We lie there in each other's embrace for what feels like forever, but somehow it still isn't long enough, I don't think it could ever be. Jess faces me on his side, and I reach up to wipe the mess of waves from his face. He puts a hand over mine and keeps my palm pressed lightly against his cheek. He holds my eyes like he wants to ask me something, but doesn't say anything as he just continues to stare at me.

"What is it?" I ask, my eyes now starting to grow heavy with sleep.

Jess gives me a hesitant look before answering, and I wonder what he's so worried to ask me about.

"We definitely don't have to talk about this right now, but..." he says after turning his head to kiss my palm.

"Whatever you have to say, I'll listen and not get mad. Promise," I say with a sleepy smile, trying to reassure him of my newfound maturity.

"Okay," Jess says, propping himself up on his elbow before answering me fully. "So, by no means am I kink shaming you, but damn, Ryan, I never thought you'd be such a—"

"Pervert?" I ask, cutting him off before he's able to say the word himself.

Jess throws his head back against his pillow and lets out a laugh before turning to look at me again. "No, I was gonna say *freak*, but I guess if the shoe fits," he says, and this time I laugh with him as I playfully smack him on the chest.

Jess continues to laugh, and I cuddle up next to him and rest my chin on his chest as he folds his arms behind his head.

"I mean, I guess it's something we should definitely talk about. I don't ever want to make you feel like you have to do something you don't want to just for my sake," I say. "Your experience is just as important as mine."

"And, how do you know that I'm not some secret BDSM Dom, huh? Maybe I'm into some real freaky shit and you just never knew about it," Jess teases, and I shake my head at him before playfully biting down onto his chest.

"Hey, *ouch!*" Jess laughs.

"I'm sorry, what were you just saying...?" I say and give him a cheeky smile.

"You're such a meanie," Jess says, and leans up to kiss me, before I rest my chin back on his chest again.

"Seriously, though, I want you to always be comfortable with whatever we do, freaky shit or not," I say and laugh.

"I mean, don't get me wrong, that stuff can be fun if both parties are into it," I say and shrug before continuing.

"Even though I was able to learn a lot by being able to explore all these different sides to myself, I think that even if the sex is great, without a true connection, it's all sort of meaningless in the end, don't you think?" I ask, and Jess just raises a brow like he doesn't believe a word I'm saying.

"For real, I'd take that kind of intimacy with you any day over anything ever. As far as I'm concerned, you're the best lay I've ever had," I say and shrug.

Jess playfully smacks me over the head with a pillow. "You're just saying that because you don't want to hurt your boyfriend's feelings," he says with a fake pout.

"No, I'm serious," I say, laughing as I swat at the pillow. "I thought I had connections with past partners, but I realize now that I was trying so hard to force things that weren't even real. I know what it's actually supposed to feel like now, and I wouldn't trade it for the world," I say. "Not ever."

"Oh yeah?" Jess asks me with a satisfied smirk on his face.

"Yeah," I say as I rest my head back on his chest and look up at him through my sleepy eyes.

"I'd go through every single shitty thing that's ever happened in my life over again if it meant that I got to end up right here, right now, in this moment with you, Jess Cameron," I say, and can't hold back the cheesy grin that spreads across my face as I stare deeply into his beautiful emerald eyes.

"You have no idea what it means to hear you say those words," he says, giving me that smile that almost makes my heart stop.

I rest my chin on my arm as I place it across his chest. "I really mean it, Jess. In the end, thank you for choosing me," I say, continuing to smile my dorky grin at him, and I wonder if anyone has ever died from being so happy.

Jess sits up to bring our lips together before pulling away an inch.

"I'll always choose you."

# Epilogue
## 1 Year Later

I'm just about finished with putting the frosting on the cake when I hear the lock on the front door unlatch. I turn and sprint to the door and jump into Jess's arms before he has a chance to even set more than one foot inside our apartment.

Jess catches me and drops his bag on the floor in the doorway, and I cling to him like a baby koala. "Hey baby," he breathes into my neck, and I feel him smile against my skin. I hang on tightly to him and inhale the faint aroma of his warm cologne, instantly feeling at ease now that he's home. He steps over the threshold and gently kicks his bag inside before using his foot to push the door shut behind him.

"Did you have a good day today?" I ask, still clinging to him as he walks us into the living room.

"Yes, but it's better now," Jess murmurs into my neck as he hugs me back tightly.

He gently tries to peel me off of him, so in response, I giggle and fasten my limbs more tightly around his neck and waist.

"Hey, let go, I wanna kiss you," he says, tickling my sides. I laugh as Jess basically forces me to release my hold on him, and I almost drop to the floor before he catches me. We laugh as we land on the ground next to the sofa, and I face him, quickly climbing onto his lap as I straddle his waist.

"I missed you today," Jess says as he brushes a piece of hair out of my face before tucking it behind my ear. It's such a simple gesture that he's done at least a thousand times before, but somehow it still gets me flustered every single time. I feel warmth spreading through my cheeks and my heart starts to beat a little bit faster than it was before.

"Oh yeah? How much?" I ask, holding his sultry gaze with my own.

"I can show you if you'd like," he says before leaning toward me, and our faces connect in a soft open-mouthed kiss.

Jess pulls at the straps of my shirt, and I lace my hands in his hair as the kiss turns needy. "W-wait!" I say, abruptly breaking our kiss and pull away from him. He tries to pull me back, and I place my hands on his chest as I push against him. "I almost forgot!" I say as I jump off his lap and run into the kitchen.

"Come back! Saaaammmm," Jess whines from the living room.

"Just a second!" I yell to him over my shoulder before grabbing the small cake off the kitchen counter and run back into the living room.

"What's this?" he asks, eyeing the small round cake plate in my hand, the other covering the words written on top.

I sit on the floor, facing him and he watches me with a curious look. "It's a carrot cake," I say, beaming at him, pretty damn proud of how good it turned out even though it's technically a "healthy" cake.

"A *carrot cake?*" Jess raises a brow and gives me a look like he's trying to hold back a laugh.

"Yep," I say and nod at him. "Just like the one Judy makes that you love."

"But I thought we were going out tonight?" Jess asks with a crooked grin as he looks from the cake to my face.

"Oh, we are. You can think of this as *first* dessert," I say with a sly smile, my hand still covering the top of the cake.

"But, I planned on having *you* for my first dessert," Jess says, flashing me with the most provocative look I've ever seen. My cheeks flush, and I fight the urge to pounce on him.

Jess gives me a cheeky smile before nodding at the cake for me to proceed with my unveiling.

"Okay, ready?" I ask as I fidget in place, the anticipation about to kill me. Jess nods, and I remove my hand dramatically. "Ta-da!" I say excitedly as I reveal the cake to him.

Jess claps his hands together and throws his head back in a laugh, grinning ear to ear as he looks up at me from the cake. "I love it," he says through that beautiful smile of his before leaning in toward me for a kiss.

It might not be the most original thing I could think of, but I decided that the cake looked a little plain, so I added the words *from your favorite pair of boobs* under the words *Happy Anniversary* in sparkly blue gel-lettering.

"I know you don't normally like a lot of sugar, so I made it as healthy as I legally was able to—for a cake, that is," I joke. "Anddd, I figured that since I put so much love and effort into it—and since it's our anniversary—you'd have to at least have one *teeny tiny* little slice," I say and bat my eyelashes at him. "For me? Pretty please?"

Jess smirks at me. "Oh, I definitely like sugar," he says with a wicked grin on his face, and I feel my breathing catch at his words. Jess gives me a half-lidded expression as he bites his lip. "I'll have some, but I want you to feed it to me."

I swipe a finger into the frosting before holding it up to his mouth.

"*Uh*, are we out of clean forks or something?" he asks, trying to hold back a laugh.

"No, I'm just afraid that you might change your mind in the five seconds it'll take me to walk to the kitchen to grab one," I say with a giggle, and wag my finger at him to open up.

The corner of Jess's mouth twitches upward slightly. "I guess you're the boss," he says, making an *It can't be helped* face as he shrugs.

Jess grabs my wrist and guides my finger onto his tongue, intensely holding my eyes with his before slowly sucking the frosting off. I feel the tip of his tongue make a small swirl on the tip of my finger and swear I can see his eyes darkening.

I can feel my cheeks burning up—along with other areas of my body—at the way he's looking at me, and my heart starts to beat even faster than it was before. When he releases me, I slowly pull my hand back, my brain temporarily short-circuiting.

"I can't believe I can still make you blush after all this time," Jess says smugly as he licks a bit of frosting off his lips.

"Oh, shut up, or I'll make you eat this entire cake," I tease as he continues to try and seduce me with his shimmering eyes.

"Promise?" he asks, his voice low and laced with a hint of mischief.

I swallow hard and try to get my wits about me before swiping a tiny bit of frosting onto the tip of his nose.

"*What*—" he says, looking at me incredulously before wiping the back of his hand across his nose, and I quickly set the cake plate on the floor and try to escape. Jess is too fast for me as he snakes his arms around my waist and pulls me back into his lap.

"You're gonna pay for that later," he whispers into my ear, and the feeling of his warm breath on my skin tickles me. I laugh and only half struggle to get out of his arms, not really wanting to escape his warm embrace.

"We'll see about that," I say, and I feel his soft lips on the back of my neck as he chuckles against me. Jess hums as he lets out a breath as he continues to hold me, and I feel so at ease that I almost forget about our evening plans.

"Shit, what time is it?" I ask, trying to lift Jess's wrist so that I can look at his watch.

"Who cares," he grumbles into my neck as he hugs me tighter, this time wrapping his legs around me too, making an escape almost impossible.

"We have dinner plans, remember?" I say as I lean back against him.

"Says who?" Jess's voice comes out muffled, his face still buried in my neck.

"Says you," I say and scoff. "Remember when I said that I'd rather stay home and cook, and you said, 'not a chance because it's our first official anniversary so we need to celebrate properly.' Remember that?" I ask, teasing.

I feel Jess's hands start to roam. "Let's just celebrate at home," he says, his voice dropping low as he nuzzles his face into the crook of my neck. I consider giving in, but the excitement of what I have planned for later outweighs my rising desire.

"Uh uh, not a chance, mister," I say, trying to pry his arms from around my waist. "You wanted to go out, so we're going out. I didn't buy a new outfit just to wear it at home," I say, laughing.

Jess grumbles against my back, still not wanting to let me go, and I'm finally able to break free from his grasp when he loosens his arms from around my waist. I stand and turn to face him with my hands on my hips.

"When did you get so whiny?" I ask as I playfully shake my head at him.

Jess gives me a *humph* and rolls onto his side on the floor. "Since you made me a horny cake and decided to wear those tiny shorts today," he says, gesturing to my blue floral print booty shorts.

Jess props his cheek up with his palm and gives me a mischievous smile as he bites his bottom lip before sweeping his gaze up over my exposed legs.

I fold my arms across my chest, which I then realize only emphasizes the current minuscule amount of clothing I'd chosen to wear today, and roll my eyes at him. "Come get ready; we've only got twenty minutes," I say before turning around and head toward our bedroom.

"Yessss, ma'am," Jess calls after me, followed by a heavy sigh and a gentle thud, most likely from the sound of his body dramatically flopping down onto the carpet in protest.

~

Last summer, after we got everything packed and settled with my apartment and classes, we ended up staying with Sophie for a few weeks while Jess got everything situated for the move. We had stayed in town long enough for me to get my stupid cast off, but decided to start my physical therapy wherever we ended up settling down. Jess was worried about me having to start over with a new physical therapist halfway through my treatment and thought it would be best to just start and finish at the same facility.

When we had left town and said our goodbyes to everyone, I feel guilty saying that it wasn't as bittersweet as I'd anticipated it would be for me. I didn't feel a single ounce of guilt leaving with Jess, knowing that everyone would be fine without us.

Sophie and Chris were preoccupied with their new budding situationship, and Judy with her own life as well. The sad reality of the status of my relationship with my dad is that it's exactly where I left it the moment I walked out of his house. The more time that passes, the more I realize just how much of a bad state I was in with most of my relationships at the time, and I'm glad to finally be free of their cyclical toxicity. Without Jess, I don't think I ever would've realized how I was giving my love and energy so freely to people who didn't appreciate or seem to want it, which I can see now was slowly killing me.

Jess had told me that we could go anywhere in the world, and honestly, the thought crossed my mind to suggest somewhere exotic like France or Spain, but I eventually settled on Colorado. Jess had mentioned to me before that a few of his buddies on the oil rig had lived just outside of Denver at one point in the small town of Weatherford and had said that it was a really beautiful place to live. Jess obviously has a thing for snow, and I really like to ski, so it worked out.

Neither one of us had ever even been to Colorado before, but we decided to throw caution to the wind and take the jump—Jess's words. Truthfully, we could've chosen to live in a van down by the river, and I'd have been happy with that, so long as I got to be there with Jess.

I figured that being in Colorado would be nice since it's still close enough that we can visit Cedar Hills by plane, and it'll only take us a few hours, which makes me feel better about leaving Aunt Judy behind. I still didn't really like the idea of being so far away from her—especially in her old age—but Jess reassured me that we'd fly back whenever I wanted to see her, all I'd have to do is say the word. Of course, Judy still has Sophie since her current college plans are on hold for a while until she figures out what she wants next out of her life.

Jess had a pretty good chunk of money saved up from his time on the rig, so he was able to find us a place to stay pretty quickly. As predicted, he didn't want me to pay for anything, but I was at least able to talk him into letting me spring for our flights. It wasn't much compared to what he'd already covered with all the moving costs and the deposit for the new place, but it still made me feel better being able to contribute, even if it wasn't a lot.

During our first week living in the city of Weatherford, we were walking downtown by some shops when I noticed a help-wanted sign in the front window of one of the small local newspaper offices. At first, I was hesitant to apply, especially since I didn't even have my degree yet. Jess eventually talked me into it, saying that I was still a journalism major and that it wouldn't hurt to at least try. He told me that even if I ended up just being an intern or something, I'd be getting real-world experience in an office.

Jess hyped me up with a pep talk and a good smooching before he sent me into the shop to ask for an interview.

As it turned out, they were so desperate for help, they hired me right on the spot. The work is only part-time hours, and I mostly write fluff pieces for the local happenings of the town, but I don't mind it. If I'm being honest, I actually really enjoy how slow-paced it is.

After our move, Jess wasn't really sure what he wanted to do for work. For obvious reasons, I was against him going back to the oil rig since not only is it dangerous work, but he'd have to be away from me for long periods of time. I told him that I'd support whatever decision he made, but I was pretty relieved when he told me about the full-time art teaching position available at the community center downtown.

I always knew that he loved to draw, but he always claimed it was more of a hobby than anything. Now that I see how happy he is when he gets home—usually covered in paint or charcoal from sketching all day— I realize just how much he truly loves it. It also makes me happy to know that he's doing something he loves instead of the dangerous manual labor he was doing before.

After Jess and I had left Cedar Hills and started our new lives together, everything felt like it fell into place for us. From our new apartment overlooking the small lake east of town, to our jobs that seemed to fit us each just right.

I see now that before I was just coasting through my life, deep down knowing exactly what I wanted, but believing I wasn't worthy of ever having it. Once I realized that true happiness and fulfillment come from within one's own self, I felt like nothing could ever stop me. I look back at the sad little girl who used to feel abandoned and unwanted and send her all the love in the world. Sometimes I picture myself next to her, holding her hand in mine, telling her that everything is going to be okay, and that she's safe to give love to herself before others.

I know that Jess was the catalyst to my self-growth, and I think about that fact quite often. I feel like I owe him so much, and he doesn't even realize it. The deep love that Jess continues to show me every day seems to know no bounds, and I count my lucky stars every chance I get that we found our way back to each other. Being with Jess and living the life that we do, together, happy at last, has me waking up every single day, beyond grateful for my life and his presence in it.

Getting to wake up in his strong arms day after day, warm and safe, my soul feels like it has finally found the peace it's been searching for all this time.

~

"You ready yet?" I call from the mirror by the front door as I finish putting my earrings in. "We're gonna be late!" I say, turning toward the living room after I straighten out the pleats of my light blue dress.

"And miss the reservations we set for ourselves?" Jess says, walking into the living room dressed to the nines. "Since when do you care about being on time, Ry?" Jess scoffs, and I give him a slow once-over. It only takes about point two seconds before I feel all of the heat in my body rush down in between my legs.

Jess traded in his usual tight t-shirt and jeans for a pair of dark brown slacks and a collared cream-colored shirt, which is honestly equally as tight on his biceps as his regular attire. Jess has his wavy hair slicked back, and even though I protested when he cut it earlier this year, I can't help but swoon over how good his new haircut looks on him.

"On second thought, what was it you were saying before about celebrating at home?" I ask as I step toward him and rest my arms around his shoulders.

Jess leans in, and before I have the chance to devour him, he smoothly brings his lips to my ear before whispering. "Sorry, baby, you wanted to go out, remember? I didn't get all dressed up just to stay at home," he says, mocking my words from earlier, and I feel him smirk against my neck.

"Let's get outta here, wouldn't want to miss our *reservation*," he teases in my ear before giving me a quick peck on the cheek before he grabs my hand and pulls me along behind him.

On our way out, Jess grabs one of his light jackets from the coat hook by the front door, and my heart swells at the action. The man runs as hot as an oven, so I know he's probably only bringing it for me just in case I get cold later.

We step out into the warm night air, and Jess swings our hands in between us as we make our way over to his Jeep.

"Remind me again why you're the one driving?" Jess asks as he looks over at me with a playful side-eyed glance.

I shake my head at him and hold my hand out for his Jeep keys as we stop in front of the spare tire.

"Because I'm the only one who knows the super-secret plans for the night," I say matter-of-factly and gesture for him to hurry up with the keys.

"Right, so, not only did you not let me plan our night, but you also refuse to tell me what we're even doing?" he says and gives me a skeptical brow.

"Correct," I say and smile at him as he finally fishes the keys out of his pocket and drops them into my outstretched palm, the metal of the keys jangling against the dog tag keychain.

"Hop in, stud," I say and wink at him before making my way to the driver's side.

Jess climbs into the passenger side of Grandpa Millard's now restored Jeep, and I hand Jess a blindfold out of my purse once we're both inside. He reluctantly takes it from me, and I motion for him to put it on.

"I wasn't expecting things to get freaky this early on in the night, but I'm definitely here for it," he says with a shrug before putting the blindfold on. I laugh and put the Jeep in gear before turning down the main highway out of our small neighborhood.

Jess nervously grasps at the door handle and dash bar in front of him with every turn and stop that we make.

"What is your deal? You're acting like I'm gonna kill us or something," I say with a laugh. "Did you forget that you're the one who taught me how to drive stick?"

I shake my head and smile to myself, remembering how *not* good of a driver I used to be in high school before Jess's guidance.

"Look, baby, I'm not saying you're a bad driver, I just know that you've never met a pothole that you didn't like," Jess says and flinches dramatically as we drive over a manhole cover.

"A girl hits a pothole a little too hard *one time*, and she can never live it down," I say and shake my head to myself. "Just relax, I promise you're in safe hands," I say as I reach over and grab his hand and place it in my lap. Jess seems to relax a little but only replies with a *humph*.

"Okay, this is officially not fair anymore," Jess says as he sniffs the air in front of him. "Is this some kind of new torture tactic you're trying out?" he asks and I tell him to open up before putting a french fry into his mouth.

"That's all you get for now," I say after shoving a few fries into my mouth and turn my attention back to the road.

"When you told me to put this blindfold on, this is not where I thought this night was going," Jess says, chewing the fry.

"I've gotta keep you on your toes somehow, don't I?" I ask and give him a quick peck on the mouth after cutting the engine and setting the parking brake.

Jess reaches for me and puckers his lips out dramatically, blindly searching for me from his side of the Jeep, and I laugh at his silliness.

"Okay, we're here," I say and watch Jess reach for his blindfold. "Uh, uh, uh, wait a sec, not yet," I say, stopping him before he can pull it all the way off.

"So, is this the part where we finally fuck, or what?" he asks, laughing, and I playfully smack him on the shoulder.

I open the door for Jess and help lead him out of the Jeep toward our final destination for the night.

"Okayyy—*now!*" I say giddily as I tug on Jess's sleeve before he pulls the blindfold away from his eyes.

I watch as Jess's face lights up as he takes in the scene in front of us. "What in the world is all this?" he asks, turning toward me.

"Do you like it?" I ask, smiling at him from ear to ear.

"But I... how did you..." Jess quickly glances around the large backyard that's lit up with small hanging lights and a trampoline that's topped with blankets and pillows.

"*Finally*, we get to have our very own Jess and Sam trampoline sleepover," I say, now realizing how childish this whole thing is, and hope that he doesn't think it's stupid.

"*I so knew* that you always wanted me to stay whenever you and Soph tried kicking me out," Jess teases as he squints his eyes at me. I just nod as I roll my eyes, knowing there's no sense in denying it, especially not now.

I take my heels off, and Jess helps me onto the trampoline before climbing on beside me after taking off his shoes as well. The weight of our bodies on the mat pulls us together so I basically end up sitting in his lap.

"Sorry I made you get all dressed up just to sit outside," I say, only half sorry since I'm definitely enjoying the view of Jess in his fancy clothes. "I didn't want to give you any hints, and I knew that you might suspect what I was up to, especially if I'd asked you to wear pajamas instead," I say and laugh.

Jess looks at me with a joyful glint in his eyes. "Thank you for doing all this, Ryan," he says as he tucks a strand of hair behind my ear.

I nervously fiddle with my hands in my lap. "You're sure it's not dumb?" I ask, feeling kind of embarrassed.

"Absolutely not. Why would you think that? This is the best surprise I ever could've asked for," he says, giving me that mesmerizing Jess smile of his, and I swoon at the sight.

"One quick question, though—and I'll go along with it if it's the case—but, are we breaking and entering right now?" he asks, looking around the backyard.

"Yes, hopefully the cops don't show up any second, or we're gonna have to either run or fight them off," I tease, and Jess just laughs. "No, but for real though, one of the ladies at the paper is out of town with her family for the week," I explain. "I knew she had a trampoline, so I asked if we could borrow it for the night, and she said yes."

"For the night, eh?" Jess says, and his emerald eyes darken slightly. "Should I go get that blindfold then?" he asks with a cheeky grin.

"Most definitely," I say and bite my lip at the thought of getting it on with Jess out in the open.

"But first, we need to eat, or I don't think that either of us will last very long," I say and laugh as I open up one of the bags of fries we'd brought onto the trampoline with us.

541

I hand Jess a burger from the bag. "Are you sure you're okay with this? I'm pretty sure that burgers and fries constitute as junk food," I say and raise a brow at him before stuffing a few fries into my mouth.

When I asked Jess if he had a preference for dinner, he'd told me burgers, but now I'm wondering if he was just joking and I took it too literally. Burgers don't really scream "anniversary dinner."

"Burgers are protein in my book, so they're allowed, and the fries are only okay since it's a special occasion," he says, eagerly taking a bite of his unwrapped burger, and I roll my eyes at his twisted logic.

I unwrap my own and take a small bite. "Aren't you glad we made it in time?" I ask and nod at the sunset that's visible just above the backyard fence.

The setting sun's warm glow paints the entire sky with beautiful shades of pink and orange, and the wispy clouds look just like cotton candy.

Jess is unable to answer, having just taken another huge bite out of his cheeseburger, so he just nods in response.

"Even after *you* almost made us late," I tease and wag a finger at him.

Jess swallows his bite and steals my chocolate shake from out of my hand before taking a gulp. "*Me?* You were the one who almost didn't let me out the door," he says with a laugh as he holds the shake just out of my reach.

"Gimmie that, you punk!" I tease as I reach for the checkered cup in his hand.

Jess finally caves and lets me grab the cup before he leans in, kissing me on the mouth.

"*Hmm*, that's not how I remember it, but we can agree to disagree, I guess," I say as I pull away and put my nose in the air before taking a sip of my shake.

He smirks at me and takes another bite out of his food. "It's beautiful out here," he says, looking toward the sunset. I smile as I look off at the glowing clouds in the distance and rest my head on Jess's shoulder.

"It really is," I say, and when I turn to look at him, he's smiling widely at me.

"What?" I ask, wondering if I have food on my face or something.

"What? *What?* Can't I just stare at you?" he says, giving me an innocent look.

"Not when you look at me like that," I say and feel some redness creeping onto my cheeks.

"Like what?" Jess asks, his eyes darkening as they slowly sweep down over my exaggerated cleavage from the tight corset-like backing of my dress.

"Like you're trying to undress me with your eyes," I say.

"Oh, I'm definitely trying to do more than that with my eyes," Jess says with a wink as his finger teases at my dress strap.

"One thing first, though," he says, and reaches over to his jacket that's hanging over the edge of the trampoline before pulling something out of the inside pocket.

"Your gift, My Lady," he says before handing me a small cardboard tube with a pink ribbon tied around it.

"What's this? You already gave me a gift," I say, looking to the gold cuff around my wrist that he gave me this morning before he'd left for work.

"I know, but I wasn't sure this was going to get here in time. The bracelet was supposed to be my backup, but I decided to just give it to you anyway," he says with a wink before planting a soft kiss on the back of my hand.

"This is too much, Jess. All I did for you was buy you a burger and guarantee your neck pain from sleeping outside tonight, not to mention that I made you a cake that you didn't even ask for or probably want," I say, and look down at the small tube in my hand, feeling like the worst girlfriend in the world.

"Did you forget about the engraved brushes you gave me? Those were so thoughtful, really," he says softly, and I look down again, lowering my gaze in embarrassment.

Jess puts a finger under my chin and lifts my face to meet his gaze. "I love what you did for me here too, Ryan. I've always fantasized about a scenario like this, and somehow you were able to read my mind and make it happen."

"And as for the cake you made for me, that frosting was damn good," he says, giving me a crooked smile as he squeezes one of my hands.

"Really?" I ask, and my voice comes out smaller than I'd like it to. Jess gives me another kind smile and nods.

"Go on then, open it already," he says, nodding at the small tube in my hands.

I remove a thick piece of tape and pull the plastic cap out of one of the ends before looking inside. It's too small and dark to tell what it is, so I turn the tube upside down and gently try to coax out whatever is inside.

I slowly draw out a rolled-up paper before handing the cardboard tube to Jess. I grab the top of the thick paper with one hand and slowly roll it open with my other, careful not to rip or bend it in the process.

Painted on a cream background is a large bouquet of flowers, different shades of pink and purple, all different shapes and sizes, neatly tied together with a brown twine string. The colors blend beautifully into each other, and I can tell that it's not a normal painting, especially from the coarseness of the paper that it's on.

"Do you like it?" Jess asks hesitantly from beside me, breaking my trance.

"Jess, it's... it's... I can't even think of the right words to use," I say, looking back at the flowers on the thick paper.

"It's the most beautiful thing I've ever seen," I say, still mesmerized by the somehow soft yet strong brush strokes of the picture. "When did you paint this?" I ask, not needing to see the signature on the bottom to recognize that it's Jess's work.

"This is the watercolor painting from the art contest all those years ago," Jess says before pausing. "I painted it for you, Ryan."

I turn to face him, and his expression is as serious as the flame burning behind his eyes.

"What do you mean? You would've painted this in high school, way before we were even together. I've never even seen this before," I say, confused by his meaning.

Jess helps me roll the painting back up, and I safely tuck it back inside its cardboard tube before putting the cap on securely.

He looks off at the vibrant skyline before answering me. "Do you remember the first time we met?" he asks, and I can see a smile come over his face as he thinks back to that day when he walked through my parents' front door.

"Of course," I say, still watching his face closely.

"Do you remember what you were wearing that day, Sam?" Jess asks, still gazing off at the setting sun.

"Um... not really. Probably a dress or something," I say, curious about his question. "I know I was pretty obsessed with jelly sandals, so probably those," I say with a small laugh.

"Well *I* do," he says, another huge smile taking over his features. "You were in fact wearing white jelly sandals, your hair was in a braid down your back, and your white dress had purple and pink flowers all over it," he says, finally meeting my eyes.

"How do you remember that?" I ask, amazed by his detailed recollection of what I was wearing that day.

Jess turns to face me finally. "How could I ever forget?" he says, smiling at me before grabbing my hands in his. "Even though I was awful to everyone that day—including you—you still held onto me with your trembling hand as you walked with me. I could tell that you were scared of me, and you had no reason to treat me so kindly, especially after seeing my mental breakdown. Despite all that, you still did it anyway.

"Ryan, all that time growing up, you never treated me like the orphaned nuisance that I believed I was, and I'll always be grateful for that," Jess says, and my heart aches at hearing his words.

It's easy to say that I would've done it for anyone, but that wouldn't be the truth. That day, I was terrified of the angry boy I saw breaking my mom's plates in the kitchen, but in my heart, I knew that he needed to be shown compassion and kindness, especially after witnessing how lost and hurt he was.

When I don't say anything, Jess moves to reach into his back pocket. "Here, I'll prove it," he says as he opens up his wallet and pulls out what looks like a crumpled piece of paper.

"What are you—wait, Jess, I believe you," I say, trying to get him to meet my eyes again as I gently place a hand on his arm.

Jess unfolds the tattered piece of paper and holds it out to me. The edges are worn, and it looks like it's about to fall apart. I carefully take it from him and realize that it's a photo of him, Chris, Sophie, and me at the aquarium. It's almost the exact same picture that I have, just taken at a different angle and without my mom in the frame. I stare at the tattered photo and, lo and behold, there's little Sam, hair braided back, wearing a white dress covered in a purple flower pattern.

I look up at Jess and can feel my tears welling as I hold his beautiful eyes with mine.

"I know you still don't believe me sometimes, but it's always been you, Sam. Even if it takes the rest of our lives together, I'll never stop trying to convince you of that."

Jess gently tucks a stray piece of hair behind one of my ears as he searches my eyes longingly. "I love you, Sam Ryan—"

I pull him into a deep kiss, cutting off his words with my mouth. I'm so happy that I feel like my heart could explode, and I can't even fathom what my life would be like without Jess in it.

I pull back and stare deeply into his breathtaking emerald eyes.

"Jess Cameron," I say, enraptured in his gaze, and wish that I didn't ever have to look away.

"I love you."

# Acknowledgements

I'll keep this brief at the risk of sounding too sappy. In short, this book wouldn't have been possible without my family. Albeit they didn't know what they were supporting at the time, I'm positive they knew I was "up to something."

My father's unwavering support and encouragement carried over from my childhood into my adulthood, and I'll be eternally grateful to him for that.

With that being said, Dad, thank you. For everything. Thank you for always believing in me and teaching me to believe in myself no matter what. Thank you for always being there for me, supporting me in ways you didn't even realize. Thank you for giving me the space and safety I needed to create freely. You have my word that I'll never give up on my dreams, and that's a promise.

And to my biggest supporter throughout this entire journey, I want to thank my sister. She stood by me and pushed me forward even when I was unsure of what I was doing. Even when I felt like I was light-years out of my league, she never let me give up. Thank you for shouldering the weight of this "secret" until it was time to share it with the world.

To my brother, literally none of this would've been possible without you. I'm sure you never imagined the iPad you gave me for Christmas a few years back would be used for hours upon hours of editing and revisions, instead of Candy Crush and Fruit Ninja. Truly, I can't thank you enough for that.

And finally, I'd like to thank myself. After finishing a task that, at times, I was afraid of never being able to complete, I no longer feel like the scaredy cat who was so unsure of herself and her future. Everything that's happened in my life—the good *and bad*—has led me to this moment, and I wouldn't change a single thing about the journey here.

And to my readers, if you've made it this far, thank you for reading my words and sharing in Sam and Jess's journey with me.

Remember that even if something seems impossible, it's not. Don't give up on your dreams. Don't give up on yourself. I believe in you.